LIFE..
LOVE..
KUMBH..

LIFE..
LOVE..
KUMBH..

Togetherness is the greatest stoning..
..Relations, the best snuff...

Aporva Kala

Srishti
PUBLISHERS & DISTRIBUTORS

SRISHTI PUBLISHERS & DISTRIBUTORS
N-16, C. R. Park
New Delhi 110 019
srishtipublishers@gmail.com

First published by Srishti Publishers & Distributors in 2012

Typeset in AGaramond 12pt. by Suresh Kumar Sharma at Srishti

Printed and bound in India

Maaji and Babuji…

….in awe...

TRIO

Upright, slender, spectacled, Sameer Bhargava, wearing a surgeon's coat, climbed up the stone stairway, carrying a blue tooth brush on which lay a mote of red, clove flavored paste. A minor squall of chilly winds welcomed him to the roof. Waves of fog clouds floated like sky ships crossing the dusky vastness with silver stars as peep-holes. Afar, the yellow sodium bulbs, garlanding the streets of the town of Haridwar, could be seen glancing furtively through the fog furrows like children playing truant. A shiver broke through him as the cold hit him like a bee sting. He walked up to the red bricked water tank; open mouthed and weed floating and balanced his tooth brush carefully on the edge of its wall, least it trips sideways grounding the paste, or worst, drop inside the water tank like a bird's dropping, he patted himself on his precision. His hands, now free from the burden of carrying the tooth brush, rubbed themselves involuntarily, surprising him. He jogged on the roof floor to keep himself warm. The tail of his white cotton livery and grey corduroys fluttered in the winds making a sound of a kite flying. Having worked up a certain amount of swelter he stopped on his wheels and rambled towards the roof walls and surveyed the town below. The cold; he thought -but for the Himalayas, this place would have been Siberia and what of Siberia? He questioned. Probably, a monsoonal paradise? Nah! A Climate Chaos. It made him whistle in a sublime delight and he felt warmness descending upon him. Grace and all, he looked skywards.

Presently he sat crossed legged on the roof floor and closed his eyes. A wispy jet of vapor spilled from his mouth as he mumbled a Sanskrit *shloka*, then stopped midway trying to recollect the lines he had forgotten. God damn it; the stoning eats into the memory, he swore under his breath. It was Jorden who suggested a little high; in the name of the *Maha Kumbh* - was his justification. Damn well he needed it; the blood and the gore and the sick and the dying on Dr. Mutthuswamy's table.

Now the hangover, once the euphoria dies down- headache, dry mouth, swollen eyes and nausea.

Annant; lasses lassoed and all, was fasting and nursed long lost grudges as he sulked on his predicament. Who cares about faith seekers nowadays? Or, for that matter, the sulking grudgers? Better be lassoed than a bull on the loose. Did he hear? No.

Annant was Annant after all; always on a knife –edge.

He forgot about the need to recollect and complete the Sanskrit *shloka* and ambled across the sprawling roof with turrets on each of its four corners and stopped at a broken down Chimney, peeping into the dark hole.

"Annant..Annant…Ay..yey.. Phony yogi… Wake up dear brother the *Brahm-Muhurat-* the hour of the spirit is here." He called shrilly. He had a womanly voice and it irritated him to listen to the rebound.

The shout echoed through the smokeshaft waking up Jorden instead.

"The doctor cocks." He mumbled and instinctively pulled at the rug under which lay Annant Bhardwaj in his morning slumber. Thrice, he shook him to wake him up.

Having failed to break Annant's cat nap Jorden ignored him and searched for the way to the roof, crashing on a wooden stool in the process. He swore under his breath and tried to adjust his eyes to the murky surroundings.

"Hey doc… Which way up? I can't make out much in the dark." He shouted as he searched for the stairs to the roof.

"Climb up as if on heaven's case." Sameer stood on the opening of the staircase and directed him through the dark.

Jorden wrapped in a multi colored hand woven Naga shawl; which lay on his broad shoulders like a scarf around the neck, fumbled in the dim light. He found the stairway after a few stumbles and then, having gazed at the huge stones slab stairs with admiration, climbed up in long strides.

"Ah! The Jew amongst us, welcome to the abode of enlightment, that my amour, is the mother we have for a river, all primed up to wash away the sins of innumerable souls, tomorrow." Sameer pointed into the now settling brume and dilated his pupils inside his bifocals. A thin coating of vapors had condensed on his specs. He took them off from the nose rest and placed them lightly in his surgical coat's pocket.

"Did you notice those patterns on the walls of the parapets? He asked "the miniature culture- camels, peacocks and Krishna, the lord himself, dancing with his muses."

"Amazing, aren't they?" The tall Jew asked instead; his eyes searching for the remains of the yore on the turrets which stood on the four corners of the roof and his hands caressing the roof wall like a lover. "Quite a task you have in mind." He pronounced as a peel of the wall came into his palm like an unwrapping of a chocolate bar; brick blockings eyeing his intrusion.

"It has to be done, nonetheless; but what has come of the scribbler amongst us. He is late for his yoga session?" Sameer sounded a tad worried and pulled out a conical bundle of

Tendu leaved tobacco cheroot from his trousers' pocket. He lit two sticks and offered one to Jorden. Both blew misty smoke clouds and watched the sleepy town.

The morning light approached lazily and with languorous steps, waking the two from their Ganja giddiness and the river town from its quietude, almost simultaneously. An orchestra of temple bells and chanting erupted suddenly like a pleasing drizzle. Both sat cross legged listening to the pious sounds. The twilight erupted from behind the lower ranges of the Himalayas displaying blue balloon sky dotted with fleece flaky clouds. A crow flew with a swish and sat on the left corner turret nibbling on a hard as a bone chapatti making a sound of crushing bones. Few swifts and sparrows flew in and out of the nests they had built on the ornate turrets and the roof parapets of the otherwise deserted Rajasthani Haveli, situated on the foothills of the Shivalik range which walled the old town of Haridwar. It looked archaic in the changing scenario. Otherwise what is one hundred and twenty-five years in this country? Where the average age of inhabitants is one hundred and forty-four years; Old Aunt Maitrey and her cycle of *Kumbh*: one *Maha Kumbh* bath in a lifetime; coming after twelve Kumbhs in a cycle of twelve years. The town believed her. She was of an age when all her contemporaries had left for the god's lair; albeit a few years younger than the Havelli; known famously as the Nanku Havelli, which once belonged to a Marwari Banker, Seth Nanku Chand, who, on being treated of an unheard off ailment (a result of excess of profiteering during the first world war, as the legend goes) by Annant's maternal great grandfather; who himself had earned some reputation on solving the insolvable medical cases(Pasteur prescriptions gone phut) in the early part of nineteen-tens; had presented it as a humble show of gratitude to his healer. It hung loose over one of the hillocks, which rose like a camel's hump on the lower Himalayan ranges and was surrounded by a smallish mango orchard kept alive by Jung Bahadur the loyal Gorkha. Its location made it tower over the busy markets, populous temples and the innumerable Ghats on the holy river of *Ganga*. One could see the people bathing and wooden boats plying on the river from the roof top and the entire town, including the national highways; number 58 and 72 and the Rajaji National Park; famous for the great Indian Elephants; if one climbed on to one of the turrets which hung to its last tethers or on the red bricked water tank or even the chimney. The building was in its last rites for the last quarter of a century and the residents of the town waited upon its demise, as if waiting for the death of the head of the family and the following change in the legacy, but it didn't come around. Eighty-eight year old Gorkha had tended it like his sick child ever since Annant's mother's mother had brought him to look after it and to save it from her husband, who, in a fit to keep alive the failing socialist dream and as a step towards internal cleansing; for, the politicking and the slimy world of contracting of the nineteen-sixties had shaken his moral moorings, had decided to donate the property to the cause of the landless under the influence of Vinoba Bhave's *Bhoo-Dan*: the charity of the land.

The two sat on the roof of the *Nanku Havelli* in the twilight in their contemplations; as the calm of the dawn coalesced with the passionate religiosity of the moment.

The yellow rays of a shivery sun, mellowed by the mist, fell on the blue waters of the river making it come alive to the wakefulness. Slowly the Bazaars rolled on and bustled with the early morning energy. Milkmen, it were, who began the commotion in the markets as they scurried with milk cans tied on their bicycles, whistling to keep the crowd at bay. School children jostled with the visiting devotees: their bags full of books as they hurried through the melee; the joys of impending holidays written large on their expecting faces. But it was the day before the *Kumbh* bath; hence the visiting devotees from all over the country, nay the world, ruled the town- a million salvation seeking souls. The shouts of "*Jai Ganga Maa*" and "*Har..Har..Mahadav*", rent the air.

The mornings are busy in all holy towns, Sameer thought. But my, what madness? He spread his lids in amazement. Good lord, save the world from this stoning, he mumbled.

"The Brahmin sleepth, what would come of the world?" Sameer stood up and walked up to the mouth of the staircase mumbling in his ruminations.

"All mothers are rivers and all rivers; mothers." Jorden spoke in a trance gazing at the vastness of existence that unfolded like budding bursts of a flowery behemoth.

"Come along you Khumbakaran- the devil god of sleep; or should I sprinkle the holy Ganga waters on you as if it were your last supper ugh...sleep." Sameer shouted as he tried to peep through the worn down ventilator into the room where Annant lay, but his small figure didn't allow him the necessary reach. "Ah! Damn, you try Jorden". He invited the much taller Jew.

Annant Bharadwaj lay awake, his warm breath burning him inside a rough woolen rug, listening to the cacophony of religion with a burden weighing on his morning enthusiasm. His mind playing with him like a spoilt player hell bent on messing around.

Her body lay among the woods; a Pythagorean pyre: neatly stacked dried wood. An incense smoke cloud hung over it like amniotic fluid- white and nourishing. She lay without any pretentiousness of presentation- Just a floral sprinkle. No jewels. No vermillion. The make up of a widow, reserved for the one who dies after her husband. In her case she had no one to own her up: A widow by birth. An unclaimed corpse even when she was alive. She breathed zest, though; when she had come to him. He had seen her thus: A vivacious soul out on a stroll that is life- relishing the journey, unmindful of any bends or terminuses. And now her ash floated along with the earthen lamps; Juvenile Journey. She was finally owned up- it took death as a price for her being accepted. What killed her? It is always what, never who. Sameer's prescription of death: Doctored- MDP and all. But who killed her? God or blasphemy. Karma or Samskar. Both. In all probability.

"Tyro *Tratak*, the sun larks with the waters, or is your heart still grieving for her? It has been a decade days now: for the sake of other people's faith, come up and bless us both with your Suryanamaskar, or do you want to dip your night's excess into the holy Ghats?" Sameer shouted again.

Annant's mind is occupied with her images: Vivid and everlasting. She had asked for his permission to touch his feet. It had embarrassed him no end. That was after she had had a taste of his rebuke on her refusal to evolve. Ambition is all I care for and hard work is my way, she had claimed. He had dig her to differ- life as a style attuned to success is imperative, he had directed. She listened to her mind ignoring his heart: her quest superimposed on her living. Becoming one she could never be. Two conclusions follow. Die a death. Live a death. He had construed her in all manners possible. She had smiled her usual smile and gone her usual way. Go away; then, he had let go of her. She had let go of life. It is better to die than carry the burden of expectations. You die every moment then, bearing situations you are not supposed to put up with.

Sameer walked up to the water tank and picked up the blue tooth brush with the red, clove flavored paste, which he ran vigorously over his teeth generating rich foam which burst out from his mouth in pink streams of spew flowing across his chin like unconnected tributaries. The pink froth sprayed, now and then as he brushed with a vehemence of a new enemy.

"Clean the grime or better still de-venom your cascade of words." Annant, with puffed eyes and white stubble patted Sameer on the back, startling him.

Sameer gesticulated with hands miming a savant's sign to keep quiet.

"The best time to meditate, when the doctor is tongue tied." Annant turned his back to Sameer and addressed Jorden,-"So you are back for the Kumbh bath? How's the old mansion? You couldn't make out much of it last night. I say- it is quiet dark in here, what with all the trees, you see; the groovy kind, but the moon lit us all right." Annant faced up to the guest and extended his hand.

"The occasion whelms me." Jorden smiled pleasantly and took his hand giving it a warm shake. "Your brother the younger; Doctor has resolved to turn the *Rajasthani* beauty around." He added with a twinkle in his eyes.

"Has he? He practices exceptions and bends the rules. But dear doctor of the dead, tell me of what grime you were talking of? I was fasting, yesterday." Annant asked Sameer.

"Of Die-motional sludge- have you had your push or you wait for the Laxative of Karma?" Sameer spoke in his gargle and then clearing his throat said "Or is it the monthly flushing of the cannon with no birdie?" He winked and then splashed water from the tank on his eyes. "Ice in liquid, do you two have a trick for a morning swim?" He asked. He soaked the water with the arms of his surgical coat and dabbed his eyes and turning towards Annant, asked "So was last night's idea useful?" He spoke hurriedly and with a lack of conviction which he tried to shadow with his impetuosity.

'Yes." both answered in unison.

"I mean we would bath for sure as for your idea..hmm..well.. ugh." Annant said. "But you raised a ruckus about and threatened to perform a Julius Caesarian on anybody who calls April the cruelest month- I was damn born out of the loins of my father in the spring of April, you claimed. Surgeon, you stood up for the month of buds and bitches like a true *Kuon Kunos*."

Sameer walked up to the stair case and then stopped. "Did I?" He asked then feigning aggression shouted "Where is the mirror in this palace, or is it the same cracked one; which you don't look into; for it brings bad omen- your mother the heretic."

He paused and observed Annant closely and continued to shout "You look beastly; white beard and acne marks, red eyes and a famished visage- Old son of a vet. Have some flesh. Or is it the other people's faith again?" He paused briefly and addressed the Jew.

"You know Jorden, he won't shave on Tuesdays, Thursdays and Saturdays, won't eat meat, remain hungry for fifty two days or more in a year, touch the spirit only once in a while, and never dare I say, visit a call house; the H.H: The Hypocrite holiness. Savoir faire dear *Tratak* or else bubble burst."

"What have you against me?" Annant was miffed and looked the other way.

He combs his hairs with his fingers and then grinds with his ring finger nail on a spot of dried yellow lentil soup which peeped like a jaundiced eye from the left front pocket of the blue Levis jeans. The white shirt had yellowed with aging and he tried to recollect the last time it was laundered. To hell and back; it is the inner scrub that matters, he thought.

"Nothing dear elder brother, my aunt's son, I am jealous of your wayward ways; I, the son of your uncle pushed into the battlefield of disease, oh! The craft of images beckons me". Click... Aim.. Shoot...Frozen moments. But yes; I have an unflinching faith in your capacity to do the unthinkable-become a seducer of words: debauch the generation that is to follow." Sameer waves his hands in thin air and frames the town bellow with his joined palms, his thumbs sticking to each other on their tips and his fingers at ninety degrees. He closes his left eye and moves about on the roof.

"Do your heart's calling, dear dreamer or be doomed forever in the fire of unfulfilled wishes- a soul disease." Annant follows him and holds him by the scruff, looking into his eyes. "What is life, if in a lifetime one doesn't do what one wants to do?"

"What brings you here into the wilderness of religion, Jorden- again and again?" He let go of Sameer and walked towards the Jew. "This isn't your first trip to this holy town I suppose?"

"To know; to experience- more so to be complete the all in all of everything: from Aleph to TAV; as my father would have said." Jorden is in his trance. He folds his hands in humility and places them on his heart then bows slightly to Annant.

"Ah! The learning! And the fun of it? Or is it the white man's burden to know more?" Annant sat down with a thud and asked with squinty eyes, his hands fidgeting with pebbles lying on the roof floor. He picked up one and threw it on the crow, which had now brought a starched Poorie and nibbled on it. The sound of its nibbling irritated Annant who swore aloud as he missed the aim. The crow on its part crowed as if pricking his attacker.

"Expect guests when a crow crows; old aunt Maitrey; the hermit heretic". Sameer said.

"We have one; unique specie from the great pilgrimage; Londonium." Annant replied tersely.

Jorden turns towards the river and temples with a jerk and stared at them. "Your religion is the perfect stoner. The hypnotic hermitage: this town of yours". He smiled then cowers on being ignored by the brothers as he roams aimlessly on the roof.

"All knowing, all doing, the white seeks salvation of the highest order". Sameer sat on the parapet as the sun broke into the open through the haze settling into a rhythm of rhyming rays.

"Does all." Annant added, rubbing the sleep off of his eyes and mind.

"Tai chi, *feng shui*, *sushi*, walk on the moon, nuclear tests, peace talks, climate change, bombing." Sameer paused for a moment and then continued,

"Oscars, surgery, inventions, writing, music, criticism, poverty, poetry: even yoga; Jorden here, of the Maccabee race is a Cardinal ugh....curator.. no.. no a preserver of the archaic- a member of the ruins on the roam limited, now SPHB – researches on the ruins of the raj and contributes to the general awareness about this country. He plans to write an anthology of ancient buildings; good for him, I suppose, while in England write or get wrought rotten rusted." Sameer informs him and then tells Annant that from henceforth, the parts of his speeches shouldn't be put under the wrench and martini scanner or chirped upon like a wren and it is his trick at practicing the fine art of writing his prescriptions. He paused again for a few moments and then continued, "I told you last night, he makes it a point to visit the holy town once in every two years..Ah! The routine..I like it ..I sure do.. the regimen of regimental fool." Sameer searched for Jorden and found him lost in the flurry of activities that the town had awakened to.

"Annant is Pickwick paperless; the hunter of wisdom and due to the Lovelace heart, a budding poet Ass." Sameer shouted at him.

"And our Londoner like all Londoners; searches for truths and writes about what lies beneath- sleaze master; the caves and temples of Lord Kama beckons him to this land of charmers." He dutifully completed the introduction.

"But why have you dear English Jew, whose forefathers fought to enter the country of the Johnny Mill; the Stuart with a little heart; saunter into Haridwar, no pubs or fish and chips' counters here; only *Ganga –jal.* The holy ale- Quaff it for the spirit and carry it to the banks of Thames in a holy grail?" He asked in mock seriousness.

It somewhat irritated Jorden and he eyed him with a calm evilness; for a moment though.

"Aya Aye..Doc. Doolittle.. Let the world lip the drop.. Drop the lip- The *Maun* of Hinduism." Jorden replied tersely. He had turned red on being slighted by the two; the ego has to be rested, he decided and took a deep breath.

Annant evaded the debate further.

That day in her purple cotton sweat shirt patterned with English Roses, *ULysses*, *OM*, blue beetle bird and Moby Dick; over which hung a yellow Stoll on her shapely twin breasts, like a door keeper and gay to the core; she had accosted him.

He asks her then tells her that one's dress tells where one has reached yours where you are heading to. She chides him saying his is gibberish of the highest order the phoenix of stupidity. He laughs her humor asks of the rumor. The mongers mangle beliefs and all would you go with them or the truth that is mine. You seriously, he says, you look a humdinger when claiming the un-faked. Be Sir-seriously lest a Socrates is poisoned over she says and arrows her joy, he bows on happiness, she rebels he eggs, she solves he dissolves, she asks he tells.

Annant walked up to the torn ramparts of the Haveli facing up to a weak sun and curling up to the cold, his teeth chattering aloud.

He watches the river wistfully and searches for her remains. The people bath with her ashes. He fears her coming back- Once gone should remain a gone. No comeback. Come back. No. Let her rest in peace at least in her death.

"Let us run to the river and belle watch wash wheedle the morn." Sameer suggested, more so to distract Annant from his despondency.

"No I won't, not for whetting my wanton wailings." Annant sat in his sorrow.

"Wash the lust forthwith in a dip- jiffy." Sameer laughed.

"I would, when is the Great bath." Jorden offered and decided to join the brothers.

Annant laughs hoarsely. "The Jew has it; now wants a peep into woman for omen, I buy you for faith, the Great Bath, though, is a relic of civilization as a culture- thou hath to bath. The Mohenjo-daro; circa 2600 before the Christ jived in." He clarified in his acerbic laughter.

"I hold my ears in forgiveness Anne; you would then take the holy dip, the duty of a Brahmin, and where is your holy thread, across your breast, or do you find it hard to follow it truss?" Sameer asked.

"Nothing of that sort; I am up to my faith and more." Annant replied in a quiet tone.

"What of your guilt? Our dear friend sits with the guilt. She died due to drowning and no more. There is a medico-legal term for what she suffered from MDP: Manic Depressive Psychosis. The guru in you detests failures I suppose."

Sameer stretched his back on the yellow mudded floor of the roof. The white coat catches the roof earth. His hands are soiled with dewy dust.

"What do you know of her or of deaths and dreams?" I am ever a learner never a teacher." He pleaded as he rubbed his hands for warmth. A whiff of sadness catches him in his mood swings. He sigh a sigh of a defeated man; the shoulders drooped with a twitch of a cynic.

"Let me be of some use to you two priests of the past: Rishi Bhardwaj and Bhargava- a blessing is all that I seek in return. Where is the tea pot Anne?" Jorden stands with servitude.

"Annant- it is my name." His anger vents in a crib.

"It counts for a lot; the blessing and one's name. Go down the stairs, turn left and you enter a scullery, the abode of Annapurna, goddesses of cheer. Light the fire and Will. Pull what you look for." Sameer laughed and stretched his limbs. "Do hurry or prepare a pyre which warms us for good."

"Strange devotee he is, isn't he?" Sameer said when Jorden had stood up to dust himself and go.

"I heard you doctor. But I would prove that my quest is genuine. Drink my ale and see it for yourself." Jorden replied and climbed down the staircase with a handful of yellow mud which he examined with curious intensity.

"Would he be staying here?" Annant asked suddenly and rather curtly. The intrusion to his solitude irritating him.

"He has agreed to help me spruce up the oldie, so he has to put up here, I suppose." Sameer replied.

"Why? Did something happen? He asked. "I do apologize for the hullaballoo over the Greeks and the literature of yore we created in the Mango orchard last night. Did something offend you?" He walked up to Annant and sat beside him.

"He asked for a fork while we were dining." Annant hissed.

"A fork!" Sameer cried. "And it offends you. This brother of mine, Annant you are impossible, next you would ban the use of WC; etiquettes dear brother, a way to perfection."

"Fork- That symbol of the British art of gluttony; but that is not the reason why I took umbrage." Annant spoke with a certain degree of firmness.

"Then what is it?" Sameer asked impatiently. "Damn he was stoned." He said.

"I know that the stoning made him more of a Brit than Jew; true and stiff. It is what he said regarding me being forked; which caused me a hurt." Annant replied.

"If you wouldn't tell me the riddle how would I know?" Sameer stated.

"He said; Annant your life was fucking forked; with divergences without coherence." Annant answered bitterly.

"Did he say that? Fucking forked- did he? The Brit: a Jew but a follower of evil Mill. I am sorry now, that I picked him up. Not my fault, though, you led me to it; Guests are gods and all; now this is what you get; Upanishads need to be rewritten my naïve brother." Sameer cried startling the sparrows, who flew chirping loudly.

"I am offended because he spoke without knowing me; standing on judgment without the evidence, after all it was an acquaintance of a few hours and there he goes with his theory of deprecating me. He is too presumptuous about the inanities of appearances, poor realities gone for a toss." Annant was calm now after having unburdened himself.

Sameer paced on the roof. "Mere words Anne, not to be taken seriously; what worth a Londoner has nowadays; that too, a Jew; in these United State of imperial times the empire piggybacks the Boss." He explained with the patience of a doctor.

"In my own country, in my town, he says that." Annant is angry in bursts.

"Wash the annoyance in the *Ganga;* let peace prevail without a wail." Sameer begged him.

"Is it your pragmatism that makes you side with him?" Annant asked. "Bloody Willy James and his doctor follower." He shouted in his agitation.

"It is important how people take you." He said as finality. "But dear brother I wouldn't offend your stone-mate, I promise I won't and the Upanishads remain the way they are."

Sameer knew Annant and his nature of being touchy when it came to people taking him seriously or not. Was he right into working up an ego when he talks of freedom from the same?

Jorden slips down the staircase and enters a tiny mess in a mess. Jars ajar, vegetable peels and peeled vegetables, a knife blunt on the *kinch,* half empty glass of over nights' coffee, lentils' soup with floating cloves, oranges, bananas, ginger roots, and garlic - a heavenly aroma emanated from the bachelor's hood. A single burner, spick as a span shining under a peeping yellow ray of sun from the torn down ventilator for air, he supposes. He lights the burner for the blue flame, pours water from the water filter half filling the pan and lets it rest over the fire. In the multitude of condiments' cans he stumbles upon the tea and sugar ones. He plucks a handful and throws it on the hissing pan. For good measures he cuts ginger roots and a few pods of garlic into small pieces, crushes cloves, cinnamon, a pink dried flower petal of *Javitri*, a slice of nutmeg, a few black pepper seeds in a pestle and pounds them with a pounder. Finally, he throws a handful of cashew, walnuts and almonds, into the pan shouting '*Om Swaha*', then with a flourish of a priest spikes up his creation by ladling it. The pungent vapors fill the small kitchenette as the broth comes to a boil.

He carried the black broth pan and three terracotta mugs to the roof just as the sun trickled through the misty morning in its full glory- A thin line of silver mercury, melted and translucent.

"The Londoner truckleth...Dare we...that too at Haridwar-O! Jesus; forgive us jejune Hindus, our only sin, but by my dye- the Posset pots right from Etruria." Sameer stood up with a flourish and bowed as he took the tea pan and the cup laden tray. "Let me, my lord, pour by the ounce and drink by the barrel." He guffawed on his feigned fawning.

Annant with eyes shut listens to the chanting letting them seep in him. She deserved more, certainly, not the way it all ended. Dreams: Discrimination: Desires: Destiny. She confronts him in his cerebrations- A shorter version of history; the trudge of a child or a nudge of fate.

Sameer thrusts a mug full of the pungent dark vapory brew on his face.

"Mull over a mug, no storms in morns,' He warned like a caring nurse. "Café Jorden- Come all for an Ayuerveda high."

Annant holds it with his palms. His shudder rests on the white surgical coat which Sameer covers him up with. The cover of death; Annant held on to the coat tightly afraid that it might blow away. The river banks buzz up with life- A sea of humanity flowing into the river. Flowers float in its waters: marigolds, roses, pansies and nasturtium: The floating saucers of the Sal leaves; oil wick burning in them like a flame of faith; a prayer to the mother river.

"All writers pen sad stories to garner sympathy." Sameer sipped the broth, occasionally whistling with rounded lips, through which the vapors blew in semi-circular patterns. "Writing is, after all, for the abandoned of the society: The ink-leech; spewing black blood and sucking innocent souls. But if you want; we can help you find a way; love or war, I suppose; or the usual immigrant comedy of errors or a trip to a nostalgic loss? Have you something in your mind?" He poked Annant.

"It shows your utter disregard for the creative, the renaissance would be no more than an interregnum and all philosophies die in oblivion." Jorden intervened. "Write you must Saint Annant to prove the doctor wrong. Start with a fright; King ... or a girl: suitable to the senses or about lovers of a Sari clad." He pauses as if working up an idea. "Write a *Bhagwad* on Krishna-*leela*, for all that that the world cares." Jorden jumped like a monkey all excited.

"The Jew shoots well." Sameer poured more of the black liquid. "Drink it to the health of the New Year, the sun changes its course tomorrow and with it the season; falling on Zodiac Aries and the planet Jupiter enters the Zodiac Aquarius. It is a gay time Annant - harpy sharpie dory; before *thanatopsis* attacks you."

Annant took the offer without much ado. Jorden stared at his creation.

"A brief history of time-my time; not the universal traveler: reinvention of a lost world, perhaps." Lines appeared on his broad forehead and he posed as a thinker.

"Ah... The passion of a creator Good Lord without the cross; come out of the master bait of intellectualism that the mind dangles my friend and I treat you to C2H5OH- roll on to the bandwagon of alcohol, pick up a treatise on human understanding on the way." He laughed and stared at Jorden.

Jorden had sided with Annant on this and Sameer found himself cornered.

"Let us go wading at a quiet bank. What do you say Jorden?" He offered sheepishly.

"Aye aye.. Watson Doctor.. ." Jorden said without looking at him.

Annant shrugged the white doctor's attire and jogged across the roof surveying the river town; A mélange of humanity. In sync Diversity-flowing as consciousness. The river sheath swarming with native immigrant birds; Wagtails, Herons, Cormorants and Egrets, and their migratory cousins; Siberian cranes, Greater Flamingo, Black winged Stilt, Common Teal, Rosy Pelican, Black tailed Godwit, Pochards, Mallards, Gulls, Spotbills and Shellducks- from far away land of Siberia, Afghanistan, Turkistan, Kazakhstan and Europe: making a Bird's sanctuary named Neeldhara. The town settlers' from the heterogeneous humans: Tibetan, Burmese, Hill, Turks, Mongols, Afghans, Persians, and Arabs, mingling with the native Aryans: Overstaying their migration through their kin and kith.

The temple domes were decked with flowers in buds and blooms. Tiny jasmine in thread forming a garland of purity: roses and rose petals strayed like boons.

An array of colorful camps dotted the river banks, like a garrison of army on a peace keeping mission. A mini India: many great nations. Different people living in the same place: An inversion of the notion of a nation.

"Hurry up good genius- the tutelary saint, least the river of time maroons us three." Sameer called loud in the hullabaloo that rose from the temples.

Annant looked towards the river and saw the remaining of the mist settle on the banks. In the clarity he sees her standing on the waters; a blithe shadow floating without aim with freedom. He waves her for the last time; seeing off a visitor.

"Let us waddle like ducks and belly flop like dolphins." He bucks up himself.

"Pray the ray, the life giver; *Enthos*- the god of ardor." Jorden cull up writer's cudgels with his livery.

"We search a deserted beech, my chum, and bath naked, no robe for a rub, the droplets caress with a missy whim." Sameer looks for his coat and pulls out his bifocals scouring them for dust and vapors.

"Only perceptions dear intern the half quack; the eyes have it. For the rest there is always the next birth." Annant wakes up to the festival.

"The Innateness notwithstanding- I vouch for sensations. Immortality: thou are a chimerical bridesmaid of life." Sameer puts on his glasses' rim on his tardy nose rest after clearing the mucus that had settled in his nose barrels with his fingers. He played with tiny grey balls of his nose excreta enjoying the subtle spongy sensations and the regularity of meditation.

"And I for potentiality, leading to the possibility of Actuality: wood is cold but has a potential of fire and a possibility of turning into ash: The flux my friends and the four stages of Aristotle superimposed over the Ashram system of Vedic times." Jorden said as he prepared to follow the two. "Ah! The completeness of the Being." He spoke gaily.

"Imposter saint; give one more than the five ways to Confessions and we will let you lead, till then follow us, we are the Brahmins, responsible for upholding the values of excellence since eternity." Sameer directed Jorden in a stern mock.

"Have you an imposter key for us benign charlatans? We may seize ourselves in your kip for a take five, as you labour it with your pupils;

the guru of Philosophy." Sameer put his left hand on Annant's right shoulder.

"The Phantasmagoric Philosophy: ineluctable bride of mediocrity." Annant joined in with his mocking.

"But a sympathetic maiden for the dismal science, it keeps you in a learning mode, without neighing on the Vet. Pile up the pelf, with the tail up."Sameer added his bit to the lightness of being.

"Old J.D.B. is a Ghandhian, deals in coins- austerity in times of ostentations. But I pull off fine; yes I do owe the bride a curtsy."

"What have you for excellence?" Jorden buzzed from behind with a new found interest of a keen student.

"Consciousness- Raise a toast to it. It is *Kumbh* time; drink deep for the nectar. Get a Pitcher full and live till eternity." Annant shouted over the top of his voice as he rushed to the left turret to climb.

Sameer held him tightly. "After the bath you can give the fall a try." He pushed him towards the stairs.

The three amble through the mango orchard dotted with different varieties of Mango trees; *Dusherri*, *Safeda* and the smaller ones; hard boned and button-shaped for pickle; four Guava and two litchi tress gave them company; all stood obediently like grown up children of Jung Bahadur. A lone Banyan tree with its branches spread like tentacles, and its roots hanging from them, covered a major part of the open ground. The roots have it-wisdom a of a banyan tree: mind over matter.

They walk as brothers' in arms, stepping on the creaky, sleepy leaves with pleasure of ramblers. One of them snaps a guava tree twig not more the size of a rule, and divides it into three, almost equal parts. They chew, rub, and savor it in as mint on choppers.

As they enter the Bazaars' bustle after crossing an unmanned railway crossing, where a timely push by an aware devotee saved them from being mowed by the chugging blue railway wagons carrying thousands of pilgrims; a procession of naked Naga *sadhus* make them wait and force them to take shelter along with another crowd of devotees in a dark alley. The procession is led by the head of the *Juna Akhara*; Swami Adeeshadannd ji Maharaj, who sat on a Gold plated throne for a Howdah with a Parasol made of pure gold providing a sun shade; placed majestically on the back of an Indian Elephant whose trunk was decorated with floral patterns in red, yellow and white and who waved it from time to time to the crowds. The Swamiji too, raised his hands every now and then blessing the devotees and throwing Marigold garlands as a mark of his love for them. He was followed by a regiment of naked *Sadhus* riding on well built shiny *Kathiawari* horses carrying silver swords; a neat line of *Sadhus* march on the right and the left flank like foot soldiers, brandishing bamboo poles. Colorfully attired Band players played popular devotional songs and lend their musical might to the procession. Some of the devotees joined them and danced to the tunes with gay abandon.

Annant shadows himself from the pageantry hiding behind the people and receding into the darkness of the alleyway. He sees her ashes floating away to the oceans of eternity. The spirit never leaves, never goes away. Immortal Mahatma. Her karma cycle comes a full circle. That day she had asked him the way to happiness, to which he had answered acceptance; she asked him about the reality of ideas and he had said Plato was real; she asked what of quality and he had answered faith; she asked the stead of religion and he answered meditation; she asked the cui bono of culture and he answered meditation; she asked the duality of reality and he answered inevitable; and then she answered his only question. Yes. She said of the promise. Will. Be.

Long haired, bare bodied ascetics, brandishing the triad of *Trishools*; silver swords reflecting the sun and mustard oiled Bamboo sticks: bellow: *Har Har Mahadeva', Jai Ganga maa'*- Thousands, an army for Hinduism; the fate of faith in the hands of believers. The shouts wake up Annant to the predicament of a fair.

"Creatiwitty I would buy a wordsmith for." Sameer stands on the edge of the alley and shouted over the din extending a hand of friendship.

"Or a painter; any day; the rebel with a brush; a bohemian artist- Strokes of consciousness." He continued.

"The words explain us all, each having a meaning in a meantime: every time for a life time." Jorden speaks up.

"Each trapping the mind forever; let the freedom come from Annant, a book on meditations. Without doubt!!' Laconic locutions. Minnie Mum." Sameer shouted about searching for Annant. Damn life and its intricacies; Atman, the only free radical. He thought.

Annant looked into the sun through the key hole of the crowd and rubbed his eyes. The peephole becomes his third eye and like Shiva he sees the world around as it is, as it should be: Cable cars, billboards, floating balloons, flying kites, wasps, birds, petals, smoke, smog smug, condiment whiff, sweat scent, peoples puff and the dust stratosphere, cement jungles, towers, poles, glow signs, fluttering buntings of many a hues, shower of petals, cloud of vermillion and the lot. He feels a surge of passion rise in him like an ocean wave. It awakens him to the present.

He sands his father's mother's brother's daughter in a time piece- A precipice of relation- destiny deduced decision. And she had accepted everything as in everything, without a fall, with no exceptions, Minnie without a fuss fuse.

"Let us proceed lest we find our entrapments here." Sameer pulled at Annant's cold hands.

Jorden holds on his own as he dodged the surging crowd; a proud Jew after all that had happened to them over a period of history for geography. The three scythe through the crowds and are pushed into a human wave of the ocean of reverence.

Their shoulder brushing, knee pushing, palm pressing, eyes glaring, mow walking, stranger strangling, priest accosting, mob ripping, hymn singing, group clawing, drum tapping, feet footing, beetle mashing, cur kicking, child rescuing, flea waving, mosquito clapping, eve teasing, elder dodging, passive smoking, sari intertwining, petals raining, peel slipping, bicycle parrying, loafer directing, tourist guiding, police checking, barricade waiting, crowd carrying, deity praying, rose water sprinkling, drain splashing, mud bathing, space competing- march: Then the sorry saying, jumping, running, shouting, mouthing, swearing, chomping, stomping and limping struggle- took them to the green river bend where the river hid from the gay crowds.

The trees hung over the river with their floating shadows. An occasional leaf fall creating micro ripples on the quiet surface of the holy Ganges. A breeze with river laden smell sails over the sluggish green water. The bright sun reflected on it in wavy reflections.

The three lay on the pious sands catching up with their breath.

Afar the gurgling white waters patted the creek like boulders on the isolated bank making a splashing sound.

Kajuli, gadera, dheroo, faketa, bagha, khosti, Anju, gagata, suhia: the fishes named as mermaids swim in nature's aquarium across the *Ganga* and into the Bay of Bengal.

Annant cupped the sand grains; the white diamond dust radiating the sun rays, and sprinkled them on Sameer:

'*Om Bhu bhurswah…*
tasya vithur varenium…
bhargo ya devese deh mahe
…diyo yo..naa prachodiyat.!

Sameer lay with closed eyes and let Annant complete the *Gyatri*

Mantra. His mind focused on the piety of the chant and the forthcoming bath.

Annant slipped into the waters ahead of Sameer and Jorden. Got to be going to the college and to Minnie, he thought. When was it? Last year? Nay, five years ago, like in fables; when he saw her: Up and close.

Minnie and friends- where were they? Hiding behind the rock and boulders; relieving themselves of lemonade and all. He shouts in a stickler's tone- come up and out and raft; follow the guide; beware of the currents, and the snakes and all: snack devour them quick; prepare the bonfire- camp curtain at ten.

She watches with intent intentions and says, "Indeed you have what it takes to care, like a mare; but can misters be one?

He disowns her statement immediately and walks away with faltering steps exploding the sands in the evening.

'Nay you be circumspect of mine encumbrances' he says in her directions, over his shoulders.

He is ignored by her and then the rest pounce on him, as a ball floats in his direction, crashing on his privates.

'You are all sons of the witches' he swears in his digress.

She rushes to him and brushes her hairs instead. He feigns pain and finds indifference in lieu: rubbing salts of disdain.

'They had connived to prick you, rise up or you are down forever- the pupil seek perfect priest.' She says in the evening sun, red rays falling on her black silken hood. Her eyes wink at him in a sly tease. 'Mr. Rip Van Winkle, be a star that twinkle". She makes a macabre face.

He straightens up with his practice, shows off his yoga, and disciplines the crowd. But Minnie appears unimpressed. To hell with you he shouts at her. But it is at midnight she bares her true fangs. The stars are gay, like you, she says and join him as he sat watching the black waters roar. Sleep off, he commands. No way and she sat through the night holding his hands.

Annant swims as a tyro, the currents push him towards the deep waters.

"Rush die roll in Padma, Annant; dare do cross limit of your limitlessness, you devil of the Dead Sea." A concerned Sameer shouted, sifting loess with his fingers; then took off his specs, pale blue shirt, grey Corduroys and the rest and felt the *aqua pura* on his stark nakedness.

'*Shanthi..OM shanthi....*' He sprinkled pious drops on Jorden...

'*Shanthi..shanthi.*' '*Shanti..Shanti... Shanhti Shanthi..*

Aporva Kala # 19

"Be quiet...! Annant called. "I am never a teacher ever a jester". He came out of the river shivering like a dry leaf on a windy day and searched for a spot where the sun shone the brightest and then in a preacher's tone explained them blasphemy and silence: saying one can be former never the later, for if one is quiet he is blasphemous anyways so the choice rests on the devil deep blue sea.

"River we choose, for our muse, bath we would for we have clock in our Leibnized palms; you the master of Carollcalls mark 'P' your students for the quarter of the day, but pray we on their behalf , free all the Telemachuses on this day and for all the days to come in multiples of infinity." Sameer shouted at Annant. When moroseness strikes it is like the vengeance of a crippling disease. Swings of Karma: Annant- the pendulum.

"Brother elder why Kant you be eternal?" Sameer spoke in a prescriptive tone as he entered the mossy sludge of the *Ganga* on the banks. "Annant, she lives on your liver- Prometheus, the son of Lapetus, you are the pivot around which the modern man would evolve, one day."

His diagnosis: Annant's prognosis- A hero's death.

Jorden wanders along picking threads of his earlier visits- Saffron robe, vermillion dot on the forehead; *Gita*; reincarnation and she; his mother of previous birth. But she wouldn't agree; he was sad. Pray I might meet her, this Kumbh, he thought, it has been years now.

"He searches his *Sadhvi* the mother of 'K'. Sameer spoke water words.

"Lay your keys on the heap Annant. Would you meet us at the Annapurna café?-The bite place of all hungry or is it fasting again, or are you having Minnie Meal today?" He asked.

Annant sat in a sudden gloom, water dripping from his naked body. He continued to shiver under the cold. Got to be going to the college and then, perhaps to Shamisstta's house, he thought of the warmth of her embrace. With disinterested movements he puts the shriveled clothes on; the sand studding them like diamond granules. A few decaying, sooty leaves form patterns on his loose yellowing white shirt. He pats his long curly hairs with disdain and lets his fingers ply the eyes, brows and the lashes.

"*Tratak*, shave or be damned; you look the uncle of my father, nay, like a writer witch; the black magician of Harpy's school." Sameer continued his swimming and bantered along.

It surprised him to know of Sameer's concern; how he gets involved and tries to put things in perspective. He hung the bunch of keys on a branch of a nearby Sal tree and walked away

"Catch you up: have to do a lot of catching today". He called in a soft voice, almost pleading. It would be a while when I wake up from this nightmare, he thought, as he struggled to pull out his feet sunk deep into the silvery sands. A spasm of pain rose in his vertebrae like a snake's rattle. He winced with swear and wanted to escape the company of his brother. Sameer was the real free bird; ethics, values, pain, form, quality, creativity, for him; existed in the realm of nonsense, it was the pleasures of living alone that mattered to him without the burden of the good or the bad, holy or the unholy, god or the godlessness, death was the end, birth was the beginning; a knife and sutures would do, screw sew saw: prescribe but do not follow; Immortality being the greatest feel good factor; Sameer lived stoned moments, hiding the reality behind the veil of smoke. My history- a marshy swamp of rules, faith, Karma, duty and the worst case of detached attachments; Krishna prescribed, the greatest surgeon of all. Annant rued his being alive, the way he lived. He clutched at his back and dragged his legs, stooping with an old man's hump. Hurry up dear years; he said a silent prayer, let time fast forward to his death. What of the spirit?- A fire escape from all for all.

Jorden in a shyness of his own exposes himself to Sameer.

"*Tis* your first time?" Sameer asked as he floated on the calm waters catching up on his breath.

"No, but I am as a custom, alone in the throes of my canon." Jorden swam in deep veneration; use to the custom which was no longer alien to him; there is no discrimination here, he thought, chanting a Sanskrit Prayer- *the Shanti Path.*

Om Dehyo: Shanti Antariksha shanti; Shanti, Prithivi Shanti..

Shanti rapa: Shanti Roshdhaya: Shanti Vanaspathaya: Shanti Vishwe Deva,

Shanti Brahma Sarwaj –vam

Shanti Shanti reva Shanti sa ma Shanti redhi

OmShanti Shanti Shanti Om...

MORNING SNAPS

Was the triumvirate alone in their bathing?

-No.

Who else were there at the bank besides them?

-Two washer women.

Did the washer women saw them?

-Yes.

What did they notice?

-Annant walking with a hump.

What did they conclude?

-Humped Baba.

Did they eye Sameer and Jorden?

-Yes: Off and on.

What did they have to say about them??

-A black and white television set floating in the *ganga* waters.

Why?

-One of them had recently bought a color television set.

Which one?

-The younger one with a blue sari.

What else did they observe about the two?

-Their coming close in an embrace.

Did they react to this?

-Yes.

How?

-They shooed away a crow.

What else did the washerwomen talk about?

-Their kids, soaps, price rise, people, Kumbh bath, *Bindi*, Rent and White skin.

What did Annant do after bidding good bye to Sameer and Jorden?

-He bought three Jasmine flowers beads.

Did he haggle over their price?

-Yes.

Did he win?

-No.

Why?

-The flower woman was charming.

Why did he buy the white flower beads?

-To counter his students' comments regarding his white stubble.

How?

-He didn't know.

Did he forget anything?

-To brush his teeth.

Why?

-He couldn't find his blue brush at its usual place.

How did he cope with his back ache?

-He let niggle please him.

What did Sameer think off while bathing?

-What were his chances of catching cold.

What did Jorden think off?

-The *Sadhivi* he had met at Rishikesh; mother of his previous birth.

What brought them closer?

-Sameer found a blue tooth brush floating and sought Jorden's opinion regarding it.

Was it the one with which Sameer had brushed his teeth in the morning?

-Sameer discussed this point with Jorden.

Did Jorden know about the ownership of the blue brush?

-No.

What conclusions follow from their deliberations?

-That the brush was not the same brush with which Sameer had brushed his teeth but that it can be kept as a souvenir of divinity.

What did Sameer do with it?

-Threw it on the heap of clothes.

What was the main concern of Jorden?

-Where to pee.

What solution did Sameer offer?

-Behind the trees on the other side of the banks.

Did Jorden relieved himself?

-No.

Why?

-Washerwomen.

Triumvirate's walk in the Bazaars.

Shoulder brushing: Sameer Bhargava's with Rajiv pal Singh, the wrestler, resulting in Sameer falls.

Knee pushing: Jorden's knee when he tries to hold on to Sameer.

Palm pressing: Sameer's palm, when he falls on the ground.

Eyes glaring: Ratna purohit's eyes, when Jorden knee rubs on hers.

Mow walking: Annant's walk, when he tries to pull Sameer up.

Stranger strangling: Ratan purohit, when he strangles Jorden to show off to his wife Ratna purohit.

Priest accosting: Pandit Bhirgu's intervention; to save Jorden.

Mob ripping: Annant's run, when he catches Sameer and Jorden and rushes through the crowd.

Hymn Singing: A group of clean head shaven youth singing Hare..Rama..Hare Krishna.., into which the three run in to.

Group clawing: the group pulling up the three for interrupting their singing.

Drum tapping: Sameer's tap on a *Dholak*, hanging on the neck of Peter, a Dutch devotee.

Feet footing: Peter's feet coming down on Sameer's .

Beetle mashing: Peter's feet falling on a beetle when Sameer removes his at the nick of time.

Cur kicking: Annant's kick on a black bog which threatens him.

Child rescuing: Jorden picking up an unattended child.

Flea waving: Sameer waving the flea from air.

Eve teasing: Annant catching a teen ager eyeing a Bengali girl in the crowd.

Mosquito clapping: Sameer trying to clean up the mess of the mosquitoes.

Elder dodging: Annant, dodging JDB, when the old principal tries to recognize him.

Passive smoking: Jorden and the child in his arms, when Ratan Purohit lights a cigarette.

Sari intertwining: Sameer stumbling into Mrs. Mitali, mother of Himansh Mukerjee.

Petals raining: From the temple when the crowd nears it.

Peel slipping: Ratan purohit slipping on a banana peel.

Cycle parrying: the milk vendor dodging Ratan's imbalance.

Loafer directing: Jyotin asking for the way to the Ghats from Jorden.

Tourist guiding: Sameer explaining the historicity of Haridwar to a group of Bengali devotees.

Police checking: Jorden handling the child to the police.

Barricading: The police detaining Jorden, Sameer and Annant.

Crowd carrying: the three are pulled by the crowd.

Deity praying: the crowd carrying them to the temple of lord Shiva.

Rosewater sprinkling: the priest sprinkling them for purity.

Drain splashing: Annant's feet fall in an open drain.

Mud bathing: The splash covers Sameer and Jorden with mud.

Space competing: the walk of the crowd of thousands on the narrow hanging bridge over the river *Ganga*.

Sorrying: Annant's to Nicole a girl doing a picture shoot for the BBC and is photographing the monkeys who acrobat on the steel wires on which the bridge hangs.

Jumping: Jorden over a cake of cow dung.

Running: Sameer from a bevy of monkeys.

Shouting: The peanut seller on the monkeys.

Swearing: The peasant seller on Sameer for pilfering his peanuts.

Chomping: Sameer on pilfered nuts.

Stomping: Annant over the stray fallen empty covers of peanuts.

Limping: Sameer from the fall he had had.

The Procession of Sadhus:

What did Annant think of the Naga sadhu's procession?

-That only if he could be one of them.

What did Sameer think of the procession?

-That only if he could be its part and allowed a puff of Ganja.

What did Jorden think of the procession?

-That his white skin would look odd if he joined the procession and what if anybody notices his circumcision.

Did any of the Naga *Sadhus* observe them?

-Yes.

Who?

- Sathyavarth, a Naga Baba carrying his Digicam; photographing.

Did he photograph the three of them?

-Yes; when he photographed the group standing in the dark alley.

How many people comprised the group?

-Approximately three hundred.

The amble in the orchard:

Who broke the guava twig?

-Annant.

Why?

-To neutralize the garlic smell.

Did Sameer and Jorden know the reason for the offer of the guava twig?

-No.

What else was there in the orchard?

-A cat waiting to pounce on a sparrow.

-A sauntering turtle.

-Ants building an ant hill.

-A group of street urchins gathering firewood.

-An eagle perched on the sprawling Banyan tree.

-Puddles under the litchi trees from last week's rains.

-Jung Bahadur preparing his Hookah.

The roof of the Nanku Haveli after the three had left:

The Terracotta Mugs:

Annant's : on the parapet.

Sameer's : Near the Smokeshaft.

Jorden's: on the third from the below stairs of the staircase.

What was in the mugs?

-Annant's : cloves, crushed ginger, a full black pepper.

Sameer's: drained.

-Jorden's: half full with the black broth.

What happened to Annant's mug?

-The Sparrows played on it pushing it over the parapet.

What happened to Sameer's Mug?

-It stood near the smokeshaft.

What happened to Jorden's mug?

-It remained on the stairs.

What happened to the tea pan?

-It warmed under the sun.

What happened to the blue brush?

-It was carried by the crow that nibbled on the hard as a bone chapatti.

Where did it carry the blue brush?

-To the river bank.

What happened then?

-It was shooed away by the two washer women.

What did it do?

-Dropped the blue brush and flew away.

POKE

"Relevancy is reverent; irreverence grows out of irrelevancy." Annant dusted the wooden chair whose spindle lay in tatters and snuggled in its loose nylon strings' seat.

I can lord over the subjects, he decides and smiles in doing so, what if it is a paradox he loathes, decries, laughs and accepts, all at once.

The last suppers' slurp of the dishes devouring the last of the morsels: the tongue the greatest scrubber. Tomorrow would indeed be not just another day- another history. Annant sat upright which tired his vertebra; five sacral perhaps or four coccygeal? Sameer's count. A spasm of pain shot through them and he clutched hard on the backbone waiting for it to pass. The wall's rest the best he concluded and walked up to the white –grey students' feet stamped wall and leaned on it ignoring the sole shaped muddy imprints. He loathed the lean too; upright are the mighty. Not so when they are burdened with the sundries of life. Maya Mother. Or. Fate fait: Accomplice on the run.

"Is the relevancy of your statement reverent?" Himnash glued his eyes on him to score a point.

"I am hungry: The sentence is relevantly reverent to the one who is; but to the one who is not; it is relevant but not reverent or irrelevant. Hunger is a matter of reverence, though. This is all there is Himnash; the matter is however, open to interpretations, because I, unlike god, am not a finality. Though, for the mighty almighty and women; reverence is the real relevancy: odds and ends being irreverent irrelevancy." Annant eyed Minnie as he spoke; good he thought as he reclined on the wall, hunger and relevancy. He enjoyed her twitch and a shrug: Like lost letters trying to be found and read.

"Does it not make this class irrelevantly reverent for a moment and irreverently irrelevant the next?" Minnie asked of her doubts like her scout.

She is the bridge with the damn class or damnest society; Annant thought.

"Or is it Relativism activism?" Moneriil the mawkish looked at Minnie with his toad eyes.

"I think what Mr. Annant means by his exposition is a certain type of Rileism." Himnash added a dash of spice to the debate.

"Mr. Himnash it is Reism you mean; I suppose?" Minnie with a look of scorn asked the tall and uncouth Himnash.

"Miss Minnie Sir is not on the side of Concretism; he likes the soft philosophies- the Romantics: The Roman-antics." He narrowed his eyes as he talked with precise words. Got to impress the girl and beat Annant in his own game.

The class slowly became a battle ground of bandy words, a free for all. Annant stood leaning on the wall with a smile on his face. The newies have it in them to argue for good for lost causes. Who was it who said something about Indians being argumentative, good soul, let him come to Haridwar and meet this bunch. Good for him too, if he adapts with age: for if after fifty you don't live the aspirations of the young; go away. Who needs spectacled snails salivating on the soma of youth? Learn dignity or live in any of the fifty-two states of the United States. Am I filled already, at thirty; midnight of a life time, very viable and yet a sabbatical lurking like ghosts of the past. He thought. One cannot live with questions alone. The answers are the lubricant of the intellect.

"Take your pick, freedom is the only contribution of philosophy worth its salt." Annant intervened as he enjoyed the reverence of a teacher despite his irrelevant teachings. What why should I damn care? He questioned his answer. Anyway there is nothing in philosophy which could be taught or imbibed. He answered his question. I could go on and on and on: lording over these seeking souls; that is what the world does. For a price, nothing for free. The universe revolves around the charge and the discharge. All types all colors. ViscousJellyWatery. RedBlueGreenWhiteBlack. And the discourses; off or on; who cares about the course as long as it putts the soul or jockey's to a win.

"What is your pick?" Ramanuj stood up with an authority of a teacher, his spectacled face making him reverently irrelevant.

Buffalo me for all that I care, Annant was irritated now; the sucking seekers and their punches as questions; like snores of a deep sleep: a catarrhal catharsis. What of my swoon? Are disturbed will disturb; the newest generation. Tad tardy toads; wanting readymade nirvana. He cleared his throat and winced in pain as he straightened his back- last night's posture- he blamed the coiled awakening. He climbed carefully on to the wooden table, the only sign of authority in the classroom and sat on it, cross legged. Posture matters, he concluded; the Lotus Posture; double definitely. It prepares one to face the challenges. He straightened his back and fixed his gaze into the centre row of the chairs; c'mon, punch me, left and right; but you cannot knock me out.

"Life is a like". He commanded his last sermon on the mound. "Relevant and reverent: True times are so. Irrelevant, it may sound, but what I speak is not irreverent." Annant fell for pleading. Dam well I did, he thought. "All are irrelevant". He tried the usual Buddha way. Give them what they are hooked into, he thought. "Nothingness is all-relevant, irreverent, irrelevant and reverent." He was happy now as the class looked bemused. Mix them up, good for them, the churning; at least they would work up an appetite for the inane. That is what the organized system of learning feeds. Universilly. Ox on ford-speed up and race but not for the mace. Sham bridge to nowhere. History tells creativity is a result of the soul song.

"*TAT TVAM ASI*". He shouted at the top of his voice surprising them all.

Nina would have survived had the system been relevant; the whole that is, not in parts. Now: the pangs of regret, retreat, retrocession, regress, remorse, repulsion and renunciation. Better let the seekers suck themselves up. It was she who mattered. Death had made her relevant and reverent; her being alive was irrelevant and irreverent. That one can suppose, is a challenge one faces, once one is fertilized as an egg. Womb to tomb. Tomb to womb. A never ending saga enacted or a spiral within another. Old Aunt Maitriy says that one dies as many times as one sees death, one is born as many times as one sees a birth- So for every funeral attended one dies and for every naming ceremony one lives. Lives within lives and Deaths within deaths. Her smell mixed with that of the wooden chairs, peeling walls, withering doors and sills, cracked panes, dim yellow bulbs, fading mercury light tube, yellowing charts of Existentialists, portraits of wandering Socrates and upright Swami Vivekananda, lone ceiling fan, gold rimmed and dust coated and the sweat of her fellow mates; whiff his nostrils and soul. Like the algae and mosses of the rainy season, nay many a season; all layered and fossilized for posterity. He could have kept her alive, made her live. Had she lived it was her life; her death making him the sole cause. I want to know all she had announced; Plato and Machiavelli, Democracy and Anarchism: Marx, Proust, Tagore, Nehru and offcourse you- her eyes danced to the tune of her search. It surprised him to know of her knowing, irrelevant all. Her flirting stuck to him. Meeeeee; he had made fun of himself. She had laughed, loud enough to disturb the system; eye brows raised, sly peeps, wanton whispers and wagging tongues. But she was what she was; made of an elemental folly of the creator. I am occupied with pre-engagements; he tossed her around, for long, long enough for him to stretch her patience. He, it was who fell for her trap. She pestered him no end, chasing him like a lover, unrequited now, in her passing by- A travel to the unknown. Irrelevant relationship. He relented in parts, never a whole, letting her nibble at the knowledge crumbs he threw on her, the ones she could absorb. Then she was gone for days on end. He would move ahead with his examinations, delving deep into his pursuit of yoga- Now when he recounts her sudden appearances like a possessed spirit coaxing him to change course. Philosophy is the key she would say, fresh from her reading of tomes on Idealism, logical Positivism or Kantian discourses; yoga for the *Sanyasis*, evolution is a resultant not the finality, her encounters stumping him. It irritated him to pick a quarrel with her. Before he could realize, she would disappear. It was in her disappearance that he lived, stranger than the reality of a mirror- but he faced up to his dilemma, getting used to the wart no longer new and hence no longer a part of disdain.

That day when she came she had a story to tell.

"Let us make this class relevant." Minnie shouted at him in her worry. Covert care; floating ovule.

"Need we?" He shouted back in contempt, it surprised him to note his contemptuousness. "Ignore the cell for the Kumbh, run along and dip your knowledge, swim or be suffocated." Annant regained his composure and felt his white stubble with his left hand. The right legged pained under the practice, he shuffled it but did not let go of his posture- the *Padmasana*.

"The college closes for a month, would we see you when we return or you are off to the greener pastures, the wildness of the west beckoning you?" Himnash spoke with irreverence.

"Sir would hit the word -press I suppose, or report the Kumbh Fair." Ramanuj suggested.

"Times Roman for his brand of neo- Transcendentalism, perhaps: Font to Flaunt." The parting shot of a logician- Minnie.

Annant smiled. Minnieemincemealtime.

The class broke in a commotion; papers fluttered, chairs screeched, knees cracked, knuckles broke, whistles of relief, sighs of parting, rubbing of the palms, balancing of the wrap on the bosom, promises of a reunion, and the call of friendship. Annant sat with unlocked legs and watched in silence, acknowledging the mute goodbyes. The sun rays peep like children wanting to enter a class they don't belong to. Higher Aspirations. He stretched his legs and lay on the wooden table, closing his eyes for succor. The legs dangled like an inverted victory sign. The quietness seeped in him calming him in the process. Minnie, her yellow wrap wrapped around as a shawl over her green Cotswold, moved her chair on the edge of the window from which the sun rays enter with their warmth. The sun made her sleepy and she closed her burdening eye lashes. The college building bore a deserted look. Stray group of students roamed aimlessly, catching up with their ensuing longings. A bevy of girls, flirtatious and cacophonous sat under a tree shade munching on peanuts and gossips. They hushed up every time a member of the teaching staff cross them by. The huge, yellow behemoth prepared for its month long annual sleep. Deserted temple- irrelevant and irreverent. An eerie torpidity seeped into the class rooms like fearful walks into oblivion.

Annant slept in his dreams, mumbling about Jorden and Sameer. His lips open in his slumber, a thin stream of saliva seeped through them forming glue like blob on the wooden face of the table. His nose made a sound of a snore whenever he deep breathed in his sleep.

"You… are you alright". Minnie pulls him out of his stupor.

Wide eyed, from sudden wake, Annant eyed her with intent and stretched himself on the table, winced in pain. "Ah! My back barnacle!" He cried.

"A late night, last night, Sameer and a Jew, Jorden, had a *satsang* of their own." He disclosed his rendezvous to her in parts ignoring her inquisitorial eyes. "The mind wandered in its whim." He mumbled.

"Or is it she again, c'mon it isn't an event you could lose the sleep over, she was close to you in a way; was she"? She asked of her doubts. "It has been quite a few days now, as far as I know you were not in her touch since last few months."

She tries too hard, Annant thought; that is her problem. Girls aren't elastic. It is the cotton strings that they are made of.

"Yes I know, but she was a dreamer in her own way, and dreamers never die, remain like a dream; paying one a visit every now and then". Annant answered her in his melancholy.

"But she is a part of memory now, not dream". Minnie said.

"I could have helped her, a leftover for a child, given her something to look forward to, I was afraid of her faith in me, what if I fail her? It was a burdensome period but it had to be lived, if only as an ode to my own childhood: a forgotten flight of fancy." Annant unburdens himself for her sympathy.

"A nightmare for a childhood! Is it a complaint or a whining song?" She asked.

"I don't know; it certainly is a cry for a lost cause, for what could have been, but never was what it should have been".

"So you grieve yourself not her?" She poked him further.

"Procrustean predilections." Annant seemed to have regained his composure and sat upright looking through the windows into the empty play ground.

"A what? She sounded irritated.

"Never mind". He yawned.

"And yours?" She asked vaguely.

"What of Mine?"

"Yes, yours; life it seems is waning from you or is it some tragic romance you are writing"?

"Write I would? Definitely not tragedy and no not double definitely a romance: if love hath power…peace wouldn't cower." He smiled; good that all have left: The pudding is all there for the take. "Gratis"? He mumbled

Minnie held his hands and pulled him out into the open. Both walk across the brown grassed grounds. Dried and flatted. They sat on the far corner, near the Football Goalpost which lay in tatters.

"I have a same story as hers, would you be there when I need you"? She asks of him wistfully- the parting making her long for continuity.

"I don't know, I need a break from all this; a disappearance for a reappearance, it is a struggle to survive and create, If the old Vet. Has his ways I would be attending to insemination of the cows; artificial and official- Breeding for milk. Long live the udders, a butterfly stroke in the white river, the land of the Butter thief, Krishna." Gayness suddenly descended on Annant as he found a common cause with the girl; and a decade separating them. To be young he thought in jest, or to be with the young, a question of elements and a matter of substance. He could now be free; no longer tied to the role of playing a Loadstar.

"You know what; I think you are a born rebel: that too at Haridwar where all rebellion ends"!! She exclaimed. "I am in for a treat, really am I? Had always dreamt of a Camusisque living minus the charade that comes with it, now, right here, in my backyard, I find you, with "Rebel without a cause" written all over, OH! My luck, a part of the planet Jupiter: But Sir you are a soul alright, an untouched feather fluttering in its excellence." She joined in his jest.

"Am I?" Bulls Eye! Annant smiled.

"That is music to my weary soul, but I am into yoga, the *Dhyana* makes me a rebel all the more. I accept all…For my rebellion." He boasted.

"Do you know what you claim or is it a boast of a teacher?" She asked as if reading his mind.

"I mean the highest form of rebel is acceptance." He said.

"In what way?" She asked with a twinkle in her eyes.

Philosophy the greatest aphrodisiac- Plato the greatest seducer for her.

"It is a stage when one does not rebel with one's self. One accepts one's ways. It is a practice, though, nothing to boast of, if I move forward it is god's will." He explained.

"Is it possible? Not to rebel? I mean what is there to hold on to if there are no notions for which you feel strongly and passionately and even negatively?" She talked fast and demanded a quick fix for a reply.

"Yes." Annant checked the queen. Anything for a mate, Maidenhead mash; today is the day. Tomorrow would be the washing part.

"Is it not fatalism? Not trying to change one's course of destiny but accepting it as a part of one's being?" Minnie with her doubts; wild blue berries; seasonal, sour and innumerable.

"Accepting is a part of the training to evolve one's self, hence it has an in built system to set up a higher goal a higher standard of living. Then again it is part practice; it should go with correcting one's shortcomings. Acceptance of the nature- the *Prakriti-* is the ignition one requires for a spiritual growth." Checkmate; Annant the grand master.

"Obliviously she didn't understand all this." Minnie lays a fresh table; a new game.

That is what the opposites do; cross the swords invariably and unknowingly.

It hurts, thought Annant.

"She did, but couldn't follow." His tierce holding him- Defense is the best offence when you cannot make the enemy see the futility of a fight.

"Would it have made a difference?" She pestered.

"Indeed, it would have. Her pursuits would have been more real, achievable and more evolving." His octave, now when the clock cannot be turned back, neither a wrong; righted.

"She exceeded herself, then?" She came hard with an upper cut; a freestyle fight; an unequal war.

"Yes, but in a direction which was not hers to begin with. A wrong step to begin one's walk through the maze that life is." He faced up to her. No ducking this time around. "One cannot be what one cannot be; she tried hard but couldn't counter the devils within, then the pushes of her prodding pricking parents towards the servility of survival. Damn what of creating? She held on till she could then…" Annant was quiet. His eyes were moist with her memories. Tough to part: lock stock and barrel. Something remains, like recognizable tastes and smells, which kindle the faculty of memory; yea- pricks the soul.

"And what is your calling?" She asked.

Her innocence is attractive; Annant thought-the best offence; Feigning an orgasm.

"Mine?" Annant paused. "Evolution; I can't see myself doing anything else, except to evolve and, if possible set an example for others to emulate. You see the art and science of growing, achieving, expanding, and the consciousness of all." He is flushed with the outpourings more for the theatrical absurdity than for making her understand. How does it matter what is life? A girl needs security; a middleclass girl needs security, conformity and rebel. Annant thought. What of premarital screw?

"You and your ambition, you follow what you deny, is there not a contradiction involved?" She braced up for the debate.

And the fine art of continuous hankering; Annant questioned her intentions. Better lay down the arms despite the man in you; for good god and more.

"Yes there is, the dialectic is a precondition for any such pursuit- A constant churning so as to reach a point where the judgments are clear." He replied in all solemnity.

"What is the point which one aspires for?" She asked and he fell for her genuine ingenuity.

"*Samyama.*" Annant said. "All in All of everything-Nothing left as a left over." Let her have it, he decided, the taste of the yoga and the power of knowledge.

Minnie kept quiet, staring into the vastness of the brown field. She seemed tired by her questionings. Her hairs danced in the river gale. She pulls them back, only to see them fall on her face. Irritant children. May I, he says and without waiting for her approval, uses his fingers to tame them. His fingers deftly; with the finesse of an artist, comb her flowing silken blacks back on to her neck. She twitches, shudders, heaves and then lies on her back. Sun stilts behind a wandering cloud. A dark spot emerge on the playfield. Amoeba shaped shadow.

"What was that talk of you writing a book?" She questioned. "Have you finally decided to be of some use and to take a step forward for us?" She comes round to the same corner;

Annant thought- A home, few kids and a good F… life.

"Me, no…No not the least; as if my life is not embarrassing enough, I write!" Annant hurried his denial.

"And what was the stunt of Transcendentalism and all that you pulled in the class, yesterday?" She leeched her way.

It irritated Annant to see her sucking his being like that.

"Nothing of that either, the more we talk on it the less we understand of it. From the subject matter view, it enriched the western philosophy, but its main source is the Vedas. Colebrook did a great service, once upon a time. He was lucky to find some authenticated text somewhere in Benares. He writes that the Brahmins never wrote a thing about the philosophy or spirituality, but narrated their views to their students or to their sons. No written form."

"How did it turn the western philosophy upside down?"

"Well, it developed a faith in the spirit and its oneness. The movement was carried forward through literature and made popular by the likes of Carlyle, Yeats, Shaw, Cousin and Elliot; Thoreau writes in Walden-'In the morning I bathe my intellect in the stupendous and cosmogonal philosophy of Bhagavat Geeta. He goes on to proclaim that the water of 'Walden is mingled in the sacred water of the Ganges.' In the twentieth century the idea gained credence through various philosophies: Existential, Phenomenology, Neo Hegelianism and it led to a renewed interest in Indian Philosophy. The spiritual quest replaced the intellectual bias of philosophy in the U.K and the U.S.A."

"What of the Realists"? She asked innocently.

She isn't; Annant convinced himself.

"Science fought its own battle to be called knowledge hence the need for knowing the things those surround us. The Logical Positivists ganged up at Vienna for the same as they went about rejecting metaphysics and even God." Annant said. Better let the bait work deep, he thought.

"Spirituality?"She asked looking at him with intent of a child.

Whorascious appetite for the inane, thought he.

"A quiet pursuit, I suppose, to each on his or her." He spoke sublimely, enough to hide his viciousness.

"Religion?" She looked the other way.

"Hmm..hmm..Kumbh of people, all together, the oneness of a prayer." He replied.

That should end; the topicality is always an escape route none can challenge. History leads to contests which none wins. Annant measured up to her expectations, so thought he.

"Would you be back for the next term?" She was emotional now carrying fresh tears like an engaging mizzle.

"No, I would move on." He wanted to add-come along, but decided not to. He rubbed his back. The pain had waned. Good he thought; when one is out of sync with one's environment even a minor irritant becomes a major concern. Class room is the real pain in the back. Good again that it all ends today. Who needs teachers nowadays- internet is the real guru. Doubly good, leaves me free to pursue without the burden of the Brahmin to teach. But *Minniee* is a real pest pestering me for last half a decade- knowing, understanding and now demanding. Suffer you duffer, he derided himself- keep girls at an arm's length, when in this country be sure to commit the crime after the solemn vow: Before the seven circles of the fire; douse the blaze of the lions at the nearest Ghats.

"Would you?" She eyes him through the corners of her kohl eyes- A moon eclipsed.

"Yes, roam for recast; the soul search, as a sole aim- Evolution my religion. Pray for my pursuit." He worked up energy as the day neared a dull noon time. Summery feel- Sun on at Ten!!

She woke up to his calling and sat with her head covered by her green wrap. The wind gained speed, carrying with it dried leaves and sand grains. She covered her eyes with her hands. Her cupped palms hid her longings. The cloud speck had travelled with the wind uncovering a warm sun.

He stretched for comfort. The air cleared his mind of the mornings' sadness. I cannot lay claim to all blame for whatever worse happens in the society, Nina sine qua non. No way. There is always a new way; all the way to Nirvana. Tough to stop the reckless reeking of the past. One has to achieve and hold on to vacuum to reach somewhere, to begin the journey and to end all…*iti..iti*.

"Sex: I meant that by transcendentalism." He said with a straight face. "It was my fast yesterday, hence the need to substitute the word." As well give it to her, he thought, she always, without fall, understood hypocrisy.

"Now how does it matter?" Minnie was indeed sad by his going away. Sadness brings the best out of a woman, he thought. For them to be happy is to gossip, he said so to Minnie.

"Is it so?" Minnie was worst case possible; un-arousal lass: Got to change course; he thought.

"How's your father, The Mr. Sharma of Sharmajii's Pooriewale?" He breaks the barrier of silence that hung for a brief moment. Fathers are the treasures of girls; more so when the girl is the only child. People cry over female infanticide; they should come to Haridwar and to the Burra Bazaar.

"He doesn't take kindly of me, has something against me but his poories are the pride of Haridwar, one can have them countless. People have them, daily as a matter of their food policy." He, the other man in a daughter's life; a perpetual enemy: Middle class Hindu fathers, worst case possible, holding on to charity after giving it away.

"He wants me to join his Poorie trade, leave my passion for philosophy for round, hot Poories". She made light of her pain. Now I know, thought Annant; why the talks of Camus and all.

"Unbelievable, but true, when it comes to you father, things are either possibly impossible or non nothings. But it sounds good. Poorie Philosophy. No half measures there." Annant laughed loudly surprising the swifts and sparrows who were the permanent residents of the yellow building.

"It is a question of my life, but how it matters to you; you move on- I will find my own way." She was flushed with anger. Her crimson color excited him into a high.

"Get married, settle down, have kids, and more… be away from all things fried; no oil to soil your soul, fly by like a bird, into the blue horizon, but behold, take a dip for the Kumbh, before you go."He laughed in a delirium of an insane saint. "Or still better, my Penelope; elope with some white pole to the distant lands of El Dorado." Annant was at his wicked best.

"I have known you to be a gender bender, but never a misogynist. You have let me down, Mr. Annant, in a way used me, now you find a crass way for my quandary. You are a … that's what you are." A Blushflush rested on her face.

It aroused him in a strange and an alien manner which even he couldn't comprehend; almost like lost causes or out-of-order escalators or like dreams without the drawn curtains- hanging hooves of horses. He moved closer and let his hand rest casually on her thighs. She didn't react which put him off.

"Minnie, be mum, have given you all you wanted, now, let me … be". He continued to laugh loudly. "C'mon, Dearie, I was jest leering, I would talk to your old man, I would, promise. Why don't you go out for research and all, and then come back to have kids? Till then be pregnant with Ideas and ides-March to glory; let thy life be an example, shine like the pole star, my friend, let there be light."

Annant turned his back to her and stared at his hands- the lines have it: head, heart, age, destiny, Mars, Venus, Sun and the mounds, thumb, fingers- If he could turn the history upside down. Would it matter? It repeats itself- all events and their causes; the Karma and its rewards. Wasn't he living a life of his ancestors? Inherited causes: Inane Activism.

"You have forgotten all about Nina now; I am sure she died as one of your guinea; on the altar of your experimentations." She was angry like Goddesses Kali- mother fury.

"Mr. Sharma, the real scientist, or more, the chiseler of destinies, I am just a child of my father, the holy with the spirit, three cheers to the great Buddha of upbringing, the middle of nowhere, leading to somewhere, but not where you desire. Oh! The sheer excuse of living." He continued his laughter.

"Is it Irrelevant or irreverent? You are a Blasphemous beast." She cried as her body turned in a spasm.

"Permit me my views, dear lady of the emergency; it is democracy we bred in; the numbers have it. As for you, think of breeding and no more, for that is your wont. Think no more, bear the children for the twenty-first century; let them inherit an empire of Poories. Cheer up young lass, the future is yours, global demand for Poories on the rise; I see headlines anew: Sharmaji's Poories- a craze with the whites of the house. Let us all go to the Downing Street of desires, have a paunch full. I am famished of fasting and bearing you all at the same time."

"This is man of the impossible and no more, it is better you run away; peace at Haridwar. Let your pyre be lit someplaceelse." She gets up to go.

"Bury me, for all I care, this is, after all a country of tombs and towers. The Mumtaj rises to bless the Shahjahans of the world. Let love be the new religion. And embrace the new Asana. Or is the Rani of the Lucre you seek for a sought? A war for the crown as round as a frown. Toss up your anger. Heads you lose, tails you are up. Cheer up Minnie, this is the last we meet, all your aches be gone with me. Be a free bird, perch in any branch you want, peck your insect, flap your wings to glory, float in the *ganga*, light a *diya*, beat a brass bell, call the gods, lie for a salutation, apply the vermillion, shower the flowers, wash the deities, drink basil curd milk, bite on god fruit, chase faith, swing to Sufi, sing for shamans, dance the night, beat the drums of divinity, do what you wish for; wear your heart for your sartor." He closed his eyes in a good bye.

"A whim; I expected that, all thunder, dusting the soul, keeping the mirror dusted, Sir, yours is a misspell name, rename yourself as Annt: the end." She walked in haste leaving him in his delirium.

Minnie walked a slow walk, almost a ramble, no not a ramble, but a nowhere saunter; an undecided stroll. She searched for aim but found none; just a vacuum lay without pretentiousness or pith. She felt hurt; by Annant and by her father, the two whom she adored or more. What now? Both had left her midway. Well a girl needs somebody to live life with. What had come of Annant? He was so caring and all to begin with and now he had fallen in to a precipice himself. The flight of Icarus: Drown for good Mr. Annant. Hell. Time to dump him for good. She ran back to him facing him with her heaving bosom breath.

"Your face is a curse." She said like a final call before the flight takes off.

Nina in her yellow wrap fluttering in the river smelling winds had a story to tell; what was that he tried to recall, but couldn't . Some of her ideas or did she say something of her new muse. Annant lay, under the wintry sun, she, his muse; wrapped in a silver foil her hand made chapattis; imperfect glories, meeting his hunger as a confluence of the hungry and the feed. You can have one more bite, she coaxed his hunger. I have had enough, he feigned his satiation, but if you insist, he was a master at relenting. Go ahead then, have all. He chews with vigorous energy, like animal, unruly for effects. What of the spirit? She had asked. Have as much as you want, never a point of cloy. No fill, just a pit bottomless. Her anger seethe like sauce, he dresses up his bite. It is the other spirit I want to know, the one, which you claim to know about, she eats her words without cherishing. I know of only one spirit, and I have let it be known to you, what else you want to know, he questions her. The bases of all that exists, she clarifies with the patience of a mother. Oh! That, say like that- ferment your predispositions, add a dash of Karma, a sprinkle of soul, a dressing of yoga, a guru for a flame, let it simmer under the fire of practice- the *Sadhana*, and lo and behold the spirit is tamed. She laughs; the guru in you is a gourmet, she guffaws. Serve it hot; the experience is ephemeral; have it till it lasts. He says.

That day she had a story to tell, his mind wanders back and forth, time travelling through a labyrinth of her memories, but he didn't find her story, now that she has become a history, the world should know of her sacrifice- he is angry now, on himself, on the whole humanity, on the old JDB, for trapping him into a teaching travesty. His hands move on the dried earth beating it like a drum, drumming up his anger. She was gone before she could tell. He remained with a wish of a story, a riddle for a puzzle. Life in its mystery, as a mystery. He groped in his darkness, lying under the sun. The white Jasmine flower beads lying as a witness to his suffocation. The sun stood like a silent pied piper, annihilating him by its rays, burning his pyre. He lay on his own smolders.

Ramcharan stooped to wake him up. "JDB calling you, wake up sir wake up." The call; like a whistle of the train, passing by. Ramcharan, the betel leaf chomping, *Beedi* smoking, *Lungi* loin and country liquor smeller towers on him; the sun hiding behind his tall figure.

"I say sir, JDB wants to have a word with you, are you there, or is it *Dhayna* time?"

"Wake up Annantjii, or is it your Annt. The end?" He carries on the orders of the boss, JDB.

A stout strong man at seventy, old JDB, whose forefathers set up the college setting up for him a life time of employment and providing the people of river town a medium of Macaulay Marijuana, mixed with the vernacular grass. He had adapted it according to the Maulana Azad's minutes, for good measures-brings in the grants, he had explained his dithering. JDB brought up on a strict diet of the best tradition of the English patterned method of teaching expected the same from his staff. He sat on an ornate chair, a relic of his legacy, in an office adorned with an oil painting of Gandhi posing with his maternal grandfather. There were the mandatory portraits of Nehru, Patel, Indira and the rest. Green curtains hid the worn out windows and the sun giving the room a damp smell and a degree of coldness. It is for the administrative control, you see, he explained his objectivity as an employer. The capitalist in him won over his role of an educationist. Cut up the corners, hike the fees, get tax rebates , remove non-remunerative courses and side by the administrative system, he would say, and you can never, not earn a profit. The various grants came by the college's way, courtesy his acumen in toeing the line of the powers that be.

"Ah! My dear where have you been, long time we haven't discussed philosophy and all, how's your Carlyle gang doing?" He greeted Annant in his usual manner.

"Good Morning Sir." Annant stood in a sulk sleep. Sin to wake a sleeping soul, but then, employers are the new gods-Capitalist Veda.

"So you would be unemployed again, your contract ends today, your father, what a man! Yes, do sit, where was I? Yes of your expiry for this term, you have to do something for your udders, feed the poor intestines, eat for your teeth, what would they chew upon? So Annant I say of your father, what a man, and what a chicken he send last night, despite it being Haridwar, he manages all this for me, I liked its juicy legs, and a bottle, despite it being banned in this holy town, Jai Ganga Maa, he is a man of real resource, I am under his oblige to do something for you, would you have some tea?" He sat and lets Annant stand.

The pause- less pundit. Even at seventy-the chug is a run.

"May I sit sir?" Annant asked.

"Yes do.. do..Why stand when one can have a chair?"

"I am not after it; Chair Chorus; the new anthem- *Jana Gana Mana* –a forgotten oldie." Annant said as he pulled at a chair. A towel hung on its back; soiled by drying the half washed hands. Multi-colored: red for Catechu, brown for dust and white for? The thought made him shudder. He sat upright without making use of the spindle. The pain reappeared with a mild intensity. "Three on the Richter- Seven for Haiti; yesterday. The world is indeed shaking like Aunt Minty's pumpkins." He mumbled under his breath.

"What will come of the youth of this country, all going the way of *Sanyas* and all; if only Ghandhiji was alive, he said work is worship, and you roam without aim, no wife, no job, no children, no life." He lamented.

Old JDB was born eight years before Gandhi was killed by passions' pandemonium; but he laid claim to the father of the nation's legacy through his ancestors-the first of the capitalists to serve the motherland.

"Sir do I get my payment for my classes for the month of December, I am running a little short of the dough, you see?" Annant used his decency to get back his money. Tough to rake out the moolah from the Mullah of business.

"Yes … yes why not, how much it is, fifteen classes at the rate of one hundred and twenty-five rupees, that is one thousand eight hundred and seventy-five rupees, am I right?" He asked.

"Yes sir, to the last R- the sun god. Will Ramcharan get a cup of tea for me?" Annant shivered under the coldness of the office.

"Rupee; dear Annant , makes the world go round, care for it and rest is taken care of, as the old saying goes- one should be in control of one's loins and one's wallet."

"It sure makes the world go in rounds; the tea sir, I am freezing in this cold." Annnat rubbed his hands for solace blowing warm vapors of his breath on them.

"Yes.. yes.. Ramcharan get a cup of tea for Mr. Annant." He called.

"What was I saying, Ah! Yes, your stipend; we will pay it up and clear your dues, but I am afraid, there will be no section of philosophy from the new session." He informed.

Old JDB with older tricks from his oldest bags: cut the culture to get ahead.

"That makes me effectively unemployed." Annant said without reacting. Old man; there are soothsayers in my gang.

"Yes it does, it makes your father a worried man, and I care for that man, what a man, arranging flesh for me right here in Haridwar , it is not sacrilege dear; Brahmins in northern India are allowed to eat meat, like their counterparts down south can marry their cousins, you see, a matter of race, but what was I saying, yes it was your employability, which you have none, as you are a philosopher and all, but since your father says to do something I would, you want to be a writer, isn't it?"

JDB standing up for the caste other than his; stranger than fiction- Brahmins are the new outcastes.

"No way, to be a writer… better be a glider… for a glide would take you to a flight…. A write would land you in smite." Annant laughed- humor is the greatest reliever of the ordinary.

"For the sake of your future, be serious, no girl would see your face, taking of the girl, Nina died, she was one of your gang, wasn't she?" He asked.

"Hmm..mmm am ..mum."Annant looked the other way.

"The matter is of your life here, I have a proposal for you- A post at the 'Khaabardar Haridwar'- 'Beware Haridwar': the local newspaper, owned by the dynamic Chaudhary brothers, be their sub-editor and earn a salary with contacts, who knows, you might get a contract in the government department to supply newsprint or even to write the speeches of our beloved chief minister Swami Shankanandji Maharaj." Old JDB looked at him expectantly- a chef cooking his master dish.

"That was a good one , I swear, I knew you worry for me , but to that extent, I couldn't imagine, this way I get all- power, pelf, prostitutes, land sharks as modern media persons, religious leaders as political scientists; Wow- writing speeches did you say? Wonderful. 'Dear brothers and spinsters; sinners and winers, I promise to abide by the rule of the benders, the constitution is my Bible, Geetha, Koran, Tanakha; we the people give ourselves the comfort of the governance, hail the democracy of faith'; let the sloganeering begin, fight election and yes..Yes..I can get a ticket too: M.L.A. Annant said that he will take a *padyatra*, a walk, across the state for the betterment of what else, river *Ganga*,.. save it man." Annant laughed hoarsely.

"Annant it is your arrogance that makes you deride things around you, the world goes like that, this is the system of the ruling and now is the time to side with them; tell me if and when you are ready to join, I would talk to the junior Chadhury." An exasperated JDB pulled a file for comfort. Paper tiger still, despite the disc ruling. Misnomer Miser.

"No not at all, I understand your helplessness, but need I care, for your care, the vet. makes me a black sheep, but I refuse to follow the treaded path, I will carve my own; novel and unique, let my ambition make a mark now." Annant hissed.

"Doesn't yoga discipline you to accept and to respect?" JDB asked.

"It is the discipline of the mind sir not of the matters worldly, and respect is for the practice, the *sadhana*."

"Son, the world is dog eats dog kind, one has to be careful in its dealings, and anyway, it is up to you, I would be waiting for your reply."

"I am waiting for the tea sir and my leaf of lucre, if you could do the needful." Annant sits in shuffles.

"Off course; it is your right, which you have earned through your discourses: were you in the bazaars in the morning? I think I saw you with that cousin of yours, the doctor- keep away from him, and there was the white guy, who was he?"

"The whitey mighty? Oh! He is my student, learns yoga from me, Jorden is his name, from London." Annant knew how to tame the master, throw a bone of the land across the seas and see the tail wag.

"Is he? Good, seems rich, ask him to take you to the west, earn dollars or Euros, my son; Ramcharan, get tea for Annant sahib, quickly." JDB is impressed and Annant presses the advantage- The home run.

"Yes it could be done, he must be rich, as all whites are or seem so, I can immigrate and be successful." Annant changes the chair choosing a revolving one –let the last rites be performed with panache of a Casanova.

"Rich? What you are talking about? They own the world, I tell you Annant this could be your big break, go to America, settle down earn money ,send some for your father, poor man, needs rest now, a bottle of wine for me would do. Can I invite him here? I have some rum remaining and your father can arrange for the flesh, even at Haridwar how he manages: perhaps he can donate a nice sum of money to our college, or call me to some foreign university, here drink tea." He offers Annant a cup half filled with tea and with a cracked rim.

Annant slurps on it hungrily, making sounds.

"Change course Annantji, no sounds lest you are termed a beast; you are going west, etiquette and what they call- fork and knife; forget Sharmaji Poorie wale, it is Pizza my dear which would bring the moolah."

"It would certainly, but let me enjoy the pleasantness of the hot broth, Ramcharan ki Jai ho". Annant said in his contentment.

"These slum wallhas have given a new anthem; Ghandhiji is the need of the hour, wish he could come back, fight poverty with zeal, but you prepare to go, pack up from India, search west and bring the goodies to this country." He directed.

JDB is the super cop, thought Annant.

"I would, as you command sir, but can I have another cup of the warm shake, before I go?"

"Yes most certainly, when are you bringing the gentleman to my house; Jorden Sir, he is, isn't he?"

"He is a Jew".

"How do I care, as long as he is of the color white. Bring him along and let me entertain him on your behalf, I have a feeling that something is going to crop up." He cried.

An excited seventy year old: a marble in a hole.

Ramcharan, smelling of ethyl spirit enters with another rimless white cup of tea, piping hot though.

"Sir you are going to foreign, all talking since morning, if you go call me I would serve you tea there, serve you the rest, just once, let me roam in the streets of the lights, Haridwar is all Ganga, and raw rum." Ramcharan slurs.

Now all need dreams and aspirations, no holding back the open India. It is Gobble up time for Indians: this Globalization.

"Ramcharan, can you arrange this raw rum of yours for the foreign guest of ours?" JDB on his arranging binge.

"Yes sir I can brew it right here in this college, it will be closed anyway, behind the library building, under the Gulmohor tree shades we can dug up a pit, I will bring the necessary spices. Can you tell your doctor brother to arrange for some Methyl spirit? We can give him a bottle too." Ramcharan chomps on his beetle stuffed mouth vigorously.

"Sameer can get you that, sir my payment, so that I make the necessary arrangements." Annant played on.

"Yes; Ramcharan, tell Kulkarni to pay up Annant sahib in cash now. Wait. Tell him to bring the cash to me." JDB the real trader- money and honey never to be shared.

"Thank you sir." Annant prepared to leave.

"Why thank me, it is your earning, do think of the offer, Chadhury brothers are the owners of Haridwar, they would make your life, move on kid, dreams can wait life doesn't, it is an old man wishing you , care for your father, poor man has struggled all his life, live up to his dreams at least, here your money." He handed Annant crisp notes.

Annant wanders inside the campus for a while then moves out into the bazaars. He decides to take a walk across the canal road and takes a bend. The canal road is deserted, which he finds as strange. Bathers want maximum fruit so they would bath at the holiest of all Ghats, poor *Ganga* is attractive in parts and on occasions, for the rest it is ignored.

She died before she could tell her story, or did she tell about him? Annant tried to remember but his memory fails him. She had a verve which he took note of when he first encountered her. So you want to know, but why, for what, he had asked. How is that your concern she asked. Well, and then get lost, for good, one who challenges my authority at the very onset, would do the same when she knows what I have to tell. You have a point all right, I want to know so that I can live a complete life, evolve, be blissful. Then I would, for bliss, the *Annand* is the final, nothing beyond. Annant had agreed. Tell me more like lore, was her mantra till she took the drastic step to end it all. Did she know that it would start all over again? Did he tell her.? Did she listen? His mind becomes restless as he sat on the embankment of the canal letting the spasm of guilt pass by.

ANNANT

I should grab some grub, hungry now, for over two days: Just a piece of Jaggery and two chapattis for breaking the fasting. Minnie could have been of some use; or not, perhaps: satisfying my hunger or what or what not. Her berries: pluck, duck, suck, muck; small but gratifying- Aunt Minty's big berries: small pumpkins; plucked, sucked, ducked, mucked. It's in the hands, uncle Josh says, the lines decide when and who would be the first one, till then, the god is in your hand. Morally it is an anathema, he warned but one can do it amorally.

I paid up that day, Brother Muldowny; white robbed with a green waistband, who caught me up with my nationalism. Dear mister Annant, pay up a fiver for you speak up-that too in your mother tongue, holy bible, is that why your parents pay up sums of money, to be wasted in a fit of the language for the plebian. I pay up, a fiver, for speaking in my own language, in my own country.

St. George's like the Saint of Aquinas. Or even Augustine, an Irish saint, preaching perhaps, but setting up a cathedral for a school, perched up on a hill near the great Himalayas; the abode of knowledge, spreading discipline and making *Chotta* sahib of all the urchIndians- imperial legacy lingering even after six decades of freedom; it will go on and on and on, so said old aunt Maitry; damn well it would, she swore to my surprise. But of this business of missionary schooling; it provided all: A church, a cemetery, a library, a music room with a piano and Ms. Sweety as the skirted music mentor, teaching us how to sing the Johnny Wakelin song.. . Sing Mohammed, Mohammed Ali, who floats like a butterfly and stings like a Bee... the Black Superman, a French teacher, three and a half feet tall not French but neither an Indian- All five star but it is the fiver that hurt me- Poor money for my movie escapade. *Oui..OUi... Je 'mapple* Annant. A door to Paris.

Of this business of Amour Bharat, I remember raiding the huge mansion- Sikhandar hall; owned by Brigadier M. A. R. Skinner- DYO Lancers. Skinner's House, representing two attackers; One settler an imperialist; the other a Greek; though an original invader- Alexander(Sikhandar, Porus's nemesis). The mansion had it from us three musketeers. Huge stones and small swears- the new lingua of the boys in late eighties, when India was more Bharat than it is now. I was not alone, had got hold of *Osho* Macgregor, he paying the price of being sounding like Skinner and hence needing to prove his love for the country of his birth before the religion gained from conversion and a Shelly Seth from Lucknow- skin the skinner was the war cry as we dodged the keeper, a Gorhka; and swung through the rebel and all- the *Gadar* or the August *Kranti*. But we were somber in the school under the tutelage of the Patrician saints and Jesus' blessings; the Sunday mass washing our sins of secret rebellion.

Aunt Minty said of me that this boy will grow up into something, a hirsute, like all saints. I think she meant Hermit. Her daughter, my cousin; the little Shammista- not of the age of berries but, working up an appetite for all things hirsute- kicked me for my hermit-ness. Tag along and I will show you what is all there all to see, she coaxes my shy.

Annant sat on the embankment as the sun beat like an afternoon sun. But the river wind cooled him. He searched for a food vendor but found none. Let the hunger eat me up; gobble the last of the leftover crumbs of me. Devour me O! Death of Desires.

That day when I had pushed the fork out of my plate; Aunt Minty with her choicest of words had vituperated me into submission-you belong but not to the family of the Bharadwaj; a wild tribe of the Andaman and Nicobar has dispatched their sin to us. You should be sent to the *Kala Pani*, the British knew how to punish, for not following their spoons and fork ritual. You are a true aborigine and a *Junglee* to boot ; Debar him dear brother, she ordered my father. Annant, if only you could repay all that the poor brother of mine has done for you, sending you to the expensivest of all schools, big building with a huge clock, like Rome church, swimming pool, cricket, and here you are no forks, in the name of the father, the son and the holy spirit. She makes a cross across her chest. The pumpkins shake under her passion. I eye. Are you blind of colors, I had ventured into rebelling, got to start it from the home. They are black as soot; I am fairly fair, I whispered. She eyed me in her sticklers' look and had her way. Fathers and brothers for teachers; none nun so life was not fun.

I would be a vagabond and all, rather than sitting in a cubicle of a class. Annant the rebel is born without slogans and with conviction. It is cemetery then, all day, with tall fir trees and an eerie silence of the dead. So the British live through their dead, I lay on the marble tombstone of my liking and ruminate. The signs of cross with the epitaphs on the tomb sound like poetry. The tall deodar and silver fir trees brood and wail in the evening wind as I sit and read them echoing the valley.

"There sleeps Col. Young..

Died when still young."
"God took her early old Mrs. Kinsley…
At ninety she was young at heart."
"There is sown Peter; tended the gardens…
With all his friendly demeanor and healthy manure."
"An angel dear Sophia left us in her teens…
Took dreams which could have been…"
"Major Shepherd fought the Indians for the British..
Lost his last battle with Cholera."
"Chris the wild boar sleepth here..
What a man!!"
"Mary left us for her abode in Birmingham…A false tomb this is from Joe…
Who would love her till Nirvana."
"There sleeps Joe.. Finally.
Died on hold."
"John Lang the Australian writer sleepth here…
Assisted Dickens and fought for Luxmi Bai."
I jot down my first then and there; on the sleeve of my school shirt- 'Ode to Camel's Back Cemetery'-

Stars say all fall..
Aft hath twinkle thee
Rains say us pours..
Hind O! cloud crinkle
Wind say thy blows…
Aft pressure prickle
Tears say thee roll..
Rear sadness cry tingle
Sun sees all shine…
Crested dawn tis sprinkle
But life I say dies…
Aft dreams a wrinkle.

Brother Aloysius, the English in charge; laughs, guffaws, rebukes and relents; the penned lines find their way to eternity, and the school magazine gets the privilege to be my first. My father is a happily flustered man trying as he did was to understand the scribble. Dribble past the post, he lampooned me. Feelings dear father, I countered, don't be mean for a mean, be open hearted and wide vision, see the bloom of a poet. I see gloom he retorted, first step towards a doom. Can I now Face up to Uncle Ruskin I ventured: Ruskin Uh…My footfall of history; why would he bond with the beast- My father the best judge for a critic and the best critic for a judge.

Aunt Minty; then with unripe berries; raw fruits and rawer intellect; sounds caution; this boy is coy she says of him. Annant focus, concentrate, waver never, job is your calling; poor my brother, paying every pie of his hard earned money to see you through, and here you are squandering a chance to dance . Be someone, she coaxes me. I eye those berries; cajoling me: 'wanna manna bite'.

I had debunked her thoughts as hearsay and furthered my agenda- a Marx in the making: A revolt against the tenets of upbringing. Live or die, but never shy, of your dreams of filling the reams. His is a scribble of gribble, aunt minty complains to all and sundry. This time my mother, a silent spirit rebukes her with her quiet eyes, silencing her for a while.

Annant wakes up to his predicament, no job for a fob that is when I am the cause for other's job, fob, lob, mob, top, and cob or whatever, he cries. He stretches in a posture of *Suryanamaskar* reciting the *Gayatri* Mantra in his mind; six sets of the yogic exercise; twelve asana in each set. On the grass he lay in a posture of the dead: the *Shav-Asana*. The mind has to be arrested, he convinces himself. Is it so easy? He questions the wisdom but continues to lie like a dead man.

A group of *Sadhus* pass by. "Old man some sleeps under the sun, should we make some provisions for him?" One of them asks.

"He looks alright, to me a devotee of the highest order." Another adds.

"He is in *Sadhana*, a great man meditating on the non-existent."

They fold their hands in unison and place a bagful of fruits besides him.

Bananas, Oranges, Guavas, Grapes, sit on *Padmasana* besides him; the sun warming them. Annant woke up with a calm mind and recited the *Shanthi Path*: the prayer for peace. His hands groped on the fruits in the saffron bag. Heaven is a reality; he shouted and peeled an orange. The juicy leaves and citric smell opened his senses and he sucks on them with a relish of a connoisseur.

Aunt Minty had finally relented, or so thought I; that day when it rained in torrents turning it into a city of sludge. I carried the black umbrella with a patchwork of brown at the centre, in one hand and the bag of provisions on my left when a gush of the wind carried the parasol away, revealing all. I wet myself in the rains, as she hid what she could, then as an afterthought she pulled me on herself, as a cover. The rains tasted sweet but shook me in my sweet-sins. I ran with a fear of a flood chasing me. That night I woke up to a strange fact; keep milk, not to drink but to feed the cat. Dreams clawed on me for the night and the rest of the night, until, Ricky came along with her winsome smile and a deadpan humor.

Annant gobbled on the guava, biting on the seeds with ferocity of a feline. Peanut cracking sound emanated from his mouth. Now is the time to pay Aunt Minty a visit, he concluded. She would welcome him as her own. Their house would be full of guests for the Kumbh bath. Would Shamistta be there with her mate Mr. Tweny(Richard, Edward or Charles; he had said. Oh! the stiff uber upper lip of Brit) ? The Brit was fun, a supporter of a universal surname, a casteless society can be attained only by inter religious and inter-continental marriages, he advocated. It could impress Shamistta, not me- A Brahmin marrying a white, Aunt Minty had painted the family colors in black. Even the old Vet. Vent his anger. I hammered a point - it is 2005 AD for god's sake, humanity has a long way to go, I announced at the family conference, not 5002: when the world would all be colorless, casteless, irreligious and godless. My father seeing his authority waning and my blasphemy gaining credence as a fact would; turned to Aunt Minty. Dear brother; she said in her tear-tone, who listens to the old woman like me, then Tweney son is not the usual white guy, he is not into those things , you know, bi- sexuality, mastering.., gigolo, and what have you and he would help Shams in her pursuit of a PhD from MIT, LSE or whatever. Old vet. Relented and funded the farce. So I thought. Mr. and Mrs. Tweney, honeymooned at London, and came back in search for a job to Haridwar. It is this depression brother elder, Aunt Minty explained. You wait; even that guy from the whitest of all houses would come at your doors to ask for one. Gates is already at your gate; Buffet lays a buffet for Bihar, and Clinton come calling, every now or then. So poor Tweney, let him, in all I say, he is family. Vet. Calls me- Annant we know you are good at nothing, but you can fool people with you philosophy, your gift of the gab and your student connection, help Tweney Brother to open a centre for the queen's lingua, give him a room at your grandmother's Haveli, and let him earn his life like lively hood, not like you, doing things for nothings, the blackest Robin of our family with your herd of Will Scarletts.

Baba calling, a part of my duty, I thought and laid a plan for Tweney, eyeing Shams in return. Name it Mr. Tweney's English: give a slogan- 'Speak the Queen's Language in thirty days'. So a board is put up and an inauguration party thrown, courtesy the old Vet. The chief guest Mr. Kaushik, the local M.L.A. hails the centre as a step towards the development of Haridwar. People can now read and write in the language of the world, he claimed, let the world know that to be English is to be arrived at, speak for pun and earn dollars with collars, he roared, the government would provide Mr. Tweney all the facility for his sacrifice to come to this poor country of ours and serve us with his English, he has studied the language from his birth and is the fighter of the guy to teach our sons and daughters the language of the highness holiness queenness. It is the effort of Doctor Sahib and Principal Sir, the Gandhi of Haridwar, our own JDB, who have inspired us all, the politician concluded. People clap, and Sameer offers a swig of the spirit to me, *Jogiji* he taunted, take *Sanyas,* before the people take you for a ride. He laughed. Shams would be nearby I hoped, forgetting the seven vows around the fire and a promise at the Church on the nearby hill station had turned her into a touch-me-not type. *Sati-Savitri*; Sameer re-christened her.

But Tweney had his imperial plans tucked away from my gaze. So in a couple of months he had moved up market: to the Pentagon Mall on the national highway renting a twelve hundred and fifty square feet of space, decking it up with glassware, sofas and technology, employed a skirt wearing, student attracting counselor and had become a Managing Director of Tweney's Coaching, with a brand new Brand name, logo, slogan, an ISO -9000 certificate and a couple of patents in how to pronounce inspissations and do *Kapal Bhati*. Drink my piss I was livid that day when Sameer brought a bottle of the red Angel country liquor. What do these guys think of themselves I shouted, having the world as their keep. Sameer –the sage: no Brits now, dear Annant brother, they are all Americans, if only for the color, the world would be a better place to live in - but a black has won the white house race , now you see, he is with us, a fan of Gandhi- peace platoon. Is it so? I slurred. What of Shamistta I asked? You have a lot, Nina, Meena and the Red angel. I laughed- Bottle best for bachelor for a pest.

Ricky of the rich, frocks, curls, shoes, shawls, sophistication and manners, caught me one day at one of the vet's party. You must be *Apu*, she asked innocently, charming me in a strange way. Yes was my answer, the lie of a lover, Annant the boy for a lover; forever. No she countered him, you are Annant, and no more, she said. Yes; was my answer. We hit along so to say, living in the maze of adolescent in our childhood. It happens when one finds the lack of years as a cause of impotency, and one wishes that time runs faster, deviating from its usual stroll. Ricky, though, had come as a grown up.

Annant laughed loud. The orange and pink undies; the micro berries in micro bras.

Annant had finished a guava and pulled at the yellow over ripe Banana. The queen fruit, dear Annant- Shamistta it was who educated me to the goodness of the fruit. Before a bite, let it light the tunnel of funnel, it is safe, fruity, can be had once or twice a day and most certainly keeps the cur away. The Vogue says that before the pill, it was the greatest symbol of feminism. Grow up and then roar your slogans, she said- the black, half a bong beauty. Annant caught the rebel bit. Ricky it was who warned me to keep off that girl, she is a witch for one, we are sober types we don't indulge in such fracas and your sister oh! What a one you have for a cousin: A Sin; telling you such slangs. But it is only a fruit; I had complained and left her in a huff.

Annant bit a mouthful and savored the sweet after the sour. His satiation making him sleepy. He blessed the *Sadhus*, this country is a blessed one and to be born here, one doesn't have to work, can sleep anywhere, move about to its corners, but for the middleclass, the import of the British, this country would have been heaven on earth. I would buy an *Ektara* and sing my way to glory and feed, he shouted at a passerby. 'Brother, even the *Ektara* sings in a false raga'. The passersby and their Veda: To each his own. A billion streams of wisdom. Billion Buddha; All smiling in their anguish.

But the middleclass bit stuck to him. Nina was the cause. His not creating was the effect.

Aunt Minty set up the tone that day. 'Brother, send Annant to some medical college, he can be a doctor, he likes flesh, but a Human one', she spoke in innocence, but the old Vet. sat upright, feeling the pinch of destiny. We should otherwise he is gone for good, bunking classes, teasing teachers, chasing *Sadhus*, and god knows not what. But I want to paint and write, I rebelled, fuelled by Ricky. 'Bull shit for a paint, do you want to white wash our family name, your great grandfather was a doctor, your grandfather a doctor of Excavations, your father a doctor of Animals and your ambition is to be a painter'. Aunt Minty, the preserver of family. 'Aunty not that painter, but like Goethe, Hussein, Leonardo, Tagore-. I pleaded. 'All quiet, he would do what is told'. Vet roared. For the last time though, for I ran away to an obscure town without telling anyone of my escapade. I was given a grey jersey and blue knickers to wear, a shanty to live in and dishes to wash. Wash I would but would not return to the cell of a school or the world of books. Permit me my life and I could create another Mahabharat; I phoned Uncle Josh, the mediating mendicant. But son, there is only one of the kind in the world, and many have retold it with impunity, now don't start one in your house, poor sister of mine your mother, is sobbing since morning to the day previous to the previous day. I stuck to my ground only to lose my job at the *Dhaba*, curtsey, the Inspector Lal that was his name, a friend of the vet. I found myself back at the school- to the Manor born: caned for the sin, for misspelling sacrilege. Replacing 'i' with 'e' and 'e' with 'i'.

Was it a sin enough for being humiliated? Never humiliate a Brahmin, he shouted loud, waking the somnolent waddle of the swans on the placid canal waters. People forget history nowadays, he lamented, that is what the ego does, making one the prisons of one's inflated present, ignoring the humble past one had lived.

But I was a hero now at the fort St. George. Ankur offered me his Enid blytons, Shailendra his Holmes, Vinay his mouth organ and Lauki his luncheon fruit. Ricky pecked me on the right cheek, my hero she shared her secret, now do one more thing, she said, hold me in your arms. I did-My Arms and my woman. Shamistta let me have a peek into her reds and pinks; I ogled with a surprise and discovered with a glee of a scientist, it takes time to ripe. Wait mate.

Annant rested his head on his squared hands. All scientists are oglers, I suppose, he thought. The sensuousness is a sine quo non of modern technology. But the spirit? One has to work on one's own. Finding a way for a complete evolution. Lest the spirit is waylaid in the science shining. All should exist; he relented to his holding on to a single spirit track.

But Ricky grew quickly, ahead of Shamistta. Taller, fuller, saucier, naughtier, loiterer. Her lips were of the bold types, requiring at least a double go to feel them in one's own. Her size threw sighs. She flaunted them in front of me. I, of the sagely dispositions, ignored her. But she wouldn't let go. One day, a typical summery day, when the afternoons are spent in the comforts of the shade, she descended on me like a cloud, raining her yearning. The cloud had roared. A gale swept flushing me to my deeper desires. It was after much effort that the release came, in torrents and squalls, though- the plenty to spare of the youth. Equanimity was established for the time being- All silent at the battlefront, with no guns booming. What the heck! Ricky shouted me out of my slumber; spoiled my new dress, can't you be clean? She asked. All spots and mess, she was angry and left in a huff, mumbling swearing- yes even girls, man it is naughty nineties and the society can be naughty if the girls are. By God they own it. Not males who are all wild boars. But come the following Sunday she was up on to it again. In the coming monsoons she was gone. Her father transferred to the land of the *Nawabs of Awadh*.

Annant winked at the floating swans. 'Do you know me' he shouted at them. "One day you would." Is it important to be known? Why can't one live life of a disappearing? An invisible man: the real Superman.

Aunt Minty must have cooked a treat for that guy Tweney, Annant thought. Past the Chandi chowk and from there I can take a rickshaw to the premwalli galli, the love lane. Then I knock and Shamistta, now with ripened and pumpkinsh berries, like her mothers', would open the door. 'Hai, it is you, and boy, look at you, getting old shold, get a girl who ...Maa it is Annant, he looks hungry and all."

'What do you know of my hunger? I sit in a gruff. Aunt Minty, looking worried or feigning her look of worry says 'Son, come and stay with us, we make one large happy family, let me cook for you, your father is a worried man, let him have rest, your mother cries whole day.'

Shamistta brings him tea; he asks for something to eat, gets Poories in return, Sharmajii's Poories, your favorite, she informs him, Mr. Sharma gives us a discount in your name".

Ricky went without much of a fuss. A quite exit. Shamistta, the know all girl, knew all. So you are finally up there to be a man? She asked. I don't know, not now, I am grieving her going, I drew a line. My thin line of hairs for a moustache attracted her. You are the real man in our family, she remarked, yet I have something to show, would you accompany me to the backyard, she pulled at my hands. I let her take me round an old fiat, left hand driven, sat in the torn down garage. Through the cobwebs and the mossy muck of the monsoon we entered a shanty room behind the garage. Wait here I will be back, she disappeared. Here take this and write, whatever you want.

She gave me a dairy and a gold tipped pen kissed me on my cheeks. I took her in my arms. Both of us stood there for a long time; till the rain drops woke us up from our intimations.

So she wanted me to write, Annant shouted. Minnie, too. All girls are like fishes needing feeding and a net. Trap them least you are trapped. There are thousands of books of erudition in our country why write one? Annant thought.

That day Shamistta let me know that it was fun to grow up. Dangers lurked round the corners, though. Aunt Minty with her power of perusal pestered Old Vet. To tighten the noose around Annant. I was send to a school with bosses for teachers. No Twain only cane, check your dick you harry, no Dickens either. No Tom Sawyers no David Copperfields, only Webster. Master it for grammar, the wren with a dash of Martini. Drink deep dear Annant lest you fail the term. I did. That was the last of the efforts that the healer of the silent made on me. Aunt Minty continued her charade. Shamistta kept me in my wits. 'Try things which you can fall in love with while doing, otherwise do not attempt,' she advised.

I fondled with her berries that day in the innocence of my youth. Colors returned to my life as I wrote vigorously for the newspapers, letters to the editors, and the news of the nature. 'Cut corners not trees'. 'Save *Ganga Maa*'. 'Five hundred trees planted by the school students'. 'Before monsoon listen to sage forest', '*Chipko* Diaries'. It kept me going.

Annant yawned, it has been a long day, he said to himself. Better be going, to the Ganga Emporium book shop, first; then to the Ganga banks, listening to the god's songs. Sameer and Jorden would be off to Annapurna café.

Uncle josh made me rebel for the second time, for the last time. Sameer would join the Medical College, he announced one day, distributing sweets and surprises. 'Good' with a grump, the old vet. Wished him luck. He was of ordinary type, you know, never into serious study, our Annant is far bookiss… only if he could focus, Aunt Minty, stoking fires. He could still make it to the medical seat, I am ready to pay capitation, vet with a trick. Fund my book and you can have the hooker..ur ..Booker, I stammered. 'You are a son of a …. That's what you are; get out and be gone before I smash you into pieces, pack up time Annant, have enough of your tantrums. Writer uh.. as if leaves can be plucked, words trapped like flies, plots created like dreams, characters bred with the sleigh of the mind, no Annant dear son of my wife, your innings ends : caught and bowled.

What does he knows of cultural history; Damn Dads. When you need an enlightened one, you get a bigoted one. It was the year when the country took a leap towards global domination of the pulp fiction-modern literature. 1997. Off course I had followed her nose pin. Diamond- struck. When will Anniee gives her those ones- my friends teased the hell adolescent out of me. The architect doesn't have a structure and yet you, the connoisseur of the Great Indian Beauty-plump, wrapped and vermillion dotted; falling for the thin mint. Her eyes, I stood up like a true one crushed one; like epitome of honesty, line lips and soft ends, her vegetarian teeth and her curly hairs. I was wonderstruck by her rebel, you need an icon when you are a teenager and in the early nineties it was must if you were to survive. Oil wars, leadership crisis, assassination of the handsomest PM and dark art. It was the last one which worried me. What would come of you Annant?

Then came a Good Win for all Indians; or so thought I; my father was least impressed and so were my friends. The god of the smallest things wins a booker. Ah! A hope. I cried. God win. Big book big heart. It didn't matter to me what the story was , I was young at nineteen years, too young to understand it, but wasn't she looking fetching in her sari; that came as a dampener to my rebellious heroine image- torn jeans despite the muddled genes- like Shamistta's Rijul or Ragini: Ruddy and Rahel : Dizygotic, binovular, dichorial, dichorionic, dissimilar, false, fraternal, heterologus, hetero-ovular, two-egg- the unlike T's. There is crankiness in mixed races; Uncle Josh told me. What off that I care of? I said. She did it for the country and the country doesn't return the favor. She is my true Bharat *Ratna*. I claimed on her behalf. It was my infatuation that was pressing me. My friends knew of it. It was around this time that My Friend Hussian had perched himself up on the nest of the hornet; the second of my Bharat *Ratna*, like the nine *ratnas* in Akbar's court; the barefoot baba turned the nudist narcissist.

"Now he is gone to become the Shah of Oman". Annant shouted loudly, "Does it make you happy?" he asked the dumb ducks. Brain drain was bearable but Art drain? LostSoul.

Mothers are mothers after all, and it was the mother of my mother, who provided for me till I pursued my love for philosophy. My only link to the family was Tweney, who stood by me like a good Brit, was it on Shamistta' insistence or otherwise, but he was there, lending legitimacy to my rebellious ways. In his royal Enfield we biked our blues away, as Shamistta bred a couple of kids as a reminder to our childhood.

Annant lay quietly now. Life is fun without mun, but today I am a rich man, he thought, just less than a couple of thousands. Save some sum, JDB and his banking habits, not to be banked upon. Could buy a present for Shamistta? He thought. Or buy a dictionary of Philosophy, by, what was the name- Andrew flew, for cuckolding Minnie, prior to the nesting? He doesn't decide. How did Nina decide? He thought; to end one's life well: what can one say to this; it can happen to anybody, the mind playing truant. If only he could have seen it coming. Unfaithfully Ours, the Time.

I thought of her as she: And she as her. The last time she came, with a drained face, unkempt hairs, unclipped and unribbionned, unwashed and knotted; Overnight hairs. A dish fermented. Her clothes, strained with over wear; uncreased and unwashed. Shoes without socks. Eyes without lashes. Lips without smile. Heart without a beat. 'What has come of you? I asked. Oh! Nothing.. nothing at all, all fine, but pray can we dine, am famished. Feed me before I vanish. Sure whatever you say, I said. Then let us go to the German bakery besides the Luxman Jhula, the hanging bridge over the Ganga; at Rishikesh. Come along then, pillion my bike, but before that, wash the face in the holy waters, see your shadow, then you would realize how haggard you look. Let it be, I have come to a friend today, could you not leave your teacher treachery just for a day, she begs, surprising me. As you say my Cheri Amour, I let the youth snuggle out of me. I carry her; she- a burden: I feel it; she lets me, I try to divert her mind, and she minds my diversion. Annant, she said, could you not be serious, I am in a dilemma, after weighing all the pros with the cons, have concluded that, I should join the ashram way of living, the world is not my cup of tea, I want to be engrossed in religious work, keep busy, now would you do me a last favor, tell me a sect which I could join? I rested the bike on its stand, helped her stand on her weary feet. Let us eat; then we decide. I said. The German bakery was full with foreigners and locals aping them. Mostly Israeli, bit others too; Dutch, Russians and Brit women. We search a quiet corner and order our grub. Sandwich for the witch, my order. Sizzler for the muzzler, her order. You are into muzzle and all, I asked, have you met someone, a man with a golden gun? She laughs, Annant you relax me, and your sense of humor is a top draw, despite your pimple face and shabby mane, you could be a clowning glory, a joker wins the poker. I nip the corners of her Sandwich, chewing on the hard crust; now tell me all about it? I had asked. Eat first, she ordered, as she grumped on the food. She had ordered a jug of fresh lime which she sipped. I lighted a cigarette. Satiation should be the only aim, I remarked. That depends on the hunger, too. Her erudition had always surprised him. Tell me about yours, I asked. Mine, don't be silly and all, sir, I want to know something about these ashrams, if you could, help me join one of them. I wasn't surprised and told her so, but why do you, life is moving ahead, these are not helpful in growth, they are the mushrooms of the monsoons, never trust an organized system, I warned. She insisted. I did not relent. She was searching for that last speck to hold on to before the complete drowning. I beg you, she had begged, literarily had. For me they all are at one par, none befitting your level of spiritualism. I have lost my battle of the bump stead, my loneliness has eroded my creativity, my parents want to truncate my life, I have nothing left to look forward to. I will see what I can do; I said it with a heavy heart. Let us sit on the banks for a while, watch the sun set and all. I asked her without forcing her, I knew that she no longer was mine, that she had moved on or more precise fallen into a quagmire of beliefs. Blind bore. Her defeat was part mine. No .no .. I have to see him, she begged me and sat on the pillion like an obedient student, drive me back, sir, it was nice knowing you.

Last words, or were they? Annant searched for a shade and sat under a tree. The canal banks were crowded now. People putting up camps for tomorrow's bath. Plastic sheets fluttering uncontrollably, a herd of children crying for attention, elders coughing and smoking, women folk cutting vegetables and frying poories.

Aunt Minty's husband , what was his name ,I forgot, yes it was a long time ago, then I must have been really young; grown up child indeed. Yes Mr. Sen. It was a marriage like an affair, short ,torrid, rebellious and with a keepsake ; a love child, in this case, Shamistta. Now I knows why a typical *bhadra lok* name. But she had it in her to charm the charming, tall and all, Mr. Sen, the I.A.S. officer not a very gentleman. These administrative guys are fit as a fiddle but for fondle. Work they can but won't, as is their wont. Rent seekers all. Now the story of Aunty Minty. This Mr. Sen Sudhanshu, his name, Delhi Bengali, posted in the god's abode, and one day, sees Aunty Minty, at the Ghats, worshipping deities. He takes immediate liking for her; the brother Vet. Assured of some on high and not so mighty in the government hierarchy, readily agrees to the match. Then after Shamistta, Sen goes a wander seeks an alliance out of the solemn. Adult try. He succeeded. Vet. Knows it before Aunt Minty. That much we should give to the old Vet. Keeping the family together; a son of honors. He fought for his sisters' honor. Sen was shown the door. Aunt Minty, with little Shamistta came to stay with us. You have a sister, now, he informs me. What is that? I, the innocent. But families should stay together, what fun! I and my growing years with people around: except for the middleclass mindlessness for the professional living.

Annant watched the campers with intent- The world a family. What fun! Nowadays the boys want their freedom, the girls theirs, as well as their husbands- but hey the children want family. But who cares! The children are the burden of today, no income, all responsibility. What they give cannot be measured. Why worry? Shamitta grew with me, ahead of me; my education, part incomplete, she the first teacher. It was fun alright. No morality- All innocence. Now she is a mother of twins, half Brit half Brahmin children: Ragini and Rijul- Lightning and thunder- Rahel and Ruddy. Like mother like daughter, Shamistta found Tweney, again on the banks of the Ganga, the all giving river; their love stood the test of time, rest, as they say is history. The English tutor and his pupil: The Veda mentor and her *Shishya*.

Annant had seen it all. He could pen his family he thought, a story of the continents all condiments for a block buster, write and get back to them, your detractors. Niiniiminnieniiniiiminniee advocates her strange ideas for a torture. You must have been trained by Chinese in the fine art of torturing. I know Chinese checkers too, she eyed him. What of I care of? Annant: a disillusioned sage. Wake up and be damned, I shouted out at her. To pick me, she angered and all. Swollen fruit.

Annant had fruits on an empty stomach, dyspepsia, the bane of us fasters, he thought. He approached the camps with eyes on solid food; but asked for the some digestive powder instead. 'Yes we have, *babu*, an old man, keen to be a part of the Kumbh offered him a spoonful of a dark brown, thinly powered powder. He gulps at it in one go and belches in Burrup. 'Look sahib, the ancient has wisdom and all, the old man smiles. Annant agreed and relieved. 'One more spoon he demanded'. Take the bottle he was given a dark glass bottle. Good souls, May god and all bless you. Annant the sage; the role of a Brahmin. This burden of a Brahmin, no one understands. The sacrifice they make for knowledge, when the world sleeps, they wake setting standards for the mediocre. But it is their arrogance that is taken note of. They have earned it, haven't they?

Now what? No philosophy. No income. No girl. No family. No name. No Minnie. No Ricky. No Shamistta. No food. No house. No clothes. No nothing. None no fun. No none none no. Now what? The thinker does not thinketh. Better to lie under the sun than to lie to one's self. The dilemma of bliss superimposed over the daily living. *Maya* versus *Gyan*. Illusion versus Knowledge. The choice is obvious, isn't it? But the choosing isn't. Isn't it? Let destiny peep. Even if it brings weep, my mother's mother's wisdom; the old lady with her betel nut cracker and a silver case for catechu, lime, areca nut, peppermint, engraved spoon for serving. Betel leaves all dressed up with lime and catechu before they found their way into the marooned mouth with red white teeth and pleated corners of the mouth; buccal mucosa slithered by the lime and bathed by the catechu juice. She would chomp nonetheless. What a country and what a grandmother? Kumbh bath is tomorrow, I would wash away my sin, if having a laugh is one.

Annant laughs in a shout. "What is it Sahib"? The old medicine man, like the color of his powder; His is the real knowledge, effective, quick, reliable, no side effect, cheap and for the spirit- The medicine man, humble, accessible and content with his fees.

"Don't call me that?" Annant warned him.

"What sahib?" He asked innocently.

The old man has his genes altered.

"Do you have a medicine for making one a white?" He asks.

"You mean Gora?" He asked in all his innocence.

Ah! Gurudev rebel Rabindra. "no.. yes .." Annant replied in haste.

"No sahib, the sun is cruel here, but you can try milk cream or apply the froth of the freshly udder milk." The old prescribed in all his humility.

But my maternal grandmother was the royal scion without the paraphernalia of her entourage. After grandfather had passed away, she took hold of all and sundry; a dynamo of a woman standing tall at four feet. Her company was a relief whenever I paid her a visit. Vast fields to run. Berries, green and sweet, Neem trees, Mango in the summers and milk from the herd of cows. Speaking of the cows, it was fun whenever I took them out for their jungle feed. *Kaali, Chanda, Nimmi, Gaghri, Doodhli*; they went by these names and moved in slow steps, regurgitating on soft grass. Then they would take rest under the tree shade. A small stream strolled down across the forest. It was fun to bath in the privacy of the animals. Their innocent ramblings, adding a color to the lagoon moments. Why one enjoys maternal grandparents than the paternal ones, I have never understood, but it was like that for me.

'*Bobuji khabiye kya*?" The old medicine man with her Bhojpuri dialect: Sweet, rustic, hearty, touchy, regional. "Would you eat? India is a region after all, not a nation. "*Aphi Khaibiye*"? Annant answered him. "*Babu kaun goan, Jaunpur*?" Inquisitive devotees. "*Bhai Himalaya.*" He replied. Sameer would have relished their hospitality and Jorden. What they look for these foreigners, coming thus far in search of solace and all? "*Babu Chah libeye*"? Have tea. Annant decides against having. Dyspepsia. But the powder worked.

Nina had a story to tell. Did she meet me after having failed in her search for the gutter of the ashrams? Yes she did. Not in a friendly manner that much I can say. Why? Because she did not fight, she accepted, not the acceptance of the Prakriti, but defeat. Her defeat was mine. 'Why '? She had asked. 'You wouldn't understand'. I had replied. Let it be, sit behind, let us go for a ride, to Neelkanth Mahadev temple, Shiva might provide you succor. She labored on the pillion seat. I drove in a silence. She sat in silence. What of your pursuit? I asked her. "What of it? I am about to discover the finality about life and living, will tell you all.' I sat on the door of the temple letting her have the Shiva all by herself. 'You wouldn't come'. No the lord seek only beautiful faces at night' .I said. She was careful of her worship. The priest helped her light an earthen oil wick and a few incense sticks. She had covered her head with her yellow wrap, her hands folded and her lips quivering under a prayer. Under the stars she sat on the cold stone seat eyeing me. Annant, she said, would you do me a last favor? I knew what she sought. My yes wouldn't have mattered. No I said. Her eyes were like glass, reflecting everything except her own reflections. No shadows passed across her eyes. Like I said, my yes wouldn't have mattered. It is one thing losing hope, it is another being hopeless, and to be hanging on the noose of hopelessness is altogether different. It is death. No amount of life would have saved her. Death had begun its slow clawing. Stealthily. Sublimely. Sweetly. She savored its might. A life just before death. It was fun knowing you, I would see you one more time before I go; she spoke vacuously. She knew I knew. I knew she knew. Shiva be with you, I said my silent prayer. In god we all have faith when distress calls. Yes, Shiva, the god of sacrifice, she spoke weakly now, almost laboring for each word. What can a fallen star wish for, but it fulfils other's wishes, is it not?" She asked. I kept quiet. It was a deathly night. Though stars lend it continuity, they would be there when we are gone. This night stands as a witness to our final good bye. But she had said that she would meet one more time. When was that?

"Annant sir what goes, lying under the sun, a new asana, perhaps, with you one can expect anything, just anything?" Pande, now what luck, of all people I meet Pande. Annant sat in a huff. "Ram..Ram.. bhai what is it ?" He was rude. Pande, a fellow teacher, half bald, with a half cheek scald, the right one, the rumor says his wife threw boiling oil on him, good, he deserved it and much more, should have thrown him out of the house, or still better, in the Ganga, a permanent cleaning of the soul; the sin and the sinner.

"Annantjii, now you are free like a birdie." Pande, the caddy; Annant in a hole. "No college no lecture, but philosophy is like that, talk anything rotten and people would clap for you, Annantji it was fun to have you in our college, now no girl would take admission. All came for you." Pande the womanizer, his scald tells the tale, pinches him as a rub. Annant kept quiet. Pande feeds the ducks the leftover chapattis he had brought. "Missus says this is to awaken the human in me, I say Annantji, am I not human enough, just my face, half burnt, but you are scarred, too, with all this, now Nina now Minnie, but she takes you as a saint, and me as a *Shaitan,* the devil, tell you Annant, never marry, never, and if have too, never sleep with her, the petticoat is the real, what you call in philosophy, determination." Pande at it again.

"Determinism, Pandeji". Annant corrected him.

"Yes.. yes that, but mark my word, marry is like a balloon, all air inside, but it is your breath that the balloon is filled with, the day you want to withdraw your breath is withdrawn."

"Keep up the balloon flying Pandeji, how's your wife, our dear sister in law?" Annant asked.

"She is a joy and happy, do pay us a visit, sometimes, drop for lunch or what." Pande the reluctant host, time was when he stood on the old vet's door waiting for the letter of recommendation for the old JDB, and now he is the king on the swing.

"I would: enjoy the Kumbh bath tomorrow." Annant calls and turns his back to him.

Nina had a complain *in articulo mortis*. Ricky had a complain *Ab irto* . Shamistta had a complain, *In deliciis*. Illicit. Ill cite. I llic it. Il lic it. I ll I c it- That I had turned my back on them all. What else can a boy do? Facing up to the whole world at a young age. Flounder father. Maudlin mother. Frazzle friends. Riling relatives. Truncated technology. Trifle teachers. Trickle time. Ascending appetite. Baulking books. Inferior inference. Pestering pimples. What can a young boy do? Who was that who said that to be young, Shelly or who? I for once beg to differ from the old young gentlemen. In memory of the great poet, but I beg to differ. The icing on the cake is the adage to be born in the middleclass. So a young boy born in a Middlemarch milieu can have a portrait of an artist as a young man, but it would be disfigured, a nowhere tale of two personalities: one side the flamboyance of a Tom sawyer and on the other the pity of a David Copperfield. If only the Renaissance had come a bit late, now, in the twenty-first century not in the fifteenth. Pico della Mirandola is the real and the first world hero that much I can give to Italy apart from the Puzo Mafia. Despite the ban by the Pope he stood for the dignity and responsibility of the Man.

Nina's was just a few days before she went away, or died. Ricky was all passion as a fashion. Shamistta's a concerned one a sinister one. Sin sister. Maybe I am exaggerating it now. If one views the childhood from hindsight one tends to inflate one's exploitations and deflate one's blessings. In my case it is true to an extent. After all she was the daughter of my father's sister. Your sister, my sister's daughter, was how the old vet. had introduced her. Why my sister? I had wondered. But it was hindsight I was talking; the Shamistta issue in a way boosted my ego. She would hold my hands and we would walk in the bazaars, intimately, right in the middle of the crowd. People would compliment us and I would turn red. She was six and I, nine. Things are bound to spill over if you fill the glass up to the rim my mother's mother often said as a warning to her farm hands. In my case it was what had happened with Shamissta . One thing was clear though, that I was a novice then and I am a novice now. Annant stood up to drink a couple of palms full of water. Minnie hangs by but haven't even …just the hairs bit. Wireless caress. In Shamistta's case it was growing in a caress. Once a year, though, I had to let her tie a thread, colorful and deities decorated and pay her up for her efforts. This is a vow for protecting your little sister; Aunt Minty would fill my mouth with a *rosagulla.* I would, anyway even if she doesn't tie me, I rebelled. But now I know why tying is necessary. It tidy up the things. It doesn't mean that I messed up anything, that much I have in me never lower the dignity of a man. Hide your might, never letting it out for the hide. Let the stakes rise then arise. I waited and waited. But Shamistta didn't. Or Tweaney couldn't. This is Tweaney, Annant , this was how she introduced him to me . Is he? I knew then and there only that pretty little young things are like monsoon lilies. Transient trams. Catch them if you can, but if you miss them, do not wail, a next one would be whistling round the corner, about to enter the *la gurre* of your heart.

Annant found the water warm. Was it his passion all flamed or something? Got to let the doctor measure the pressure. Shamistta was not all passion though, unlike Ricky, all passion. Her demands sore, soared with her puberty; Ding dong bell berry on the swell. Once the old vet: took me to the land of the Nawabs: Lucknow. I want it to be done up with you once and for all, right here. Here, I burst out laughing. We were sitting under the roof on the roof, the staircase roof. So what keep it short, sweet, simple; silly: safe and smooth. She was as keen as a bee. But am I an expert in matters like these, I rebelled. What you have been doing then, all these years, she demanded of me. You live in a town of nirvana, can one have nirvana without this, and she snuggled against me. Now, what is nirvana got to do with all this and with a fifteen year old, I never understood. It must be that girl Shamistta, I told you she is a witch, a Bengali black magic, but at least kiss me, and she put her lips close to mine- when her mother, with curly hairs and burly walk accosted us in her Sherlock swagger. You two come down and have *Pakoras*, they are hot, and her eyes smoldered on us. We were hot too, auntie, smoldering under nubile desires. I knew you were good for nothing, Ricky with her hunger, no *Pakora* of the world could satisfy. For me though, they were a savior. A Krishna for a Draupadi. I had kept myself draped, no sacrilege. It was the last time Ricky approached me.

Shamistta must be feeding Tweney, now, thought Annant. Poories from Sharmajis'. A bite of berries after the oil. Sweat dish. Sweet dish.

Swadesh. No boil for the Brit. They adapted once they would adapt now: Anything for commerce and love. I better be moving lest Pande returns, Annant jogged around for a while eyed by the campers. A few children joined him shouting…there goes the train..there goes the train… *chulk,, chukl…chukk*…nearby station says..*rulk..rukl.. rukk.rukk*…

Brother Benedict was the true Catholic, suave, erudite, inflexible and prone to quick disillusions, when it came to winning matches of cricket. Before the monsoons would set in, in the hill town, where stood on the hill, known as Foxes' hill, St. George's college, the centre of activity would be on how to win the local cricket tournament. My school with blessings from coaches and umpires would get passed the local teams with ease, in the preliminaries. It was then that Big Brother Benedict would have those butterflies in his sucked in stomach. He would bite his nails, shout about, walk in a stupor across the vast fields, direct the players in their practice sessions, and as I said, like a true catholic, pray for the team's success. All we had to do was to mind our middle stump, and the rest was in god's hands. In the name of the child, the father, and the Holy Spirit. The players never took his word seriously, though they played to their potential, sometimes winning, sometimes losing. But the dear brother of us all, sweated with beads, praying no end. The gods are really crazy when it comes to prayers. They listen to some sometimes and do not listen to some sometimes. But the whole world prays, nonetheless- All the time.

Annant teased the children, they teased him in return. *Budda baba* they called and whistled- The old man and his tale. Tail snatchers all. He shooed them away like monkeys. The brown medicine man shouts at them and they relent. Annant sat in a gruff with complains simmering inside him. In today's times complaining is a sign of aging, he thought. Death is the last of the complains. Alas! It is only after death that one realizes life. Nina's death. Other's life. What a way at self correction? Like testing a vaccine for a new bacteria. One's life other's guinea. The sun would be strong now, he concluded. Winters are as good as gone. A spring in the cold. But it the Kumbh tomorrow, he is reminded of the great event by a procession that passes by. A walk on the ramp by the mendicants. The whole world clicks them for their posters in the drawing room. 'Look at my snap, before you snap'. 'It is a world all together different my friend'. 'We are as exotic as Hispanics'. 'Look at those biceps of the baba'. 'Wear a rudrashk for luck and F…k'. These Nuevo riche Indians would do something for Hinduism, Annant thought. Money BagsBaba. Currency Prayers Bells of Coins. But what of it, the world changes, as JDB baba says. Follow or get f.. ck F…allen.

Annant was not the fallen type though. He stood his ground whenever something shook. That was Annant. A fighter to the core, never giving anything without a good fight. But he had let go of Shamistta, ran away from Ricky and a few days back lost Nina. What a fighter?

Defeat makes a man, no not my mother's mother this time, old aunt Maitry, it was who supplied these gems like Marcus Aurelius. In that year, a year when the young Prime Minister was shot dead, we lost the local cricket tournament to the Rock blue stars, a star studded *Changh* drinking team (*Changh* is the local drink which made the Tibetans stay in India, in case the lesser informed didn't knew). They beat us by five wickets(wickeds for Mr. Bhatnagar). Men in white robe; A pint of rice *Changh*; Cheer girls; Blessing of local deities; Chaucer choker dice. Brother Benedict was crestfallen, his Catholics and faith and all lost in the grime of local charms. Mr. Bhatnagar, the Billiards(trouser variant) rookie among the brothers, picked up the threads on his behalf, the next day. Let us first address the five wickeds; one by one, number one: put your own men in white, umpire them with pelf; number two: have lots of drinks but not *Changh* so black Irish tea would do, same result; Number three: cherry girls, but we are a boys school, we have to take town help get an outside supply; number four: built a temple of Local deity right here in the school compound; number Five: Bribe the rival players: he was serious, so was Brother Benedict, as I said he would do anything for cricket. Anything? Next year we won the trophy, without the *Changh*, no bribes, no local deity, no cheer girls, and no white robe robbers. It has remained a mystery to me, a catholic magic, I suppose. Faith is the best *Googly* one can bowl: God; the proverbial third umpire.

Annant searched a shade to sleep. But he was reminded of his task, a book for Minnie to molest her with philosophy, Chadhury brothers for power, pelf, prostitutes, eating time at Annapurna. The day is long, he concluded. His hands played with the white stubble for a beard. Should I? Or should I not? For effects, perhaps. He had the money. What of a new jacket? Five hundred rupees and no more. Banghaji I have this much. Annant sir don't pay anything, this is your shop, he the owner, a Punjabi with a perfect grin. Brings the moolah, he confided to Annant one day. How much this one the off white one? Oh! This not fit for you Professor Annant, just a thousand of the most humble rupees, but see this the blue suits you, or this light red, goes well with your acne face, a color to die for, buy it , fifteen hundred rupees only, pay later, or Doctor Shaib is there, you take it , Annant bhai the new season is here, it is Kumbh too, lot of stuff, you need something hot;

packet it you chapatti chompers, he calls his team of sales men.

That Bangha chap is the real new India, selling Ludhiana to London and Hissar at Haridwar. Annant lies under the tree shade for a little longer. Shamistta was sorry for what she had done to me, after I met with her Tweney guy. But we couldn't have stayed together anyway, she said. Your mother stays with her brother; I was blinded by the erosion of my territory. I want to settle down, she shouted in all finality, as for you, you wouldn't do anything any way. That was what girls are made up for, settle down and beget life, no more. The seeds are sown in their genes I suppose, Prakriti predilictions. Sham Shams: And I with a jilted jiggle. She was alright with me though, feeding my imaginations with her dressing and undressing. Her smell lingered even when she went away on her honeymoon. She came back in a few weeks time. Mr. Tweney the guy who won, was Charlesque in swagger and of a stooping height, though, Shamistta was no Diana, all Bengali black beauty, but he for one kept the color business at an arm's length and held her hand despite all. But I would not convert, he could put his foot down when need be. No need, the vet. With the largest heart, we are not like that, the boost of a Brahmin, no conversions, keep up your faith, the doctor proclaimed impressing him. Annant sulked, could have noosed him in this religious issue, but for the old vet. The two got married according to two faiths, two cultures. For a church we had to go to the nearby hill station, no British at Haridwar. That was the Raj, left Hindus free to profess, practice and propagate Hinduism, in their own country, in their own language. The marriage reception was a huge affair, secularism won, was the war cry. Now the prime minister can be a white. No foreign, now all are global. The Brahmins have opened there wares for the west. It was sloganeering at its best. I knew it is the itch between the legs that causes everything- Wars, Religions, Marriages, Elections, Families, Globalization, Trade, Literature, Science, and for me, Philosophy.

Annant laughed aloud, for the second time startling the ducks and the campers.

Annant caught a nap, the left over sleep, or the carried forward one. He slept among the cacophony of the crowd. A short sleep, intense and sweet, like a drink of cold water on a hot day, or a wink to a beauty, or a shy of pubescence, or a call of the peacock, or the awakening of the soul.

Short sweet sublime simple smooch.

Life like little lingerings lingering langourously.

ANNAPURNA

Two men blew vapors on the chocolaty foam that made a concave mound over their over-sized mugs. Pits appeared on the brown puffs of coffee cream. A dark liquid peeped from them. One of them drank in measured sips. The other watched the poker patterns over the brown puff of his mug.

"Go on." The sipper said. "Not like it is in Sydney cafes, but then this is a Hindu to the tea, town." He patted his back for the pun.

The other gave a tentative look, then dipped his middle finger and tested it for warmth. Licking the finger from which hung tiny droplets of the brown liquid, he made a silly face and pushed the mug to the centre of the table.

The other continued to sip and moved his right hand over his throat as if he had had a dose of cough syrup.

He cleared his throat with a sound of gargle. The other watched him closely, his eyes closed in a squint. He rubbed his hands against each other and held the coffee mug with his palms and tasted its content, this time with a tentative sip. His face bore a sign of disbelief, he took another swig, this time a more seasoned one and the look of disbelief widened. He looked behind his back as if in a search. The other gave him a look of enquiry. A questioned hung between the two for a moment.

"Coffee?"

"Drinking Chocolate." The other replied.

They were small time businessmen from Delhi, owners of a Sari shop at Karol Bagh. The first one went by the name of Mr. Jas Arora and the other one by the name of Mr. Luke Meherotra. Jas a shorter and an anglicized version of Jasmeet and Luke stood for Lakhwinder. Both were well educated; play school and Convent, followed by a degree from an Australian university. Both were at the Kumbh fair to expand their business and tap new markets.

"There is a potential here, we should open up a showroom before some foreigner comes with his Mall- Shall concept, I tell you brother this won't work in this country; the women here want to be felt by the salesmen when they try new saris." Jas said.

"More cotton I say, not the costly silk type, Kanpur supplies, or from Banaras." Luke said in a thoughtful tone.

"The investment?"

"Ask the bank to finance it."

"I mean, the Banaras ones are costly; would anybody buy them here?"

"My friend, not the real Banaras Sari; the fake Banaresi one; you now- the game under the name."

"Pochampalli, Mysore, Dacca, Assam, Kanzivarem, Banaras, all made in Ludhiana?"

"Then imported to Delhi, from there you can export anything to anywhere; you see- the stamp of the Asoka." A laugh followed.

"You got it brother, a Rolls Royce without the royal roll; now call the Waiter."

"Hey waiter… waiter come here." A call follows.

"Like this Coffee; make out what you want- except tea."

Both laughed heartily and with a masculine authority.

"Ha ha…ha..You are smart, *Sydney ka chailla*; the Casanova of Sydney, that's what they called you; didn't they?" Jas smiled with a wink.

"So all Ludhiana in the country; but as you said; name is the game- Haridwar silk for Kumbh, take bath in it and earn blessings of the goddesses Ganga."

"Hey.. Waiter. Come here." Luke called.

"Brother, now people like fake more than they like the real stuff, all fake no shake, the real is for *leal.*"

'What is *leal?*"

'Ah! My friend another fake." He laughed.

"Yes sir, what is it that I can get you?" The Waiter waited upon them.

"Is this Coffee?" Both demanded in a threat.

"Yes sir off course." The waiter replied while picking up the empty mugs.

"But it tasted like drinking chocolate syrup." Both complained.

"No coffee?" The waiter asked.

"No." Both replied in unison.

"But your order was coffee?" He asked.

"Yes." The two replied in a chorus.

"Then it is coffee; drink one more mug and you will find the coffee taste, search it man, this is Haridwar, no search no find." The waiter had vanished before they could complain, thrusting a bill on Jas's hand.

Should we? Or should we mingle with the crowds? Pay up, they decided. Better be honest with this coffee business with a sprinkle of *Moksha*; it is Kumbh time, after all.

The owner, Mr. Jugran, as if reading their minds, gives them a threateningly macabre smile, and extends a cold hand of commerce, come again, his was an open invitation, after the payment. Fake friendship. Both bumped into Jorden at the entrance. Both excused in a hurry. Is he real? They discussed him once they had walked into the narrow alley eyeing the decorated shops with a hungry glee.

"So this is, is this the abode of the goddesses of feast?" Jorden asked. "It certainly is all decked up like a bride."

He looked at peace with himself, neat, and spick with a span of his own, for aura. Last time when he had come here, a few years ago, this place was dark, dull and dirty, like the owner Mr. V. Jugran. It was cheap, pure, simple and scrumptious, like the owner. The tables were wooden and warmly smoked. The curtains were multipurpose, shadowing the sun rays and drying the hands of hungry gentry. The cutlery was to be carelessly used and for every broken piece there was a pat from the serving Waiters, who were the friendly hill folks. The cook was a master of local cuisine. Order him anything exotic and he would churn up your salivary glands. It was known as '*Annapurna Bhoj*'. Now the place is brightly lit, neat, and laden with the paraphernalia of the modern hygiene system. A LCD plays overtime, music and cricket; the crowd favorite. The Rexene sofas are bright red and luxurious. The table is clothed with crochet finery of pinks and greens. Bamboo chicks adorn the windows giving it a corporate visage. The air is conditioned to the temperature of eighteen degrees centigrade. The waiters are liveried and Tweney trained. Mr. V. Jugran is a corporate honcho with a glass cabin of his own. The food is expensive and inter-continental. That was what Jorden found when he surveyed the Menu, one hundred and fifty- one items in all. The taste was a matter of debate. He wondered how Pizza would be like. The name, he whispered loudly; 'Annapurna Café'.

Sameer sunk into the Rexene with an aristocratic flourish; His wet hairs dripping with the holy drops. He eyed the modernity around. A place meant for the old and turned into a hangout for the young. Reverse mellow. He liked the new look though, Mr. Jugran does have a finger on the pulse. Young India- Besant; the old lady had seen it coming almost a hundred years ago.

"Have you known Aunt Annie Besant?" Sameer asked.

"The one of the Theosophical Society?" Jorden sat facing him.

"Theosophy is the real religion you see Jorden; knowing to know the nature of god, and all. They have blended Hinduism into it, giving a mystical dimension to the practice of religion."

"And also Platonism, a concoction of reason and faith, it sure is worth a read."

"Contrast it with Anthroposophy, and you will find that Aunty's was an adapted version." Sameer said and eyed the scurrying waiters.

"Ah! The Greek! They my friend, are the original, what did they have to say? The wisdom about man; was it?"

"Yes, later Steiner developed it for us mortals: the cultivation of man's evolving spiritual perceptions is the most important task facing humanity, says he?"

"Like Hinduism, if I dare the Brahmin in you, the key to knowledge and the understanding of the universe lies in us all: The *Panch Tatva* of evolution. Five elements versus the rest of the ..."

"Listen to Annant on this, I tell you Jorden, he- a dear friend of us would; one day make us all, very proud." Sameer is flushed and famished, as he stands up and waves at Mr. V. Jugran.

Mr. V. Jugran, a stout, strongly built forty year old; two wives, one daughter, three sons, came up to them, keen to be introduced to Jorden. "Doctor Sahib, how goes life? Your friend? What can we treat him with?" The Tweny trained honcho. Like all hill folks he stood at around five feet. A slight paunch of forty had started taking shape. To beat the stress of managing an eatery, he had taken to sucking at tobacco balls mixed with lime, kept under his lower lip. He wore a brown jacket with red pullover inside and an olive green baggy.

"What Jugs no waiter on this table; we have got a guest at the Kumbh, send someone brother, and by the way, this is Jorden, a globe trotter." Sameer said.

"Haridwar welcomes him and so does this café, all yours Mr. Jorden." He shakes hands warmly.

Old Jugran in glimpses; One can't keep the nature out.

"Hello." Jorden extended his hand. "I had come here, say, a couple of years ago."

"This is the Maha Kumbh, the mother of all Kumbhs; the first of the independent capitalist India; as Annant sir says." Jugs mugs up his selling skills.

'Now brother; something to eat; send us your most efficient caddy Deepak, please." Sameer insisted on his favorite waiter.

"Sure Doctor Sahib, you are the pride of our city, with Annant sir; he has something in him, though, always short of cas..." Jugs lugs for dough.

'The guest, Jugranji." Sameer winked at him.

"Yes..yes...I am off."

"He has indeed come a long way Jorden; running away from his village in the mid eighties to running an empire of Pizzas here, a long way, indeed." Sameer said.

The crowd had thickened now- Varied tastes, one hunger. More people queued up: All vegetarians eating before the bath, the next day.

"*Samadhi,* is it then, which Annant aspires for?" Jorden asked.

"Ask him, I better keep mum, on matters of the spirit, you see Jorden, nowadays all are talking on yoga, and this is the real sacrilege." Sameer replied. "He calls it *Samyam.*"

"Why? Is not knowledge a matter of fundamental right?" Jorden asked

"Because, to understand the knowledge of such magnitude, one needs a thorough understanding of the intricacies of how the spirit can be experienced; that much a lay man like me can make out, but now everybody talks of yoga, A billion dollar industry, they say. I say; my foot- that is the problem with capitalism, killing the person's ability to think for himself, but following the diktats of markets and the nexus between the producers and the marketing agencies and what do they sell?- Half baked concepts, ill treatments and addictions of things unnecessary. No dear friend there is nothing fundamental about knowledge; a tough way to attain a level, one has to sacrifice all. No readymade solutions available in the market." Sameer gets excited.

"Calm up dear doctor, we aren't reformists but we are hungry; swimming works up a nice appetite."

"It does, but that was fun, except that Annant brooded over her." Sameer relaxes a bit and stretches on the sofa, feeling the spongy seat.

"Her?"

"Nina."

"Some..

"Well a girl, one of his close mentee in matters of the spirit; died a few days ago and our dear Annant has taken upon himself the blame for her death; that is what keeps him occupied, he could have written a magnum opus, otherwise."

"Hmm..mm."

"I tell you brother, all he should do is to immigrate and lo and behold, he is published. But it is his rigidity that worries the hell out of me; write I will but on my own conditions; now tell me Jorden; can anything be done without an Agent. You are from London and what was that city but a trading centre frequented by the agents of Europe." Sameer pumped his fist on the table.

"That steward of yours, Deepak I suppose; he hasn't shown up. Call him and feed me then I would present my views."

"Deep...Pak.. hey brother were art thou?" Sameer shouted about.

"Sir, I am coming." A sound echoes through the bustling of the café and a lean boy with cotton adolescent hairs on his soft face, rushes towards their table.

He is carrying an aluminum tray with two glasses of water. He is wearing a saffron *kurta*, with the *Gaytri* Mantra printed all over it. He dodges the tables, guests, his fellow lackeys and reaches the duo's table without spilling a single drop of water. A sense of achievement reflects on his face as he places the glasses on the table.

"Ram..Ram.. Sir, here is your lime water, as usual." He saluted Sameer and stood obsequiously.

"Lime, I hardly see any limeness in it". Sameer surveyed the glasses which contained fuzzy liquid.

"The boss dilutes all, but the flavor lingers sir; have a bottle of lemon, otherwise, coke it up or pep your sip, should I get one?" He challenged them with the offerings.

"How about a hearty breakfast, Deepu; something for the famished souls; not a drop of the grub since last fifteen hours?"

"Sure sir whatever you say, the Menu says it all." Deepak stood in attendance.

"Choose your pick, Jorden, the shop belongs to you, c'mon, do us a great service by picking up a healthy food for us all, but, I dare say, it is all veggie and all." Sameer is perked up once again.

"The world would ultimately come to that." Jorden replied.

"Would it? People like kidneys and all, blood hound for men, it is in the region, they say."

"Put on an order or do I do the needful?" Jorden asked as he read the five page menu.

"Order what the place is known for, for the rest, god it is who will have to vouch."

"You mean one out of one hundred and fifty-one? And what that one would be? Aloo poorie, Potatoes with Pooriees?"

"Eureka! Jorden you are the Archimedes of the hungry era."

"So be it."

"Sure, Deepak, hop along, we have exercised our freedom of the will."

"What was that you said about the writers in the morning?" Jorden spoke coldly.

"Me? What was it that I said to prick my friend here?"

"That the writers were ink leeches, sucking blood."

"Oh!, that!! Not for you, it was meant for Annant, the beast, that he is, dying to be one, it is that, She-devil Minnie, would kill him some day, you know Jorden, men won't work until their women coax them to do something, but our devil writes well, that much he has impressed me and with his ways with lasses."

"But I felt the pinch, no writing no nothing: Histories, Philosophies, Literature.. … , you cannot brush the power of the words under the carpet of ignorance."

"That is what worries me, the power of words, hold them for your dear life and be damned. Jorden, words are the bane of the modern society; arrows too narrow, missing their mark…. Leading into the dark."

"But not all are like the way you say, some change life, some give life and some give peace, the word, *Shantih..Shantih*..is a word too.."

"Agreed my father of the soul, take me as your younger brother and forgive me for good, here I hold my ears, both of them and count till five." Sameer holds his ears and rises and sits on the sofa, for five times, counting them loudly. A slight commotion rises in the café as people turn their necks to peep at his dramatic act.

Himnash with Minnie and Monerill in tow enter the café and add to the ensuing melee. He searched for an unoccupied table as the group wait. A scuffle breaks between him and the Bengali *Bhadra lok* . Mr. V. Jugran, comes out of his cabin and tries to restore order.

Sameer sits, feigning anger. Sulking Samurai. Jorden reddens under the embarrassment and takes a swig of the lime drink. Sameer gets up to intervene.

Heckling, nudging and swearing goes on for a while till order is restored by Mr. V. Jugran, through a threat of the police. "I would, to the gods I say, call the orderlies, our Deputy is one Mamata, without any of the motherly feelings, you sons of your parents, she is as strict as a stick, behave or be behind bars." He threatened.

"Bar at Haridwar! Jugs want mugs, c'mon, they are the youth of this country, allow them some rebel, Annant would approve of this." Sameer intervened to douse the flared tempers. "On behalf of the Con Dress party, I apologize." He raised his right palm miming taking an oath and turned towards the Bengali ladies. "You are the epitome of our nationalism; the country of the Kumbh is at your disposal."

"Jugs, take things chill, you have indeed the crowd of a mill." He puts an arm around Mr. V. Jugran and tries to placate his anger.

" Sameer sir, these boys would spoil whatever name we have earned for this place, but your couplet was fun. Doctor Poet, yes that's what you are." The owner smiled.

"There is only one who fits that crown, Annant's father, listen him sing and recite his original limericks and you would then know why he kept all the animals in good spirit, Dr. Bharadwaj, the vet. PBS. A Shelly shocked."

"Sir these boys, I would complain to JDB." Mr. V. Jugran did not relent.

"You are the king of this empire, need you ask for outside help, here let me call them and let them offer a mea culpa." Sameer said.

"A what? No legal wiggle, doctor sir, your word is enough, I forgive them." Mr. V. Jugran runs his hand over his tummy and sat on his pedestal chair with a huff.

"It is settled then, let me handle things for you Jugs, you count the dough." Sameer moves into the café hall and smiles at the Bengali devotees, sipping tea.

"Thank you sir, this is the second time you have saved us." A pretty woman, with a huge vermillion dot on her forehead and wearing a beige sari, looks at him with intent.

"Second time, I didn't get you madam." Sameer fawned and drooled.

"In the morning, among the multitude of people you guided us to the right path for the morning bath." Hers was the sweetest of voices.

"It is all right, I knew it was in me to be a perfect guide, but my father, the medicine seller was not convinced, pushing me into the world of organized sophistry, of the white flannels with ear stethoscope; but pray, enjoy the town's best Poories at Annapurna." Sameer smiled and let her sonorous vociferations trail him to his table.

"I tell you Jorden, these bongs have the best vocals, it is the amount of sweet they eat, I suppose, have you been to Bengal, the Brits were fond of the place: hey Minnie…" Sameer waves at her.

"She is the current object of our dear friend's afflictions." He addressed Jorden.

"Afflictions? She looks harmless to me, all pretty in her yellow suit and green wrap." Jorden observed.

"That, my friend is the trouble; like wild flowers, never touch the ones which are bright, small, in the shadows and innocent: Poison!" Sameer stood to greet Minnie.

"You with this gang? Now dearest Jorden we finally are blesseth to have the Mermaid in the Tavern." Sameer laughed a stately laugh.

"It is my gang of no choice, Annant sir, your friend is laid low with a fever of defeat, but you have an interesting guest here, hello sir how do you do?" She ignored Sameer and eyed Jorden instead.

Jorden stands up to greet her, impressing her with his etiquette.

"Sure enough, the west knows how to respect the woman, here in India, all talk, nothing concrete to show, all crass people, I am Minnie, pursuing masters in philosophy, and you are?" She asked fluttering her long eye lashes innocently.

"Jorden."

"Ah! The river flows into the town of the Kumbh. Hey Himnash and Moneriil come along, the Doctor is here with the source of confluence, see it to believe, Jorden flows into the Ganga." She shouts at the top of her voice to call her friends.

"Dear doc. What has come of our dear teacher, he has become a Baba, and all, walks like a man possessed, or is it the Kumbh vibes getting him?" She asked Sameer.

"What of I know, you know him better than I do, but yes I agree, he is into his churning, it is about that girl, too, the one who died last week, what was her name?"

"Nina. But why should it worry our respected sir, none of his ways I suppose?" She eyes him in suspicion.

"None, I can wager my last penny on him when it comes to the matters of the upright; it is his childhood that comes back, soul of his poor soul, he tried to guide her to perfection, and she was waylaid by her .... Come along, Himnash, you look a dude, an earring on the left ear, diamond, is it?" Sameer shifts making space for the boy.

"Sir, hi." He shakes hand with Jorden and Sameer. "This is Moneriil." He introduces a rather quiet and shy boy, who lurked behind him. "Minnie we have ordered for you, too."

"Join us, your teacher's friends, let us break our fasts together and talk our hearts out. What was that commotion at the door, Himnash?" Sameer asked.

"That, Doc; Nothing, he peeped in to her wet... you know what." Himnash bounced the ball in Moneriil's court.

"It is the balls and you try to court them without a referee, somebody would blow a whistle, Monrerill, no back hand only foreplay..ur..rr forehead..Fountainhead....Forehand."Sameer warned him in jest.

"I..Me.. Never such thoughts occur to me not at Haridwar, this is sin, I take your leave, Himnash; I came with you not be a part of this charade. Why would I steal somebody's balls?" Moneriil is red with anger.

"It is only a game they are talking, Monu; relax; Himnash don't blame the poor soul." Minnie intervened.

"Then what happened?" Sameer wanted the Pornosophy of it all.

"I saw a small opening, just a glimpse of oval moons, and the V-trident dangling, the holy waters stuck like sweat and the black round berries, purple ripe pointed me the way; would somebody let go of such a chance; dear healer of the starved foreskin." Himnash spoke with glee.

"So you wanted to pluck them?" Jorden joined the debate.

"No..no.. not here just a feel ,to know the ripeness, you can't know until you twiddle them." Himnash; the graphic designer of pornography.

"Did you, or did you not, ply the dessert?" Sameer asked in his eagerness.

"Would you stop this gibberish of yours, or I sit somewhere else." Minnie was crimson and more beautiful.

"Feed us before we die of hunger." Jorden wore a look of innocence.

"I did; from a vantage point, just below the amulet of lord Shiva: ripe raspberries, well fed and well washed, just then, the man, threatened me with a duel, I tell you Doc. Bengalis are the real armies of our country, fight, alone, Guruji's call, '*Ekala chalo be..*' taken seriously by them." Himnash; with a sleigh of words, hoodwinking all.

"So you did lick; by luck; who knows the god of coition; Kama may bless you- keep up the pole pointing to the north the Kumbh has just begun." Sameer laid his erudition.

"Blasphemous beasts, you all; like Annant sir, he is the one to make you all the sinners, and even the gods would not help you all, no never." Minnie stood up and ran towards the door.

" Jorden, my brother, the Mother Kaalii is angry, do the needful, douse her fire; we always need an outsider for mediation, do hurry before you lose her in the crowded alleys of the pacific of people, that this town has become." Sameer shouted at the Jew.

"I would, your command, Sameer, you are the god of gone with the wind, let me merry her- the Tess of our dear friend –the D' Aubervilla of desires." He chases her and accosts her with his white charms.

"Girls enjoy this pornosymphony and act as if they have been bitten by a snake; seeking charmers and being afraid of the bite." Himnash spoke bluntly.

"Brother what happened?" Moneriil asked as he adjusted his spectacle to the unfolding spectacle.

"Nothing, we were over caring of her, that's all; should have given her straight, but Annant would have killed us all, he is a dog, demarcating territories with his ordure." Sameer stands up and waves at Minnie. .. And then mimes for forgiveness, by holding his ears with his fingers.

"Minnie, it is the festivities that got to the doctor; he is a good soul." Jorden pleaded with her.

"I can't stand such profanity, no Mr. Jorden, this is not the Hindustan you wish to explore, go away, the culture is dead, people are all apes from the planet west land; go away, please." Minnie shouted her anger.

Poor Mr. V. Jugran, rushes to the entrance, for the second time, this time in exasperation. "Quite please', he begs. "This is guest time, fight out into the open, settle the issue and then come." He whispers.

"No..No.. This issue has to be settled here and now, in what direction are we to progress?- The misogynist gang of Annant and the doctor or the sobriety of a white?" She stands up for her right.

"White rule was a failure; they ran away when we needed them the most, suck till the arteries are empty pipes, then? Run without looking back." A man in white safari adds his mite before the bite to the ensuing battle. He is the husband of Himnash's object of fascination, to which Minnie objected and of which Sameer and Jorden riled upon; Mr. Biman Basu.

"But did we civilize once they went away? No we did not. What do we do of our freedom? Make fun of woman -Treating them as an object of F…in ridicule."

"This is fun, see Moneriil; I told you, with Minnie you can expect the most unexpected, hey Doc. She used that f… word; she pines for not swine but divines. Minnie this is a land of Kamasutra, too, if you don't believe, ask sir, or ask Jorden, he is white and you would believe him without any proof.' Himnash laughed and shouted in glee.

"You mind your tongue and mind, Jorden, this is our new generation, all bulls on the run, chasing, no not dreams but hide. This is Haridwar, for god's sake and Kumbh, fair and all these suckers of the society do is to ogle at beauties in water."

"Did they try molesting you, let me call the police." The husband of the lady who started it all says.

"No police, please, this is guest time, you are my daughter like; now go to your seat and I will serve you the best breakfast, go please, all free, no money." Mr. V. Jugran, is worried about a dip in his collection.

"Ah! Bribe another scourge the males have invented. Call the police now; I would give a testimony against all."

"Minnie, please." Jorden stoops and puts his arms around her.

She suddenly becomes quiet and walks in slow steps towards the table. Jorden pulls a chair for her and she smiles on seeing relief in his chubby face.

"Let the treat be on me, a *Dakshina* for savoring the might of rights and religion." Jorden offered in magnanimity.

"No..no..Dear brother, Let me, you are our guest." Sameer hesitates in his offer.

"We split the bill." Minnie's way about; a truce after the altercation. "Call up that guy, let us order."

Himnash without a shame shouts. "It is on the house, courtesy, Minnie and her Broadway ways."

"I want to go home." Moneriil is exasperated.

Meanwhile, away from the scuffle and the drama, Mr. Tweney had entered the Annapurna café with his wife Shamistta. They occupy the corner seat and Shamistta lifts the bamboo chicks to look out into the narrow and crowded streets. Between them a question hangs: A continental breakfast or the usual fare of Poories.

"It is a little late for breakfast; let us settle for a lighter bite." Mr. Tweany suggested.

"I am hungry as a hole." Shamistta countered as a matter of a wife right.

"It is continental for me then, as for you; take your tickle."

"Let me see." She picked up the menu for a study of the dishes.

On the other corner; the one facing east, a heated debate broke out over the trends in the development of the river town.

"I tell you, modernity is the only reality, one cannot, I repeat, cannot escape it." A passionate Minnie spoke with a definitiveness of a defiant.

"Agreed." Himnash nodded seriously.

"Who stops you from modernizing?" Jorden asked.

"No one." Sameer said.

"Then?"

"The direction matters; modern life is a necessity, but to what extend can we compromise our traditional practices?" Sameer replied.

"I feel that all this talk of traditionalism is hogwash to stifle the pace of development, man! Let us open up everything and have fun." Himnash suddenly became a rebel.

"Let us search a new name for Haridwar first, call it Haris, or Harcelona, Hardon or Hoscow: brother what of the variety in the globe. Now all the places look alike. Same brands adore the skyline. Same food. Same dress. Same people. Same music. Same movies: worse- same rebel without causes." Sameer opined.

"That is one of the Marxian dreams which have been fulfilled." Himnash said.

"I see what you mean, doc. The death of localism is what you fear."

Minnie said.

"Why would Jorden and his ilk visit Haridwar if he doesn't find something uniquely of Haridwar. It is a mindless race to globalize. They are killing the golden goose, I say." Sameer said.

"The worst import is the food items." Moneriil broke his silence.

"I ditto you." Jorden came in support. "Hey Deepak bring poories for all."

"Minnie here has a Poories empire as a legacy; do you know that, Jorden?"

"Is it.?"

"Yes, my father the friar of the flour; but my calling is philosophy." She boasted.

"Any favorites?"

"Ooh! That my friend is for the tyros, I seek to have my own tenets."

"Freedom to lay the rules." Sameer said.

"She is joking; she quotes Annant sir." Himnash interjected.

"She wouldn't; hers is an original view. But Moneriil has a point, Pizza at Haridwar- soon we might have this KFC, thing, what a development!" Sameer laughed.

"We have to take good with us to the bed, though." Himnash opined.

"This trend is the world over, one just has to study how the Islamic societies are changing, adapting a lifestyle which was once alien to them. No longer now. The media has bridged the gap." Jorden said.

"The balance is shaken resulting in dissatisfaction and the resultant violence." Minnie added.

"The consumption patterns are changing too; creating an atmosphere of undefined tastes and preferences." Sameer added. 'Black with white and brown without a crown.'

"I would have a Pizza." Minnie demanded.

"Me too." Himnash seconded.

"So the way to the west begins with an Italian breakfast, have your tastes and be free, and you Moneriil, say what you wish for, it would be fulfilled forthwith."

"Whatever you are having; I say we cannot survive in this country until we live according to its tenets- *Bharatiyata.*" Moneriil smiled, happy at being given a chance to speak.

"So there we are- to each his or her own; Place the order dear Jorden and let there be disorder, all over. Long live the chaos of the universe. Order has gone for a toss, but what do we care for the loss." Sameer waved his hands trying to gain Deepak's attention.

"Aye aye sir; let the world be one. That makes all of us a party to the development of a universal spirit. Annant would have much to say on this, I hope." Jorden said.

"What has he to add? He lectured us on relevance and irreverence, today." Minnie said.

"He moves away from philosophy to a more holistic system of thoughts; the yoga of evolution, that Minnie is a feat worth taking note of." Sameer replied.

"But from next term we would not be seeing him much in the college, the philosophy department is defunct now: lack of a proper strength, the management says." Himnash says.

"So our dear friend finally has the time to pursue his passion for yoga and, maybe write something on many things." Sameer sat cross legged on the Rexene sofa. "Sure, this place has become popular, taking long time to meet orders, more demand less waiters."

"It is the Kumbh time; the crowd is building up by the day." Jorden opined.

The café was brimming with expectant devotees. Most of who sat with smug faces waiting for their food to arrive. The liveried waiters except Deepak, who wore his religious fervor, lined up outside the Kitchen, waiting. The chefs worked up frenzy. Frying, cutting, laying, shouting, thinking, mixing, their culinary to achieve that perfect blend for a perfect eating experience. Well trained and well versed with the art of building up an appetite. This was the secret of Annapurna café. Let the guests wait upon their hunger. It is like the way mothers do, keeping the children waiting slightly longer so that their shouts enthuse them to cook their best and also when the time for eating comes, the food tastes divine. Hunger is after all the best dressing.

Hari Bhai, the chief chef ordered his junior staff. 'Rahulji, hurry up with that base, dress it up man, put more cheese, yes, Mozzarella, now tomatoes, onions and capsicum slices. Hurry up, into the oven'."Tea it up, Amit, all would want a cup after their food.' 'Adarsh, don't stop your pooriee parade, nice round hot, like the butt of your …' lay it for serving, it is about time'.

His team responded to the crises. Order was taken and food prepared to be served at one go. The waiters grinned for expecting tips and a pat with bonus from Mr. V. Jugran.

The dining hall murmured its approval. An occasional demand of more water broke the dull continuity. The café was like a packed stadium waiting for the kick off. Hunger the chief referee. A simmer of discontent hung over a few tables, though. Wrong order. We can change, if you want? Now eat whatever is ordered. Had I ordered my favorite rolls, not bread but spring? Children argued, cajoled and then begged their parents to change their orders. Parents wanted them to confirm to their order. Order.. order. A group argued and then petitioned for a more widespread menu card. No Jalapeño no olives on Pizza dressing, some told some one. Mrs. Nauti used the washroom thrice, in quick succession, cold she explained to her daughter-in law, Mrs. Nauti. Mr. Tweaney sipped water and listened to Shamsitta's banter. His eyes shifty, lest Sameer catches him with her; should have gone to Sharmaji's for Poories. No Sameer there.

Sameer eyed the wholesomeness of Minnie. Breasts before breakfast......two- thrice daily, he thought. Macho Medicine. Himnash let himself be angry on himself, the devil Annant, how does he manage it- The ugly duckling bastard; girl chaser and what not.

Jorden , from the corners of his eyes watched a group of Nuns, disbelieving what he saw. Eyes cannot be trusted, he was convinced. The Bengali bunch waited for their southern fair of Dosas. The southies are the real food masters: Dravidian knowledge; light, simple, digestive condiments and lot of soup, Mr. Biman booted for Dosas. Soon it will be the number one export from our country. A world of dosa, he said overruling Mrs. Basu's demand for Noodles. Children, younger lot, changed tables. Swapping parents. The older searched for their pubescence infatuation. Ephemeral Affair. Waiting for dishes, the waiters discussed the day's crowd. Rati liked Minnie, he confided in Matee. Rumpy was keen to talk to Mrs. Biman, but the table is mine, dare you; Devendra threatened. Mr. V. Jugran, made a mental calculation of his earnings at this hour. Good going, he prayed for a Kumbh every year.

"Is sir on a roll? Writing his heart out or what?" Minnie exposed herself a wee bit.

"Is he? You should know. You are a confidante of his; we are lesser mortals." Sameer replied.

"He is trying to leave the shores, right Monreiil?" Himnash was jealous.

"No. He wouldn't do such a thing. One has to be rooted for creativity and yoga."

"Why so? Travel does add to the oeuvre of a writer, doesn't it?" Jorden asked.

"I meant literature." Moneriil spoke laconically.

"The food man, for the thought; which maketh a writer, chomp something will write." Himnash aired his view.

"We all are waiting, aren't we?" Sameer said.

"We are." Himnah eyed the Bengali beauty once again.

"Do you have a class tomorrow?"

Shamistta asked.

"No, the administration has asked the institutes to close down for major bathing dates." Mr. Tweany answered his wife.

"You won't mind the oily stuff, I suppose; or we can get the usual bread butter breakfast for you."

"Whatever you order I would eat, I would manage." He said.

"I can't stand this boiled system. The whole England is hooked to this curry merry."

"I have withstood the deluge of your cooking. I am well prepared now. My stomach hasn't yet met its waterloo."

"What do you say; Annant would get published somewhere; in future?" Shamistta asked.

"I can't say; People have varied tastes. His yoga writing might just click with a few. I say, he should write on India and its muses. Or a biography; people need titillation."

"Pornofiction, you mean, well he could give it a try." Shamistta suggested in her smile.

"He quite likes you." Tweany guessed.

"We share a childhood, I fatherless and he father-infested."

"His rebel, I suppose, those were the times when communism exited; now it is capitalism. The west has, in a way legitimized the way one substitutes earnings with the fine art of rebellion. Yes, Shams, I say until one rebel one cannot create, the energy, the dedication, and the fire comes from disagreements and denials." Tweany is worked up for no apparent reason. Only if I could have an English breakfast for a day, he thought, I would donate a hundred and one rupees to the nearest temple, he promised.

"Annant in your head, dear, no wonder you spent time with him, what has he got in his mind nowadays: religion, yoga, philosophy or literature?"

"Everything- his is a kaleidoscopic Karma."

"And you? Coming all the way and falling in love and siring a mix breed for children."

"I don't know. Past karma I guess- Reincarnation roulette."

"Do you believe in all this?"

"One has to have an explanation of things beyond reason."

"Let us go back to your town. London would be fun. Like it was when we honeymooned. It was a long while ago." She is pensive.

"I like the spirituality of this town. Being brought up in an English society I felt that I was missing out on something. You know: a lack. Then my parents died in that attack at WTC: poor workers of capitalism, innocently attending to daily chores- That, for me was a defining moment. I questioned my existence. What is my purpose? What should one aspire for? Where is this mindless pursuit of the ego leading us all? What is death? The spirit? In the cluttered mind I saw the vision of death, my death. I could feel life slipping away, like sand from palms. Go away you weary soul, it said. It was then I came here and met a friend of my friend from Washington; Agastatya. A few words of mumble solved my riddle. Then I met you, the unsolved one. Life is like that I feel; riddles which one could solve and some; one can never solve."

"Do you still love me?'

"Why do you ask? There is no way I can; not but not love you."

"So you do. Kumbh really is a looking back time. Reminiscing remembrances. It keeps coming back- A cycle, never-ending and in a vortex."

"Yes. That is life then. We don't have much of a choice but to live it to the fullest and beat it in its game."

"How is it possible?"

"By living and believing in a moment." Tweney watched the miasma of humanity through the slits of the bamboo curtains.

Orders had started trickling in- like wishes after the prayers: The smallest the first. Tea. Coffee. Drinks. Then the more substantial ones; dosas, pizzas. Pooriees, burgers, idlees, Sandwiches, uttapam and ras malai. Order was restored. People joined in the chorus of eating. Murmurs stopped. The only sounds were those of the cutlery beating on each other; the spoon on a bowl, glasses clinging on teeth, steel plates rubbing against each other. Or those of eating; chomping hurriedly, sipping in a splutter, sucking with a swish, shoo hoo.. after chilies on the palate. Diners eyed other diners order. Some reflected on what could have been. Others planned a reorder, to keep up with the neighbors' order. Still others ate in silence, accepting their order as a matter of fate. Children tasted their parents' order as well as their new parents'. Pseudo parenting. Slowly hunger made a quite exit, like an unnoticed guest packing his bag ones his task has been completed. An air of satiation hung loose. Men searched for a smoke. Women washed themselves off the grime of leftovers. The children ran hither thither, away from the grasp of their parents. They were caught by their 'for the moment' parents and handed over to their permanent ones. The battle won, it was payback time. Mr. V. Jugran stood behind the cash counter, adding and then subtracting with an astuteness of an accountant. Crisp notes found their way into a large iron box, he called tijori. The amounts were rounded off to the nearest denominators; thus Rs. 151.50. Became Rs. 152 and Rs.157.50 became Rs. 160. No change ,sir, he smiled in the most innocent of smiles and handed them little orange toffees instead, for the kids ,sir they would suck them for glucose. He would advice them. The dosa was not crisp. Jugranji, a frequent visitor complained, to which Mr. V. Jugran, blamed the balmy morning. Come tomorrow, and get the crispest of them all, he smiled to silence the critic. The place has become costly; another frequent visitor complained; taxes, this GST or VAT, sir then the price rise, the government is helpless, I am a small fry; without oil, too costly, he laughed, the old Jugran laughter, reducing the complaints' bill by twenty percent. You cannot keep the nature out.

"Ah! Tweany bhai, your lectures are the best- these beasts from the hills are now becoming civilized. Bhabhiji, ram..ram..you don't visit us anymore,' he complained, 'you use to come regularly with Annant sir, now, you don't. No payment for you Tweany bhai. You are the chief patron of this café, no payment."

"I insist, please." Tweaney puts a hundred rupee note on the cash counter: A proud Brit; damn well we were the rulers once; he thought and hurried outside pushing Shamistta in the process.

Mr. V. Jugran, doesn't mind and shifts his focus on other clients. The bath is the real money spinner in this country, he thought.

So did Sameer and Jorden. Deepak, the waiter with a difference had served them well. All extra helpings of the pooriies and potatoes with pickle and curd. Lime water to gulp it, followed by tea to beat the cold at bay. Odd couple. Tea with lemon. Sharmaji's is better, Himnash opined, more so to rub Minnie. But Pizza is for real. Good cheese, pulpy tomatoes and soft capsicum, he said, savoring the crusted bake.

"They are all right, but Jugs should import the base, the cheese and other exotic dressings, you see the variety is the key to a restaurant business." Minnie said.

"Ah! The Restuentreprenuer." Sameer exclaimed. "It is in the blood Jorden."

"Aye Aye..Aryan." Jorden licked his fingers in delight. Merry Masalas.

"Did he have a mini meal; Annant our recluse saint?" Sameer asked Minnie.

"What is it that you mean? As if I am a dumb doll. No Mr. Sameer, I won't take your sexist statements lying down. I have no truck with that friend of yours. Filth philosopher. His is a half baked vision. A nowhere destination, and worst, he guides the juvenile in to a dark cave. Poor Plato must be ruing his parable, in his grave." Minnie hasn't forgotten the morning raga.

'It takes an understanding of the highest order to understand people of his caliber. Tell me in this era of globalization and professionalism, he talks of evolution and leading a more rewarding life. He doesn't ask for money and stands by his principles. What is more he listens and corrects; that, according to me, are the two things a teacher should do. It is up to the students to find their own way." Moneriil spoke with his eyes closed.

"I told you juvenile judgment. Brother Moneriil, we are not riling your teacher, but his boasting gets me, sometimes. I say let the world judge him, not the way he judges himself. I am the King types."Minnie defends her point.

"What he does, only he can understand. The world is ignorant. Did it understand Socrates?- A man way ahead of his times. I tell you Doc. One day the world would remember our Annant sir for the way he re-laid the tenets of yoga and philosophy; for the betterment of the world at large." Moneriil stood up in anger.

"Relax, Monu, woman have to have their daily dose of gossip and derision; here take a sip of the coolest of lemon drink and forget her diatribe. It is the chilies in the curry which got her." Himnash pulled at Moneriil's arms.

"I didn't mean to hurt you: maybe I wear my critics' hat, rather seriously." Minnie becomes quiet in repentance.

"He is writing something on the Kumbh or what?" Jorden asked.

"No, he jokes of his ability to pen his thoughts. He wants to travel, perhaps; Away from this all: Needs a break. But he will come out fine that much I know of him, a fighter to the core, without wanting more." Sameer rhymed.

"Let us all break now. I have to go to the shop to assist my father. The crowd must be building up there, too." Minnie stood up to go.

"The bill, who foots it? The cat..Who bills it?" Himnash laughed.

"Move on the bunch of you three, we would do the needful. And pray, if you find our dear friend Annant, tell him that we wish to see him for lunch and all. Would you?" Sameer said.

"Aye Aye.. Doc. Come let us roam into the fair. Do you want a hair pin or a jasmine bead, Minnie?" Himnash asked. Minnie eyes him with a glare.

Wait Himnash; till I get back to you, she murmured under her breath.

AGASTAYA

With her it is different. Her life is many a lives. Ah! How staid a man's life looks as compares to a woman's; who leads many a lives within one- a girly zephyr in her early years; a brewing storm of adolescence letting the menstruating bird to fly; a fecund lark for a youth; a temptresses for a wife quenching thirsts with sips of wild forest fire passions; a mother chasing the sublime purity of life; a period of gracing follows the explorations preparing her to lord over the social mores and glories; finally floating on faith boats with somber aging- but the man; nay a poor soul leads just one- clutching on to his vanity like a layered dirt over an out of use mirror.

Who decides the extent of the vanity in a man? Certainly not the god. Ego definitely-that appendage of disdain and loathing; Ah! The tumor of the truncated soul. So what does a man do? Isn't it all too visible like the morning star? No it is not; a glance couldn't; in all probability make things clearer. It needs a burning desire to extinguish the conflagration that spreads like a menace of an epidemic. Agastaya walked into the cloud of white fog. Tiny drops condensed on his brow like flakes of fresh snow. The forest is silent for a while, he thought, the cold gets the Avian too. He smiled and waved an imaginary fly away. Life is indeed a continuous process of learning and unlearning of falling then rising of moments sad of moments happy. One needs to meditate upon one's; opening the self for an enquiry. Weeding out the unwanted till purity is achieved; till the ego is annihilated. Aditi has no such qualms. She was a multitude of quests. Even painting the holy river ganga with its Ghats and bathing devotees. Making an art out of religion. She has a knack for colors ,an eye for details and a sensitivity to create. Just that....

A black skinny dog gave out a low bark breaking his morning powwow with the self. "What's up with you"? He asked the dog. A tail wag and a few barks answered him. "What are you doing here in the wilderness, the town is agog with food and fervor, go on live a life of plenty?" He scratched the dog's neck. "Run along old chap...

The dog followed him. He let it be as he took a detour and entered the forest which formed the part of the National Park. The air was heavy with fog. The dawn trickled in like a blessing, breaking through the misty darkness waking up the birds who chirped signaling a start to the search for their insects' and wild berries' manna. A flock of crow flew crowing a cry; must have lost a dear one. It is with the crows. They fly alone but unite to face a tragedy.

A few Jungle Mynas chirped *keek-keek-kok-kok* making the sleepy surroundings come alive. He caught a Great Barbet perched in meditation on a lowly Sal tree branch. A couple of Magpie-Robins and white throated Thrushes flew without encumbrances. A crimson sunbird crossed the road in a salubrious flight; its brilliant colors and whispers of *chichwee.. chichwee* made Agastaya to stop for a while and let the nature seep in him. Of what we look for? All that has to be had is here- a fulfillment and more.

"Ho..haa..ho… sha sha..hurrr.. tck ..tck..".A tall, loosely attired and red bearded shepherd belonging to the *Gujjar* tribe herded his buffaloes for the morning feed; a long bamboo pole acted as his staff whose directions the cattle heeded.

"*Adab*, how come you are in the park area?" Agastaya waved at him.

"*Addaaab Miyan*… for the feed; we are allocated a hamlet here. But the Government officials are a lot of nuisance Babu, they round up the poor animals who trespass into the out of bounds area then demand money for their release. For an animal there are no boundaries, they own the jungle and the fodder." He replied in his lamentations.

He was Furkhat Ali who along with his fellow tribes- folk practiced transhumance. In the winters they camped on the foothills of the Himalayas and as the summer would settle in they would begin their climb to the grasslands on the higher Himalayas- the *Bugyals*.

"*Accha Bhai..ram..ram..*"Agastaya bid him good bye.

"*Addaab..ram..ram..*" He replied.

The dog tailed the gypsy. Good choice, dear friend, I still need to learn to meet the ends, Agastaya smiled. And why not? Have family look after it. Aditi and her demands are certainly not a part of her disdain. A need is nothing but what it is; a lack. Food, shelter and clothing form the basic. More than them, there is no limit. How much a clerical job pays me? Not much, just to suffice. Now it won't do. When aspirations are on an upswing then even contentment is poverty. A system changes in a spiral. Capitalism was inevitable what with a burden of socialism pulling us back. False start. Now in every three months the country changes. Even a quaint and religious town of Haridwar becoming a hub of industries and modernity; pushing its historicity in to the background-Kumbh fair brings back the ancient glory of the town, the tradition of bathing and congregating for a dip goes back to three hundred B.C; some claim that it is as old as five hundred B.C.; that is very..very old indeed; Vedic period, probably, or even before that!

Embrace we must whatever the times we live in has to offer, just morph it a little to suit our culture. And yes do not forget traditions. The deep rootedness is a sign of strength. Aditi, though is a rebel, still. Her art forms a part of her expression, only a part, not the whole. She hasn't learnt to let the hair down or to immerse as a whole. Something …a minor block hangs. But then when you are up there or want to be up there a minor is major folly. She doesn't listen- To full to be a good wife. It is with a woman, she argued last night, to wanting to want more. Thank god she is genuine; he smiled as he neared the colony a furlong away from the cable car station of the Chandi Devi temple. Kerrie was his worry, not hers; she had had an off and on relation with the girl, not wanting to forget the way she was conceived. Force, she explained. Destiny he had countered. An unwanted wart for a child- she would shout in her frustrations. I think she gave her child the childhood she inherited.

Agastaya moved in reflective steps. Perhaps I could take a lead; should; I am the provider. This role hasn't changed even if choices for a women have increased, pulling them out of the veil and pushing them into the rough seas of competitive living.

A place to muse, to listen to the cackle of birds and play with the freshest petals of life- letting the fragrance linger or the evenings teasing with their whims. Mr. Srivatsna is how a government official should be- encroaching upon and feeding on the frailties of the common man. With me he might be a wee bit considerate- he calls me a Collectrate man.

He neared the government colony housing the class three employees. A two storied building complex; yellow painted, one bedroom, one drawing and cubicles for a kitchen and a toilet; the entire compound wanting repairs. The paint peeled, the walls are weather beaten and bricks snarl as the cement had fallen off like exfoliation of the skin; the lampshades are devoid of bulbs and the poles of the electric current; the park at the centre lay like an unattended guest, squirming in its uselessness, as weeds had taken it over; though a few cattle lay there regurgitating on the dry wintery grass.

Agastaya opened the rickety, rusted and creaky gate and entered the colony premises. He treaded carefully the tattered stairs and peeped into the drawing room which doubled as bedroom for him, Aditi and Kerrie. Duty first, he had justified allocating the only bedroom to his aging parents. She had agreed, she was a new wife then. Now she was a weather-beaten one. Pester, demand and nag. She had made a choice;

tomorrow she would take her free will to a logical conclusion. Delhi was a not so good an experience. She didn't listen. He hurried to the kitchen. Hasty, energetic footsteps on the roof danced in a perfect symphony. Atleast she was joyous, he thought as he pulled at the outer leaf of a green, round cabbage.

Aditii dusted the overnight's dew drops which had settled on the assorted set of clothing that hung on an aluminum wire tied to the two bamboo poles stuck between four squared bricks-on the opposite sides of the roof; a distance of twelve feet between them. The roof had a three inch boundary and a makeshift wall made of broken down furniture had been put up as a safety measure, least someone fell down twenty-five feet below. Aditi felt no such danger, this being her house for the past five years. Things might; why might? Will change for the better, she thought. Times are a changing, she chimed and happy days are here to stay. If only Mr. Tulli does the needful. The twilight had not yet broken through the haze that had engulfed the town since mid-night. It would take a while before the sun-god smiles, she thought. She sang a soulful tune and tussled with the clothes; beating some against each other and some against the wind. The ruffled ends were straightened and each piece of the attire matched with its other half. Thus the sari went with the petticoat; the white Kurta with the white pajamas; socks with their pairs. She was happy with her art. All art is perfection; she smiled and changed to another lilting tune; enacting the steps of *Bharatnatyam* dance; beating her feet on the roof floor, with the rhyme of her lilt lyrics. The sky was still dark and the haze cloaked the stars in its warmth like children under duress. She continued to murmur the lilting tune as she adjusted a fresh set of washed livery on the wash-wire, which dropped a loop under its weight. The poles danced; threatening to bend to kiss each other. She deftly used her left hand plucking at the dried but dew wet clothes which she had arranged but which still lay on the left corner of the wash-wire : two cotton saris one young with yellow and blue flowers, the other an ageing piece of six yards cotton cloth, grey with golden pattern matched with their petticoats: a white cotton Kurta, yellowing , pocketed at the heart and the matching pajamas: one blue frock- camels on its gait, starched : two pair of woolen socks, dew soaked and dripping, one grey and the other dark blue : a wrap; green georgette mixed with cotton: one poplin bed sheet in royal print of Rajasthan; elephants, camels, belle in jewelry, dancing. Her ambidextrous skill saved the clothes and the poles from falling as she lay the collected clothes on her right shoulder and freeing her both hands, spread the new ones: A pale brown jacket with the letter IBM printed in bold red on its front pocket near the heart : a pair of white, cotton kurta with pajama; pink flower printed cotton livery along with a blue wrap of the size of an arm's length: two saris both pale yellow with saffron borders: kitchen dusters, turmeric yellowed and chilly reddened, oil spotted and with gas stove burnt holes gaping at her. The water dripped from the novel visitors as they shuddered under the chilly Himalayan winds. Red, blue, yellow and white cloth-clips made them secure against the river squall. Having freed herself from the burden of her early morning routine she rubbed her blue palms for warmth and threw mouth vapors on them cupping the hands over her lips. Shoo.. Shoo.. She sounded. Her wet hairs danced under the icy gale. She pulled the royal Rajasthani bed sheet from the bunch of clothes on her right shoulders, spraying the rest of the clothes like flower petals on the roof flooring. She quickly wrapped the bed sheet around her and bent down to collect the fallen clothes, swearing under her breath.

"Better be numb than dumb". Agastaya smiled on her, assisting her in her endeavor.

"You woke up early today?" She asked in her gayness. Her eyes shifting from her immediate chore to him.

"The quilt was sweet warm and I found it hard to leave the heavenly comforts." He answered with all his sincerity. "If one trades it with the morning air then it isn't a bad bargain to leave the coziness, though." He stretched himself and wandered on the small roof from which the town was partly visible.

"Comfort, what thou name is the bird of?" Aditi smiled a lemony smile and followed him.

"You are balding and graying all at once, but there is an aura around you which pulls at the strings of the heart" she added as an afterthought.

"The sun, does it arise from the usual east or is it from the west today?" He asked in a silent sarcasm.

"West off course it is your birth day!" Aditi rolled her wet hairs in a bun and tied it with a thread of a disintegrating towel that was wrapped around her neck.

Agastaya took the clothes from her shoulders and carefully laid them in squared heap. She handed him the Rajasthani bed sheet and shuddered as the windy morning welcomed her.

"Keep it if you want." He offered her the bed sheet. "These are slightly damp still; do we take them downstairs or leave them to air?" Agastaya asked of the rest of the clothes.

" No.. no." She didn't take his offer. "It is not fate we are deciding, are we?" She smiled wickedly. "As you say; do your calling". She continued to arrange the freshly washed clothes on the wash-wire, spreading them for maximum sun and aeration.

"I would leave them for a while." He placed the heap on a broken chair and watched her with intent.

She blushed like a newlywed and hurriedly arranged her sky blue cotton Sari, covering her bosom first then arranging it around her belly-button.

"What is it "? She asked.

"You look a darn; a piece of heavenly finery." He replied as he stretched his hands skywards.

"Do I? Now that I am going away for a few weeks, you find time to look at me; otherwise it is your yoga and Karma". She complained in her sonorous speech.

"You are my world." He answered her.

"Which world? The one you reside or the one you aspire?" She asked.

"All and more". He replied. "When do we leave?" He asked.

"At 1 pm tomorrow; from the Jolly Grant airport; then a connecting flight to Mumbai at 5pm from New Delhi." She informed him.

"Are you sure of what you are doing? Not like the last time when the whole thing just blew off with a whimper; it is sought of embarrassing." He said.

"Aren't failures a part of all that we live for?" She asked.

"I wasn't talking of failing, but of ill preparedness." He said.

"For you I will never be prepared." She sounded irritated.

"Better be perfect before entering the markets. A good home work prevents the last minute blushes." He suggested.

Aditi kept quiet. It is how husbands are, finding faults with their soul mates. Want them for a mate and all.

"I wasn't prepared for all this, nor was I ready for you, not now not on that fate full day. You have come to trample upon my dreams and my very being. Kerrie…Kerrie… get ready you devil. The two of you have connived to stifle me". She harangued.

Agastaya roamed about on the roof watching the town's skyline and listening to the faith music that the wind carried. The dawn broke through and the tepid sun rays appeared bathing the Shivalik ranges.

"Would you watch the sun rise?" He called Aditi.

"I would; not now not today; your uncle and aunt are arriving for the kumbh bath, I have to make arrangements for their stay. Did you, perchance, enquire about the Low Income Group apartments the Haridwar Development Authority is constructing near the Bharat Heavy

Electricals Limited Company? Kerrie is growing in leaps; *Babuji* wants to write his memories and demands a study; *Maa* needs a prayer room; our relatives have all become devotes of deepest reverence since you have set up a base here." Her piping voice tunes him to the rhythm of a family. "Arrange all, please, now you have to shoulder the maximum: till I find a foothold in the world of the metro." She pleaded.

"I would do the needful; have had a talk with Mr. Srivastana of the H.D.A .about it, he says he will find a way; they have two roomed flats with attached toilets, a luxury which I feel is a necessity now; but we need the top floor, for the roof you see, Kerrie is the outdoor types, like you, then Haridwar is fun if explored and unbound from a perch." He explained in a way of understanding.

"Is it an assurance, I don't see anything concrete emerging from…." She picked the arranged clothes in a huff and prepared to climb down the rusted iron staircase, swirling under the wind.

"Be careful, lest you burden the poor stairs with your demands." Agastaya barbs her.

"Your yoga is my burden, Aagi, I have shed all my dreams like the skin of a reptile, expecting a newer life but your ways have waylaid me." She complained a wifely prick.

"You have your play of paints, the chime of colors, and the laughter of Kerrie to keep your sanity intact." He countered.

"Your father's whim and your mother's sarcasm; your relatives' visits and stomachs to feed; all in your paltry pay and to top it- an inferno for a home."Her eyes are moist with anger.

"*Parnams*, Maa Kaali; the Devi of wrath, I bow to your anger and much more, forgive me, a poor soul, but pray, learn to live in whatever the god ordains. It is my birthday and you demand presents?" He asked as he eyed her and then continued, "Poverty is after all of faith, trust, honesty, ideas; never of money. Can one be great wearing expensive clothing and wads of notes?" He asked and pulling her from the staircase fell on his knees. "You look beautiful, early in the morning, wet hairs, sticking to the skin sari, angry eyes and a flushed face, the sun won't rise today; your face is my ball of fire. All you need is a Jasmine bead for your hair bun."

"Can you get me even that?" She freed herself and swayed down the creaky staircase leaving him in his befuddlement.

Agastya turned his eyes to the pale hills as the first rays of the sun fell on them breaking through the brooding fog. He let the rays bath him. Flocks of birds flew to and fro across the town's skyline, chirping chants of their own; the natives with the migratory ones. The river becomes visible in its flowing splendor; a sea of humanity bowing to its charm. The town throbs with an unkempt energy akin to a spiritual awakening. In the chaos he could feel the all pervading calm of the religion. He stood under its spell, dumbstruck.

"Baba… baba ..baba." Kerrie in pink frocks and green oversized sweater reaching her knees; pulled at his pale Kurta.

"You are on time; the sun is out for you." He said and picked up the little girl.

"It is your Happy Birthday; mine in the last month, yours in the first month of the year." She said as she comforted herself in her father's bosom.

Agastya looked into her eyes with awe, and then brushes her hairs with a fatherly caress.

"Your mother and my mother; wish them, for they deserve the greetings more than I, but say, are you planning a party?" He asked.

"I would have two- two daadaji, dadiji, our house will have crowd. Then we can celebrate." She replied.

"All the more fun; look at your town, full of people; millions, I suppose." He spoke softly.

"How many a millions Baba?" She asked.

"Stars in the sky." He answered and hid her in his arms, letting her cling to his bosom.

Warmth of familial love mixed with the religiosity of the moment descended on him. He sauntered on the smallish roof patting Kerrie on the back.

"Is it your school day today?" He whispered in her ears.

"Half a day of school then I am free. In the evening we go to the ashram of the old Ekaba. Would you come? Maa has called Punditji for Pooja at the ashram." She said.

"Has she? I better hurry my bath, lest she bares her fangs again. You too get ready for your school before you incur her wrath. She is on the boil today." He said.

"What's new? Let her, but would you come?" She asked.

"I would try." He said in a matter of fact tone.

Kerrie climbed down the dilapidated staircase like a trapeze artist; then came back running, surprising Agastaya. "Happy Birthday". She said and pulled him down, kissing the cheeks - first the left and then the right.

"Thank you". He mumbled in his embarrassment, not use to such a show of emotions. "Hurry up now your mother is on fuse today; beware." He smiled and patted her.

Kerrie laughed and ran back with happiness written on her face like a glow of a firefly on a dark night.

Agastaya took out his pale white Kurta and proceeded to pull a bucket- full of water from the synthetic water tank on the roof and poured it on his half naked body with a flourish. He let the iced water cut into him, awakening him from his laziness. Without worrying for the rub of a towel he faced the sun and sat cross legged in the lotus posture; the *Padmaasana*. His eyes are transfixed in the vacuum that lay ahead of him.

His senses are slowly absorbed, dying in his mind: sight, sound, smell, taste, touch: then the mind itself.

Aditi lighted an earthen *diya* in her small wooden temple nailed to the wall on the right corner of the kitchen and mumbled her prayers in hurried tones. She signed off by playing the brass bell vigorously and applying vermillion dot with a few grains of rice on her forehead. Kerrie, who tailed her, demanded her share of the color dot and the *Prasadam*.

"Have you packed your school bag"? She asked as she applied the vermilion dot with the thumb of her right hand and mumbled a Sanskrit *sholaka*.

"Yes Maa, I am waiting for my Tiffin box." Keerii replied.

"Wait a minute. Let me serve tea to your Grandparents first." Aditi said.

Babuji and Maaji sat on the small balcony on a jute charpoy watching the suburban forest and the interplay of the sun rays through the trees. They talked of things in general adding their sagaciousness to the everyday events, the people, their relations, god's purpose and life in its entirety.

Aditi; stumbling in her sari, served them tea, breaking their flow of conversation for the moment.

"Daughter-in-law dear; thank you." Babuji blessed her as she stooped to touch his feet with her head covered with her sari. "*Sada Shaubhgyawati*'. He blessed her for being eternally married.

Maa repeated the same and offered her services in preparing breakfast. Aditi declined assuring her that she could manage on her own and returned to kitchen where Kerrie sat on a wooden stool waiting for her breakfast.

"Maa what's for the party it is Baba's birthday." She asked.

"He is a cook in his own right why don't you ask him for a treat?" Aditi riled her in her taunt.

"Maa are you angry?" Keerii asked.

"No". Aditi replied and lighted the gas burner. She put an old wok over it and searched for a few red dried onions. Dam, she swore under her breath, where have I kept them, she continued to murmur, in the basket perhaps or under the stool.

"Kerrie look for the onions under your stool." She shouted.

Kerrie did as told. Then turned a bunch of jute bags. "I can't find them. Maa..Maa...the wok is black." She shouted.

"I know no onions now." She put the gas stove off and looked at Kerrie in amusement. Both laughed in a chuckle.

"Can I come with you"? Kerrie asked suddenly.

"Where?"

"Where you are going with Baba."

"What will happen to your school?"

"It is a month's holiday."

"What will you do there?"

"Be with you".

"What for?"

Kerrie thought for a while. Took slow steps in the small kitchen, scratched her head and then sat on the stool with her chin resting on her palm.

"Where would I be then?" She asked.

"With your Grandparents; a pair of them now." Aditi replied.

Kerrie looked despondent. She kept quiet, thinking vigorously.

"I could help you with your paintings." She suggested.

"How?"

"I can take care of them when you are busy. They have always seen me around."

"I am taking only a few; they would be packed anyway."

"Packed!! You mean covered?"

"Yes."

Kerrie looked disappointed.

"I could still be with them so that they are not alone." She said.

"No."

Aditi took out her pink lunch box and searched for a box of biscuits. She put a few in it.

"Would they suffice?"

Kerrie took it and toyed with it.

"I could look after you." She threw a dice.

"Would you?"

"Yes. You need someone like me." She boasted.

"Your Baba is there."

"Oh, he; don't trust him. He would leave you and roam about teaching yoga to all and sundry."

"Would he?"

"Yes. Let us both go and he can remain here."

"Would you manage with these biscuits, they aren't bad. Cream and jam stuffed."

"Maa I want to come." Kerrie was in tears.

"Alright, we will decide it in the evening. Now hurry up for your school, Your Rickshaw would be there, let us go."

Aditi took her right hand into hers and pulled her downstairs. Kerrie took labored steps wiping her tiny tears.

"I will manage from here, you can go." Kerrie succeeded in breaking free as Aditi's grip loosened.

"Bye Bye..Take care; remember we have to go Ekaba's ashram in the evening." Aditi called.

"Yes Maa." Kerrie uttered in an indifferent manner.

She stood on the opening of the secluded housing society and waited upon Badde Miyan's rickshaw. A sense of despondency had engulfed her. Tears reappeared on her brown eyes and she sobbed in her anguish.

Aditi climbed the swinging stairs and entered the kitchen rather apathetically. Living is all tiring and little else; Oh! The grime of house holding, she concluded. She lighted the fire again and poured mustard oil on the wok. The vegetable tray lay with a heap of finely chopped cabbage and sliced potatoes. It impressed her; Agastaya sure has a knack for perfection. The oil burnt emitting strong mustardy vapors. She threw cumin seeds in and they crackled with a sudden burst of smoky whiff. She hurried with draining the vegetables and placed them on the wok. The hissing stopped and she proceeded to open a red lidded condiment holder; a small spoonful of turmeric, red chili and coriander powder and two spoonfuls of salt went into the vegetable heap. Having ladled it to her content she covered it with a steel lid. On second thought she pulled out the lid and poured three ladlefuls of water. The potatoes; she justified her decision.

From a brass barrel she measured six bowlfuls of fine wheat flour and laid them carefully in a heap on a huge round bronze plate; to which she added two bowlfuls of *ragi* flour from a plastic jar. With her deft fingers she mixed the two and then sprinkled water over it from a blue jug. In right earnest she started her kneading, pouring water in spurts. The red and white flour turned into sticky dough at first and then slowly it gained in spongy texture as she vigorously kneaded on it. She pounded hard on it with a regular beating adding water whenever the dough started sticking to her fingers. Like an ingenious sculptor she creates a crater hill out of the dough and filled it with water. She broke the symphony of her creation and watched the caldera-like dough. With a slow pounding she restarted her knead. The veins on her hands bursts into blue snakes and her muscles become taut. Her wet hairs irritate her as they peeped in her work of art by falling on her face. She continued to knead the flour with the passion of an artist pouring her energy in bursts of whims. On her forehead sweat beads erupt like juvenile pimples. A strange force overtook her. The ball of dough, over kneaded and over beaten faced up to her wrath as she let her anger seethe in the early morning whisper. She beat the ball with her hands like whipping the back of a child for a deviant behavior. The small scullery reverberated to the sounds of a whip or a cane. *Phatt..Phatt…Phatt…*

"Poor vegetables would have suffered the same fate had I not cut them." Agastayaa entered the kitchenette in tip toes, his face aglow with serenity of yoga.

It broke her flow. She seemed irritated. Locking spontaneity; what is there to living if there are schisms at every bend. She rounded up the dough and placed it at the rim of the bronze plate and poured a bowlful of wheat flour near it.

"You are done up from your meditation?" She asked.

"Yes. And you?" He asked.

"Me?"

"Yes, yours is a more deep and wholesome yoga-the family yog."

"Something is all wrong Aagi, things are not gelling, a vacuum exists; it is a quagmire of…." She lamented.

'Of life? This is what we call living."

"What of one's pursuits for arts, for creative, for philosophy, you know the soul rest; the sheer banality of it all catches me in my brood; superimposed on it is the struggle to survive to breed and to bred, the times are a changing, each desire has an end now, Sartre and his possibility hang like a hangman's axe, the markets shape our selves ,the personal in us, and I cannot ignore it come as I do from a humble background with humbler needs, all corporeal, despite my passion for paints, I find being left on the wayside in the race of life, like stones tied on my feet and I try to swim. Then is Ekaba's way the way, the *Sanyas* and all; leaving everything to pursue the supposedly greater goal of *Moksha*? Or is this grime the way forward? If it is, then I don't seem to arrive anywhere, just the everydayness of the family; you know Aagi, I was never keen to fall into the trap of this all, not for any reason, not for the soul of it no..no.. not even for Kerrie, I don't feel for her as a mother would, she is an appendage ..a tumor for a daughter, I don't say it to pester you with my dreams but can I not be wanting bit more of my life? Zing, in return for the round the clock service I do to the family; my art remains decimated. It is like losing a voice, when one knows that one can speak; my mind is numb, my heart doesn't carry the enthusiasm of my youth, what is the use of a life when one can't do what one wishes to do? Now when I do get a chance, a strange guilt tugs at my heart like an inherited burden of the previous birth. Would it be unbecoming of me as a mother to leave Kerrie? Yes. So I don't go. Then I languish in a nether world of underachievement."

Aditi closed her eyes. Her hands brush her hairs leaving tiny balls of the reddish-white dough on the loose strands. A thin wrinkle line of aging appeared on her forehead, as her shoulders drooped in submission. An aroma of burnt vegetables suddenly fills in the kitchenette; both coughed in spasms under its influence.

Agastaya was the first regain control and put off the burner. With the help of a cotton duster he lifted the lid and plucked a piece of potato; chocolaty charred. He blew air on it and then placed it regally on his tongue.

"Tastes like a Potato pudding, sour and bitter like you; so it is a birthday dish with a wish?" He humored.

"You would never understand; age is catching up with me, am no longer young lass, but am still a nowhere girl." She whispered.

"Aditi", he puts a comforting arm around her, "This is your achievement, all that is in here, the microcosm of the *Brahamand*- the universe and beyond; we are all your subjects, you as the sole creator of our worlds, not god but you as one."

"That's what I had expected, give a woman a god-place and she would be your servile servant forever, no Aagi, I want to be treated as plain woman with all the humanly traits and desires, with all the need for love and care, respect and attention." She sobbed.

" You have a family, that is the greatest creativity one can aspire for; anything beyond it is a lesser pursuit; still if you feel your calling lie someplace else; listen to it, I have the same rule for all, including myself, so exercise your freedom to choose. Now only if you could Tiffin some chapattis for me; wrap it in a paper I would eat them at my office, six or seven of the sweetest and roundest of your moon, baked to the precision of a wife- angry and surviving, my dearest I am, not the wordy type but I know that things change and if they don't, then all the better, all one has to do is to accept them as they are served, round red chapattis with a half bunt vegetable, part complete, but hey why bother , I would eat it as a king's supper , for you have cooked it , my wife, of whom I have a faith as blind as only reserved for god, it is my sincerity that speaks and I know you would forgive me for all my incompleteness, but also that today is my birthday a day before the Kumbh bath, as for your complain of the modern system of desires of which markets are the behemoth, then all I can say is that I have never been a part of it never would be, call it what you may ,but, I tread my path for I have faith in it, though I don't profess my practice. Tomorrow, who knows; your destiny smiles on you or on all of us." Agastaya is surprised at his flush of the face. Was he worked up too? When called upon to face the change? Was it the stickiness of a routine of last six years weighing him down?

"Ah! A sermon at this cave-kitchen! And your wish for a birthday-six or seven of my moons with the vegetable of my frustrations?"

"The real Kumbh; my nectar my lector all rolled in one… the Aditi… Advaita." He smiled more out of habit.

Aditi rolled a flour ball; pats it on a round white marble slab, dusting it on the flour powder, twice and proceeds to flatten it with a wooden roll. She places a concave iron griddle over the gas burner and searched for the matchstick-box. It lay under the stool. She lit up the gas burner, letting it warm and then placed the round raw chapatti over it after giving it a final shape with her claps. She paused for a few moments and turned it on the other side letting it simmer. The half baked flour cake puffed as she placed it directly over the blue flame; lifting the concave iron griddle with her left hand till the chapatti puffed to her satisfaction.

Agastaya munched on the first of the puffed moons, burning his palate; "you must have swore under your breath." He said; laughing.

"Why under the breath; I can swear out of the breath if need be, but I won't, one of us has sermonized enough for the day and for the rest of the days to come, I suppose." She returned the smile.

Under it though, she simmered like red coal, not the blue flame of her gas stove. Her conclusions would follow her desires, let them go to hell for all the care in the world; her world, what of it, nothing at all, it was the survival that mattered, for which she has stepped out of present impasse; into her freedom, a space of her own. She: un-owned and the master of the self. Then all, or the rest of them would chart their course, Kerrie, Agastaya and his parents. Her hands rolled on the red flour ball, decimating it into the submission of a round moon, like the vermillion spot on her forehead. Wait until the flight, tomorrow, she told herself, to convince her swinging.

"The old woman thinketh!" Agastaya wakes her in a huff.

"Aagi, would you come a little early today, Ekaba has called us all in his Ashram, he could help, I value his sermon, your parents are coming, too, I will take Kerrie along." She pleaded. "I have arranged for a worship of your planetary configuration." She informed.

"The old man is all at sea". Agastaya spoke his sarcasm. "Would hope to make it if nothing surfaces; but all promises are dumbbells, no sound all fury."

"Now..now what have you against him.? He is a man of solemn faith, divine integrity and great erudition; why do you treat him as one of your cussed muse? I owe my life and much more to him." She wrapped a bunch of chapattis in a day's old newspaper. "Buy some vegetable from Sharmaji's; let the burnt vegetable be hidden from your colleagues in the office; like most of the things are in this house for a home."

"Old Ekaba is a bird; a joke for a butt, fire his rounds, aim ... hit the bulls eye of the spirit, a dish served like a fast food, your marketing guru of faith; but his is a funny money way, the way to subway... diddle way. Wheedle way, sideway, short way, Ha.. Ha.. , permit me my blasphemy, it is my birthday-right to speak the truth; my lordie, nothing but nothing false, no sermon, only silence for the soul, I seal my lips for the day." He laughed loudly.

"Here is something for you to mull over, though, a list of wishes, bring them all and show us all the mettle of the male in you." She relaxed as she handed him a paper roll. "Your humor, a case of sour grapes, I suppose, but it sure serves its purpose." She smiled as she busied herself with churning out chapattis and putting them in a heap in a bamboo bark basket.

"My sad part, my humor: you talk of utility; good if it makes me laugh with you. Dare I bare my flippancy and be called the town's clowning glory." Agastaya twitched her cheeks with his fingers and stood up.

"Let me find some in the fagging forgotten family of mine." He placed the chapatti- wrap under his arms, plucked the keys of his bike from a wood rest and stepped into the verandah; as the sun blinded him.

"The discipline of the office, is it one of your whims or something to hold on to?" Old Mr. Vashisht, glued to his newspaper commented just as Agastya enters the sun decked small opening of the house from which the National park forest could be seen as a view of a bird's eye.

"*Mataji Parnams*". Agastaya ignores the old man and touched his mother's feet. She blessed him and enquired about Aditi, to which he replies that some things should be left alone so that they chart their own course, a natural heal way; he assured her. Old Mrs. Vashisht, sixty-five and asthmatic, complains of disease and old age, questions the wisdom of god in inflicting pain to its subjects, then hurriedly folds her hands, closes her eyes in a silent prayer. Next, she picks up on her soul mate and blames his youth, full of lethargy for the present predilections, the usual pastime of a male she says, friends, drinking, travel and the extended family, the ego of a man she calls it. "And how is your Devi?" She asked.

"She does fine, her colors are off today, but like a good painter, she would hit the aisle, soon". Agastaya assured her again.

"Ekaba will only find a way; he has a huge system and a following to match. There is a *satsang* at his ashram, would you come? Your birthday is it?" Oh the age sure makes one forgetful, gods bless you, I will get a black thread for you from the old tantric that we have, save you from her evil eye, it will." She let her motherly affection brim his cup.

"Who the hell is her, *Maa*?" He asked.

"The witch of the household, her black magic has ruined you for good, no job, no income, sitting like a *sanyasi*, poor Kerrie, she cannot have a new dress, nor a cable television to watch, my medicines are, courtesy of Ekaba.. is she leaving for good, tomorrow?" The old woman coughed and enquired.

"I better be gone, lest I am ousted from my job, too." He climbed down the stairs out in to the open taking deep breaths and swinging his key in the small finger of his left hand. Indian mother-in-laws have to have an upper hand. For them daughters-in-laws are witches controlling their sons; and what of the daughters-in-law? A question of cutting the umbilical for the Indian male-a task impossible. The man and his destiny-his woman; a cry for owning.

A black motorbike, sits under the staircase, dewed dried and dust patterned. He settles his food roll on the backseat and stoops to open an olive green jean bag tied to the back wheel rest. From it he pulls out a cotton duster and wipes the bike clean, with slow and measured movements. Next he dusts the duster and folds it into four folds and puts it at the same pocket of the olive-green jean bag. He opens the bag's side pocket and carefully lays the chapatti wrap roll in it. He secures the bag from all sides and double checks it. Once the strings of the bag are checked for their safety, he frees the motorbike from its stand rest and wheels it out into the open. He again puts the motorbike in the stand rest and eyes it with a sanguine pleasure, his soul mate, without utters and mutters. He eyes the sun and runs them across the locality absorbing it in his stride. With measured movements he climbs on his black vehicle and snuggles in its seat, adjusting himself into a perfect position. His right leg moves with a flourish over the kick which he kicks in a rhythmic movement. The vehicle comes to life with a soft gargling sound. He puts it in the gear with his left knee and releases the clutch complimenting the release with the right hand working on the accelerator. The motorbike moves with a shudder and slowly gains momentum. He settles into its rhythm; attuned to the surroundings that drove with him, his senses mingled with them. The small alley opened in to a busy road. He drove with a degree of authority dodging the vehicles and the people who thronged the drive way. The carts were all mechanized now. Times have indeed turned over their heads, he smiled. Now, one is trapped between guzzlers of oil, honking their impatience with impertinence: a jungle in the real sense of the term, poor animals, bearing the infamy. A price for development, perhaps, the roads broader, buildings taller, lights brighter, markets colorful, religion ostentatious, and people robotized: yet a throbbing energy of evolution can be savored. The country has kept up to the pace of progress; all types. The old garb of Fabian socialism slowly peels off in the wake of capitalism. Good for all, at least the system opens up opportunities' doors for all. Technology doesn't have class barrier, neither does the capital. What of the poorest? The state has to have a logic for its existence; working for an equitable distribution. But if one has talent then there is no penury. He whistled his approval as a tractor trolley carrying sugarcane rams the cycle rickshaw from behind and brakes in front of him like a school teacher accosting a renegade student: in this case with thousands of canes; a sugary punishment. Sugar on the run before it is churn. He laughed aloud as he braked in a hurry. The sudden stoppage of the traffic flow led to a commotion and then to a brawl between different parties, even those who were not a party to the entire happening and finally to a show of strength between the state represented by the police force and the tractor trolley driver and the cycle rickshaw puller, who unite on seeing the common enemy pouch on their fracas. Siren blared as a blue jeep carrying a pose of policemen screeched to a halt and demanded their share of the settlement rights. The sugarcane trolley is overloaded they pass a judgment; pay up or be damned. The cycle rickshaw is overloaded too, four passengers when the administration allows for three. A boy escapes from the rickshaw and sits on the pillion of Agastaya's motorbike, relieving the poor puller, but burdening him. Meanwhile, the people had started pulling at sugar canes, sucking the sweet juices, as the policemen and the tractor trolley driver sweat it out in their logic. Can I get one for you, too, the boy in his preteens ask him; in lieu of fare till the Chandi Devi Chowk. Agastaya smiles as he pulls a long stem of the sugar cane and offers it to him. All are content, the police for its timely intervention and subsequent hundred rupee note worth a lot, the morning begins well they laugh and drive off, *Jai ho..Kumbh*. The tractor trolley driver is happy to be let off at a bargaining price; down from five hundred to three to finally just a note worth a note; he would quote two to his owner, the fat rich Mr. Mullick, the passersby, for an impromptu treat of succulent stem, rickshaw puller for a lightened burden and Agastaya for his expecting a succulent sugar cane stem for his new job as a motorbike carrier.

"Uncle, pull up, the traffic is diverted from here; you have to drive through the Rajaji Park if you want to reach the heart of the town. Beware of the elephants." The boy; now his nephew-newly mushroomed relation; whistles him to a halt. Agastaya parks the Motorbike and lets him jump off the pillion.

"Too slow uncle, speed up ,gurrrr..gurrr… it is not a bicycle." A parting shot of a freebie. Agastaya rues his not asking for the fare and watches the boy vanish in the crowd with a long sugarcane stem dancing in his hands like a mallet.

Agastaya wondered about the relic of the raj- Uncle and all, Nephew!! The Brit never left the country- English the new mother tongue or rather *Hinglish* the official language of the new generation. What of the joys of morphology? De-morphed. Conversation needs a free flow of understanding- language then is back seated.

He took a detour from the Chandi Bridge. A makeshift rubble road led him on the other side of town, into the nearby Rajaji National park; known for elephants and Neel cows; deer and boars. The entry would be from the other side of the town, drive straight through the park and then take the first turn you come across, a police man in blue dress informed him. Agastaya drove in silence following the instructions and tailing the trail of vehicles which searched for an entry point in to the river town. He relished the fact that an entire humanity had descended down for the dip in the river of faith. The sheer enormity of the idea made him humble in his faith. People cannot but be faith bound. That is the tying thread for us all, he concluded. The drive was through the thick Sal forest. An occasional elephant cry emanated from the deep jungle. Young foe with their families drank water from the little streams on the way. The haze hung in the forest, refusing to drift along with the morning winds. Lingering laziness. The birds chirped still in their early morning slumber, refusing to wake up to the maturing day. Children on the loose. Peacocks with peahens in tow moved about freely among the blaring horns. Family on a business. He pulled his bike on the roadside and let the convoy of vehicles pass by. He counted them for fun. Stopped at exactly hundred. Then he climbed down the elevated road structure and sat on the banks of a small stream. Crystal clear water of the stream reflected the pale sun. He drank a few palms-full and then sprinkled the cold water in his eyes. He reveled in the sublime sun, letting the rays thaw his numbness. Aditi must be busy, his mind wandered on to his wife. What have I done for her up till now? What of her dreams? Would this struggle for existence ever end? Tomorrow life begins anew. Is acceptance not the only way? Why doesn't she understand this simple fact? What of parenting Keerii? She, off whom we are the sole- keeper. Would the little girl ever live her life freely or would she be bogged down by the internecine discord between her parents? How to conjure up enough to lead a satisfactory life? Why conjure when one has a choice of accepting whatever is on offer from the gods? Isn't satisfaction the key to happiness? Would Aditi ever understand? He felt hungry and was tempted to take a bite of the chapattis, but decided against doing so. On hindsight, she was right; one has a freedom to pursue ones dreams. Her need to grow and flower cannot be truncated by a family. She should move on. Family can wait but dreams shouldn't. What is there in life if one doesn't fulfill one's dreams? What becomes of the one who ignores the call of the consciousness? Are they separate; dreams and consciousness? What does one become? Aught, blank, cipher, crumb, diddly, duck egg, extinct, fly speck, goose egg, insignificant, naught, nihility, nix, nobody, non being, non entity, non anything, nullity, obliteration, oblivion, shoutout, trifle, void, wind, zero, zilch, zip, Zippo, zot.

He smiled. It takes a lot to be all that. He sure knew. His struggle with his consciousness had led him to explore the subtle world of the spirit. Not the *tantra*; but the path of knowledge, the yoga of existence for existence. His was a total involvement- a complete following of a spiritual way of living. And Aditi and Kerrie made him complete. That was the real *Sanyas;* he was convinced. He was aware of his *Rishihood-* The acme of knowledge. Not as a part of the ego; but imbibed in the spirit of daily living. What was life if not facing up to the challenges on a moment to moment basis? But Aditi's is a way to run away. Leave things hanging, like honeycomb, with honey inside but not a drop to lick; running away from the battlefield, the easiest of the wars to be won-a pseudo victory. Acceptance, the only weapon- The *Brahm-Astra*. But she cared none of that. The idea is to have a complete freedom. She said. No strings. Then how does one live? Isolation Ischemia. Relations are the breath of life, he argued.

Creation needs isolation; she was categorical. Universe is essentially dualistic, he said. That my dearest husband is a male-view: a male-twist to the story of life. So your calling, dearest wife, the world is free, he had decided to let her go. Why women rebel by being feminist? Exploitation doesn't see gender. It is what it is. Exploitation. Aditi sees him as a competitor, he concluded. Togetherness is all there is to existence. Create in its cacophony- The brush of connection with the stroke of genius. Paint a pint. Let you be wild. He had failed, he knew. Would I regret my meeting her? No. I had no hand in it. He thought. Destiny strikes you when you least expect. It tests the ill preparedness. The unheard parable making one a folklore.

Agastya watched with intent the hanging nests of the Weaver bird and the little avian flying in and out of the altered abode conducting their chores with a sincerity of worshippers. They flew in and out from the tunnel shaped opening, feeding their young ones. Their chirping rent in the jungle. Animals are free, he thought, the nature makes them so. They don't demand it; they have it as a matter of right. Despite their frailties and susceptibilities, they learn to enjoy living. But we human cut this chord and then aspire to be free. No one can possibly curb another's right to live. One is free as long as one annihilates the mind- ego. Would she understand? Aditi's lack was his defeat. Agastaya thought of their union and subsequent arrival of Kerrie. Destiny plays a truant with us all, he concluded. What of it? Life has to be lived by facing up to the challenges, not running away from it. He would save his house from disintegrating, he concluded, even if it comes at a price. He would sacrifice all he has to keep his flock together; he a shepherd in the making. Part of yoga education, he thought as he stood up dusting his clothes. He took a large gulp of water from the stream, gave a wave to the nests of the Weaver birds and joined the convoy of vehicles. Tomorrow he would stand by his wife, but today, he would search for a home: a place to begin all that there is to living and more; Meditate-hutment; he pledged under his breath. His left hand patted his heart, the wish list giving him a solace of a differing bliss. He drove slowly on the periphery, without intending to reach anywhere in particular. Letting the moments hang around him like prayers of the soul. This is a positive of a government job; the flexibility it gives to pursue one's own path; and the security of a salary. Kautaliya was right when he advocated the job of the state. He was a blessed *Rishi*, laid the foundation for a modern state along with an individual evolution twenty-five hundred years ago. The freshly laid pebbled path took him to an over bridge. He checked in his motorbike through the police barricade and showed his pass. Inspector Baamji, led him in. "What say sir, you have a meeting at ten I suppose?" He asked. "Yes, *Namaskar* brother." Agastaya replied. "I would take the narrow lane from here to the collector's court. Would the Bhaki-tilla lane be shorter than the Gokarnlane? He asked for the sake of conversation. Relation matter.

"The Bhakti-tilla, one." Inspector Baamji replied and waved him in.

Agastaya cut through the maze of devotees, driving carefully, avoiding any running into the horde of devotees. He entered the compound of the yellow building which housed the office of the district administration.

"*Ram Ram babu*, how are you?" Kripa, the guard cleared the path for him and helped him find a parking space for his motorbike.

"The Kumbh, brother, I had to take a detour, through the park. It takes time to move about through the throng of the devotees." Agastaysa lifted his bike to put it on the foot rest.

"True. The entire town is under the siege. But you have a pass, don't you?"

"Yes, but I thought it was a good opportunity to pay a visit to the animals at the park, least they feel left out by us humans." Agastaya said and walked in measured steps towards his office room.

FAIR

This is no ordinary day. Mr. Yash Dev Bardhan concluded as he adjusted the knot of his blue stripped tie; dark blue strips over light blue base. He winked to his mirror image. It goes well with the grey suit; the blue stripped tie. He was the chief administrative officer in charge of the Kumbh fair. This was his biggest challenge thus far, in the twenty years of his life as an Indian Administrative Officer: To conduct the baths peacefully and smoothly. Terrorists threats, the conflict between various Akharas over who would bath first at the *Har-ki-Paudi*; the holiest of the Ghats, crowd management, general law and order problems and V.I.P. movements; were some of the problems that occupied his mind. He whistled loudly. God would manage best, he spoke to the mirror.

"Hurry up with the breakfast Jeetu." He called out to his man Friday. "And polish my shoes, too."

"It is almost ready, wait a while." Mrs. Bardhan it was who answered his call.

She was a plump lady with the stately trappings of the *Memsaab;* the lady-in-waiting of yore- trudging along, the legacy of the Raj. Her green sari with the work of *Zardozi* on its borders and her gold ornaments gave her an impressive look.

Mr. Yash Dev Bardhan eyed her and smiled. "You look like a decked up bride."

"You and your talks, I don't care, here take a little time out for breakfast; your whole day would be spend in meetings and endless cups of tea, all acid if you don't have a full stomach." She said.

"How do I look?" He asked.

"You had a way with western outfits. Now sit and eat, Mr. Spike." She commanded.

Why wives become mothers to their husbands? Mr. Y. D. Bardhan stood in a sulk. A man never gets old and seldom acts fatherly, but a woman; always a mother, never a lover. He applied a fruity fragrant gel on his hairs and carefully combed his graying hairs. He readjusted his tie and moved towards the dining table.

"Wash your hands first." Mrs. Bardhan said sternly.

He obeyed her and pulled a chair, dabbing the watery palms with a cotton towel offered to him by his wife. "Why don't you eat with me?" He asked.

"I would, after you." She laid a plate for him and placed two Potato *Paranthas* on it.

He nibbled on them and sipped curd water. Mrs. Bardhan added one more to the heap. Mr. Y. D. Bardhan looked askance but kept to himself. Why bother about a tiff early in the morning. The day is a long and burdensome. He ate three of the stuffed fair, felt heavy and belched twice, in quick succession.

"Take a sip of water." Mrs. Bardhan directed.

He did as ordered. "Jeetu, my shoes; I am getting late." He shouted at his attendant.

"Would you come for lunch?" Mrs Bardhan asked.

"No." He replied in a relief.

"I would send Tiffin; send your driver." She said.

Mr. Y.D. Bardhan hurried towards his car; crèche for a home, he murmured. He sat in a rage and loosened his tie. The ways of a woman, making a man wasted once motherly duties catch up with her. She would not belong to you then. She becomes a universal au pair.

"Sir, *Memsaab* says that I have to collect your Tiffin at two ." His driver, Ratan rubbed in. "Shut up and drive." Mr. Y.D. Bardhan would have the longest day of his life. A father of two and the boss of the greatest congregation on the planet being mothered by his wife; she is shifting her menopause on to him. I won't tarry; life begins when you are fifty or when you wield power; and the power of religion is the greatest euphoria. He had cut out his retirement scheme; join Ekaba; for how long the old man would breathe? Swami Chintannand ji is siding with him. Mr. Y. D. Bardhan relaxed on the backseat catching a wink before it all unfolds.

"Drive to the City Control Room." He directed his driver.

"But the meeting is at the collector's office." Rattan murmured.

"Tell the senior clerk to call all the officers to the Kumbh Fair Camp-CCR." He directed the driver and dialed a few numbers on his Mobile.

The white ambassador; with the hooter blaring, sliced through the crowd and reached the CCR; city control room on the east banks of the Ganga, facing the Har-ki-Paudi ghats. Mr. Y. D. Bardhan rushed into the conference room and found it thinly populated a couple of peons and the head clerk, Shyam Babu.

"Where are the rest of them?" He asked the head clerk.

"Sir, the notice was a little late, but don't you worry, they would be here by any moment." He was calm. He brushed his crumbled white hairs. Officers are maniacal when it comes to meetings, he thought. They can discuss the butt of Bollywood sirens, for all that he cares.

"Sir, a cup of tea, if you want I can order black coffee?" He asked.

"No, Shayam Babu; something for this acidity." Mr. Y.D. Bardhan belched again.

"I have a mixture of black salt, black pepper, cloves, ginger powder, *Trifala*, Asafoetida, and other herbs; have a teaspoon and as they say: what a relief." Shayam Babu fawned.

"Give me some; had three of them. Last night I had a peg too many."

"Sir, was it Black label? Here take two." He handed the plastic bottle to Mr. Y. D. Bardhan.

"No. Blue; Scotch. It hits you afterwards; it was smooth while having, so I lost count." He gulped two teaspoons of the blackish brown powder with a swig of water and burped twice in quick succession.

"Expensive it must be; Foreign? The Chaudhary bash it was?" Shayam Babu hazarded a guess and his utility in the greater scheme of things. Who doesn't need a secure future? I can't be a governor, but he can be. Why not? It is democracy after all, all have unequal opportunity; the mighty come first and are served first, the spoils of the state.

"Yes. My brother-in law who lives in the states wanted to meet the duo." Mr. Y.D. Bardhan reclined on his chair and closed his eyes.

"Sir your talent is for the world. Once you manage this fair affair, then you can apply to any multinational company and earn in dollars." Shaym babu spread his board.

"I have applied for a study leave, three years; let us see what comes of it. But the real MNCs are here, these huge Ashrams. Religion is the business of the future; A new way to look into corporate evolution of Hinduism." Mr. Y.D. Bardhan spoke excitedly like a child playing a game he doesn't know and hence doesn't fear losing.

"Sir if only Chankaya was alive. He would take you in as his worthy successor. Is it the Siddeshwari Akahara skirmish you have in mind? It is a virtual goldmine, sir." Shyam babu could make a move-the right move, he corrected himself in his confab.

"It is too early. But yes; Chintannand ji has an idea of it. Ekaba has an aura which would be tough to discard. If only he ......and then there is Kashi, his trusted....keep..err .. Shayam Babu real dream is to see the country develop but not at the cost of Hinduism- it is a world religion in the true sense." Mr. Y. D. Bardhan let the cat out of the bag, but slowly.

"Aditi; I hear is a greater threat." Shayam babu gave a sly smile. "Our Aagi Babu's wife." "How's Madam? Does she know of all this?"He asked.

"No." Mr. Y.D. Bardhan replied. "Mothers look good when they wait upon their children." He smiled. Shyam babu could be trusted with secrets; he thought. One can't keep one all by himself.

"What of her? She is just a housewife. What does she know of running Ashrams? I hear she paints."

"She is close to Ekaba, had stayed with him in the hills." Shayam babu talked in hushed tones.

It was just then that the district level officers started trickling in. The city of Haridwar was dived into different zones and put under the chief Administrative officer: Mr. Bardhan- designated as Mela Adhikari- the Fair Officer.

The chairs were pulled, pushed and adjusted. The clothes were brushed and unruffled. Bottles of mineral water sprang up like monsoon insects. A few convector heaters were switched on. The attendance was full- Forty- two officers representing various departments but united for the purpose of conducting the world's biggest religious fair. They worked under the supervision of the District Administration and the Special Kumbh Fair Authority- S.K.F.A.

"Are we prepared?" Mr.Y.D. Bardhan began the proceedings like a teacher, addressing errant pupils.

"Well… Almost…A few minor hiccups..But we will iron them out soon." Mr. T. Namagyal the District Collector of Haridwar answered sheepishly.

"Better we remove the bottlenecks now, rather than waiting for tomorrow. Are the check posts being manned by the Rapid Action Force? Mr. Y.D. Bardhan asked.

"Yes sir, we had requested twenty companies of the RAF, we got fifteen, but we would manage. Ten companies of Indo Tibetan Border Police have also been deployed. The state police and the Home Guards are manning the various Ghats and the camps of the devotees." Mr. Aseem Singh, the Senior Superintendent of the Police informed the gathering.

"Fair enough, we should manage well. Now the sector Magistrates have to constantly monitor the Forty- two sectors. Have I made it clear?" Mr. Y.D. Bardhan asked.

"Yes sir." The motley group of officers replied in consonance.

"Please brief me in detail. One by one, please."

The district level officers, of different departments, who had been given the responsibility for managing each of the forty-two sectors, detailed Mr. Y.D. Bardhan.

Agastya quietly entered the meeting and sat in a corner, on a red plastic chair. He listened to the discussion and jotted down a few notes.

An hour into the conference; a need was felt for a break. Tea was served along with a few rounds of biscuits and baked peanuts. All munched. The room was comfortably warm now and the group of officers relaxed.

"Pankaj Bhuria." Mr. Y. D. Bardhan called on the newly posted Indian Police Services' officer as Assistant to the Police Superintend. "How do you like this challenge of being a part of the team which is conducting the grandest religious fair in the world?"

"I am humbled by this all." Pankaj the twenty- five year old replied with all sincerity.

"That is how one begins the public services; with the faith in the general good, but in a few years' time you would realize that these fairs, meetings and riots are for the administration, by the administration and of the administration." Mr. Y. D. Bardhan gave a wry smile.

"I gave him a personal briefing on this matter, yesterday, Sir." the SSP, Mr. A. Singh intervened on seeing his privilege being encroached upon.

"I have to keep up with that new recruit; Ajay Pradhan, the new Sub divisional Magistrate; He has lot of questions. Like all Indian Administrative Services guys have when they enter its portals, the usual high idealism and nationalism." Mr. T. Namgyal said.

"But where is he?" Mr. Y. D. Bardhan's eyes searched for the trainee IAS officer.

"He visits ashrams and camps more than the district office. Once they read that chap Upmanyu *sutra* all of them think they are all the anti-hero; Agastaya and can get stoned by Ganja and give the meetings and the protocol, a go by. Talking of Agastaya; where is our own Agastaya babu?" Mr. T. Namagyal looked around. He found Agastasya sitting with his back to the meeting and looking out from the window, sipping tea.

"Agastaya babu, let us also have your humble *Darshan*. We all seek your erudition". He was sublimely sarcastic.

"What can I say in this court of the Indra Dev himself with his lieutenants? The gods meet to decide upon the fate of millions of humans." Agastya stood up with hands folded in greetings.

"Only Agastya Babu understands out true position and predicament." Mr. Y. D. Bardhan said.

"Indeed. But tell us Pankaj how do you find the professionalism in the services now? In our times it was just saluting the ministers and seniors. One had to have an alignment with these parties.' Mr. T. Namagyal turned towards the youngest participant.

"The times have changed; for the better I hope. We were trained to solve the problems of everyday nature. The focus is more on service rather than rent seeking. It will take a while before the reforms set in." Pankaj Bhuria replied with a calm enthusiasm.

"One has to be career savvy, too. What of your ambition, Pankaj?" Mr. Y. D. Bardhan asked toying with his tea cup.

"This is my ambition- To serve the nation." Pankaj Bhuria replied in humility.

"Ah! Good old idealism. I like you man, I do. Do come sometimes to my house, for tea or something." Mr. Y.D. Bardhan seemed impressed.

Agastya listened without adding anything to the general discussion. The meeting resumed again. Each of the Forty- two sector magistrates gave their presentation. Mr. Hari Singh, sector number one. Mr. Devesh Kumar, sector number two. Mr. Adarsh Thapliyal, sector number three. Mr. Kalu Ram, sector number four. Mr. Dinesh Pandhi, sector number five. Mr. Anupam Ganjee, sector number six. Mr. Nilamber Bidhoi, sector number seven. Mrs. Deepa Mahara, sector number eight. Mrs. Chitra Singh, sector number nine. Dr. A. C. Bhardwaj, sector number ten. Mr. B.N. Chettri, sector number eleven. Mr. C.C Tharu, sector number twelve. Mr. C. S. Mathew, sector number thirteenth. Miss Rajini Kant, sector number fourteenth. Mr. Dev, sector number fifteenth. Mr. S. S Napalchiyal, sector number sixteenth. Mr. Prakash Kalia, sector number seventeenth. Mr. Dela Ram, sector number eighteenth. Miss. Bela Singh, sector number nineteenth. Mr. A. Pangti, sector number twenty. Mrs. Asha singh, sector number twenty-one. Mrs. T. Suman, sector number twenty- two. Mr. A. Jhori, sector number twenty-three. Mr.Prafull Kumar, sector number twenty-four. Mohammad Ansari, sector number twenty-five. Mr. Peter D' Costa, sector number twenty- six. Mr. S. Thapa, sector number twenty-seven. Mr. A.K. Kala, sector number twenty-eight. Mr. Rakesh Singh, sector number twenty-nine. Mrs K.S. Dorjee, sector number thirty. Mr. Wagdup, sector number thirty-one. Mrs. Suhasini Maitra, sector number thirty-two. Mr. Ram Lal, sector number thirty-three. Mr. A.P. Muyal, sector number thirty-four. Mr. D.C. Tyagi, sector number thirty-five. Mr. Chunni Lal, sector number thirty- six. Mr. Bal Bharmchari, sector number thirty-seven. Mr. Kanti Lal, sector number thirty-eight. Mr. Ratan Lal, sector number thirty-nine. Mrs. Suynyana Singh, sector number forty. Mr. Satish Chandra, sector number forty-one. Mr. Thusaar Kumar, sector number forty- two.

Mr. Y.D.. Bardhan listened to them all in rapt attention. Mr. T.

Namgyal made frantic notes. Mr. Pankaj Bhuria, the new recruit was awestruck. The Babus accompanying the officers prepared minutes of the meeting. Shyam Babu wrote a note for the press. Mr. Aseem gave his intelligence inputs. Agastaya yawned.

The meeting broke for a recess. Rounds of hot tea and Pakoras followed. The officers mingled with each other informally. A sense of camaraderie ensued.

Dr. Bharadwaj searched for Agastaya. " Ram..Ram..Agastya babu, how goes life?" He asked.

"The Kumbh is a challenge for us all, isn't it?" Agastaya asked for a reply.

"Yes. It is twenty- four hours' duty. But the holy Ganga River and the sheer religiosity make it worth." The Doctor vet; now a district level officer, replied.

"The fear of the administration is palpable. Poor devotees would be controlled anyway". Agastya observed.

"One has to be careful. There threats from terrorists and all." The Doc. Replied.

"True. But they wouldn't strike here; too sensitive for their comforts." He replied.

"Agastya babu, what do you say of that son of mine? He has gone haywire. The more I try to make him understand the more we drift apart. It is like he thinks that I am his enemy. You know me well enough, have I done anything to harm, anybody? He is my own son. Would I?

"You are a nice soul. So is he. Let him be free. He would come along.' Agastya comforted him.

"When, Aagi babu, when? He is thirty –two. He doesn't teach, doesn't write for the newspaper, 'Beware- Haridwar', and what is worst he roams about with that ill gotten cousin of his Sameer." Doctor was visibly upset.

"He is learning yoga, I suppose. He guides alright. His students are a successful lot." Agastya defended the doctor's son.

"But what of a practical living, is it a part of yoga education to be illiterate about the prudence of commerce and economics?" Agastya babu, what does he earns? Is there a security of his job?

"He has talent. Knowledge is the actual earning of a Brahmin. He has taken time out for evolving. Relax Doctor Sahib, he will come through". Agastya comforted the doctor.

"Hey Doctor, yours is sector number ten? Mr. Hari singh accosted them with a tea cup in one hand and a biscuit on the other.

"Yes' Dr. A.C. Bharadwaj replied. "Yours is number one, I suppose?" He asked.

"Yes; The most sensitive one. Har-ki-Paudi, falls in it." He mumbled under a mouthful of a biscuit bite.

"Agastya Babu, this is how the children treat their parents nowadays. I have told him a thousand times; get a foothold son, but he wouldn't listen, go to hell, for all that I care, but a father is always a father." The doctor resumed his complain of Annant.

"What is it Doctor Sir?" Hari singh asked.

"It is Annant my son. He has gone astray. He will become a Sadhu or a Naga Baba." The Doctor lamented.

"Good for him. Look at the pomp and show of these Shadhus. They are the real export form our country. He can set up a sect. Even the chief minister salutes them." Hari Singh became excited.

"This is what I get. I send him to the best of convent school and here he is dabbling with Hinduism and all. He says he is a Brahmin and Brahmins pursue knowledge. Who does one eat? Alms, peas and nuts. Damn Nut" he shouted.

"No he won't. Let him complete his practice of yoga, and then he will come through. But that Brahmin logic even I agree. One has to be true to one's caste, nation and causes and his cause is Yoga; he is a Spiritual Activist, Doctor Sahib." Agastya said

"Be quiet. This is a secular nation and a secular government. Dare you talk of the caste business?" Hari Singh said without differentiating between religion and the caste.

"It is a part of knowing one's dispositions." Agastya replied. "It helps in a better understanding of one's self. The true knowledge is to know thy-self." Agastaya said.

"What of survival, Aagi babu? How does one survive in this world?"

"That much even the gods smile. But I am with you when you say that one has to work and I think he understands that. Be patient. How are Mrs. Bhardwaj and Shamistta and Mr. Tweney? He asked.

"They are fine; a little worried due to this son of mine. Do drop by sometimes for tea or dinner." The Doctor was calm now.

"I would." Agastya said.

The meeting resumed after the break. Albeit, with a thin population and in small groups. A few Sectoral magistrates excused themselves on one pretext or the other. The IAS officers made one close group, headed by Mr. Y. D. Bardhan. The junior officers sat in a huddle. Some deserted the meeting for urgent but unexplained chores.

Agastya watched the crowd gathered at the Har- ki- Paudi, across the river. The stream of devotees seemed never ending; Colorful and gay to the core. Satisfied Souls. They seemed well behaved and disciplined making the ongoing meeting look insignificant. Faith is the greatest disciplinarian, he thought. But people need state for order and disorder. The Civil Services, though, a relic of the British Raj, has, over a period of time adapted to the needs of a growing nation. Good for us, he thought. Like all systems, it needs to be constantly reformed and upgraded. Is it easy? No. The oligarchic nature has led to its decay. Add to this the need to create an empire of their own, the civil servants, have replaced the *Zamindars* of yore. Faustian Feudalism. For, they framed rules, only to overrule these very rules. People are the best managers of people. It will be the same in the river town. The police poke in; in matters outside its ambit: the army of administrators over them. A change is imminent. Ajay Pradhan and Pankaj Bhuria represent the new breed of civil servants; honest and upright. Only if they do not fall into the succession trap of the big fishes: Mr. Y. D. Bardhan and Mr. T. Namgayal. It isn't nineteen- sixties: the working of the government is more transparent and accountable. Indira Ghandhi wanted a committed Bureaucracy, when she attained power in the nineteen-seventies. What it meant was the commitment to ideals of the constitution but what it resulted in was the behemoth proving its allegiance to the Congress party; giving rise to a nexus between two pillars of the state-the party and the Bureaucracy. Her clarifications fell on deaf ears. The politicization was complete. No more. Liberalization and globalization throws up different challenges. There is a need to adapt. This century would give a new paradigm; A service bureaucracy. Long live the Minnow brook mannerisms. Agastaya called the attendant and asked for a cup to tea. He waited upon it, watching the crowd movement. The murmur continued inside the conference hall: Louder from the Mr. Y. D. Bardhan group; a little subtle from the sector magistrate group- Hierarchy akin to Casteism.

Take your pick. The Administration is all about Hierarchy. Through proper channels; the common refrain. He held on to his warm cup of tea with both of his palms, savoring the vapors of the cardamom. Democracy, then it is; people are the shapers of modern nations. Give them freedom and they would change the face of this country. Gandhi was the true knower of the nation; his nation, after all fathers know the best. So a modern India would be governed by the grass roots. The meeting seems to have forgotten him. Can a home survive without listening to the wisdom of its forefathers?

Every age has a challenge of its own; Agastaya took a sip of sweetened tea. And every father has one; to manage his sons and daughters. Like Dr. Bhardwaj. But things should be left free. Evolution takes time. Every era took hundreds of years to crystallize a concomitant philosophy. Age and era: the long and short of existence. Many ages one era: Many eras; one history. Agastaya opened the window. A gust of chilly wind disturbed the officers; they protested; he relented. To open up is a thought. Does anybody know? How to live naturally? None. What can be done? They are the champions of the development, but what is development? Do they care?

Democracy is to open up from the mind and the heart. Bureaucracy stifles: Little mind little heart in a nation with large hearts and open minds. Raj relic rusted tool. Agastaya moved out of the conference hall, into the open and sat on the newly painted aluminum pipe railing with his cup of tea. Power; all types, wrenches the soul; sucking at the humility of a man. In the world only the relative can survive. Absolute is non-existent. The conference is for absolutism. Wanting without deserving; the system would fail then. Kautilya calls it *Matsanaya*; the big fish devouring the smaller one. Can a nation survive on the basis of such a thought? No. Governance has to be relative. People as the Nuclei, rest would take care of itself. The Kumbh fair is relative, too: Nothing absolute about religion. It is a part of the larger system of the human society: the World Family. *Vasudevh Kutumbhkam*. So two conclusions follow; one, the evolution of the self: two, the evolution of the world family. Since it is evolution that is the catalyst, there would no absolute, because the absolute is a stagnant concept. Only relative is free and moving; like the river Ganga; holy, pure, ethereal. Step in it and one is pure. Religion, then indeed, is scenery of the soul; a reflection of life. Things would move for the better, though. The thought made Agastaya happy. He smiled and waved to the devotees. The dialectic is at work. The travel through the triad is a never-ending journey. One cannot shy away from philosophy; even if it is a fading image of spirituality, he thought. A few devotees waved back at him; mostly children. They are receptive; absorbing all that is on offer. Growing old is the anti-thesis. Being young is the thesis. Maturing is the synthesis. A nation or the self cannot stagnate in its early years; it would be death. Either one is old or one is getting older; but then age is a matter over mind, one can be forever young if one devotes one's life to learning.

"Agastaya Babu....Aagi Babu..." He heard a calling among the din of the devotees. He walked into the conference hall.

"Agastayaji, please make a draft of the minutes of the meeting; only if you have time. How is Aditi madam and her painting? Are you leaving tomorrow? Rajesh Kumar was telling that you had applied for a loan from your Provident Fund." Shayam Babu asked with his usual suspect look.

"Yes." He answered with a pleasant smile and took the loose papers and stapled them; making a neat stack and clipping them together according to their order of importance. He put them in a jute bag and prepared to leave.

"Can I help you in this regard?" Pankaj Bhuria, the new IPS recruit offered his services. "I have to be well versed with the office work, you see."

Agastaya handed him the jute bag and walked slowly to the parking lot. Pankuj followed him.

"In the morning, this boy sits in my pillion and offers me a sugar cane stem as a fair; which he had pilfered from a tram-truck." Agastaya narrated him the morning incident as Pankuj cozies up on the pillion.

"Did you accept?" Pankaj asked.

"The boy ran away with his booty before I could ask him. It is tough to leave the thing one has either worked for or got through thieving." He laughed. "So Mr. IPS, would you be comfortable riding with me in a, not so, hip hop motorbike?" He asked.

"Not an issue, not at all, Mr. Agastya." Pankaj replied in all solemnity.

Agastaya kick started the motorbike and put it in the gears; accelerating it slowly. "Where to Pankaj; you are not intending to go back to the district office at Roshanabad?" He asked.

"How did you guess?" Pankaj laughed.

"It is your face. Like all faces of the world- The gateway to one's heart." Agastaya replied.

"So you are a face reader. Your reputation is for yoga. I have heard of your folklore." Pankaj was unabashed about his admiration for his teamster.

"Let us go to Rishikesh, then. It is just a short distance from here."He suggested.

"Wonderful". Pankaj settled in his pillion seat.

They drove through the bazaars, crossing the make shift bridges and barricades. The sun has broken through the haze and had settled into a rhythm of the pre-summer season. It was a bright day; full of fervor, both religious and otherwise; Loudspeakers blaring devotional songs and sermons of the religious heads of various commune and sects. The river town was decked up in a floral maze. Colorful Collage. Agastaya drove through the labyrinth of humanity and reached the Moti- Choor railway crossing; which also is one of the entrances to the National

Park. The gates were closed. They waited. A blue train chugged uphill, hooting a welcome horn. They waved at the passengers who sat on the doorway. It disappeared in the thick Sal forest and the gate was opened for the traffic. They resumed their journey, driving through the forest road. It was wintry green. The trees were dew laden, hidden from the beating sun. A few rays seeped through the denseness and lighted the forest in isolated spots of radiance. They drove in silence living the journeying moments. The chilly winds put their mind to rest. Another railway crossing made them wait. A journey had to be not hurried; undertaken for the heck of it. Just like that. Why worry of what would come of it? Agastaya, hurry up, we would be late, what sort of man you are, hurry up. I am a slow man, I say. It is only a marriage function, a little late wouldn't matter, he says. What do, I care? She was adamant on her insistence to speed up things. Aditi fast forwarded. He would tell her to take it cool, will make you a better creator, of oils and wills. He said. She was not the listening types. But she has in him to do something worthwhile. Good for her if she acknowledges his role in her life. If she doesn't? Then let things be. Who needs it anyway? Karma for the sake of Karma: the fruits, be damned. Good if they come on their own. If not? Then let things be. The other day, not so long ago, she had cuddled in his bosom like a child. Her snuggle arousing in him a need for filial life. What of a family of our own? He asked. We already have one, she answered. Kerrie. Yes. There were two now, lest he forgot; the little one and the little bigger little one: Two too much. But life is fun, he thought. It takes two to make the world go round. What of her decision? Go away, if she wants, but Kerrie would remain with him. A girl without a mother is a tough one. But why can't Aditi be a little reasonable. Life is after all adjusting with all and sundry. Her pursuit can take a form of her family; it is a creative process, too; bringing up a child. What freedom does she seek? It lay in one's soul; a subjective vision. Why search it outside? Living life with all its ups and downs is freedom. All the rest is a Tin Drum rebel; A crank.

"It is lovely morning, Agastaya; can I call you that?" Pankaj spoke in hesitation.

"Uh..mm..What ..yes.. yes why not, a name is the pole of identity of all." He said. "Are you tired?" He asked and without waiting for a reply pulled the motorbike on the pedestrian pathway. Both got down, stretching their limbs and rubbing their palms for warmth.

"The air is chilly, right from the Himalayas. Where do you come from?" Agastaya asked.

"Bihar. You belong to the hills. Don't you?"

"So you have had a peek into my personal file; an IPS at work." Agastaya poked him.

"No..No.. People talk of you."

"What? That I don't work? What is there to work in government? Few people, who are best in doing this work should be allowed to work freely and the rest, do what is best for them." Agastayta said.

"I feel a little stifled, too. The hierarchy is palpable. Rules are killing. Not to be overruled, even in a crisis. The bosses are an incompetent lot. Like Peter said, rising to the maximum level of their incompetence." Pankaj sat on the dry grass, with hidden drops of the night's dew.

Bihar you said? The land of the Ganga. People there have seen the struggle of history. Which district?" Agastaya asked.

"Gaya."

"The land of Buddha: Great. You must be used to the river Fairs and all, then?" Agastaya asked.

"I was sent to a boarding school in the hills. Here in your state of Uttrakhand; The railway school up in the hills. My father is in the Northern railways, an engineer from the IIT Roorkee." Pankaj detailed his life to Agastaya.

"You are occupied, as I see it. Now that you have been posted here, enjoy till it lasts. It is Kumbh Fair time; a chance to know something. Let the gods bless you." Agastaya said and sat beside him.

"You are right. I am privileged to have been posted here. But there is niggle in my soul; that is what I feel, which makes me seek something else. What it is, I don't know, but there is definitely something. I want to seek the unknown. Fathom the unfathomable. Catch the uncatchable. Touch the untouchable. There is a seething anger in me on my failure to achieve what I look for." Pankaj was flushed. "I hope you don't mind my sharing my thoughts with you?"He asked.

"The weather is a blessing for us. It rained last week and we thought that this Kumbh would be washed away. God is gracious, enough for us mortals." Agastaya said.

"Philosophy throws out more questions than answers. I tried all. Read all. But I am where I began my journey." Pankaj continued as if in a trance.

"Did you enquire the self? Knowing what suits you. You could be your best judge. None can provide you with a readymade answer." Agastaya suggested.

"It is a piquant position. Here I am bound by my sense of duty towards the state: my employer and on the other hand; the duty to the self. If and when, and I am sure it would occur; a conflict arises, then my judgments would be called in to question. Would I be able to hold my own then or would I be dictated by the terms set up by my predecessors? This question baffles and makes me all worked up." Pankuj continued to open up.

"Then all you have to do is to develop your inherent skills to take decisions." Agastaya said.

"It takes a lot to tread a new path. If at all, it is new. Every such path comes with a need to rebel. The times have come to such a pass; normal is rebel." Pankaj lamented.

"Be normal even if it takes to be abnormal to do so." Agastaya proclaimed.

"What do you do? I mean; what does it take to be..ur..well."Pankaj looked skeptically.

"Have you, perchance studied the philosophy of life?" Agastaya asked.

"Hmm.."

"You see living is all that matters and a change of vision. You start your explorations and reach the point from where you began; but with an entirely different perspective. That is what a discovery mean, finding anew something which, at the first glance was not visible."

Quietness hung like a honeycomb. A pause to absorb the soul symphony. Magical Musings.

"Let us resume our journey. I hope you are not being missed much by the administration?" Agastaya disturbed the prevailing silence.

"Let us. No; no one would. There are plenty who wants to step in my shoes. Kumbh is the time to show one's allegiance to the state; more so, to the immediate bosses; political and otherwise."

"Hop along then, forget the state and make merry in the bosom of the Ganga." Agastaya rode the motorbike like an expert racer.

They entered the town of Rishikesh. Thin in attendance but high on fervor. Here religion takes a back seat. It is the inherent enquiry in to the matters of the spirit which keeps the visitors occupied. Foreigners have a liking for this river town, giving it a Bohemian color. Beatles came here to Mahesh Yogi's Ashram and created one of their best music with the help of Ravi Shankar. Their songs reflect the free spirit of living and portray life as a journey; never ending and everlasting. The town can be rightly termed as a *Hinduised* version of Amsterdam. Open minded and self- focused. The Ganga River slows down here in languorous splendor, winding its way to the great northern plains before finally flowing into the Indian Ocean at the Bay of Bengal. Despite an array of temples and ashrams; the town reflects a culture of yoga and natural healing system. They entered a narrow lane overcrowded with devotees and the clean shaven headed priests. Agastaya parked the motorbike and guided Pankaj through the busy by lanes. They walked at the crowds' pace mingling with the human sea and flowing in its rise and ebbs. Colorful shops selling religious paraphernalia gawked at them; amulets and talisman; portraits of various gods and goddesses; crafts' bazaars and ascetics' clothing shops. Heavy incense smell; a mix of jasmine, sandalwood, Mogra and rose hung in the air. Priests waved at the visitors asking them to undertake '*Tarpan*', a cleansing ceremony for the forefathers. A few soothsayers shouted about on the passersby, asking them to know their future. A parrot saint claimed to tell the happenings in one's life by simply letting his parrot point at a scroll; which supposedly contained the past and the future of the person. A hand-reader sat, cross legged, inviting the devotees with his tall claims.

"It is more to do with the art of praxis not building up an edifice of monolithic-knowledge. When one applies what one has learned through teachers or books then one widens the base of one's knowledge. It is imperative to live practically: the science of living yoga with experimentation as the focal point. In a way, religion then becomes the applied form of living." Agastaya spoke loudly, over the din of the bazaars.

"I am getting you Agastaya." Pankaj replied. "The resplendent alleys are unique here; In fact all over the country. I find India basically a religious country."

"Which isn't?" Agastaya observed. "All major cities are actually pilgrimage centers. Or they are marts turned metropolis. It seems the two basic needs are satisfied by cities and towns; faith and food."

"You have a point. They converge at a point. Human histories have added another types of habitations; learning." Pankaj said.

"Yes. You come from such a place Nalanda, Gaya..

"Modern economy is, though, need based. Hence modern cities are economic centers."

"Yes. Add to that the health and tourism sectors and we a complete picture of the global geography. Here, let us cross the Ram Juhla; the hanging bridge ascribed to lord Rama; who visited this place during his sojourn in the jungle."

The narrow hanging bridge, swinging under the influence of gushing winds, took them to the other side of the river. The duumvirate entered the narrow lanes which were over flowing with devotees; keen on paying their obeisance to the temples of various deities dotting the river banks. Agastaya took Pankaj to a few of them saying that one can assimilate what one capable is of. "You see it is how one approaches the religion or the deities, with the aim of Bhakti as bliss or gods as symbols of religion: have your pick; open minded or parochial. All gods and all religions are deep down one; each thriving on others' insights." Agastaya said.

"That is the broadest way of understanding. But does one believe in it?" Pankaj asked.

"Does it matter whether one believes it or not?" Agastaya counter questioned him.

"No and yes; if I speak of myself I find no need to clarify my faith. But when I talk from the point of view of religious Philosophy then I am bound to question the tenets of various religions."

"And have a bias towards one's own religion?" Agastaya asked.

"May be; No study could be without a bias. Then what is the away out?"

"An objective assessment of what benefits one's own evolution."

"If one's evolution requires more than one religion then should one practice more than one religion?" Pankaj asked.

"Why not take evolution as a world religion, subsuming all the others?"

"What of the parochial, which you mentioned a little while ago? Would the leaders of various religions agree to your point of view?"

"Religion derives its legitimacy not by its leaders but by it being rational, scientific and leading to the ultimate bliss-the *Anandam*. As also by its capacity to treat ills that ails the society at large. It is the society, as I said, the largest conglomeration of human." Agastaya said. "No religion can be above the *Brahmandaya* society- the all inclusive, living and non-living."

"Well...I have my doubts with that.. But yes.. One needs to think with regard to this. As we all globalize we need to re-form religion. A world religion, is that what you talk of?" Pankaj stood for a while staring at the crowd.

"Let us focus on Karma instead of Dharma; without its fruits; hurry up and stand in line here." Agastaya directed him to fall in line in front of an ashram where food was being distributed.

Their turn came soon and in a leaf plate they were served potatoes' vegetable, sweetened flour mix and Poories. They carefully walked to the river banks, saving their food from the jostle of the crowd and sat on the banks eating hungrily.

"God provides breakfast. It is good that you are new to this place, had the people known that you are the new police boss in town then you would have been meted with exclusive treatment." Agastaya said, munching on crisp poories and licking greedily on the potato broth.

"Fawning public; perhaps." Pankaj replied.

"Respect for the state. It is in our system to acknowledge the sacrosanct place of the state and the people who represent it." Agastaya continued devouring his food.

"Without knowing the fallibility of the very people who man the government posts?" He asked.

"Whose sin is it?" Agastaya asked.

"The food is divine. It is up to the officials to pull up their socks." Pankaj relished the simple fair.

"It tastes so because it is given as *Daan* and accepted as a *Daan*; the divinity of giving and receiving. More so, it comes without the additional sprinkle of the *Masala* of Ego. So with your food you have eaten up your ego." Agastaya laughed as he rounded up his feasting.

"Strange logic you have. Like the way you are. Subtly growing on me like monsoon moss.' Pankaj observed.

"Now ..now.. we forgot to dive into the Ganga.. oh!.. mother.. forgive us for we are famished souls, ignoring you for our hunger." Agastaya knelt before the river.

WANDER

Life is nothing else but a journey. It cannot be anything more than movements in moments. Not a stagnant trice. You stop and all ends. Try terminating it and you end up kicking the bucket. Die. Death, not go the way to the flesh; but that of the spirit. Annant woke from his slumber in haste. Time to move on, he thinks. Where to? Destinationless has its challenges along with its charms. One has to just get up and go. Where? Why worry? What of where? Ignore ignorance. There is a subtle suspense in it all; almost spiritual, nay, in fact spiritual. Is the unknown and the knowing of the unknown same thing? Nope. The unknown exist outside you, the knowing is you. Can I be unknown? Annant wished for his annihilation. Wuthering wishes. Whistling wails. Wonder warts. What of this stigma of being? Nina was one; until she succumbed to the allurement of death. All it takes is to jump into the bosom of the holy river. Sacrificing? Sacrifice? Death: an offer to the *Yagya* of life? The final ablutions. She lived mole years. Unwanted and expendable. Why did things come to such a pass? Hers' was a dream for a life. Have them chase them, she poked him. Go on, but cut the umbilical, I could only advice. No need to do that, she was adamant. Dreams are after all universal; no ownership; no monopoly: I dream I achieve all are blessed. She said in all her humble humility. I wouldn't, agree, no less, I said. She pursued her dreams I pursued her.

It was the festival of colors, that day, when she met me. Discolored and disoriented. *Bhang* said she; have a glass and let Shiva take you over, she laughed hoarsely. Her face was painted black; her hairs were silver streaked with acrylic paint, her dress was splattered with blue, purple, yellow and red water- A muddled statute. Her smile was what remained as her own. It is *holi*, she laughed as she rode a bike, accelerating fiercely. I feared her. Holy, you said, I interjected. *Holi* silly; the festival of the wild; sensuous and promiscuous, she was evil in her talks. A girl opens up without any inhibitions, I concluded; if and when she opens up. She wasn't alone. He was there. An unrecognizable face all colored and masked behind the gaiety of the festival. Meet my friend; she let the name hang in pauses. I took his snaky hands, unfaithful, I concluded. He was on a high, though, Ah! Mr. Annant, THE...Mr. ANNANT; sir how do you do, Nina talks of little else but you; he was forthcoming. Well does she? I asked. That day I was jealous but couldn't do much of the same. She read my thoughts and rubbed red color on my face. I let her have her way, like always. She got to win, have all, without surrender. That was she. I saw a wish in her eyes, as they glanced from behind her macabre mane. I know what wishes are, Nina, I know what dreams are; life is wonderful without the burden of dreams and wishes. Who cares…. Was her response. Age is getting you sir, she said with finality- Snob. I agree and more, I said. Now be nice enough to leave me for good, I pleaded. We part ways. Let things die. Let time coat our friendship in the colors of longings. You are free she blessed me with raised palms, *thathastu.* So would I be; she was prophetic. The sixth sense of a woman was it? That day I felt a part of me die a slow death. I was overcome with the grey color of brooding. It is hard to let go: Harder to hold on to.

Annant bid goodbye to the campers. I better buy that book for Minnie, he thought.

Aunt Minnie like Aunty Minty. There are things of childhood which chase you, like clouds. Why it all happens to him? Why? Buy a book for her to woo her. 'Any book on philosophy would do', she was nonchalant- Western, Eastern, Cocktail. She had laughed in her demand knowing well that her wish would be fulfilled. Girls have it in them to know when to pull strings. They can fathom their hold on men. Once they know of the hold they go all out to scuttle any chances of the freedom that the man may yearn for. Good to be tied, it is far better than having no one to tie you up. Life cannot be lived without irritations and angers: fights and placations. A cycle of Karma; wheel of succor. Annant strolled into the town. Rubbing shoulders with unknowns; smiling at unknowns. Building relations without relations. Humanity binds all. He moved in aimless saunter, waving small acknowledgements to the everyday people, the town relatives. The betel leaf shopkeeper Chaurasia; the General Merchant Oberai; the flour mill owner Radhe Shyam; the ticket collector in the local Cinema theatre Mangte Ram; the cycle repair guy, Ali; and many other nameless but recognizable faces .Smile sharers all. He walked intermittently, tarrying at shops scouting for stray items, nothing in particular. A wooden craft; a miniature bicycle; assorted indigenous musical instruments; *Ektara* a two stringed violin, *Damru*, the Musical drum like a time piece which Shiva plays while dancing his dance of anger: *Tandav*, a *Dholak* and flute in different colors and sizes.

He decided against buying. Keep up the dough for a rainy day; no income in near future. But future is non-existent. So the present is his parable, he thought and whistled his approval. Turn left a blue attired policeman directed him; a procession of Sadhus would cross this lane; he warned. Lesser mortals walk into the darkest alley. It would be, it is Kumbh time after all, where the Sadhus are the chief partakers; millions of them decked up in floral and Rudraksha beads, bathing naked and bawling war-cry. He did as directed, following the rule. Why mule? Walk... walk... walk. Swap an alley but don't swap goals. What if one doesn't have any? Fun... fun... fun. Freedom from achievements, failures and living; a breath of the freshest of air-meta breathing. Annant walked jostling in the narrow alley, his second such jostle in the last few hours. One can fall in love with the crowd if one is free. How? What does it matter? Knowing the whys of the how and the what of the whys. Walk till you can. But the book for Minnie is his prime concern. Would she then allow him to... or add to his dismay. Maybe? Maybe not? He can force himself on her. What of will? Will. Not.

Hurry up man; a man calls from behind startling him. I am but the crowd is overwhelming, Annant pleaded. He is suffocating under the pressure of people in his life. Dr. Bhardwaj. Minnie. Aunt Minty. Shamisstta. Sameer, Aditi, Agastaya and Nina. Let the time pass. He convinced himself; falling back on hope is the saner way about. Justifies all the mistakes one makes in life and yet leaves a gaping hole for redemption. Mistake miss take taken amiss mist cake miss taken mistaken. Empty Rhetoric; post Aristotle. Commit one after another till it reaches a self correcting mode. He missed a turn. Left turn for Kumbh District; the right one for the town of Rishikesh. Off course a town outside the town, a river linking the two; my tale a tale of two cities, tailing my destiny like faithful wives. He hurried for open spaces. The narrow alley ended in a Auto-rickshaw station; they have a new name now; Magic. He hired one for his journey. The air was cool and frothy, river smelling and incense fragrant. A few devotees joined him. He adjusted. He would buy that damn book for Minnie, the damn dream of his life, he admitted in his secrecy. Why need a dream? Nightmares would do. Nina the dream merchant died of asphyxiation due to the inactivity of her lungs. A Water borne death. Nightmarish ends. Ghostly Goof-up. She was fished out like a whale. Then burnt in a pyre and again immersed in the river. Ashes. Ages. Annant.

Agastaya turned left into the cave like temple entrance. Inside, assorted deities sat in meditation. Pankuj Bhuria followed him. Both sat on a jute mattress, crossed legged. Closed eyes and folded hands. Incense smoke filled the air. A dim yellow flame lighted the sanctum sanctorum. Bare chest and tonsured hair priest sang hymns eulogizing gods. The duo sat in rapt attention listening to the Sanskrit prayers.

Faith crept in with a feline felicity. The temple bells tuned their soul to a sublime ecstasy. Pankaj felt peace pervading his being; a silence to be heard. It was a while when both opened their eyes to the surroundings. The priest distributed white sugar balls with puffed rice grains and flowers as a keepsake blessing to all.

"Religion is this ; a prayer, a song, a flower, a white sugar ball, a chime of the brass bell, the rendering of the mantra, closing one's eyes: Meditation." Agastaya spoke softly.

"Indeed, an experience and no more; ephemerality giving it eternity." Pankaj replied.

"You have a way with the temples and the patience for a prayer." Agastaya observed.

"My childhood was religious; I stayed with my grandmother; and the old lady prayed twice with elaborate ritual." Pankaj said.

"Good for you, it sure inculcates some semblance of religiosity. But you must have followed it with zeal?" Agastaya asked.

"It is a part of my inquiry; to know, to fathom, more so to experience." Pankaj said.

"The yoga of being." Agastaya said. "Let us visit the Tapovan; upstream, where the Rishis meditated; the name of the town comes from them- the Hairs of the Rishis-RishiKesh. There is the second of the hanging bridge over the Ganga called the Laxman Juhlla. It seems as both the brothers' were keen visitors to the holy towns. We walk. Do you mind?"

"No not at all. I have had my baptism in long walks up in the hills. Going back to what you said about evolving, how does one go about growing and learning?" Pankaj asked.

"The journey has just begun. It takes a life time to evolve. But your inquisitiveness impresses me no end." Agastaya hurried in his steps.

"That much I give to myself, the quest for the unknown. Do tell me the way or path or whatever; a guide a book or some such sort." Pankaj walked behind him.

They walked through the fruit trees, besides the river, upstream. The path took them to the Shivallik hills the foothills of the great Himalayas. The climb was a slow gradient and they walked with labored steps. Each lost in his thoughts. Silence prevailed. The occasional chirping of the birds broke through the quiescence. Agastaya laid his mind at rest and savored the freshness of the river breeze. Pankaj thought with an attached mind. About his goal, his search, his aspirations. He feared his failing to reach where he wanted to. He wished for a foolproof plan; a path without the pitfalls or bottlenecks. Was it possible to have such a path? Is life then, a struggle for attaining a state of bliss? Is it worth? What worth worth? He thought of his meeting with Agastaya; a matter of chance, a moment from the heart. Now that he has the attention of the master he wouldn't let go of the opportunity to pore over whatever he could.

They entered a small muster of shops selling amulets, religious books, frontispiece of deities, yoga dresses and mats, colorful clothing and exotic bakery products.

"It's the foreigners who come here; from Israel, France, Britain, the U.S. of America; who have given the town a look of a mixed culture. Their hub is the German Bakery, on the mouth of the hanging bridge on the river Ganga at Tapovan. We would go there, indeed we would. Buy a few books from the shop of Bhattjii ."

"That would be nice. I would like the same." Pankaj answered.

The sun shone brightly now. Agastaya stopped at a water tank and drank a few palms full of water. Pankaj followed suit.

"It is round the bend now, just across the ashram there." Agastaya pointed to saffron painted building at the entrance of which stood a huge statute of Shiva.

"So idols do have a role in religion?" Pankaj asked.

"One can have one's pick. Like in life; I am bee." Agastaya smiled.

"Sucking flavors; you are right in a way, have the best of the beast, for all that matters." Pankaj added.

"And now for some boatmanship; let us watch the mother river from close quarters."

Agastaya climbed down the steps to a bank where a lone wooden boat floated aimlessly on the placid waters, tied to a mast. The boatman collected devotees for a ride to the other side of the river bank.

They paid up their fare and sat on a bamboo mattress. The boatman called out for other passengers. He was successful in attracting a few of them and finally started the small motor to pull the boat. It was a short ride, fifty- five meters to the other side of the river. Agastaya watched the fishes jump at the boat. Pankaj watched him.

"We have a return ticket so the boat will drop us back to where we started." Agastaya called out loudly to him.

"I am all at your disposal, Agastaya, I needn't worry." Pankaj replied. He stared at the river and let the wind play with his loose hairs. It surprised him to find himself at such a predicament; right in the midst of Kumbh taking a boat ride on the river ganga with a man he hardly knew. But then that was life. Maybe relations are predestined? It was his search which forced him to play a dice with this man. A mystery for a man. Can one be learned without claiming to be one? No need to claim, for light shines nonetheless. But of himself he wasn't much sure. Why? One feels raw when one has had half a childhood. Half? No, one by two. When one has two parents. Never a pair. Father trying to be a mother. Mother, trying to be a father. It was long ago, long enough for his nascent memory to not to recollect. It is pain that doesn't need reminiscence. It remains as a part of one's being. Would that pain go? Why that bit of emotionalism is critical to one' growth? Why childhood with half a house is not a childhood in the real sense of the term? Hoodwink Child. Can one relive the years gone by? They did provide me with the shelter one needs when one is of a dependent age. Why something more is required to make life that bit enriching which adds the required depth and stability to it? Father, the builder of canals, couldn't stitch the leak in his family. The mother, a teacher, took it on herself to look after him. Life was lonely in the hill school. Tough to lead a normal life after something abnormal happens in one's life. Marathons, cricket, debates kept him busy. Without a father one cannot really learn the cover drives of the game or the pauses of the speeches. But he was a marathon man. No need to seek guidance from anyone to trudge along. Mother kept a safe distance from the father. To each his or her then, for all that he cared. It is in the adolescent when the burden of a career strikes. And the enquiry for evolution, trampled between the old and the not so young. He slogged for a youth. Emptiness, though lingered in him, refusing to die. Here he was with a stranger for a guide floating on the waters of the Ganga seeking salvation, more so filling up the hole in his living.

"You seem to enjoy the float?" Agastaya asked.

"I carry a burden, somehow. In me which refuses to be relieved." Pankaj replied.

"That is why you are here with me. Isn't it?"

"I, a product of broken home, can seek what else but emotional moorings. Is all this system of attachment a folly of human?" Pankaj asked.

"If it is human can one be non-emotional?" Agastaya asked.

"But it is all a part of attachment; the *Raga*: Krishna says in Geeta." Pankaj replied.

"That too is bliss if you practice it in a detached manner."

"Is it possible? The detachment, that is."

"What is it which is impossible?" Agastaya asked.

The boat brought them back to the bank from where they had started. Both got down and moved about on the hanging bridge. The crowd had increased, adding to the festivities of the moment. "One cannot do much with the past. One can live the present so as to reshape the future. Past is non-existent. Future presents us with a challenge. As one says it is in the future that mankind lives. It is in the future that mankind would die." Agastaya mumbled under his breath. Pankaj picked the words floating like cotton fluffs. Future...future...an obsession of sorts. If only all was present. What of past?- A tumor refusing to go despite a surgery of sorts.

"The mind it is where all reside. Apart from it there is no existence." Agastaya said.

They walked through the sea of humanity till they reached a full to capacity German Bakery. An array of foreigners queued up for their breakfast. It reflected an intense activity of an industrious hub. People, who had come to far off lands, are nostalgic of their tastes. Or they seek conformity of some kind; carrying their attachments with them. Have India while in India. Have Rishikesh while at Rishikesh. But the India of Indians. The Rishikesh, of the people who know Rishikesh; not of them who cash of the market of spirituality. Agastaya moved fast, climbing the stone stairs and waving his acknowledgements in reply to people who waved at him.

"Come up fast. This is the place to be in Rishikesh." He laughed. "Here Hindus are convinced of the universalism of their religion when they see a few white skins rubbing saffron. No... no nothing to laugh at, it is a serious matter." Agastaya feigned his anger. "Would you have a mug of coffee?" He asked.

"As you wish; I am on the house, as they say. Is this the book shop you talked of?"

"Then we won't. Sip lime-water instead" Agastsya suggested.

"Right inside the book shop?" Pankaj asked.

"Why not?

Both entered the book shop and were greeted by Mr. Devraj Bhatt the owner. They browsed through some of the books, sipping their lime juice.

"Aagi Babu you come after a gap of many a months. Are you looking for something specific? Can I be of any help to you in this regard?" Mr. Bhatt asked.

"The kumbh, my friend; meet Mr. Pankaj Bhuria, the new Superintend of Police of Haridwar." Agastaya introduced the recruit.

"How do you do sir? I am the owner of this book inn; that is what I like calling it. Any specific title you are looking for?"

"None in particular, Mr. Agastaya is there to guide me in this regard."

Pankaj shook hands with him.

Agastaya took him to a shelf of books on yoga and Ayurveda. "All these are simplified version of the original texts; buy a copy of '*Pantanjali's Yoga Pradipika*', useful for meditation. For *Asanas* you can buy a book on '*Hath Yoga*'." He suggested.

"Are you by any chance into literature; Chaucer or Yeats; or Indian writing in English?" He asked.

"Not much in the writings of the yore. I do read a lot of contemporary writings of Indian authors. Roy, Seth, Ghosh, Rushdie." Pankaj answered. "Now that you have introduced me to the great Indian texts of knowledge: my taste changes." He smiled.

"For tastes you can trust him, for the rest, I would look elsewhere." Annant whispered.

It startled Pankuj who turned back to face him.

"Yes mister what is it you want"? He asked in an officious tone.

"Is the questioned meant for me or do you ask yourself the same?" Anannt countered.

"I ask you and have a right to do so." Pankuj said in strict tone.

"You dove-tail the old man like a honey bee." Annant replied.

"You look my grandfather for today." Agastaya laughed. "Shave-off the white bristles or be doomed to be a nowhere guy; he is Pankuj, the ACP and here is the light and life of Haridwar, Annant- the master philosopher."

"I am just a humble follower of the Daedalus of Yoga." Annant said and extended his hand which Pankuj took with much consternation.

"Did I lie? He has gained in mythic proportions now, Pankuj direct all your queries to him and a readymade reply would spring like spring flowers; he is the champion of the doubters." Agastaya smiled.

"Way to go to the spring, Aagi Baba, we all shudder under the wintery zeitgeist." Anannt eyed the books' counters.

"A philosopher polyglot; Annant you were ever a mystery to me. What brings you here? Aditi waited the other day. She had cooked your favorite- *Malpuas*; lot of Jaggery and fennel seeds. You do need a carminative cooking, it seems, going by the famished look of yours."

"I just dropped by..err...for breakfast." Annant replied evasively.

"Join me for lunch; Aditi has packed Chapattis too many, would suffice for us both."

"I would try." He replied.

"Mr. Annant it would be a pleasure to spend time with you; your erudition is attractive." Pankaj said.

"Is it so?" Annant asked in a laborious tone. "I am in a hurry today, maybe some other time."

"Whenever it suits you, I am a freebee." Pankauj said.

"What brings you here in the midst of the Kumbh Fair; time you attend to the official chores, once in a while." Annant addressed Agastaya.

"We bunked the meet and drove up to here. Yes you are right, indeed I should pay due respect to my sustenance." Agastaya said.

"You see Pankuj when it is Agastaya one can expect something of that sort of unsought." Annant smiled.

"Is this your day of Blasphemy"? Don't pay any heed to him, Pankaj. He can take you to a roller coaster ride of philosophy, literature, religion and even girls." Agastaya spoke on the sly, hiding behind a large book-rack.

"That is what his wont is; what can one do but to listen. And you Mr. Pankaj, the officer of the Police, what brings you here and that too with him?" Annant asked pointing towards Agastaya.

"I am posted as an assistant commissioner of police, under trainee, for the Indian Police Service, conducting the Kumbh fair and investigating a few cases." Pankaj replied. "Agastaya takes you as some sort of an authority in matters of writing."

"Me? Does he? Well, I read philosophy to teach, but I am afraid that now is a part of my history. As for literature, well all I find European literature theology in a garb of folklore." Annant replied.

"And the contemporary writings in English: McEwen, Martin Amiss, Pamuk, Coetzee; and the Indians; Roy, Seth, Rushdie, Chandra, Desai, and all? Pankuj asked.

"They are good till they last. More so they are all sob stories about the lost worlds, too formulaic for my liking. All are alike. They report well. If, in a world of today, things have come to such a pen then god must rewrite some of his creations. But thank god that god is not a writer." Annant laughed and narrowed his head.

"But some of them are brilliant; Hossinie from Afghanistan, Murakami from Japan, Monica Ali from Bangladesh." Pankaj suggested.

"It is easy to judge one's country when one stays outside it; A non-residents' idea for a fact is akin to fiction. It is sin. Take the eastern society as close to the western ones and write about the gap in the freedom- a false idea of free will. It is a mere concoction of blurred visions and half truths." Annant was flushed with excitement. "You didn't mention the ever growing list of India bashers?"

"I told you here is the man with some originality and the power of being indifferently different. It is altogether a different matter, though, whether this energy is used to create or to deride." Agastaya said.

"Derision is based on factual premises. A writer is not just a person creating. He or she has a responsibility towards the society at large. If a book is disturbing, even if it challenges the defined moorings; it should not be responsible for disturbing the peace of mind." Annant said.

"What of the sheer entertainment or the joy of it all? Or the churning that such books result in leading to reforms and social upliftment? Pankaj asked.

"For entertainment we have Agatha Auntie and Uncle Doyle. For joys read the Epics; The pulp of the fiction, god save the world of letters. Remember we all should, books are for teaching; Not voyeurism, not, at any cost." Annant stuck to his point.

"But writing has to be contemporary, reflecting the issues facing the society." Agastaya suggested.

"Agreed; But what of the goodness of the people? Pick up any book and what have we? Sadness, incest, sodomy, kinky sex: all ingredients to disturb all: More so, adversely affecting the nascent minds. A skewed intelligence for growth!! I have my doubts." Annant said.

"But they are all stories, after all, mere figment of the writer's imagination." Pankaj ventured hesitatingly.

"Are they? When they win accolades they become social documents, when they win awards they are hailed as major work of Art and when they are criticized they are mere stories. Nah, Mr. Pankaj, I would beg to differ; most, if not all are autobiographical in content with a dash of market masala." Annant said.

"I think I get you. In fact all fiction that has been passed to us is actually the biographical sketches of the authors; nothing like pure fiction. All blurred. The statistics show that most of the contemporary writers are or had been either journalists or critics. Then what is the way out Annant?" Pankaj asked.

"Isn't it inevitable? After all the inputs are provided by living." Agastaya intervened.

"Add to that; a new breed of publisher-writer have cropped up with no fear to not to get published. This is how mediocrity has set in, in the literary world. No, dear friends, creation is the soul at work. As for your query, Pankaj, let books die their natural deaths; a few which remain deserve to be immortal." Annant spoke with passion and paced across the shop, then stopped and stared through the door across to the hanging bridge over the Ganga, " It is Gresham Law at work, 'Bad writers drive out good writers from circulation'. He sighed, 'Genocide of creative hearts at the hands of imposter bards.'

"You have become some sort of an activist, Annant." Agastaya held on to his arms. "Relax and suggest Pankaj a good coffee table book."

"The Encyclopedia of everything or anything or whatever." Annant spoke with a flourish of a critic. "As for your luncheon invite, I can't promise. I would definitely try .Now if you grant me leave. Good bye." Annant made the necessary payments at the counter and hurriedly left the book shop.

His mind occupied with Minnie's thoughts- Got to find her now. Girls have a way to feign their anger. What if, if she is real angry? If she goes away then there is nothing to hold on to. In this Fair of millions it is she who keeps me busy, Annant laughed. Om Shvaha! He ran in small steps more so from fear of being chased by 'That Man' Agastaya and his new disciple. He looked over his shoulders and was relieved to find a throng of colorful attired devotees spread like kites behind him. Not that he detested Agastaya, the 'that man'. But he needed time to think and yes to search Minnie. The new guy, some police guy, he was. Looked the usual types, read a lot, read a lot, knows all, most of it if not all, would follow if not full follower , find that elusive dream, the EL Dorado; Nirvana or the rest of the mumbo jumbo. Try as he might, he will fall short, Annant swore. These silver spoon guys have the time and money to try anything. Anything. Heaven Even. As for him; hell or heaven, how does that matter. ? But his emotional outburst stuck to him. It made him a little ashamed of himself. Got to control my passions, he swore under his breath. Let juvenile write, for all that he cares. What of Gresham's law operating in all walks of life and not just money- Bad money drives out good money from circulation? Bad writers drive out good writers from circulation, bad girls drive out good girls from hearts, bad politicians drive out good politicians from governance, bad actors drive out good actors from theatre, bad teachers drive out good teachers from classes, bad parents drive out good parents from nurturing, bad friends drive out good friends from company, bad fashion drives out good fashion from haute couture, bad breath drives out good breath from life; the spiral goes on; like an inverse cycle of Karma. But bad emotions drive out good rationality from living. Cry.. cry shabby baby. Next time I would be careful, he promised, no use opening up in front of all and sundry. One becomes a butt for a joke. Secrecy Mystery. Why all expect me to be tagged like a domesticated dog wagging tail at the slightest call? Why can't I be free of this burden? Let me lead my kind of life, or, better, let me die. Why live when one can't live a life of one's own liking? Annant searched for an auto-Rickshaw. The crowd had grown to unmanageable proportions. Good, he thought, easy to hide. No one to hide from. No one on a lookout. One can then lead an invisible life. Superman. An old man with an Auto-Rickshaw in shambles agreed to ferry him to Haridwar at a mutually agreeable fare. Midway it breaks down and the old man of a driver, smoking his cheroot and coughing hoarsely cursed him instead. Why blame me? Annant kicked the rusted body of the Auto- Rickshaw and cursed his luck. If you have it you have it, if not, then god help. Carry bodies of the dead, he shouted on the old, shambled Auto-driver. No choice. Good. One has to walk then. No choice. He trudged along the freshly bitumen-laid road, with a yellow line running in the middle like a birth mark; entwining through the forest. This was his wont; this was that he did when he left the conformity of his middleclass nestling. There was Aditi and Kerrie on the way; they must be busy with Ekaba's gang. Why not join the old Yogi? He walked faster fearing someone's prying on his escapades. A secret is to be held on to. Nina was it? Who said so? Never keen to open up despite being frank on most of the matters. Who was he? I had asked. Who? Was her reply. Holy sir, it was *Holi*, could be anyone who has a way with colors. Aditi does. But you are of a graying age. Color *Moksha*. You should try *Vanprastha*; the fourth of the life's Ashrams; forest dweller without a reveler. She laughed. Someday I would beat you in this game of spirituality, she said. Some day Some Wish.

"Want a lift Mr. Decent guy?" A female voice with a twang startled him in his perambulations.

A Jeep, decorated with colorful buntings and saffron flags screeched to a halt, a few meters away from him. Faith music blared from the loudspeaker perched up on its roof. It carried a few foreigners. The driver was a Sikh with a yellow turban. A tall, lean girl with curly hairs and a vermillion dot on her forehead and wearing a loose on the neck saffron gown got down and waited upon Annant.

"Hurry up man." She shouted.

"Me." Annant shouted back.

"Now..now..you aren't going to walk the whole of the remaining Nine miles to Haridwar." She said; raising eight fingers and hiding a thumb.

"I will get a lift." He replied as he neared her.

"I will give you a lift up. You look downcast." She countered.

"Am alright, let it be, I enjoy the walks through the trees." He sounded pesky.

"You didn't get me. Did you?" She eyed him narrowly.

"No."

"You saved me my disc space in the morning when I was clicking monkeys on the bridge across the Ganga. Remember you said sorry very decently." She drooled.

"Did I? I did. Yes I did. So you want to return a favor?"

"Take what you wish but hop along before my companions cry foul." She pulled him inside and placed him besides herself. "Let us go Balwantji." She cried happily as if a wish had just been fulfilled.

The Sardar pulled on the gurgling Jeep. Annant collected himself in the space, avoiding any touch of her. Her hairs, black with strands of brown, brushed his face. He twitched his nose and then scratched on the irritation.

"Where are the other two of the Triumvirate? She asked carelessly.

"Did you notice?" He asked.

"The third eye of a photographer." She brandished her digital camera.

Annant laughed loudly.

"You look as if you have attended a funeral?" She asked.

"My own." He whispered and then turning his back he wished the other travelers. "Hello to all and *Namaste*." He tried to be jovial but clutched at his back. Not again, he rued his decision to journey to Rishikesh. Damn Minnie and her never ending demands. She would have my blood in her hands.

"Hello."

A chorus sang from behind, followed by naming session: I am David; Me Chapman; hi there myself Melville and a whispery Schmidt.

He tried to call out his name but words stuck at his throat. A spasm of suffocation arose from his stomach. He gasped for air and strained his neck outside the window. Cool splashes of wind slapped him hard, like a giant wasps wings; brittle and needled.

"Oye..Oye.. Boss don't stick your neck too, far." The Sardar driver and his wisdom warning him.

It is already too late; my neck is on the guillotine. Shhhatkkk. A river of blood splurging on the faceless Shiva.

"Heey..I am Nicole."

"Nee..cool." He repeated.

"Nicole, Dammit." She pestered.

"Nic Ole."

Nick cool."

"Nilcoke."

"Nickole."

Both laughed.

"Annant."

Ant ant."

"AnnNt."

An tant."

Atant."

Antntant."

Both laughed again.

There is a child still in me, Annant thought. It would never die or wither away. Got to live the nascence of the essence. Who says death is inevitable? In these little moments we all live. The driver halted to Pee. Schmidt, the shy one strummed his guitar.

.....black serpent....never ending....

A serpent black ....

Without end.....

Life....take me ...take me..

Take me....life....roading...roading...

He strummed the strings delicately and sang in whispers.

For the Soul: Ears are dumb Eyes are blind Mind is a juggler.

"Tea." All shouted forcing Balwant to stop for the second time at a roadside Tea-hut.

He didn't ask because he didn't want to know. If you know, moments die an instant death. Nicole held his hand in hers; hiding them like a pearl; her coral eyes ensconcing his pain.

"Quite a weirdo your friend Annant. Something has got into him... Or?" Pankaj asked.

"Kumbh". Agastaya laughed. "Even if he has a point, it is pointless to talk of what the writers write. What matters is what one reads."

"In parts, though, he seems to be right. For the rest I wouldn't care. You do have a point as to what one reads. And what may that be?" Pankaj asked.

"Book of life." Agastaya replied.

"The greatest thriller, you are damn right; you have made my Kumbh." Pankuj was laughing.

"Once a police man always one; searching the thrill. True the markets shape writings. But creativity should be the primary focus of what one is writing. The problem arises because if it is creative it is not marketable and vice versa." Agastaya smiled at his pun.

"So save the blushes of the publishers and read thyself; right, *Gurudev*?"

"If you insist, I can bless you-*Ayushman*." Agastaya waved his hands in the air.

"Now for some book buying spree; I would take Pantanjali's Yoga text and the *Bhagvad Geetha*, though I have a copy of it, Mr. Bhatt."Pankaj picked up the two books from the shelf and took them to the cash counter.

"Supplement it with a spirit of enquiry and talks from persons who are an authority of such matters." Agastaya directed.

"Whatever you say. So books are after all incomplete in their nature; a half a priest?" Pankaj asked.

"An addition to books should always be welcomed. We need experts to solve any doubts that emerge from our readings. One has to tread the path but clarify one's confusions on the way rather than carry them as a burden."

"Till I am at Haridwar you are there. Then there is the internet, a good way to connect and learn. Pankaj said.

"Pack the complete set of the *Charak-Samihita* for me Bhattjii." Agastaya requested the shop owner.

The crowd had gathered in the town since morning; people making use of a day before the great bath to pay obeisance to as many deities as possible and make the maximum of the pitcher fair. Rishikesh being just a few miles away provided the perfect religious getaway. The duo entered the mêlée. Pankaj carrying his books wrapped in a newspaper sheet. Agataya followed him. They became a part of the motley crowd; colorful and boisterous. Pankaj walked with a spring in his steps. He felt light, like it is when an old deformity has been treated and life begins anew. For him this was the Catharsis at the Kumbh. He had found what he was looking for. The old Engineer can carry on with his canal building. The teacher can continue teaching. He was free of his filial concerns. He savored the chance destiny had provided him with, to annihilate his childhood stigma. In all the need to evolve reside, he thought, all it requires is a catalyst to initiate the process. He walked with faith. One has to believe in god, he thought; otherwise what is there to hold on to. God makes things happen and it is up to us all to add our might to what we are doing.

Agastya felt his knowledge coming to some use. For him it was not the problem of acceptance but to check his extent of knowledge. He was content that god had given him a chance to make a difference in someone's life. He was impressed with Pankaj's awareness; needs a little polishing, and that is all. Then again one is free to work but without a concern for the rewards. That is what freedom is, freedom from the fruits of labour. It helps one work in a detached manner; without hopes and aspirations and with a complete devotion to the almighty. It was a part of the surrender which leads to the total neglect of the ego, the identification with the merits or demerits.

"That is what bliss is."He shouted, startling his fellow devotees.

"Some insight or what, Agastaya the Archimedes of Yoga that you can now be crowned, unofficially and unliterary?" Pankaj jested.

"No…no.. Yes, you should know. Nishkaam karm, Sri Krishna says to Arjuna in the Geeta; work without the expectations of the fruits. I just realized that to ensure a blissful life, this is the only philosophy. Work without wishing for fruits to win over death and Study to attain the nearness to the almighty." Agastaya said.

"True. But is it easy to practice? Are we not attached to our actions? Can one be without a lingering hope in his or her heart?" Pankaj asked.

"It isn't. Practice is never an easy virtue. That is what, my friend is Yoga; the fine art of practice not a demagogy of professing." Agastaya replied.

"Is it? You mean there is a constant challenge to our conscious state of living due to the Karmic cycle?" Pankaj asked.

"Yes. Our predispositions challenge out state of consciousness; the everydayness, the problems of our emotions, the attractions of the passions and so on. There is a constant pulling at our state of conscious. We have to be prepared to overcome such challenge and come out unscathed from such pulls and pushes." Agastaya replied.

"And there is the art and science of yoga to keep us all at a maximum level of our consciousness?" Pankaj sought a clarification.

"Indeed. My friend you have got it now, all you need is to walk the path. It won't be easy but you have won half the battle if you have resolved." Agastaya said.

"That is what Pantanjali says in his book; the aim of yoga is to raise the level of consciousness by arresting the mental modifications of the mind."

"Doesn't it make the everyday living a matter of disdain, without any utility of its own?

"No, consciousness is to be expanded to include all- Living, non-living and the everyday living. If one is conscious one is conscious. That is all I have to say." Agastya seemed tired.

"Let us now have coffee to digest this all." Pankaj suggested.

"Indeed". Agastaya seconded the proposal. "Foot the bill as a part of *Guru-Dakshina*. Will you?"

"Indeed; anything and more; whatever you say, my life included." Pankaj spoke with humility.

They had tea, instead; with lot of ginger and a dash of crushed black pepper. At a small makeshift shop, one of the many which had cropped up during the Kumbh fair. Bamboo huts tied to pine poles, with red, yellow or green plastic sheets forming a canopy for a shade or a roof. They sat on a wooden bench, sipping sugary tea and letting the silence imbibe in them the spirit of yoga. Their silence made them open to each other. Words didn't transpired but they read into each others' thoughts. It was in a spur of a moment in which Pankaj opened up to Agastaya.

"It was a nightmare that I went through, Agastaya, what with my aspirations being buried under the friction in my family." He said.

"In an age when a boy needs a father, I had his schedule to look after. His absence grew long, lonely and tiresome for my mother. One day she blew over. Went to work in a hill school and took me along. They didn't separate legally, clinging on to a hypocritical relation. It was I who dangled between the two opposites; till I found a need to have my own share of the proverbial sky, my own space. But I cannot leave the two at this age. I have to look after them and chase my dreams, too. It gets tiring, sometimes." Pankuj bared all.

"Like I said, carry on with your duty without any expectations, you will be never tired." Agastaya smiled.

"Yes. That, it seems is the only way." Pankaj said.

"No there is a million ways. This is a fruitful way- The one which maximizes the peace within." Agastaya summed up. "Now for our own duty; official. Would you drive? Agastaya handed him the keys of the motorbike.

So I am not alone. The world has a distribution of misery. Pankaj is what Kerrie would be; A broken childhood in a broken home, not like Pankuj's, but the life in a city is different. Kerrie needs a mother now. She wouldn't wait. Problems are compounded by egos and ambitions. A right way does exist but how many opt for that. One cannot run away from one's duty. If one does what is left to live for. This is spiritualism at work. It doesn't require jargons to describe the soul. Annant says soul is a simple. Aditi does have a point; how does one create in the muddled environment of the family. Why not? Amalgamate all. Imbibe the spirit of everything. A consciousness of everything. Then one can create everything. Be what one wants to be. Painter. Writer. Poet. Dancer. Anything. For a mother..no..no..or a father, children are the creations. How does one define creativity? A unique way to do everyday work. Not something which overwhelms someone. But something which challenges someone to achieve, to grow and to seek. I have the severest test of my life, Agastaya thought. It takes a lot to build up a relation and nurture it. One has to make sacrifices and adjustments to carry it to a desirable level. It is a work of an art. Life at its creative workshop. Come out at your own risk. Today I have a date with Mr. Srivatsana, Agastaya resolved in his will.

"Take a turn to the right towards the pebbled path; we bath in the small tributary, the Suswa River." Agastaya guided Pankaj to a stream for a river.

The water was chill when they bathed, floating on the waters. They lay under the afternoon sun drying their bodies and resting their souls. Both lost in their confabulations of the mind. Both promised themselves a fresh beginning.

"Aagi..

"Yes"

"You know...

"What?"

"I am engaged."

"Good for you."

"Got engaged the day I completed the police training at Hyderabad."

"So..Congratulations".

"I ....

"What is it?"

"She is just seventeen."

"Hmm...

"Out of my caste....

"Hmmm...

"I don't know her all that well."

"Then...

"Still, I am marrying her."

"And...

"None of my parents know of it."

"Hmmm...

"I didn't tell them."

"Why?"

"To give back to them what they gave me."

"Revenge?"

"Yes...

"Hmmm..

"But...

"Now what?"

"Well..err...

"It isn't sweet?"

"It is..was…now..the girl is too young; I wanted to marry her so that I could control her, subjugate her, so that she be mine forever and serve me. Not run away like my mother did. Or not the way my father couldn't control her."

"Does it make you happy?"

"Now.. after today…no..Remorseful."

"Why?"

"I don't know."

"What do you want to do now?"

"I don't know."

"Is she pretty?"

"Well..ughh..passable."

"Now you lie."

"No."

"Yes."

"Now what?"

"Now what what?"

"Aagi…

"Yes."

"Was I right?"

"Were you right?"

"I would go to my father tonight. He is old now."

"Just a few miles separate you from him."

"Yes."

"My mother is here with me; for the Kumbh."

"The Fair brings all together."

KARM

A middle aged couple sat on a wooden bench, which lay like an unattended carcass on the verandah of the Collector's office compound. Occasional wails of a bony brown dog cuddled under it, with its tail curled between its legs, disturbed their soporific sitting. The man wore a green woolen jacket and the woman huddled in her carrot colored shawl. They talked in hushed tones, shying away from anybody who tried to converse with them. It has been over an hour; the man said. He must be coming, it is Kumbh time, the woman replied in a tone of understanding. Should we go, we can come tomorrow, the man suggested. It is the first auspicious bath tomorrow, the whole town is closed, the woman replied. Should we go to his house then, the man asked. No, the woman replied categorically, you can go if you want, I would wait, she said. Both sat in a grumpy silence. Would you have tea, there is a canteen here, the man asked. No, don't worry, I am alright. Don't repent now, he said. Why should I, she replied him arrogantly, she was going astray, anyway, good she ended it on her own. A curse for a daughter that was what she was. Good that she is no more, at least we are saved from embarrassments.

A sudden flurry of activity broke the somnolent mood. Cars and jeeps moved in and out blaring sirens and horns. The compound was soon overcrowded with khaki clad policemen waiting for their deployment at various check posts across the river town. Safari suit clad clerks with files under their arms shuffled from one room to another preparing papers and getting them signed from their bosses. Trays of tea were served by Ghanshyam; the canteen boy. A few peons sat under the lone Banyan tree; smoking cheroot and gossiping.

A white ambassador car entered the compound and Mr. T. Namgayal, the District Magistrate got down in a hurry. He raced through the corridors and barged into his office.

"Call Agastaya Babu, and hurry up, Dinkar." He ordered in his authoritative articulation.

An emaciated, thirty-three year old man rose from a wooden stool and rushed to the adjoining room.

He searched for Agastaya and asked about his whereabouts. We don't know; was the common refrain. He was here in the morning, the guard Kripa confirmed, and then he left for the meeting at the city control room, he added. Dinkar searched in the canteen and came out murmuring about Agastaya's disappearance.

"Sir Agastaya babu has not yet returned from the meeting." He reported to the District Magistrate.

"But it has been over an hour since the meeting ended. Has Mr. Pradhan returned from the Juna Akhara camp?" He asked.

Dinkar ran out again to find the new I.A.S. recruit. He returned in a few minutes.

"No sir, he has not yet come back from the Camp." He answered in a grave solemnity.

"It is tough to make people work. And then there are Mr. Bardhan's vexations to keep up with. It is Kumbh time and our senior most Babu is out on a stroll. What can one say to a yogi?" Mr. T. Namgayal sighed and sunk deep into his leather upholstered chair and closed his eyes.

"Can I get you some tea, sir?" Dinkar asked.

"No, you go and find Agai Babu." Mr. T. Namgayal sounded exhausted.

It has been a sapping day up till now. The work of the state takes a lot from you. It was easy to speak out against the state. Those were the days at Jawaharlal Nehru University; he could still hear those slogans. When was it? Nineteen-sixty-nine. The red flag was then the symbol of rebel. Good old days, those were, Mr. T. Namgyal relaxed under the influence of memories. That is what it is with nostalgia; it makes one relive the sublime past. His eyes shone under its whiff. He could sniff at the smell of his college days- The bonhomie and the blasting of Indira culture. The rise of the left, in the south and the east, gave them the necessary push. The blood churned then. He was a pale shadow of what he was then. But of this chair, he patted it with his hands; he would be a non entity. He detested this hiding. Agastsya was a free bird; pursuing his dreams even when familial strings pulled hard. How he was jealous of him? He thought. But the man worked for all that he has, he acknowledged. Youth strikes you the most in your old age, he thought. J.L. Nehru University was his youth- Philosophy, rebel, poetry, fun and Malashri. She was the fire behind the fire; his fire. Until calamity struck them both; "you cannot marry outside the tribe." His father announced his verdict.

"I cannot marry outside my tribe." He narrated his helplessness to her. That was before he cleared the Indian Administrative Services exams. It would have hardly made a difference. She moved on, with Safdar Anwar; an exponent of the *Nukkad Natak*: the street play; espousing the cause of street children, rights of the common populace and humanism.

He is a poet at heart, she told him. Yes he was; a liberal Marxist to the core; an anti-authoritarian. He spoke against the emergency and fought an artist's war against the over bearing state. Malashri carries forward his legacy further, even after he was brutally murdered by goons of the government while performing a street play; twenty years ago.

Mr. T. Namgayal sighed and sipped water. She trudges along, while I am the part of the same state which killed him. It wasn't easy then, nineteen sixty-nine; the year when man took the first step to conquer the space; India was embedded in its ethnicity. A Brahmin marrying a Muslim; Malashri was an immediate outcast. They; he wasn't alone in this; had helped her elope and got the two married in a temple and in a mosque; Abdul Ali had insisted; faith and all, he said. But an artist has only one religion: Humanity. So the man had it in him. Of the four of us: Two live the legacy- One after his death and the other in her present. Abdul joined the Indian Police Services, but is upright and strict. He shot the hooligans, a few belonging to his religion, during the Aligarh riots; and always paid up for his bills! Not sparing Sadia, his wife. Malashri? I got to meet her. She must be in Delhi; busy with her People's theatre movement- making the public aware of their rights, and letting the state know its limit.

The Kumbh Fair gives time to reflect. It made Mr. T. Namgayal happy. Now that he was approaching the evening of his life, he could write his memoires; to garner sympathy and to get back to his detractors? Or to re-live the past? With a sprinkle of what happened during the emergency. Where was he posted? Allahabad, as the Sub Divisional Magistrate. Indira Gandhi's legacy; and Nehru's; from JNU to Annand Bhavan; a loyalists that he had become; that he was, until disillusion set in. He could write all about how the state functioned during those dark days. JP rekindled in him the old fire. Jai Prakash Narayan, the Gandhi of Bihar. He was awestruck by him, wanting to join his movement. But? The doubt; derailing his plan to rebel, once again. It is the family who pushes one back. Who would look after your wife and your son? Now he has a daughter to look after; a daughter for a son, now that his son has migrated to the United States. She is like me; he smiled, impetuous and rebellious. A matter of the genes, they would strike the DNA. She sought something new, something mystical. He had suggested Agastaya's name. Malashri would listen to him.

Dinkar wandered on the lawns of the office campus. He smoked a cheroot, and then went to the canteen. Kripa treated him with a cup of tea and salted cumin seeded biscuits.

The middle aged couple wore their impatience stoically. The man sipped tea and the woman sat in silence. It is about time he comes, the man said. Yes, now that we have waited for so long, let us wait for a little longer, the woman opined. What parents have to go through for their children, nobody can understand. Both lamented. At least the sun god is smiling, otherwise we would have turned in to ice, the man said. No last year was colder, the woman contradicted him.

Do you know them? Dinkar asked Kripa. Somebody known to Agastaya Babu, he answered. He is in demand, nowadays, our Aagi Babu, Dinkar smiled. They are her parents; Kripa said in hushed tone. Are they? How come they want to see Aagi Babu?

Pankaj drove into collector's office compound with Agastya sitting on the backseat. He parked the motorbike. Kripa hurried to the parking hut and helped him to do so, saluting him at the same time. Agastaya moved towards his seat, bidding Pankaj a warm good bye. Both promised to catch up with each other sometime in the near future.

Dinkar entered Agastaya's room before Agastaya did. "Saab wants to see you." He informed him.

"Get me some water to drink Dinkarji; what of the D.M Saab?" He asked. "Is the matter on the boil, like our Boss?"

"I don't know. But he is waiting for you since a long time. And there is a husband with his wife who wants to see you. I think they are her parents." Dinkar speculated.

"Whose?" Agastsya asked.

"Nina's; the girl. Haven't you heard of her?" Dinkar answered.

"Tell them to wait a while. I will see the Saab, first." Agastaya spoke with a quiet authority.

"So you took Pankaj Bhuria on a ride to Rishikesh. Anything specific cropped up or just like that?" Mr. T. Namgyal adjusted his spectacles on the nose rest as he spoke.

"That depends on the perceptions sir. What a chance journey gets one is a matter of individual conjecture." Agastaya replied. "They are the young guns; Top guns."

"Agastaya Babu you are an irrepressible soul. It is not the official work that matters; it is the philosophy during the Kumbh that is the primary concern. And you are an authority on it."

"In god we have faith. It is his will. I do agree that it is the spirituality that matters."

"Your hard work; your *Sadhana*, Agastaya babu. I have a personal request to make." Mr. T. Namgayal said.

A pause hung between the two. Neither made an attempt to break the monotony of the silence.

"What is it that occupies you?" Agastaya asked the officer.

"It is to do with my own limitations with regard to keeping up with my pursuit of the matters of knowledge. Then when, at my age, the realization comes that I have become redundant it makes me aware of my stagnancy which puts me in a piquant position when I relate with the generation that follows me. That fault lies with me alone and I cannot but owe up this lack. It is people like you who hold on the fort for us. It is like the good old system when parents used to pick up the Gurus for their children." Mr. T. Namgayal spoke slowly and with a degree of conviction. Like a person who has found someone to have faith upon.

Again a pause hung for the moment, time to think and to add; a distance between two points- The logic of a conversation with the power of listening.

"And then people like me seek people like you; to add that essence in our lives." Mr. T. Namgayal was forthcoming.

"You have not yet told me about your problem or can we say; the challenge?" Agastaya said.

"Malashri, my daughter has a bouquet of doubts for you. She doesn't know you, though, but I have a feeling that you could solve most of her questions."

"Such as?"

"Philosophy, Spirituality and Politics; hers' is a strange taste.'

"Let her find her way into all this." Agastaya suggested.

"She meets people, that was why I mentioned you and there she was all keyed up to grill you. You wouldn't mind. Would you?"

"What is there to mind in all this?" Agastaya asked.

"I mean you are busy with your pursuit, would you have the time to meet her and talk?" Mr. T. Namgyal asked.

"What is the use of all this *Sadhana* if it is not put to some use? But are you not enough for her, I mean your name stands for the great teacher: Tarkeshswar, the lord Shiva?" Agastaya jested.

"It is the generational gap, Aagi Babu, children have a way of a rebel with their parents. Malashri won't listen and moreover I fall short of her expectations from a father. She may be right, but she has a fire that I had in my youth. I want her to have a vent for her quest, not die without a fight, or an enquiry." Mr. T. Namgayal spoke passionately.

"Then I would most certainly give her time." Agastaya said and stood from his chair with folded hands. "'Now can I take your leave Sir?" He asked.

"I much obliged Aagi Babu, you have lifted a huge burden from my shoulders. Yes.. Yes.. Please do, I would ask her to call on you." Mr. T. Namgayal stood with gratitude.

Agastaya sat on his chair besides the window through which sun rays trickled in. He had had a busy day. The more one grows the more work one seems to have, he concluded. Now that he is an authority in matters relating to an enriching living more cases will come to him, he foresaw the challenge. I would make a system, I need to, he thought. A system, however has its foibles and follies, why not let the work be free? He questioned his wisdom. Or let a system evolve with time? Who knows what destiny has in store for him? He afforded a smile. Some days are like that. He searched his pockets and found a crumbled paper- Aditi's wish list on his birthday. I had to meet Mr. Srivastana, the CEO of the Haridwar Development Authority for the flat. What if Aditi decides to shift base to Mumbai? That Tulli guy has a way with words. Destiny Dance. He would make an effort to correct her misgivings; he would complete her wish list, as a first step. He tapped his shirt pocket, near his heart and felt the warmth of his wife's wishes. He loved her. He knew he did, right from the moment he met her gaze on a February morning. It was a long time ago. Long before; since then Kerrie had been an addition to their togetherness. There was a disturbing streak in Aditi which didn't make Kerrie's life easy going. The little girl had to fight for her mother's care and confidence. Aditi, though, took her as a sort of aberration in her life. Shouldn't motherhood come naturally to a woman? True that creative pursuit is important but so is one's duty. And then there was her mindless pursuance for religious beliefs bordering on to dogmatism; rationality gone for a toss: Ekaba, as her sole faith pole. True that she owed him her life, but not at the cost of one's family. When it is family it is family; the rest can wait.

How can one leave a scientific enquiry? True, that faith is an inward passion, but can it be mindless. Why can not one approach god with *Bhakti*- the total surrender without reward. Aditi is doing fine; she teaches, paints for the Art galleries and looks after her family, agreed it is not a commercial success or as glamorous as it is in the metro cities, but it more fulfilling. River town does provide one with a moment to reflect and find solace within. That is the primary input for any creativity. Agastaya closed his eyes and fell into a slumber.

The middle aged couple waited for Agastaya to wake up. They sat still, least the creaky chairs wake him up.

Agastaya's tiredness put him to a deep sleep, deeper than he had expected. He woke in a daze. The presence of the couple added to his surprise.

"*Namaskar Babuji.*" They wished him in unison.

"*Namaskar.*" He replied in his wonderment.

"We are Nina's parents." They again spoke in a single voice.

"Yes." He was still in his stupor. The laze clinging to him like dying hopes.

"We wanted to talk to you." This time the lady spoke with the calm of a convict.

"Yes." Agastaya said and then called Dinkar for a glass of water.

"Can the matter not wait until tomorrow?" He pleaded and waited for the haze to clear from his head.

"We need a few moments only then we won't bother you." The middle aged woman pleaded in return.

Dinkar brought a jug full of water. Agastaya poured a glassful and drank it in one breath.

"The cold makes one more thirsty, contrary to the belief that it is the heat which makes one so. A lot of water is lost due to vapors from the mouth." Agastaya carried forward the conversation.

"Your daughter, it was. God had ordained and we mortals have no choice but to accept the same." He said.

"She was a student of Aditi Mam; learning painting from her." The lady said.

"No..no..We have not come for complains or anything like that." The man was defensive.

"She had left some of her belongings to your house- A blue brush and a box of water paints. An aisle too, I suppose, I am not sure." The lady was more forthcoming.

"You could ask Aditi; for I am unaware for such matter." Agastaya was irritated and spoke sternly.

"Please bring the items with you here, in your office. We would collect them from here, or ask Dinkar to get them from your house." The man suggested.

"I generally do not interfere in my wife's work." Agastaya let his anger to be shown through his terseness.

"Just once; your wife would create a scene. She blames us for Nina's death. But what could we do? Destiny is cruel. Why would we kill our own blood?" The woman began crying.

"I would try but I cannot promise." Agastaya nipped in the bud a budding farce.

"Thank you Aagi *Babuji*." The middle aged couple took his leave.

It was a subtle pressure that killed her. Agastaya thought of his first and the only meeting he had with Nina. She was the bubbly types not prone to waves of despondency. It was raining that day and she had painted her white sheet blue, with her blue paint brush. ALL- She had given it a title. He hadn't asked for her logic but she had supplied it nonetheless. ALL- a drop. She had said. He hadn't understood but admired her courage to communicate; must have been tough when one isn't accepted by one's family. He knew that in her was a disturbing streak, a freak for a girl; A soul like a peck on the cheek of life. Purity personified. You have a way with colors; he had answered her logic thus. Yes, very true, I could paint the world blue, for all that I care, but? She had stopped short of total emptying. He knew it, that sooner or later the conformity of her existence would question her quest and pull her back. She would have to fight on her own for her survival. Let her rebel and then she would bud as a bloom, he decided. Annant was there. Her death was Annant's failure too. It is tough to come back once one has lost a battle where a win was just round the corner. That was what was eating Annant. He would find a way. But Nina didn't .Or did she? To end it all. It must have been a tough call for a girl who lived life to the full; sought a complete picture to be painted by her blue brush. Now her parents' major concern was to get back their daughter's symbol of expression; nay rebel. They were out to rub her footprints from the sands of time. Not a speck of her to remain for posterity to turn her into a hero. Yes, she could be a symbol of an uprising of the soul, a call for a rebellion. Against what? What of conformity? To what extent was one to not to rebel? Agastaya exhausted. It is one of those days when the chain of thoughts never ends or finds its logical conclusion. They go on and on until one is engulfed under their influence. Thoughts have existence in thoughts alone, not a part of reality. Like he had told Pankaj, apart from the mind there is no existence. He meant the existence of the spirit which is different from the existence that is due to the mind. Mix up the two and what we have? A pseudo living. The spirit is not the mind that is why it never dies, is always in a state of bliss and seeks the ultimate. What is the ultimate? Can all, I mean all, seek? And get what they seek? Agastaya's mind worked up a claustrophobic argument. He detested such working of his mind, pulled at his conscious state, challenging it constantly. Now Malashri, seeking a spiritual living. In the sixties and early seventies it was the red rebel, more of the Marxian variety now it was the rebel of the soul. The White revolution: Annant Baba's Euphemism-

The color of the *Sattva*; the essence of all. This generation is certainly aware of the need for a spiritual development, not the generation previous to it; who had to focus on the 'earn-your –bread'- syndrome. Spiritual education is an intricate process, hence not everyone's cup of tea. If it does not have the necessary devotion, it could have an adverse effect. Globalization has it perils, too, with everybody trying what they could never do. Doors are available and so are the keys, which key is to be used for unlocking the door doesn't matter. A matter of master key. That is what is with capitalism, searching solutions which are readymade. Like the clothes one wears. One size fits all. All even. 24. 26. 28.30.32.36. Odd!! Everybody wears an ill fit. Or fits into what is available- The markets becoming the voice. And the universalization of tastes; one pushed down the throat of all. What of the particulars? The Individual is insane. That is what conformity is; it starts from the house and ends up in the market. Try something new and chances are that people would rebel against it-A Pseudo rebel. There is hope though, Nina, or her sacrifice. Every generation has a hero who withstands the wave of 'the given' and vouch for 'the Unknown'- the: 'To be found'. That was what should be one's quest. To know. To live. To create. Rest would follow; if not success at least peace- And Peace Matters.

Agastaya was abruptly woken from his languorous thoughts about all by a commotion outside. Now what, he asked himself?

"We would not take this laying down the state belongs to us and if this is happening to our people then there will be an agitation. We will not allow the administration to take our demands for granted. Every citizen has a right to safe life. We are the government and we will run it for the betterment of our people." Mr. Ramakanth Saini; a six footer Jat and a Member of the State Legislative Assembly from Haridwar roared.

Mr. Ramakanth Saini had come to the District Magistrate's office to collect a few passes for access to the bathing Ghats reserved for the V.I.P. s; along with his supporters. One of the supporters pointed out the presence of Mr. and Mrs. Papanaya, the parents of Nina; the deceased girl, at the office of the District Magistrate. Seeing it as a good opportunity to rake up a local issue, Mr. R.K. Saini asked them about the incident and whether the administration had done any investigation to find out the cause of the girl's death. The couple showed their tardiness to publicizing their daughter's death. But he would have none of it; not the one to let a chance go to waste: hence, the impromptu speech.

"It has been ten days since her body was fished out from the holy

Ganga and still no arrest has been made, neither a proper enquiry conducted. I warn the administration that if nothing is done with this regard then we will call for a state wide agitation. It will be a peaceful one but we cannot ignore the violence factor." He threatened.

One of his supporters pointed out the demand for compensation and the M.L.A. again spoke at length, directing the administration to pay a sum to the poor parents of the deceased girl. The local press had arrived and the correspondent of the paper: "Beware-Haridwar', clicked photographs to the delight of the crowd that had gathered on the premises of the district collector's office.

A section of the crowd started shouting slogans against the administration.

Agastaya sat on his chair trying to catch a wink. Mr. T. Namgayal, though, was a worried man. He sent for the Sub Divisional Magistrate, Mr. B.P. Kandhpal, but seeing the situation having a potential to turn into a violent one he offered to have a meeting with the delegation of the local citizens led by the M.L.A.

Agastaya was called, second time during the day to record the minutes, which he, for the second time in a day, didn't.

"We demand a through enquiry and a payment of an interim compensation to the parents of the deceased." Mr. R. K. Saini said.

"It was a prima facie case of suicide as our investigations have revealed." The District Magistrate defended.

"The investigations are incomplete. She was last seen with a boy. Did the police track down the mysterious chap?" Mrs. Dey the not so local and yet Haridwar's own social worker who took up such cases and who had hurried to ground zero, said.

"We did. Mr. B.P. Kandhpal has all the details. Let him come." Mr. Namgayal sought time.

"We have been waiting for the past so many days. Take action now, you are the head of the district. Or are you under pressure from the opposition?" Mr. R.K. Saini was quick to score a point.

"No.. no.. not all sir. We will try our best. List me your demands and I will see what can be done." He said.

"A compensation of fifty thousand rupees and a thorough investigation into the crime." The demand was repeated.

Realizing that he was cornered on a sensitive day on a sensitive issue Mr. T. Namgayal relented.

"Alright then, we will pay an immediate relief of thirty thousand rupees to the parents Mr. and Mrs. Papanaya and a team of police officers would start the investigation today itself." He announced.

There were shouts of joys and Mr. R.K. Saini was carried on the shoulders by the crowd. The correspondent made a hurried note of the breaking news. Agastaya waited for the people to leave the room. Mr. And Mrs. Papanaya sat grimly, undecided as to whether to leave or stay. After a while they decided to go.

"There is always a chance of an emergency cropping up, Aagi babu. Now whom should we send for this investigation business?" Mr. T. Namgayal asked.

"You are the boss. What do you have in your mind?" Agastaya asked.

"I was planning to send Inspector Rawat for the preliminary investigation. Though the police has no *locus standi* as there was no complain or a First Information Report, yet the public has to be placated." He put things in perspective.

"Fair enough; let the new I.P.S. guy Mr. Pankaj Bhuria accompany the police team." Agastaya suggested.

"Good advice, the presence of a senior officer would lend credence to the enquiry."

"Pankaj would handle the matter sensitively. That is my belief." Agastaya said.

"Agai babu, this business of administration is a tiring one; makes one old before the age. Too much of pulls nowadays. If all the citizens are made aware, then how the official works would be done?"

"It is Democracy sir and we all have to share the price of the freedom that comes with it." Agastaya stood up from his chair to take leave.

Time for lunch, he thought. Aditi had packed the chapattis and he had invited Annant at the Sharmaji Pooriewale- 'the Ancient shop of Mathura'; as the sign board on the shop proclaimed. Both were supposed to have lunch there. It is late I better hurry, he thought. Have to walk the distance, through the Bazaars. Good the color and the gaiety would be soothing. He opened the brown bag tied to his motorbike and took out the packet of Chapattis. He walked outside the office compound and breathed freely. The ways of the world would never end, he convinced himself.

Mr. And Mrs. Papanaya, the middle aged couple made a quiet exit. They walked through the decked up Bazaars eyeing them with forlornness. Now they could buy a few of the things they had wished for. Mr. Papanaya suggested that they save. The suggestion was however shot down by Mrs. Papanaya, no she said let us buy that small car instead, adds to the status, she reasoned; we too have dreams, she gave a final call. But what of Shalini and Mala; he asked? Got to get the two married, in a few years; the cycle of Karma wheels without a pause. We tried it with Nina, didn't we? But she wouldn't listen. He was rich and a fool to boot. The woman said. They argued and walked past the sweetmeat shops. Will you, now that all is well; Mr. Papanaya asked Mrs. Papanaya. What of the blue brush with Aditi? She asked. Oh! We will get it back now; any day, he replied. What is there to fear? Nothing, she paused; alright then let us. We haven't had anything since morning, she said. Worth the wait, though, when god gives he gives without any bars. Mr. Papanaya entered the shop and prepared to place an order. He knew that she had it in her to do something: if not in her being alive; then in her death.

Agastaya walked a hungry walk, through the colorful and crowded bazaars. The packet of Chapattis rested in his pale white, IBM imprinted Jacket's pocket. His hands were ensconced in the warmth of his olive green cotton trousers. The crowd was a mix of Gujarati, Rajasthani, Bengalli and the South Indian devotees who, like him, roamed the narrow alleys searching for specific cuisine. It surprised him to note that the Bazaars of Haridwar reflected a pan Indian taste. One could have a bite of foods from all parts of the country. A part tourist and part pilgrim, he smiled. But it the Poories with Potatoes which are the specialty of the place; that too, from the Sharmajii Pooriewale. Agastaya found his hunger alien to him, even after the Daan for breakfast at Rishikesh. Perhaps it is the exertion of the day, or the cold; whatever it was but he felt the sweet pangs of hunger rise in his stomach. The site of an array of displayed food intensified his craving. He stopped at a fruit vendor to buy Oranges but decided against it. Why kill the appetite, he thought. He took a detour from the main passageway and entered a linear lane to the right. It opened in a dark corridor, which he crossed and reached the Har-ki-Paudi. Despite the hunger he spent a few minutes sitting there and watching the swelling-by- the- moment crowd. He scooped a palm full of the Ganga waters and drank it. Three times: rubbing the wet hands over his head. Calmed; he walked into another lane, one among the many, like arteries. In the lane within the lane was a tiny shop with the old world charm and a loyal clientele: Sharmaji's shop, claiming to be a branch of the ancient shop of Mathura. The man himself was busy as a bee or what. Mostly directing and shouting to two oiled clothed boys, not more than nineteen years of age or whereabouts, who served with panache of base ball players. Passing the *Melu* leaved manna with dexterity and wit. A fat and oiled , half clad, middle aged, bald headed man sat on the thick cotton mattresses, rolling the kneaded flour balls into small round pan cake shaped moons and pouring them into the boiling oil. They crackled and hissed when they made contact with the oil. He took them out after frying them for a half a minute, catching them like fishes on the net shaped ladle. He was Punditji, the lone chef and the secret behind the unique taste of the Potatoes' vegetable, the sweet and sour ripe, yellow Pumpkin paste and the incomparable crispiness of the Pooriees.

"Agastaya Babu *Hari Om*; blessed are we that you have come to our humble outlet. It has been a long time since you tasted Punditiji's culinary." Mr. Sacchidanand Sharma, the proprietor welcomed him without leaving his seat.

He was a few years short of sixty years of age, an age when even the government retires its employees, though, with the changing times, even sixty is considered a not so old age; with a tuff of white hairs peeping through his predominantly still black hairs. He was of a smiling demeanor and good old world charm of stately humor. He wore white cotton Kurta over a brown cotton trouser. A woolen shawl hung loosely over his shoulder. He sat behind a worn down counter collecting the fare for his ware. He never boosted of his ownership of the shop. Never. That much one has to give to the old Poorie trader, always emphasizing the fact that the shop belonged to all those who worked for it. Our shop, he always said, never, my shop; thought Agastaya; a communist without being a card holder.

"Namaste Punditji. Yes, very true, it has been long since I entered the bazaars." He answered.

"Now that you have come do sit and let us have a pleasure of serving you. How are your parents? And Kerrie?" Mr. Sharma asked.

"How is Minnie? Where is she?" Agastaya asked instead of answering him.

"Busy with her world of thinking- shinking. But do come inside and sit. Hey Bholla, bring a glass of water for Babuji." He ordered.

Agastaya sat on a wooden stool and sipped water. The shop itself was small, smoked and dilapidated; untouched by the glamour and the glitz of growth. Unlike Annapurna café; it had retained its grace which comes with aging. The shop had been set up by Mr. Sharma's father in the early fifties in a partnership with a chef from Mathura; when he had migrated from Lahore to Delhi and finally to Haridwar. Since then the shop had seen many ups and down but had survived the onslaught of all. The Mathura chef, Ram Bhajan, had no heirloom and hence Mr. Sharma was the sole owner now. It still was the favorite eatery of the town. But the young preferred the more upwardly mobile Annapurna café; Mr. Sharma often complained. He planned to give his shop a face lift. A little glamour would not harm, he argued. His only condition was that Minnie, being the sole inheritor, should take more interest in the proceedings of the diner. She was of a different breed altogether; Mr. Sharma had just one complain in his life. That if only he had had a son. Things would be different then. A son understands the value of an inheritance; a girl wishes to leave, and have a house of her own. Girls are like that, he had worked up an old age cynicism and it has soured his relationship with his daughter. Minnie was a boy for him, always and he had treated her thus. Her womanhood, though, shone in her beauty and many a suitors knocked on Mr. Sharma's door for her hand in marriage; and add to this was her love for pursuing philosophy and what not. Is it a career? He had questioned her wisdom. Is career and be all and the end all of all? She had countered him in her rebelliousness. What can one say to a person bent on committing hara-kiri.? It was that teacher of hers, one of his father's long lost cousin's son's son; Annant Bharadwaj; who had waylaid her. Wait till I get my hand on him, he was agitated in his thoughts, and then I would teach him a lesson or two. Wait till she completes her studies in the college, then I would teach the bugger a lesson. After all he was the best guide in town, Mr. Sharma abided his time.

"You seem occupied, Mr. Sharma?" Agastaya asked.

"No..No.. not at all. Punditji, prepare a plate for Aagi Babu." He directed the chef.

"A bowlful of vegetables would be enough, I have Chapattis with me." Agastaya took out his packet from his jacket pocket. "Did Annant Sir come here? I had invited him too, for lunch." He asked.

Mr. Sharma's face contorted for a brief moment, and then, he replied calmly, "No, he didn't. He is a nice soul, Annant sir, but he is troubled nowadays. It is that girl, Nina, people gossip. But I don't believe in all this, he is the best guide in town, he indeed is."

"Yes you are right, it doesn't matter when people gossip, but when one's own people say all those things then it sure becomes a matter of despondency." Agastaya countered.

"Yes ...yes.. Very true, hurry up Punditjii, Babuji is waiting." Mr. Sharma shouted in his shiftiness.

"I would rather wait for a while for Annant." Agastaya spoke tersely.

The people thronged the little shop and ate with relish, sucking deep into their fingers and smacking the lips in acknowledgement of the aftertaste. Outwardly it appeared to be a dingy and almost dirty eatery but Mr. Sharma was an expert in hygiene, using his local wisdom to keep the shop as well as the alley, where it was situated, clean and free from sludge.

He has a point, Agastaya thought; the new generation has a way with the shining. No harm in that as long as one is tied to his or her roots and learns the traditions as well. Go and conquer the world but remember to come back to sleep under the cool shades of the banyan tree of your courtyard, his grandmother said. He agreed with her. There is one thing that worried him, though, the blind race for greenbacks. It eats into the time and energy which could be used for one's evolution. Where there is *Luxmi*, the goddess of wealth, there *Saraswati*, the goddess of learning is seldom met with. Old grandmother of seven and the mother of two; was right. Capitalism has its own fallouts; alienation, ostentatious, status consciousness, mass-identity and the Brand chase; eats into thc individual identity and invariably leads to a certain degree of unfair trade practices by big corporations.

Minnie was a rebel in her own way. It begins at home; father first. Like the state versus the individual. She had in him something vulnerable which attracted around her an army of her followers; charmed by her plenitudes and parables. She found a common cause with Annant; both separated by a decade years. But what has age got to do with rebel? The two made a contrasting pair- One silent the other boisterous; one reflective the other pre-reflective, but both impatient. There has to be a common point to gel. A Poorie empire for poor Minnie; Mr. Sharma had in him to surprise one and all. He was right to the extent that inheritance should be kept preserved, but Poorie for a legacy was taking the legacy business a little too far. Or was it? In this way the world would change with every generation. There will be no history. What of nostalgia? Should memories be then burnt on the pyre at the Ghats of the holy Ganga? History has a way of repeating itself, though. Pooriees would be back, wait for their time.

"Aagi babu, it is getting late for lunch, should we now serve you the vegetable you had asked for?" Mr. Sharma woke Agastaya from his thoughts.

"Yes you are right; yes do serve me your famed Potato vegetable and a piece of lime, if you can." He said.

"Have a ladleful of the Pumpkin paste, Punditji, it is like a tangy Chutni." Punditiji, the chef called out.

"Certainly, I have a tongue for the sour, helps in digestion; do serve it to me Bhollu Ram." Agastaya called out his approval. The chef is God and more.

Bhollu served him the piping hot potato broth, freshly chopped coriander leaves floated over the faintly red mish mash. Sautéed cumin and coriander seeds stood anchored on the corners of the dried leaf bowl. A splash of the reddish-yellow paste made a blob in his *Melu* leaves plate. The aroma struck Agastaya with an intensity of a flood; he unwrapped the Chapattis in a hurry and plucked a large chunk from one of them. He dipped it in the thick potato mash and placed it carefully in his mouth. His right hand's ring finger scooped out the pumpkin paste, which he sucked at. He chewed on the gobble, slowly and swallowed the glob and hurried on to his next swallow. Aditi has a way with care and all, he thought, almost mothering him along with his parents. Kerrie, was her prime concern though, and rightfully so. The sweet flour-Ragi cakes satiated him. One needs a company of a woman to attain the state of bliss, the *Annand*. Today she was under some sort of pressure; Ekaba, perhaps, cajoling her to join his ashram or her memories or her quest for creativity. He would fulfill her wish list; he tapped his shirt pocket for the tabulation. Close to his heart. He loved her and yet he felt tied with his own set of prejudicial thoughts, Agastaya found himself in a quandary. I got to get out of this piquant situation, he resolved. He would try his best, buy her things, go to Mr. Srivastana and tutor a few students in the evening. He could begin with Malashri, Tarkeshwar Maharaj can pay. Yes this would make her happy. It would not change him, though, he believed in spreading the legs to the extent of one's blanket, not more. Adjustment; have little will manage. It was a challenge in itself, keeping one's wishes within one's reach. Unlimited dreams have their own joys, definitely, they have. Sky is not the limit: that would make us human seek the ultimate. Go for it Agastaya, go for it. He gulped the blob before it could choke him. The chilies were a little strong today; he cursed them under his breath and drank the water. Bottoms up! He placed the glass on the wooden stool and sat as in an interregnum. Mr. Sharma was doing a yeoman service; indeed he was, providing food at an affordable price. Even the taste was divine. He was an efficient creator. Why can't he be like him? Why can he not take charge of his household and be the provider in the real sense of the term? He would. He resolved. How? When? She leaves tomorrow, he reminded himself.

Agastay re- wrapped the left over chapattis; Annant's share, and paid up for the vegetable- Rupees five only. Not expensive and yet not so cheap; a middle path for the middle class. What he had witnessed a little while ago was a part of the middle class farce. The couple had got a price, Mr. Saini earned a mileage, District Collector got a chance to lord over the body politic, and the correspondent from the local newspaper earned a sensational headline for tomorrow, apart from the Kumbh bath bit. What of Nina? She should have held on. There is absolutely no point in ending it all. In her death was a political question which hung like a spider's web. Politics is a detachment in effect but panders to emotions in practice. That is why people love democracy- A rational emotion. He opined. Poor Nina- Humanism at a loss. Who would stand up for this discrimination? No one. For it is a service in the real sense of the term. Annant would. He has it in him to stand up for evolution of mankind and more.

Got to hurry, he thought, Mr. Srivatsana must be in his office, got to catch him before he leaves. It was a matter of a few lakh of rupees that he can draw from his provident fund, for the rest of the amount, he can approach the bank. His monthly installments could be managed by his tuitions. Agastaya was surprised how much he lived in the future. It was not him but he could make a concession for his family; for Aditi, for Kerrie and for his parents. For, what was life without a family? He had decided to broaden the oeuvre of his spirituality. It was a matter of making a little effort. He lived in his dreams for a brief moment, till he returned to his dwelling in the present. He let the aftertaste of his resolve linger for long as he walked through the bazaars; then turned at the railway crossing, towards the office of the H.D.A.

"Aagi Babu, I had told you earlier too; got to crooked the little finger of yours, then you see how you pull out a handful, nah, a bucketful of butter." Mr. Srivatsana spoke with a stately air.

"What of the usual way, the right Way, of getting a good deal quickly?" Agastaya asked.

"This is the usual way, Aagi babu. Tell me any other way to run this country and I would become your follower for life?"

"The legal way, I meant. I have applied for it. It is almost a year now. What is the progress?"

"Government chugs and you aim to disturb its saunter. No Babuji it is not done. Because you are our man I had told of the other way. Apply now and do get a letter from the Chief Minister and I would allot that old bungalow, besides the canal, near the Irrigation Circuit house; a perfect place for your yog- shog."

"Why would the C.M. do the needful for me?"

"Why not? Oh! I got it. Is it the male ego at work? It happens, brother, but you got to use her for once and then you can lord over the whole thing." Mr. Srivatsna ordered tea.

"I didn't get you."

"Get Ekaba to talk to C.M. Shankanandji; or write a two liner. Then see how your file flies." He guffawed at his line.

"Why would Ekaba write a letter for me?" Aagi asked.

"Our respectful Sister-in-law would ask him to."

'What if I want it the legitimate way?" Aagi stuck to his line.

"People wouldn't stop talking, would they?"

"What do they talk?"

"Well, you should know Aagi Babu; about the impending changes in the Siddeshwari Akhara."

"No I don't."

"The whole world knows. It is like darkness under the light."

"I am not aware of anything in which she is involved."

"Does she have to be necessarily involved to be involved; this is Haridwar brother, the Karma befalls without knocking?"

"What is it that people talk of?"

"Well, that Aditi would be involved in the management of the Siddeshwari Akahra."

"How?" Agastaya was surprised but did not show it.

"Mr. Y.D. Bardhan, though, has a different plan. That is why he sought transfer in the Kumbh. Don't you know? You are a naïve soul, brother. But now no more; even the walls have ears."

"When would those flats be ready?"

"I don't know. The next four months are devoted to the Kumbh fair; then we will see."

"Could you suggest me another way?"

"I have, already; the best way. Our reverend Sister-In-Law can do it in a jiffy."

"Well..hmm...

"Why think. Now your times are changing for the better. Don't forget us once you reach a zenith. I would be your humble server, as always."

"Hmmm....

"Beware of Mr. Bardhan and his coterie. He has the confidence of the Home Minister. That much I can tell you and no more."

"Thank you. I have no choice but to wait."

"Things are no longer in your control Aagi Babu. Flow with the destiny, as they say. Strong walls are the most fragile in times of distress."

"That depends how deep their foundation runs."

It was the sprinkling of the rain which welcomed Agastaya as he emerged out of the suffocation of Mr. Srivatsana's office. Pure drops hit him with motherly pats. A gentle breeze calmed him. He walked with a lingering gayness; his aura tailing him like a halo.

DRAG

"Large animals do not cover theirs and have two reasons to do so: it is bulkier and it is manure in the shape of feces, works best when left in the open, you know oxidation and all, the rest of the animals do it in small quantities and some of them, the pedigreed ones, cover their carp." Sameer adjusted his spectacles on the nose rest like a teacher.

"Right; the smaller ones have just droppings: goats, hens, birds ..." Jorden agreed.

"Some do not excrete at all; they have some internal mechanism to recycle the waste." Sameer said.

"All animals are the outdoor defecators, all except, the Humans." Jorden savored the soft push; pulpy and yellow. The food makes it so, he thought; a vegetarian delight.

"Elephants have the bulkiest fecal matter, followed by the cows, then the rest but they are the best organic muffins the plant world can have, that much I can swear by my grandmother's grave. Dung up as she was, not on Elephants, I suppose, but good old domesticated cowplops." Sameer said.

"About this open business, though, is it advisable to cover up the crap, as per your instructions, or leave it in the open, uncovered?" Jorden asked.

"Manners brother manners; like pedigree dogs, till it turns into a perfect manure cover it with mud. Compost, they call it in organics." Sameer replied.

"The whole world, is then, an open toilet?" Jordeen asked.

"Rabbits suck their feces from their anus to recycle; not a drop of waste: good vet. Annant's father says in his research on Angora and all other species. But you are right, the whole world is indeed an open toilet, what matters is what is it that one intents to excrete." Sameer paused for a moment and then elaborated; "Yes, yes and an eatery, too; for us humans, like our cousins the animals are ordained to complete three tasks on a daily basis: Eat, Sleep and Defecate." He paused again as he pushed a lump of brownish pulp. Ah! Black diamond with jaggery, he smiled in his relief. "And to these three may be added the fourth one, though, not on a daily basis, as the previous three, Procreate through Fornicate; which, contrary to any known such case: all animals do, but according to the quarterly Journal of the NYF; some humans don't. The Not- Yet- fornicated and without any encumbrances miss a quarter of the pleasure that is what the quarterly journal of the British Society for Pro-recreation says. It adds that man in the west fornicates for fun; while in the east they do it for increasing their numbers. India and China collectively; they mention, would take over the rest of the population of the world, by two thousand and forty-five." He proclaimed a truth like a savant on his hunches.

"Like animals, who do it seasonally and only for procreation, is it? What of the easterners; do they do it more like beasts; time, season and the final aim of progeny, being their primary concerns? The westerners are the cowboys of copulation; seeking pleasure before procreation. But the advent of rubbers, what say doctor, has it put a spanner in the number game of the east or has it built a bridge between the two civilizations? United they stand in the seeking of the pleasure of fornication without the duty towards procreation?" Jorden asked on length as he felt a nagging pain on his calf muscles due to squatting.

"True Jew, now you mew like an erudite cat; your questions flow like your muck; good for the world, I say, through you it will know of this sermon of defecation. Well, it is a deep thought that you think; a byproduct of your outdoor excretion. But I agree with you that rubbers form the thread which ties the west and the east, like brothers-in-penis. Now the easterners can fornicate without the fear to procreate. A thousand times in their lifetime; for if they fornicate to procreate then they can do it only a few hundred times. Pregnancy and child care taking a toll on the life-term for fornication. Now east has indeed met the west and the twain shall fornicate till eternity." Sameer continued his contemplative tone. "But seasons and the time are gone for a toss. Tolstoy had a lot to say on this; must have influenced the austerity of our grand old man-the father with a notion."

"What does your indigenous wisdom says on this semen-sensitive matter; a true global concern?" Jorden asked with passion of an inquisitive student.

"Let not a drop of semen goes to waste. A drop of it is the rarest of all elements available in the universe; it is irrigated by the blood, dear Jorden, one's own blood. Whatever we eat goes to the stomach for digestion resulting in digested juice. This juice is digested again for five days and forms the blood. The blood is digested for five days and then the flesh is formed. This flesh is digested for further five days and tissues are formed. The tissue is further digested to form bones. The bones are further digested to form *Mazza-* which is digested for a further five days then my friend; the semen is formed. It is estimated by the scientists that forty kilograms of food makes one kilogram of blood and one kilogram of blood makes two ounce of semen. Would you waste the power behind your aura or would you preserve it?" Sameer asked.

"What can I say? Dr. Vatsanyaa; the guru of Kama; the Epicurus of the east, must be winding up in his grave listening to your sermons on the hunches." Jorden said.

"It is priceless possession of humans do not let it go to waste. The west and the apes of the west, have a death wish by fornicating for pleasure. By every semen drip they near their death. Master the bait of the pleasure; measure up to your passions; dear Jorden. The Sage Vatsannaya and his book '*Kamasutra*'; I say is the most under understood of all literary works, apart from the '*Annantsutra*." Sameer proclaimed.

"Is he writing a Bible? You sound like a true Christian soul." Jorden stared at him like the one who has seen one's own reflection whirling in pools of dismay.

"Do I? Save me then; dear Jew of the highest purity; the Saint of Haridwar. I shall let go of all that I said. Push in the open and savor the might of the light." Sameer relaxed under the influence of outdoor ooze. "A-*Brahma dewtuo nasty*.....

"It sure is a sweet feeling, squatting near a stream, among the trees, hiding behind the bushes and letting the cool wind beat your butts." Ah! The excitement of even being caught with the pants down by the eavesdroppers or innocent animals; Sameer you are the real doctor of the universe- the Phd. on Human Evolution." Jorden bowed while on his hunches and fell with a jerk.

"This is the idea of heaven, dear Jorden:
Out in the open we stool....
With the air so cool....
Let your fart drool....
and let the mind mule...
who might say, an idea may indeed barge...
Before you are over with your discharge."

"Be quiet lest you attract the attention of passersby....
Who might catch us in our intimate excrement.....
The world is unforgiving, my friend....
Till you say the final goodbye...

Jorden shed the final ounce of his shyness as he pushed a large lump of solid brownish excreta.

Both squatted with pleasure of children who has been allowed to have their way, if only for a brief moment. The spices in the Potato broth were purgative in nature but divine in taste, add to that, a bowl of the thickest of the curd and one can have a loose stomach. After devouring a plate too many, the two decided to visit a quiet stream on the nearby hills known collectively as the Tiger hills, to let out the heaviness of the tummy. They rushed through the various alleys of the Burra bazaar; across the Krishna Street and through the busy Gyani road, till they reached the mouth of the Chandi Devi Bridge. Both crossed the overpass on the river Ganga and took a narrow forest path leading to the isolated and thickly forested assortment of low hills. On a base of a hillock a pristine stream emerged from the thick mass of the Sal trees. They climbed upstream, and squatted under the tree shades. Sameer guided Jorden through the act. First dig a narrow hole with a stick, you are tall hence a deeper hole is a must, so dig deep, then put two flat stones on either side. Use the mud for covering it, he gave a parting advice- do not throw it and use it to cover the carp. Jorden did as directed. Sameer sat just a few meters away from him. Both hid behind Lantana shrubs, saving themselves from the prickly stems and branches of the weed.

"One of the imports of the British, this Lantana; is suppose to be a mosquito repellant."Sameer sounded irritated as he rubbed at a red boil which had erupted on his back due to a stick of prickly Lantana brushing against it.

"Is it?" Jorden asked.

"I am not sure; though of *Neem* tree I can vouch that it is the best repellant of the class *Insecta*; then there is the lemon grass shrub, which too, has the qualities of repelling the biting beasts. A weed is after all a weed. Now this Lantana has spread onto the fertile lands like tentacles of the untamed: a menace to the farming community." Sameer complained.

"Do you blame the British for all this and other ills: Democracy, Middleclass, Communalism and...?"

"Closed toilets of the stand and deliver variety. They had a knack of un-understanding the indigenous knowledge and a cleverness at making fun of the same." Sameer said. "One cannot superimpose the material excellence over the quest for spirituality, which they did with impunity of an imperialist."

"Did they not make an effort to save the disappearing wisdom? And have they not modernized India?" Jorden asked. "The Railways, the canal and drainage; code of laws and Jurisprudence, law and order system and the Westminster model of Governance; the list, I am sure is long."

"They did: Railways and the canal system to drain the wealth. A nation is known by the wealth of knowledge and the depth of culture. It is here that they played sly traders. As for they being the preservers of ancient wisdom; every household in India does a lot more than an empire did; for preserving it, we are doing it right now; by excreting in the open. For them it was a win- win position; to appear as reformers and take up the cause of modernity: it served their imperial designs. Hence, their effort to superimpose their own value system over the already existing social mores and practices." Sameer said. "As for the idea of modernity, dear brother, this country was modern in the true sense of the term long before the west took shape or gained political prominence. In fact once India became India, the floodgates of all ills were open: but let the churning continue, we relieve ourselves of the excess baggage and let the lightness of the being take us over. Have you done up with?" He asked.

"But they helped the Social reformers to bring widespread reforms in Hinduism itself- abolishing Sati; the widow burning on the funeral pyre of her husband; bringing up education for women; working for the down castes." Jorden said without answering Sameer, insisting on his acceptance of his ideas like an irritant reformer.

"Rename the country as Bharat Mata and see the change. What should we care for all, we are thinkers and visionaries not the political hypocrites, so, dear brother; it is the time of the Kumbh, clean it up; have you? I am done up and washed, no paper for me, the freshest water soothes my burning back: Those red chilies.....*Annus Horbilis*." Sameer prepared to wind up his session of defecation.

"Indeed. Mr. Jugs pours them by the mugs." Jorden covers up the matter with the mud scooped out of the hole he had dug up.

"Wash the hands with the earth, Jorden, dearest brother of mine; Detergents are the second most deadly of the inventions that came out from the stables of the science: post, the world war two, Plastics being the first." Sameer said.

"Indi-genius." Jorden said. "The indigenous style of life; I say, Doctor, you are a teacher par excellence; blessed is my soul that I ran into you last night. If only I had met you and the brother of yours Annant Bharadwaj; in my last trip for the Kumbh Bath; I would have been worth the weight in Nobel or a Booker."

"Blessings are the best prizes: No bells to toll or No Boo to the Cur of creativity; the tail wager to the west; my friend; work without rewards, as the good soul Krishna says. Mark my words; be with a Brahmin for company and the world is your class room. But what of the one we all look up to; the power behind our power? Annant a saint, quite like Saint Augustine; adding the fourth pleasure: Fornicate without Procreate, before the vow of Celibacy. Talking of the Saint, did you per chance, saw that English man at the café, the one with a lovely woman?" He asked. "A devout Christian: Pope with a noose: pegged back by a she-Brahmin; Shamisttha, Annant's cousin."

"I did notice a few foreigners; I don't know of whom are you talking about." Jorden replied as he washed his hands with the brown mud, rubbing it gently on his palms.

"The one with the red sari clad woman with a huge vermillion dot on her forehead, wearing a white shirt and sky blue woolen jacket matching with his navy blue trousers; he is a true Brit, a lover of this civilization Saint Twenny Baba. Never mind, but the sari clad was our saint's first." Sameer informed him.

"Is it so? And Minnie: the young lass?" He asked.

"The guy, an enlightened English man, married Annant's cousin Shamistta; who now runs him like the slave Yakub of the Princess Raziyya, the daughter of the slave emperor: Illtutmish; the builder of the Kutub Minar: taking revenge on behalf of all Hindustanis-Imperialism in a household. Our saint, though, has a way with girls: his cousins, notwithstanding. Culture my friend, resulted in another unrequited love: no incest in Hinduism, but inter-caste and inter-culture and inter color marriage is allowed: the usual hypocrisy of middleclass Hindus. Ill-bred, English read. Hence the new find, Minnie, but a perky bird tells me there is a bottleneck, there too." Sameer said pulling his pants up and jogging up to let the blood flow through his legs. He stretched and arranged his clothes with a relief written large on his face.

"What of that?" Jorden asked.

"It is a family history, a history of war vulgar enough to be remembered; listen to the folklore in the best tradition of Bharat Mata: Circa Nineteen thirty-nine, An Archeologist, the father of Annant's father, marries one of the distant cousins of Minnie' father. The good old Vet. is born circa nineteen-forty two; the year of Gandhi's call for Do or Die against the British. All goes well till his father, the excavator of civilizations: including Mohan-Jo-Daro, a part of the Indus valley civilization, the earliest of Hinduism and all; excavates something in his wife, an illness of body or soul or that of virtue, though, not of a serious proportion, but he, nevertheless, decides to leave her. Annant's grandmother goes back to live with her parents but later marries a second time. Since then it has been a decree in her village that marry an untouchable but never in the family of the Archeologist. Dr. Bhardwaj has a lifetime of ruse, that of being left to fend for himself and has declared his unflinching hatred to his mother's family. Poor Annant now becomes the part of a curse." Sameer spoke with a passion of a story teller. "Caught in the cross fire of internecine family feud like the fighter son of Subhdra and Arjun; Abhimanyu, in the battle of the Mahabharat. But Minnie's father, the great Pooriee trader has a secret plan up his sleeve, I can smell a rat as fat as a mat, or whatever: for he allows the two to get intimate and all. After all our Saint Annant is the best guide in town. He is a trader for a Brahmin, you see, so the deal; once the deed done, let the Saint be ordained as blasphemous, quite like Jesus."

"And the fact that she is actually his Aunt." Jorden added. "No carte blanche for Incest."

"And the fact that he does nothing for a living and more; so the world thinks and rumors of him. I tell you Jorden this country has come to such a pass, that the Brahmins and moreover, a creator Brahmin is expected to earn money or pursue a career; cashing the Karma, poor Krishna gone for a wing. It is knowledge that they earn and collect and it is for the guidance that they can be sought. All this is ignored for a system of the markets. In this regard of providing a direction to the society, creatively, Annant does alright." Sameer washed his face and sat on a boulder.

"What now?" Jorden asked.

"Now what?" Sameer added.

"To the banks or to Annant's college finding the Saint of Haridwar and then roaming about in the river town?" Jorden said.

"Would he still be in his college? He runs away from the old JDB. He isn't with Minnie, that much we are sure of." Sameer added.

"Let us find him and take his blessings." Jorden stood up to go.

"It was his pay day maybe he lends us a few hundreds of the greens to buy an ounce of the Black Diamond- Ganja." Sameer said.

Both walked out into the open. They re-entered the bustling Bazaars and lost themselves in the sea of humanity. From the Shankrachary Chowk they hired a cycle rickshaw and directed the rickshaw puller to take them to the JDB College on the outskirts of the river town. The rickshaw puller huffed and puffed his way up the slight gradient and deposited them on the gates of the huge yellow building. They entered the silent premises looking for Annant. The beauty of small towns is that all places are like backyards, just at an arms distance. Close Knit. Like a Crochet web. Or a one huge family under a huger banyan tree.

"Who go there bugger two? The college is closed from today so *Rukkoo.* " Ramcharan, the peon accosted them at the main entrance, wobbly with his speech and emitting a stench of a mixture of tobacco and country liquor; red catechu lines marked his chin like congenital scars.

"Bhai…Ram..Ram.. Is Annant… Sir here..We..we are his friends?" Sameer took a tentative step inside.

"Hush up fella… there is trouble….But Annant Sir is god…" Ramcharan slurred, "Hush up even the walls has ears."

'What is the matter? You are drunk. How do you manage it even in a prohibited town of Haridwar?" Sameer asked in awe.

"I am the son of a Brewery and the father of the bottle. But don't talk of Annant sir that Inspector Rajendra Singh Rawat was here enquiring about that girl Nina. I tell you these girls what they want they themselves do not know, then it is the good people like Annant sir who has to bear the shame." Ramcharan sat on the ground and lit up a cheroot. He offered the conical bundle to the duo. "You are Sameer docturrr, are you not?" He pulled hard on his tobacco stick.

"Yes, I am his brother and am here to save him like *Bal Bhadra*." Sameer took the cheroot bundle and lighted two dried brown tobacco leaf rolls, offering one to Jorden. They puffed deeply, letting the smoke out in circles and spiting on the ground, the aftertaste of raw tobacco.

"But where is he?" Jorden broke the lingering silence.

"Who are you?" Ramcharan shifted his attention to the white skin. Then as if recollecting asked again; "are you Annant sir's student, the white man; well, JDB is keen to see you. I can get you a bottle of the kick but only if Doctor Sahib supplies the spirit." He smiled in servility.

"But where is our sir?" Sameer asked with a worried tone.

"Oh! He; he is sitting under the Gulmohar trees' shade behind the canteen; it is his last day in the college; from the next term he will not be here."

"Why so? Never mind." Sameer stood up to go.

"Wait sirs let me guide you to your friend." Ramcharan stood up and walked in unsteady steps.

Both followed him. They walked through the breath of the brown grassed ground and turned left. An old dilapidated structure greeted them with rowdy sounds emanating from it: Boys baying and beating the wooden tables and moving plastic chairs. Loafer Choir. A small garden with Gulmohar trees with stray summery red flower still hanging on a few branches and a circular pond half full with water with dead lotus tubes floating on it like swollen carcass: stood like an oasis of peace. Annant sat under the shade of one of the trees with eyes closed.

"Old chap, why did you not call us? What is this police matter?" Sameer greeted him with his doubts.

Annant kept quiet.

"Speak up Saint or is it you *Maun Varta*; the Fasting of silence?" Sameer shook him.

"Is it something serious? Can we be of some help?" Jorden joined the questioning.

"This country, I tell you, is being run by the Lord Rama himself: *Ram Bharose*; nobody works, the administration is a mother-fucker and the police are fucking their own sisters. Now if anybody touches Annant sir, I tell you, rivers of blood will flow in this town of the Ganga." Ramcharan suddenly let out his alcohol agitation.

"Take on the government, we would, Jorden, my brother of past births; Ramcharan, here has a point. Now relax Ramcharan, go and arrange for some more of your heavenly Soma Rasa; the divine drink of the gods; we are here to add our might to your concerns." Sameer calmed him. "You get the daughter of the liquor; a bottle of the freshly brewed stuff."

"Oh! The usual interfering of the inane and the uneducated careerists, searching solutions without delving deep into the malaise." Annant spoke softly; barely audible words.

"Allow us to take up your case, Dear saint, and see what we can do. We will shake the roots of this nation, we will stop the Ganga at the *Gaumukh* itself and let the entire humanity damn well thirst for spiritual manna, we will....just for a few hundred rupees we will, make ten million of your followers, I swear on the Gita Bhagvad, that I will not sleep, not touch a lass or have a drop of the spirit, till justice is meted to our hero, our pride, Annant Bharadwaj; the son of my uncle." Sameer came up with an impromptu speech.

"*Inqualaab Zindabaad*!!" Ramcharan shouted with clenched fists.

"Long live the revolution." Jorden shouted.

"Blood comrades, it is blood we will shed. Give me blood and I will give you justice, *Sonar Bangla*; *Ekla chalo re*.... as the world sleeps, we wake up to our tryst with the soul. Dare anybody lay hands on Yogi Annant and we will shake the foundation of this state, nay, this country, nay nay, this world, nay nay nay the *Brahmand*: Universe". Sameer proposed in his speech.

"I second the proposal, let us march up the Tiananmen Square of Haridwar, the police station and let them see what is meant by the power of the voice of people". Jorden lent his might to the brewing agitation.

"*Rokkoo*..Wait! I am the Pall Bearer, I am *Amirika*, let us get stoned first. I put my Betel spit mark on the war. Let the spirit flow, Fushuck eet MMannn, I am white ..Ready for the fight. *Ratt..tta..rattaa..boom.. boom.. swisshhh..vroom..booommm.* But we have a Mir Jafar, this white man, get out you son of a daughter fucker." Ramcharan shouted in his alcoholic drool, and moved menacingly at Jorden.

"Wait comrade; let us not fight amongst us, Jorden has been hit by the leer of the west, so he seeks us Brahmins for the path to salvation. But we all are Ghandhi's sins.. sorry comrades..Forgive me my blasphemy, I meant sons: so we will be non violent and March peacefully and without arms in the pockets…let us go." Sameer stood up on the wall of the garden and waved to the unseen audience.

"I am Amerika so I will leak first." Ramcharan stood on the other side of the wall and pulled out a quarter of a bottle of the liquor and took a swig.

"Let Annant be the new Che….blood brothers, let us castrate oops, sorry holy blunders, Castroise all, least they fiddle with us. Let the hero swing and the heroine sing the songs of valor." Jorden pumped his fists in the air.

"No my friend, no women for a just cause, not for our hero, for he had had too many of them: let us not forget Aristotle's advice to the young: if you want to conquer the world, then keep away from the women. Conquer the woman before the world." Sameer shouted and snatched the bottle from Ramcharan and took a swig himself.

"But how do we run the world without the fairer sex?" Jorden questioned Sameer's wisdom and Aristotle's. "But was it Aristotle, really, who said so." He sounded disappointed but the sight of the bottle perked him as he too, took a swig.

"No sex wex no..no..no we want real women, the nautch girls will take up Annant sirs' case." Ramcharan shouted with a flushed face.

"Yes indeed it was Aristotle and he said much more about the fairer sex of yours; like they are ….I don't remember, he had some unkind remarks for them. But that is not the case here. It is about Annant Bhardwaj; the Rishi himself. We have to pick up the cudgels on his behalf, just like Plato and Crito did for Socrates. No hemlock for him, dare they nail him, our own Jesus; and we will carry self immolation." Sameer suddenly became agitated.

"We want Maneka.. we want Menka…we want Miinika..". Ramcharan shouted and snatched the bottle back from Jorden and took a large gulp of the brown liquor.

"No we want our own queen Phoolan here. Woman are the real

warriors, my wife beats me blue and black, the Kali Maa. I say Dogturr, it is all a conspiracy of that Rajendra Singh Rawat, the Inspector, who questioned our Sir's character, calling him a *Charitraheen*, the loose one. But now it is time to unite. Look what they did to our queen, turning her into a bandit. Arise you two, follow me to the Dilli."

"I second his resolution. Let us leave Annant sir to write another Mahabharat. Let me be Arjuna, you Jorden be our Krishna and Ramcharan, you are Karna fighting, this time with the Pandavas, the wronged ones. March to Kurukshestra, the battlefield and lay our lives for a just cause. Let us become immortal, like Gandhi clan and all." Sameer shouted.

"Who are the Kuravas; the evil ones?" Jorden asked in all seriousness of a seasoned Charioteer.

"The ruling elite; the public is but the helpless Dhritrashtra; the blind father of the evil Duryodhan." Sameer suddenly became serious. "We need a reincarnation now for the twenty-first century. Krishna you have come in the form of Jorden, like you promised in the Bhagvad Geeta: whenever there will be an excess of evil I will be born to re-establish the order of righteousness. Hare Krishna..Hare Krishna..."

"Let us re-establish the dream of our Father: mine too, for ,from now on, I am an Indian, nay, a Hindustani; like pretty woman of ours; Miss Julia Robhearts; and re-establish the *Ram Rajaya*, the rule of the lord himself." Jorden was flushed with excitement.

"This is the real resolution of the U.N., the league of the notorious; let us form a world government, with its capital here, right here, at Haridwar. Resolution number one thousand six hundred and twenty-eight." Sameer proposed.

"Let Annant be the Prime Minister, then" Jorden said.

"Agreed. And you can have the foreign portfolio." Sameer was accommodative.

"And me? You mother fuckers, sister fuckers, have you forgotten the leaker. I will be the president of the world- The Obama of the all friends of the daughter of grapes, the followers of the tipsy. I will booze my way to victory. Let the Ganga River be laden with the spirit. Drink for free and to the fill. Drop and re-emerge with a hangover drink again for the Final *Moksha*." Ramcharan swore on the empty bottle and threw it with all his might. It flew with a whistling call and crashed against the wall, spraying the shards of the rough glass like a hundred reflecting mirrors.

"Be quiet, everybody and now let our hero, our leader, the prime minister of the world say a few words of wisdom." Sameer climbed down the wall.

"Shut up." Annant said as he lay on the grass and yawned, thrice, in quick succession.

The three of them fell in a stupor, under the influence of the liquor sun and the exhaustion of an innocuous rebellion.

The canteen with its bunch of boisterous students had fallen silent, like quietness before praying.

It was that time of the day when its future course is undecided, a day when the routine is conspicuous by its absence and the people search for a cause to justify their whiling away the moments. The sun was hot now, an effect of it entering the tropic of cancer. The foursome slept a summery sleep, coiling lazily on the damp grass with red Gulmohor flowers sprayed carelessly. The college building stood forlorn like a yellow tomb, waiting for someone to light an incense stick; a sign that it has not fallen on the days of total neglect. This is what happens with public places, if they are not visited upon on a daily basis, they quickly fall into the realm of the oblivion. Imagine a railway station without a horde of passengers glancing for their trains; desolate destinations. Or a cinema hall without an audience: a flop show. During the vacations: it happens with the schools and colleges: empty classrooms and unoccupied seats stare back with a sadness born out of an oversight. The long corridors were eerily silent. Ghostlike. A Cemetery Seminary.

The river winds gushed, swirling through the vast emptiness of the yellow structures. A few whitish-grey pigeons, who had made homes on the roof tops of the double storied building, flew in and out, finding the silence as an aberration to their normal living. Some sparrows and swifts chirped to break the monotony of the dead air. Rustling leaves lent their might in keeping the lull at bay. The campus had been isolated: like someone standing outside a line. Can anybody enjoy life without being a part of the crowd? Can anybody crowd out crowd from his life? People who are left alone tell the story but are never a part of it; those who are a part of the crowd or are in a melee, are story bound, acting upon the role assigned to them in the theatre of living, longing and loosing.

A speck, not just a speck, but a large and bulky nimbus cloud; though, just a speck when viewed from the perspective of a complete schemata of nature; flew in with the gust of the wind and covered the almighty sun. All of a sudden it was dark. Like an early evening; or an unexpected sunset. With it the cold set in; a chill cutting through the bones and marrows.

The foursome shivered, almost, in sync.

Ramcharan was the first to wake up with a stagger. He rubbed the sleep off his eyes and surveyed the group. Jorden followed suit and sat on the green lawns of the small garden.

"Sir, good morning." Ramcharan was sheepish in his wish.

"Good morning in the afternoon. We must have slept for a good hour or so?" He asked.

"I say, more than that. It is three- thirty now. Our principal, JDB wanted to see you. Would you take me to the land of the white Ganga; Amerika, I can do anything, cook, wash, brew and all?" Ramcharan made use of the opportunity he got and asked for a favor.

"This is a wonderful country. Just a few hours ago you were advocating making this city the capital of the world." Jorden replied.

"One has to go about visiting places." Ramcharan philosophized in his somberness.

"True. Let us see". Jorden answered laconically.

"Wake up the brothers Karamazov." Jorden called out to the cousins.

Sameer woke up in a trance. He gave a look of enquiry to Jorden and then shifted his attention to Annant. "Dear brother elder wake up to the beauty of the evening, let us find a shelter before it rains. The clouds are ready to drop.......wake up my dearest of Fop."

"Doctor, do little of your theatrics....least you may be counted amongst the heretics.... I am awake to the world and its way....nobody dare hold me under a sway." Annant retorted.

"The saint speaks a poem, we are blessed listeners, indeed we are, now my Pal in times of gloom; lend us crisp brown note of five of the hundreds rupees and we would sing your lullabies across the whole Gangetic plains." Sameer stood on his knees and folded his hands in a mock prayer.

"I am but an unemployed rogue, a burden on the mother Earth, how can I pay up? And what it matters if I be famous or infamous? My identity is a microcosm of the universe." Annant said.

"A sad saint, dear brother let us jack the sack up, Ramcharan here is a crisp note with Gandhi smiling and Reserve Bank of India underwritten; run along and find a Sadhu who can enlighten us to a lump or an ounce of the blackest of the Ganja; the diamond black." Jorden offered.

"A Stoned Saint!! I would take one any day. Yes our brother Ramcharan kindly hurry up and be done up with; in the name of our Guru; Saint Annant, tomorrow is the first of the Great bath a good dip will clean us of the sin." Sameer seconded Jorden's proposal.

"I am on my way, a hundred more for my country bottle; *Lal Pari*: Red Angel." Ramcharan stood with a jerk and dusted his clothes. He back combed his unruly hairs with his hands and straightened his crumbled loin cloth.

"Here is your hundred for the red Angel." Annant handed him a crisp note.

"Keep this, Jorden." Annant returned Jorden's investment on the lump of stoning.

"You are our guest, our God." He said.

"I told you he has a large heart, like this vast brown grassed field." Sameer pointed to the empty fields.

"Hail the Saint Annant, bless us with your blessings." Jorden pocketed the five hundred rupees note and bowed his head.

"Now tell us your *Ram khahani*; the story of your estrangement." Sameer said.

"Which one?" Annant asked with a jiving smile.

"What do you mean; this Inspector business and the inquiry?" Sameer said.

"Oh! That. I thought you would be keener to know the Nicole saga."

"The Nickool saga!! What is that you hide my dear brother, some script for the night before the bath or just one of your proclamations of the humors in your lament?" Sameer asked.

"Alright, if you aren't keen to hear I would give it a go by."

" No.. no…we are keen to listen; whatever you say are golden words for our famished years. Go on… on you go Annant." Jorden intervened.

"I had gone to Rishikesh to get this book and on my way back I met her. Just by chance, you remember her; the tall, curly golden brown hairs, white female with cameras dangling across her neck like necklaces; who was shooting the monkeys on the dangling bridge in the morning; she, A Jew from Harvard, a drop out for effects, is deep in the Hindu philosophy; she was with her companions." Annant told the parable.

"Go on, is there a setting Mon Cheri; am I in it?" Sameer was excited.

"Sameer, your hunger is palpable and vulgar. She is a *Sadhivi*; the pure one, like the Ganga herself. With me though, she was.. errr.. hmm"

"She is a Jew, so I am in with a chance." Jorden speculated.

"You are a Hindu now." Sameer contradicted him.

"She has the loveliest hairs and the mesmerist of eyes, if only..." Annant closed his eyes.

"Then…

"Then what, this religion business is taken too seriously once these people are at Haridwar. She took me to Ekaba's ashram and into her room."

"Room." Both shouted in unison.

"Yes, her room decorated with portraits of deities and floral beadings all around, she lighted an incense stick and made me read the Geetha Bhagvad. And then.."

"Then what.. the Karma …

"Yes. She fed me."

"Did she?"

"Yes; to my satiation."

"I told you he would do something worthwhile this Kumbh, now you are a liberated soul Annant; the real Saint." Sameer hit the air with his clenched fist.

"Congratulations!" Jorden clapped.

"But this Pankuj is the real spoiler."

"Who is this pimp Pankuj?" Sameer asked.

"The one who is conducting the enquiry." Annant answered.

"What of him? If he is a pain in the ass let me morphine him." Sameer suggested.

"No; but it was a farce that the administration plays with her death." Annant was sad.

"Tell us the whole story." Jorden sat cross legged and in rapt attention.

"Old JDB called me that a police party is questioning him with regard to Nina's death. I rushed back to find inspector R. S. Rawat, the baiter of Yogis, in heated argument with the old chap; I immediately intervened and told him to keep off the Principal. He picked up on me then and threatened me with cases under the Indian Penal Code, section so and so; I was at my wits end already and blew out swearing on him and all that; Punkaj, the new Indian Police Services guy calmed us both before we could get our duel underway, the damn inspector that this Rawat is, a rat and what, he started abusing me; I abused him back; a tit for a tat. It is a said affair of things, I told Punkaj; that the law lacks the sensitivity of the issue. Why did and did and how did and what did and when did and where did: does it all matter, now that Nina is no more. Would they or anybody understand why she left us all in the prime of her youth? Would it matter to these insensitive bastards? Or her parents? She was killed, yes indeed she was. Her death is a sacrifice of the soul for rebelling against the preconceived notions of upbringing. I see myself in her. She couldn't handle the pressure and why would she, when she had a choice?- To end it all. How? Offer herself to the mother Ganga; the life giver and salvation giver; then this newspaper and television guys dropped by trying their slurring tricks for cheap titillation. I fought for her, even in her death and shooed them away. All fuckers of their mothers; acting as if this country is their private domain. I pity her; she doesn't have peace even after she has become a part of history. Poor girl. But she was a dolly and cheerful. Oh! How I miss my poking her, time is cruel my friends, cruelest of all; consuming everything that comes under its sway. Her smile still chases me as I make my way through the lanes of the river town. Her words still reverberate through these yellow buildings, which now, resemble a tomb and no more." Annant spoke with an intensity of a lover.

"Between us what it was? I couldn't fathom, till she was gone; certainly not the mundane attraction or what; but a Platonic bonding, which, still lingers in me. She was my pupil and I her guide; but as I got busy with my own search I gave her less and less time and there was a fault in her too, she wanted to prove to me that she could do without me and that she had someone else. She did. A guy of her age but certainly not of her intellect, who was her pupil, that was what she told me, then something happened between her and her parents. Slowly she drifted from me like a deadwood. Slowly and slowly she died- A case of slow poisoning. Who poisoned her? Annant asked aloud.

"The society is the killer of the non-conformist." Jorden opined.

"The home was her grave." Sameer spoke in a murmur.

"The country of the blind: Wells and the frogs." Annant said.

The three bore the melancholy, stoically. The day was gloomy as the clouds build up an imminent rain. Somewhere, far away, deep on the hill range, lightening struck. They saw the silver streak first and then; it took a long time, for the sound to travel through into their ears and into the souls waking them from their brooding. Rain drops danced a deathly dance drenching the three. It rained for a few moments, before the winds carried the dark nimbus in its motherly bosom. It was enough, though, to wash the three from their grime of grief.

The sun broke through in its revengeful intensity, drying them in a jiffy. They sat like statues, waiting for ants to build nests on them. Waiting for annihilation to come to them. Now. They wanted the end for a fresh beginning. It is easy to begin anew, rather than try to redo the existing. The slate should be clean. *Tabula Rasa*. One has to hold on to a vacuum to reach somewhere, to begin a journey and to end all.

"This business of stoning, I tell you, is something one has to revel in." Sameer confessed his fondness for the black substance.

"It hits you all right." Jorden agreed.

"A matter of consciousness, dear brothers not addiction; but yoga is a better way." Annant noted.

Ramcharan served them well the drag. A terracotta pipe, just a size of the palm, with engravings was filled with coal and the Ganja. They inhaled the joint, one by one- thrice, in quick succession and then a break to savor the lightness. Light grey fumes, sweet and sensuous, made them forget the lingering melancholy that had engulfed their merry souls. Each took a swig of the Red Angel drink from Ramcharan's bottle.

"We can set up a factory of this right here, sirs, we can, I swear, beat the guy Mallaya; next we will fly in the beastest aircraft and cruise on the Ganga." Ramcharn spoke with a hic. "United Breviaries: the *thekka* of the lord."

"Leave the brewing to the fellow; we will drink it for cheers and also because our friend, here, Annant, is off color. Inhale for all you care for this uncaring world, inhale". Jorden added.

"*Jai shiv shambu*". Annant sucked deep into the Chillum.

"*Jai* Shiv *Shambu*..Jai *Shiv Shambu*... Sameer and Jorden repeated.

"*Bhole Shankar..Bhole Shankar*... Ramcharan chorused.

"Annant, do you pine for her, still?" Sameer asked in a whisper.

"There was a life before her, there would be a life beyond her; what hung in between was an ephemeral union." Annant replied vacuously.

"True." Jorden added.

"Creation truncated; perhaps." Sameer opined.

"Her tears still lay, unattended; on my bosom...I wouldn't wipe them...for she might stop paying me visits." Annant could feel a spasm of emotion rise in him. Let the dam be broken and let the eyes turn into the Ganga.

They lay on the green grassed lawns of the college garden taking turns at the drag. Ramcharan passed out first.

The three saw the warning sign and decided to put an end to their intemperance.

"We got to fill up our stomach before we follow Ramcharan; the stuff makes the stomach crave for food." Annant spoke incoherently.

"Aye..Aye..Saint Aquinas. What is it that you have for a head rest?" Sameer spoke with a threat. "Haven't you had your fill with Nicole?" He asked viciously.

"Speak with reverence to my Guru." Jorden spoke with a quiet threat.

"You shut up, the white for a man. No pigment all ligament." Sameer retorted.

"Be quiet doctor, before I let go of my control, be quiet." Jorden eyed him like a hunter.

"You have the guts to threaten me in my own country, in my own town. I challenge you to a duel, right now. Arise and fight the *Parshuram*; the Brahmin who annihilated the Rajputs. I challenge you." Sameer rose menacingly. His five foot and something figure trying to match the six foot and plus Jorden.

"What goes on you.. mother fuckers?" Ramcharan opened his eyes for a brief moment and then passed out.

"Doctor, call an ambulance before I start bashing you up. Dare you say anything to the universal Guru. I will break every bone in your body, all two hundred and fifty of them." Jorden towered over Sameer.

"Ha..Ha…Ha.. the white without a right.. Dear shylock, keep up with the counting, two hundred and six bones. Ha. Ha..ha..".Sameer laughed. "Have my flesh instead black and Hindustani, but remember, to kill a Brahmin is a curse for which there is no repentance."

"Easy for me fewer bones less time, now be ready to get the bashing of your life." Jorden clenched his fists.

"Hark! My valued pupil; stop. Let the angry Doc. shout in futility. Who cares for an angry one: poor doctor needs to treat himself first. Forgive him and earn points for salvation." Annant said.

"As for your question, regarding my head rest, see it for yourself." He handed Sameer a parcel wrapped in a day's old newspaper. "What Nicole fed me wouldn't be of your taste?" He said.

"Oh! A bible for Philosophers and all: Russell William Arthur Bertrand: A History of Western Philosophy. I see. For whom? Oh ! Guru *Amma* of all; Minnie with her wonderful drupe; I say our Saint is a maniac of flesh." Sameer spoke with a villainous glee.

"I say stop doctor or else.." Jorden moved to hit Sameer.

"Chill.. dear pupil; the doctor couldn't digest the drag, let him pour out his venom, let him become pure in our company." Annant intervened.

"So what was that with Nina? Guru of the Mislead; leading all the misses to their downfall; come out of this farce Annant, come out. You are a swindler of faith and all, that is all there is to your knowledge." Sameer spoke with vehemence.

"You have hit the nail right in the coffin, Sameer, indeed you have. I am what you claim. I am." Annant spoke calmly.

"Guruji give me your permission to break this blasphemous doctor's neck." Jorden said.

"I am hungry." Sameer said suddenly.

"Ditto here, it is the joint. Let us lunch on the roads of this holy town and watch the bathing beauties at the Ghats." Jorden proposed.

"Then the three of us; the Musketeers of Muses; the Brothers-in-hunger, proceed to douse the fire of the belly."Annant roared in his intoxication. 'We are the Shiva's stoned triumvirate; yes we are the trident of the lord of animals."

"And the fire of the loins, dearest guru; what do we offer to the *Yagya* of passions?" Sameer asked with a sly smirk.

"Take your pick dear doctor, if you are hell bent on whiling away your youth." Annant said.

"For me it has to be something spicy, like in the morning; I love the feeling of the rectum under fire; it sure keeps the stomach light."Jorden said.

"It is better to throw out than store the trash." Annant observed.

"I want like Minnie's, round, jumpy and succulent. But, tarry, it is in the discretion of the lord himself, if we are to taste the forbidden fruit." Sameer poked Annant.

"A woman belongs to all; no mine or thine: she, a mother of the world. Gods and Demons, alike." Annant spoke calmly.

"Aditi, is it? The mother of the Devas; the gods. You are lucky and a bastard to boot; Girls. Fatherless. Motherless. Writer. Oh! The world has conspired to keep you in a state of bliss. And your poor cousin, I am left to rot in things I detest. I wish for a freedom. My father; your uncle Josh, has forced upon me this curse of medicine, nipping a budding artist in me. How I wish to create, like you do, dear elder brother of mine; the writer amongst us?" Sameer lamented in his trance.

"I know what eats you up, Sameer, but let destiny run its course; till then create with sutures and pills. To provide a balm on the sufferings is Devine creativity: dear doctor Dante." Annant said.

"I want to be free, too." Jorden announced.

"We are. Suck on the joint and float on the skies of eternity. Let the tyranny of that chimerical bride: destiny, not ruffle our feathers. Swoon like an eagle….fly like a bird. The life, my friends, is best lived by accepting what one has; it is but acceptance which makes understanding redundant. As for your lament Sameer, I know at what cost I have bought my freedom. And as for the girls; one can't trust them, not at all. They want to settle down and have children; that is all." Annant said. "It is in their nature and one cannot counter it."

The three snuffed the joint and got sufficiently stoned. They walked with wobbly steps on the by-lanes of the town searching for a food joint. The lanes were washed and clean. Crowds surged for the bath.

They mingled with it and were carried away under the momentum of the mass. Sameer stopped at a food trawler; where a dark skinned middle aged woman was frying round Poories in the boiling mustard oil.

"Here my friends, is the real Avatar of the Goddess Annapurna; the goddesses of the bite. It is here we are going to break our fast; Mata, feed us, the hungry souls, we have been fasting for last three days, feed us O! Mother." Sameer pleaded with folded hands.

Annant and Jorden sat on the wooden bench, stoned; eyeing the bustle in the bazaars with a glassy look.

"What do the sons; long lost, of mine, want?" The woman asked.

"You're choicest of plum cakes." Sameer laid down his demand. .

"I don't have cakes or shakes, have pure Hindustani *Khana*." She laid three plates.

"You have and they shake. But anyway, serve your wish and we follow the command of your culinary. An artist, after all should be accepted as she is. Please do serve us, till I get an eyeful of you." Sameer said.

Annant and Jorden watch the crowd swaying to the beat of religious music. Both tap their feet and close their eyes waiting to be served.

"Hurry up Sameer, hurry you swine ..Serve us the dine." Jorden swore.

"He peeps with motives ulterior, god save us from his evil eye." Annant said.

"I am working overtime so that you two can have the best street food in town, and you, yes both of you, haven't the courtesy to be patient. Dear friends, patience is the real faith." Sameer said.

"We know what keeps you busy, dear doctor; patient of the protoplasm: treat it before you die of denial." Annant said.

"I serveth two masters and none pays me by the buck: A deer on the run without fun. O! Lord of Kama, the cupid; arrow me out of my sorrow." Sameer cried.

"Babu you want it spicy?" The woman asked.

"Who doesn't?" Jorden shouted.

"Yes..yes… lots of them; set afire, from the gut to the gutter; a river of inferno. It is water that engulfs me; I want the bosom of Agni; fire goddesses." Sameer shouted on the small crowd that had gathered to listen to their banter.

"Self and control, lest one forgets ones vow: Celibacy and Austerity; twins of Saints." Annant noted.

"Baba Gandhi is back with *Bhang*. No dear *GuruDev* we seek yoga of union; not that of renunciation." Sameer spoke in matter- of –fact tone.

"I agree, let us go to the banks and ogle at the bathing beauties. I say, the music in the background adds to the charms of leer." Jorden said with a flushed face.

"What? Lear? Shake a spear, yours alone, and spare us from the tyranny of the tragedy. Poor King was a father of daughters three and died of the youngest' ambition." Sameer said.

"All writers are my brothers and sisters and I shall lay my life for their honor; of them Lear, the greatest, not nonsensical but the master of the limerick is my path bearer." Annant stood up and raised his left hand in mock address.

"Writers my foot; a bunch of bastards scrawling their innards to titillate and no more; I say should there not be a code of ethics for these; ink leeches, that is right, the ink leeches of the society?" Sameer demanded. "But all writings are honest deceptions; that much impresses me of the scribbling saints.."

"I second the resolution." Jorden stood up. "Food, stool, drool, nool, snool, zool, aool. Ooool."

"Tis your fault doc; for you take the books seriously; all books are books of nonsense." Annant announced.

"Then all writers must be Jokers of the Arc; what say the Jew, should they be all torched at the clock tower at the Har-ki-paudi for heresy?" Sameer spoke his observation.

"Fry them in mustard oil with a coating of the peas' powder and eat them with chili paste, see how they burn your anus in the morning." Jorden swung between brothers' for loyalty.

"Be quiet, let Annant scribble the ultimate tome on all heresies and provide *Moksha* to Gutenberg; then let us lit the pyre of the worlds' presses; for once let the holy Ganga be black as she drinks the ink-venom, *halhala*; then and then only the humanity would arise from the horrors of its histories." Sameer turned towards the crowd and waved to them.

A section of the crowd clapped on his impromptu act. Some shouted; "*Jai Maa Ganga*, "*Jai Shiv Shankar.*" A commotion ensued. Couple of policemen; with their stick swirling like a cricket bat, entered the scene and demanded the reason for the riot.

"Shun off, shut up, disperse, disperse, what goes here? I told you Dhungi Bai, set up your *thela* someplace else but you wouldn't listen." One of them sounded the mobile kitchen with his bamboo stick.

"*Jai hind.*" The three saluted the policemen.

"Who are you?" the other enquired.

"He is Quattrochi." Sameer said pointing to Jorden.

"Who.?"

"Saint from Italy." Annant announced.

"Oh! *Namaskar.* But you should be in some five-star. This is a rundown place." One of them asked.

"This is a seven star place; Lonely Planet says so." Jorden replied with humility.

"Is it so? How come we are not informed of this star wars? They asked with a tinge of rebel. "Serve them well." They warned the food vendor and went away.

"Babu, the food is served. Have it till it is hot and piping." The woman served them the manna.

"We like it hot; it keeps us glued to each other. But say, does anybody want it cold?" Sameer asked.

"Babu, the old ask for the cold and laid Poories; not the hissing and crackling ones." The woman replied.

"A case of doused fire and excess of all. Denial, my friends is the best Aphrodisiac." Annant gnawed on an oil dripping Pooriee.

"What did you say about laid Poories?" Sameer asked in mock seriousness.

"The Poories which have been fried beforehand and kept to cool." The woman chef explained.

"Poor souls...out on the cold. But Poories should be freshly fried and dripping with boiling oil." Sameer added.

"Virgin. Marry before they are spent. One more please. Hot..hotter..hottest." Annant said.

"Sure. My daughter cooks the softest ones in town, she is busy with this dates." The woman answered as she dropped round white moon shaped dough in the boiling mustard oil.

"Is it her date that keeps her away? Is it cramps? I am a doctor." Sameer offered his expertise.

"Bathing dates Babu. She is healthy and eats a plate full." She replied.

"What?" Jorden asked in all innocence.

"What else sir, but food, but you are a foreigner, good, they come to me for all hunger. I am cheap." She answered.

"Would she come to London with me?" Jorden asked.

"What? Don't you have sisters at home that you speak like this? We are not in these businesses of importation and deportation. Mind it". She threatened.

"He is a mother of all Tresses. A social worker; caressing the alighted souls. He meant no harm, Mata; just a Jew, he is and no more, would take your daughter to the queen." Annant calmed her.

"One more of the queen Poorie." Sameer demanded. 'Me too; two." Jorden was stoned for good.

They ate with a motley crowd ogling at their hunger.

"Let us call it quits, friends, leave some space for the sweet. Poor woman, we can eat her up, too. It is the Ganja at work." Annant sought to infuse some sanity into the proceedings.

"We want more of the same. Call your daughter and we will eat her, too, her cooking." Sameer revolted.

"Guruji is always right. True words teacher…true words." Jorden stood up to wash his hands.

"My apology to you." He said to the woman. His hands folded with piety.

They sauntered through the busy streets, satiation reflecting on their faces. Of the many Ghats at Haridwar; they sought one at the end of the lane on which were situated the leading ashrams of various sects of Hinduism, like various units of an army standing on attention. An atmosphere of religious fervor was put together through the constant chanting of mantras and religious songs. On the gates of every ashram, guards stood, waving to the crowd to move on and keeping the visitors at bay. Huge Billboards had cropped up proclaiming the qualities and uniqueness of various religious gurus and God-Men. Some espousing the cause of Yoga; still some championing the love for one's nation; a few coaxing the people to come together to fight the menace of Globalism. One of them advocated the need for protecting the environment. A Banner proclaimed that Hinduism was in danger of losing its identity. Soothsayer Cynic.

The entire lane was decked with Marigold flowers and colorful buntings. Lime lines clarified the boundaries of the lane, giving it an officious look. Sweepers and rag-pickers worked in haste to keep it clean.

Into the lane the threesome entered, like a royalty on an inspection.

"Good that they keep it spic with a spanner." Sameer commented with his hands inside his grey Corduroy trousers.

"The genie is out of the bottle." Jorden said.

"Once a year all of them show up in the river town to collect donations and increase the membership of their cult." Annant said.

"Aladdin rubbed the lamp." Jorden spoke in a trance; his eyes blood red and his forehead shining under the red son reflecting on the sweat beads that had collected on it.

"Most of them are controlled by women of the highest virtue." Sameer said.

"Good for them and good for the society. It is charity they aim at." Annant said.

"Ask a wish and it will be granted." Jorden spoke in a trance.

"All are beautiful and in need of a punch." Sameer spoke incoherently.

"It is some good they bring to people, but they lack the necessary depth and insight in the Hindu culture and Philosophy." Annant observed.

"Three and no more." Jorden said.

"All they need is a nice sec..sermon and they will be fine." Sameer continued his wobbly replies.

Stoned, threesome reached the banks and sat on the stairs of the Ghat. Annant splashed water on his face and then some, on his companions.

"I will take a dip." Sameer announced.

"The genie refuses to comply with the demands." Jorden continued with his blabbering.

Sameer pushed Jorden in the water and followed him with his clothes on. Annant laughed a hoarse laughter. "Turtles all'. He shouted. "Drown for good, like Nina. Go..go..go..swim like a fish and die on a dish. Savor life without a trite. I am off to light your pyre." He stood up and rushed through the lane and out into the open leaving the two frolicking in the Ganga.

The sun was slowly setting behind the Shivalik hills. The evening arrived slowly; very slowly, like an intermittent breath; in fits and starts; in bits and pieces. Small light bulbs, yellow, green, red and blue, mingled with the redness of the sky. The river town waited for the morning, foregoing the evening in their preparedness, which stood like a guest who is about to leave but is searching for someone to see him off; least he goes away without leaving an imprint or waving a goodbye. Despite the enchanting atmosphere and the religious gaiety; sadness lingered over the town. Why? It is nobody's matter: To stop and give the passing day a thought. Who does? Nobody. For all are tuned into the future. So the evening stayed on like a stump. Unwanted womb. Without the freedom to wash the amniotic sack. A matter of survival: letting the crap remain.

Such was the evening. Such was the day. A day before the day. Millions and millions expectations hung over the river town. One river. The sole fulfiller of all. Salvation. Moksha. Washmysin. Getajob. Free my soul. Want wife. Last wish of mother. First in sevengeneration to take dip. Save me from ghosts. Treat my pain on the left leg. I want eternal life.

The redness hung for a long time well into the night. Who cares for the dark when one seeks enlightenment? Millions formed a mass of humanity. Nothing mattered. Color. Caste. Creed .Sex. Religion. Region. Age.

Faith was all that mattered. It was indeed a fate to be here, amidst the aura of oneness. Spirit stood sublimely for seeker.

SWING

Annant Awakened. Annant stoned. What is a life without a little of inebriation? Or more? Who decides the limit? Or the what? I? No? No one? Freedom is inevitable: it is only the matter of the form, in which it occurs. I think that it is not the freedom per se that matters but the capacity to absorb it. I could have it without any determinism and yet undermine its value; or I may not have it and yet enjoy it- A freedom in determinism. What could a stoned soul think, nay, not think. Why think? Love is the greatest freedom for all that I care of. Annant: a Rebel lover over heels. Love as an acme of living and dying.

What if I am? One heck of a lover. It runs in the genes; this DNA of love. Passion Protein. Virus of attachment. Congenital disease. What can one do? Fall? In. Love. Fall. In? Love. Fall. In. Love? Stoned sex. Lost life. This business of love is one hell of commerce of emotion. Tear bucks. One can't buck them up. Morose. Morbid. Melancholy. It hits you with a vengeance of an inherited enemy. Laying low for a brief moment; when you win. If you lose then you become the hunter. Waiting for the feline pounce. Today; if not today; tomorrow. Hunt the amour down. Cage it for good. The beast of love. Annant held on to Russell for solace. Would she? Wouldn't she? Could she? Couldn't she? He had rebel other peoples' rebellion. None had sown wild oats for him or on his behalf. Minnie in a mince. Mice in burrows. Hidden wars. Guerilla guises. Fake farts. Master baits. Oasis mirage. Twin desserts. Minnie nipple on her berries; the apple of my sour eyes.

Annant walked in stoned ecstasy. Among the crowd of millions, he mattered. Only. The only mattered to him. Iconoclasm. Iconoclastic. Icon. Annant walked in haste. Eying the details of all. Maya magic. God the legerdemain hand. Handsome rewards for re-wars of love. Inamorato. God loves all his creations; Brother Ayousious said, circa nineteen- ninety five; two doubts arose; All and His. Does all include all with him in it? He was alone, no god to stand up for him; not up till now. God as a He? What of Goddesses' love? Impossible. Brother is right; the avowed Patrician Christian. Nevertheless one has to try; even if one doesn't succeed. The narrow lanes looked alike. Sameness of existence. Conformity is inevitable. So is search. I have to move on. I have to. I have it in me to excavate the essence. *Sat. Sat* for *chit. Sat chit* for *Annand.* Bliss. What else? Kiss. Minnie Mum fussy, fuzzy and I muzzy? Your lips and mine, I would say. My lips on yours I could say?

I have chased her long enough to deserve a peek: sans sartorial nonsense. Why cover the cover? Naked soul with auratic splendor. A peck is not a speck in the rye. Why should it hurt? Tearful eyes; women weapon. He could insist. He would insist. Rape of the unlocks. Lip locked. Lips locked. Annant in a dock: Twice before the Kumbh. I have it in me to charm and all. Always did. Ricky charmed. Before her Shamistta. Before them Aunt Minty. Youth was enough. Oh! To be young or what not. But now? At thirty either you are perfect or nothing. Am I any? Both would do: Perfection or nothing. Siamese Twins. Conjoined couple. In the land of Shiva I am none. Hell in heaven. A reverse gear. Only if Minnie succumbs? Would she? If in doubt don't get stoned: Sublimation of intoxication.

Annant walked, leaving Sameer, leaving Jorden; leaving all else. He entered the bazaars with unsteady steps. Snuff lends the lightness to the being. He took short steps for balance; leaning on the crowd for support. White beard, deep acne scars and dry lips gave him a ghoulish look, like a Melanesian mask hanging on his skull. What the heck? In a relationship one of the two has to be ugly; so that it has longevity; beauty kindles passions enough to strain the strings. She was the lovely moon and he, the spot on it. He thought. Got to find Minnie; before the vacuum sets in. She must be at the Ghats for the evening prayer. It is almost dark .No not yet; red glow of the sun; like her blush shadowing her wheat hued cheeks. He longed for her as the day wound up to an end. Why love has to be intense? He thought. Women's love isn't. It is a male contribution to a relationship. And what does a woman contribute? Children Continuity- Intentional Immortality. Annant took a few careless steps and disturbed the mob of devotees. Some swore on him. Some fell on the wayside. Annant jostled ahead, trying to reach the main Ghats. His eyes searched for the yellow wrap over the green dress. Go ahead, the signal said it all. Yes, he should go ahead. Should have; long ago. A yellow attired woman accosted him. Who are you? She asked. You are Minnie, he answered. Just like that. She fumed and threatened exhume; right here, before the Kumbh bath. O! By Goddesses: leave me alone for good. Annant shouted without the words flowing. Leave him; poor he; must be deaf with dumb; the crowd sided with the disabled. Annant wished of their words to be true. Two out of five. The senses assimilate the world; the Maya of god. All gods: Tweany's, Jorden's, Brother Aloysousis's, Agastaya's, Sameer's . All one. Just a utopia; perhaps? People create their own gods so that they could compete with other people's gods. It is not the humanity that fights but human gods. God War. Good War. One needs a longing to live; and enemies make one long for them. I long for my love; Annant shouted. Again without the words coming out from his mouth. No fallen blessings. But he shouted and he heard his shout and he feared it and shouted back asking it to keep quiet but he didn't pay any heed to his shout and shouted with renewed vigor. One shouts the shouts which one listens. Annant stumbled onto a cycle-Rickshaw and swore .Wordless though. The cyclist saw his rickshaw swirl and tilt towards the drain. He swore, though, Annant didn't hear.

I must be D-Two. Ditto. Deaf dumb. Death and devil. Good. Now I can finally live. This was one of my earliest wish. Soundless speechless sorties of life. Minnie would understand the Sadhu in me. Won't she? She won't. Had she; she would have; five years is a long, long time in the history of time. Indeed. Yet I hope and hop around. Fire in the lions; Sameer has a rascal idea; catch her if you can, if you can't; snatch her, if you can't; latch her, if you can't; leave her. It is as simple as that; the doctor always prescribes the approximate, for there aren't a perfect set of treatments for disease; and yours is old, deadly, decaying, fatal, dear Annant; you are fsucked up. My poor cousin dies of sin; which he never committed. Never mind, dear brother, in the name of the father and the son and the Holy Spirit, you, the Jovial Jesus, shall die for a cause. Love or sex: Decide before death. Saint Sameer ordained. But before crucifixion let us go for fornication; a nurse nurses the ambition of all; she or she's she or she's she's she: suckers can't be pickers. Would you? Dear brother, Annant, the prisoner of your underwear, would you? Wait or pick up the bait? Sameer; the pompous pimp. I was sad for things coming to such a pass. Virginity blues: knocking me black-blue. Trap of the mighty sheath of the foreskin. Letting the Pole out of the closet; lest it falls prey to Darwinian- death out of disuse. Swim in the River of Kama-Agni: take a dip if you are a fire eater, otherwise Ganga is there for free. Minnie would do for me, I announced. Sameer laughed, she wants kids and that's all, my innocent brother. She is Social Camus; the damsel who was once upon a time, in distress: Now no more. Wait for a few months and she would ditch you like children throw cloves from there soup; Sameer the soothsayer. It is wrong, I argued, cloves are the best anti-oxidants. Annant, let the nurse nurse you back to the worldly ways; loosen your knickers and you will not regret, it is the word of a Brahmin, Sameer cajoles. How much? Don't worry, my brother, let me sponsor your ejaculation of this middleclass hypocrisy, Sameer the son of a representative of medicine; Uncle Josh. What if we are idiot boxed, stung by the camera of the digital age;

nano eye? I ask. Ughh!!.. Media; the sincerity of mediocrity; making known the unknowns and working up a hero worship of all zeros except Arayabhatta's; Sameer was calm. Camera is not a third eye that can peep through our rendezvous, he assured me.

So it has been decided, I will pick you at eight; Sameer Coursoe; Robin on a song.

Eight. Eight! Two O's together. Or two zeros. I had no choice but to do it with Sameer's pick. The nurse has a link, with all; press, police, politician and public. No fear to be caught while in the act or with the pants down, Sameer brewed confidence to con all. Still I feared for my soul. Sole cry of sanity. Sanitize before ….all and all. But it is eight: post meridian, I worry; all nervous and sweating. I am like that. Even with Ricky or Shamisstta. My fire reserved for the fire of the *Kundalini*. Now this nurse is the *Kundalini* coiled around my Self. I dream days together. Is she like she? Comparisons are inevitable, her face resembles her, he is like him, and this old man is like that old man. This is taking it too far. All old men and women are alike. Aging makes no discrimination between the beauty and the ugly. But she, what of her? Like a queen? Marilyn Monroe? All beautiful women live a gearless life and die horribly. Now if she is beautiful then what is she doing here? Seeking Nirvana, fulltime and suckers part time? If not, then what am I doing here? I am Annant; Swami and more: the thousand headed *Shesnag* on which lie Lord Vishu himself with Goddesses Luxmi; as his consort. How can I then go for a pest in the bed? I have noticed one thing; whenever a doubt arises, there are two voices voicing two ways. Always. One has to choose. I have noticed another thing; whenever two voices shout, one tends to pick up the one which is closer to the heart. No. It said. Did I hear it? No. This is another thing I have noticed with regard to the voices. One can Un- hear one and hear the other. WhichEverOne. Heart is the biggest liar. It is. It lies and gets away with lying. It beats the hell out of rationality. Pontiff Puppet. Draining blood. What would a philosopher do when faced with such a sorry state of affairs? What have the yore philosophers done?

Descartes' Meditations; doubt rise and results in clear and distinct ideas; all in the mind and all innate. Spinoza bakes the best cake; love god intellectually. Oh! God! He should have stuck to polishing glasses; or gotten married. Then dear philosopher, we would see what your mettle is. Soren Kierkegaard is the king of leer: Life is a disease unto death; he proclaimed till death claimed him early. He didn't get a nurse to nurse him out of his hypocrisy. Wait. He did but she left him because of his Philosopher tag. Poor Soren; come again and let me teach you a thing or two in handling these damsels. And Nietzsche? Following Schopenhauer's Superman- was nursed by his sister despite crying foul of the female race and died a wreck man. All theory no practice. Sartre was better, loyal to Simon de...the author of 'the Second Sex'. Both lay together in Paris, next to each other, without marrying. Minnie wouldn't listen, this is India not France, she says. What is the difference, I ask. It is no longer Bharat, so we move nearer to Europe, moreover, India and Farce are no different, I say in my deep erudition. She isn't impressed.

Sameer is the real Philosopher. My brother intern, a half a doctor, but not, in any way inert. I listen to Sameer's solution. Doctor knows best. Nurse provides the healing touch. Floor wrench in the night end gale; Passions know no bounds, sisters notwithstanding. Lie on, play on. Labour for love is lost, so kiss the bum and hide her face.

Eight is far. It is just seven. Darker night: colder and lonelier than the usual ones. I walk hither thither as if preparing a solo act. Rehearsal Reversals. Sameer had given his words; will get the best tampons: foreign import. No fear for a bastard, he laughed. Lineage lingers. But I will get the best available; the whole world does with it. I am impatient; like one is, when one looses faith in one's self. How to begin? Doctor Vatsanyaya would give a last minute Sutra. It is nothing to do with the arrow; use your cannon, be a fighter, score a goal. Sameer says. I am pacing up and down and am wet with sweat in December. It is seven-thirty and Sameer is nowhere to be seen. I am worried not that I may miss a shot at fame but at carrying the enormous task, alone. Could you? I had asked him. Whatsthefucskingsoul! Sameer shouted. It is not done in our blessed Bharat Mata. No Poporn. Crackle it alone, with butter and a sprinkle of black pepper powder. Savor the dish, my friend; brandish your knife and let it slither through. I am ashamed of discussing the details of the act which I have never committed. For doctors flesh is for cutting and sewing. Tailor made solutions on the operation theatre of life. All's the world is a hospital and we all play our illnesses till ordained by the superintendent- in- waiting. Master Doctor taking a roll call; to each when their time comes. Serve your term and go on; no tarry once the final knell has been sounded. Sameer is god. I pace paces, filling up spaces, in my mind and in the weakling I have for the heart, which flutters without a thump. Seven-forty-eight: The noose is tightening: hangman cometh. I wrap a shawl around for effects I tell myself. Romeo and poet visiting the consort of Lord Indra: *Menka*, the angel of my first night. Orgasm gasps. The organ plays a soulful tune. I shiver; it hides between my thighs like a dog's tail. Power Cower.

Then at eight or half past eight or nine, I lost the sense of the clock, Sameer comes; stoned to the neck. She is with Shamisstta: our nurse; your cousin is in labor about to deliver twins. Then what? I am relieved and yet the pomp of valor can never be hidden. I am ready for the strike, I say, Oh! The erection hurts: Pole ready for the waltz across the wall of hymen. A tipsy Sameer is the truer Sameer. The nurse nurses your juvenile amour he says. Now what? I shout more out of elation than out of complain. Should we go to Shamistta's laboring her delivery, I suggest. Shut up. Sameer, the sentinel of the valley of moroseness shouts. Letting none fall into the trap of emotions. Shun up and shut up, he shouts again. Let us visit Jamuna Bai, he directs me; she dances and sings her way into the hearts of many a men. A real paragon of broken homes; snatching men from their domesticated bitches, he snarls. But before the plunge snuff a joint; Sameer the cocaine snorting saint directed. I say alright; if you take me for a coward then I am not. We take a cycle-rickshaw; who cycles stealthily through the narrow lanes in the dark. A few dogs sing in their woof. Omen for us men. Bad Faith. Heidegger's prick it is; the existential quest and all. Mine is angst. Against all, for exploiting my good faith; use and throw; types. Sentry caught napping once the cycle is complete. King of good times; Pauper in times of his need; if I support you will become a useless log; Saint Minnie ordains my punishment. A blue attired policeman stops us with a glee of a sucker. His eyes had bulging pupils and a bamboo stick jutted out of his left hand. In the name of Shiva what are you doing at this hour at this lane and stoned at that; he questions our illegitimacy like a moral judge. Sameer the savior says, we are going to our Auntie's house, she is ill, I am a doctor, got to give her a pill. Prove it, the impolite police man insists. You are suffering from jaundice, your liver has a cirrhosis, the left eye has cataract and your heart skips a beat every now and then; Sameer's diagnosis as a prognosis-death. The police man is a butter man; melting souls. How true, he exclaims; save me if you can from the fast approaching *Yamaraja*; the god of death, look here he comes, riding his oxen. The guru will provide you a balm; Swami Annant Maharaj; Sameer bows in obeisance. I! I stammer, I eee? Yes, Sameer says and then shouts; *Jai Gurudev*. The police man touches my feet. I bless him. He pays up my fees, the *Dakshina*-Hundred rupees and one. And lets us go. Does it behoove of us Brahmins to be visiting such places; I asked? Are we not human? Do we have no need for needs? No Cousin it is not a sin we commit, but if we check our steps now we will be branded as cowards. Let us hoist the flag and win the fortress of desire. Sameer behests, in cry of war for freedom of the inane. False Freedom.

We reach a building, falling apart, probably due to the ravages of times. Ignored Idea. Creaky staircases take us to a dim lit corridor filled with multitude of smells, almost suffocating, like balmy days of the monsoons. No wind to bring in the air. Airless life. We entered with wide eyed pupils. Pupils hurrying for the class; Annant the sophomore; Sameer the Mentor; Trembling Telemachus in an Odyssey of the nether world. A sitar tunes up and the beats of the *Tabla* greet and guide us through the dark corridor. My mouth is dry and my hormones are drier. Never mind, Sameer, the doctor says. First time is like that; in everything he emphasis; Everything. I listen to him but tremble due to my own voices. Two, like always. An old man greets us with a bowed back and betel red smile. Welcome *Hazoor*, he says in the truest tradition of a Mughal court, right in the bastion of the City of joyous Hindus. This way please, he directs. We enter a rundown hall decorated with cheap lights and stray colored candles. A lady sits on a Persian carpet, faded and jaded. She is, however, dressed in a shimmering sari and is heavily artificially jeweled. Welcome doctor sahib, she greets us, with a smile which is oh! So real. Who is this young man? She lies for charming me. White stubble is worst than a white beard; more so when it is interspersed with few grey growth. A half full stop stopped. A few of her benefactors look at us with a tinge of jealously. He!! He is the great philosopher, the Plato of love, himself, has come for your *Darsan*: An eye of the most beautiful woman; the angel. Sameer drools. You exaggerate, doctor, she blushes. A cat among many a dogs. What is it you like? Annant, that is him, Sameer adds. Yes Annant, what would you like to listen? She asks. Listen, I answer, I want to do something worthwhile, I brag. Tarry, dear philosopher, she says. Hafiz Ali tune in your table, *Bade Miyan*, chord your Harmonium. *Insha Allha*..One of her paramour shouts. *Irshad..Irshad*...all choruses. We sit on soft velvety cushions with round head rests. She starts as I eye her huge watermelons. Knighted through a regal *Banarasi* Sari, gold brocaded and silvery embroidered. Huge floral patterns with leaves and climbers tug at my heart. She clears her throat. Once. Then once more. The *Sarangi* player plays the string instrument accompanied by the settling of the chords of the Harmonium. Hafiz Ali moves his deft fingers over the round face of the table. *Thak ..Din..Thak..Din..thak din din...thak ..thak..*

I close my eyes and try to settle my thoughts to the night. My heart searches for something else. She sings; ...

"The intoxication of these eyes...
Behold many a lovers...
I am a light....
Around which many a moth fly...
It is but hard to linger for long....
The fire can engulf them ...
As they burn in incomplete desires...

I catch a few words which flow and stuck to me. Suddenly I get up and leave the sitting; running through the darkness like a possessed soul. A few shouts chase me for a distance then die down.

Annant walked through the alley of street vendors selling vegetables. A herd of cows accost him blocking his way. He swore. He picked up a stick and shoo them away. I got to find her, he shouts; again without words.

Sameer was sour on me after the fiasco. You coward soul, he shouted, Jamuna Bai is the best in the business. I am a saint, I defended myself. So was Augustine, he exampled. The truth was that I knew I was one of the two: coward or a hypocrite. The second one, I suppose, for I am strong enough to accept that I am the later.

Annant sees the sea of humanity and his heart sunk to the depths of desolation. How to find Minnie in this wave of euphoria? Call her dial her shout her whisper her soul call her telepathy her? No. What of chance? She was angry: lover's anger or something else? Annant found himself tearing a bit. Like it is when one feels the need to cry but tears fail him. False nimbus. A missed chance in expressing oneself.

The red evening was darkening with alacrity of an approaching mishap. Where all escape routes have been closed and the destruction is inevitable. His heart sank, further, searching for its nadir to rest, finally. Lost Cause. Snake Lotus. What else can one do? Order Tea. The tea man tried to strike a conversation. He kept quiet. That one can always be. Tortoise for a cause- slow motion. Life is but a journey; one keeps moving even when one claims to the contrary. A tea cup is thrust into his palms. He holds the cup without taking a sip. Smelling it for comfort. Ginger and tea leaves. His senses are finally invigorated. He submits to them. That is what is with the senses; engulfs one and all in a jiffy. Soul *Causa Sui*. That day Sameer was cross and yet saluted him. Some other time old chap, he said. I can live with my virgin thoughts, I said. I have had my chances but never took a liberty to swim with the tide. You're the proverbial anti- force, Sameer said, the rebel in search of a cause. Storm without norm. I heard him as always.

Annant sat like a defeated drunkard. Repeat; he shouts to the tea bar-man. Right away, he gets an immediate reply. Cocks' tails up, mine Darwinised for good.. Another cup and a few sips after he is awake. Forget the bitch; he decides. Roam like a Roman: *Sadhu* and the night with the *Nagas* and the *Dhooni*. Ash smeared existence, like being hidden from all and sundry. Like running away from friends and the families into the awakenings. Who need relations anyway? It use to be ten for two, now twenty for two; double whammy of capitalism. Knockout of poor; poverty of ideas. What should I worry of? They haven't asked me. Addiga has dug up two nations of my own. As if it was easy to understand the one we had, add one more. But where are the poor? All are rich in spirituality. One has to come to these river towns and see it for oneself. Mumbai or Delhi, you will find all types, the rich needing the poor and the poor needing the poorer and so on. But the Kumbh proves one thing that India would always be Bharat. He saunters again towards the Ghats following the jingles of the bells and the chanting. Religion is a good time pass, better than philosophy; he concluded and a million times better than love: love is wastage of an era. My grandfather's affair was unrequited, too. As I said, it runs in the family. The excavator has a huge cache of hidden treasure which I happen to hunt just a few weeks ago. Lo and behold what I find: my grand old man's photograph, he reclines, surrounded by five writing tables and three chairs, two stools and a the family bitch; Timsy: a Nicholas Roerich adorns the wall; the painter being a personal friend of my grand old man had painted a portrait of my grand Aunt as a gift, which hung right over his head; my grand old man is posed as a writer, thinker and what not. But it is at the back of the Kodak paper that I find the scribble:

To my love and dream...
To my soother and partner...
Without strain...
You are in my soul...
Pictured in my eyes and heart...
My dearest beauty....
You are the most precious being..
Of my life.

So that is my inheritance, I think. If it is then I am destined to fall in and get my amour Cheri.

Annant walked the slowest walk; Just a wriggle of a snail. A walk till the life time passes. No milestones to look for, no stoppages to expect like deadly infections after an epidemic. A pace which is quite pace less; where anybody can take one over; a lost race. Annant followed just anybody in the crowd of millions. Oh! The joys of linger. A breath without the effort of breathing. Why should one inhale when one knows that one doesn't require insufflation for inspiration? One is born mortal if one needs to gasp for a zephyr. Annant means no end: immortal. The crowd has started giving him way: he thought and smiled. Walk slowly when on a high. He smiled; this time in his own smile. Wriggle in life; life in a jamming session. Annant was at a nowhere: if one considers an iota as just nothing.

Legacy proves one's mettle and one's karma. Predispositions predatory. So I am the chosen one to complete the cycle. My grandmother left the grand old archaeologist in love for someone rooted to the present: A Rajput for her rebel against the tyranny of her paramour. Yes. True love is imperiousness at its truest form. She lived her past through my father. But it is I who is taking forward the business of ardor amour.

The tiny bulbs are in full bloom like lilies in the pre-monsoon climes. Devotees are hurrying to the Ganga Ghats before the mass Prayer with a million earthen Diyas begin. What of all I care? Annant walked a free walk. Minnie or no Minnie; what does it matter? I better consign Russell's History of Philosophy in the holy river; he thought and quickened his steps. The newspaper wrapped bulky packet had become his symbol of being chained and throwing it was a way to the freedom of his weary soul. The dark waters gushed along inviting him to drown his fetters of the broads in his life. He searched for a quiet Ghat but found none. In the overflow of the humanity he decided to let go of his yolk. "*Om Namah Swaha*"...he shouted and lifted his hands to throw the book when at precise moment he heard a distinct feminine cry. Twice in double quick time.

"What are you up to now? Some old trick of yours is it or an act to put Shakespeare to shame?" Minnie pulls him by the scruff of his collor.

"I wouldn't be surprised by your drama; never would I be; chasing me after the fight and before. Can you not live without a tiff with me? Annant asked in his quandary: to throw or not to.

"What are you up to? Let me see the packet of your ashes; hurrying as you are to immerse them for salvation." Minnie was not the one to leave him. Climbers don't leave their support system, Annant thought. What of parasites?

"What of that you care? It is break off time dear Minnie and I am your Guide so keep within the limits of decency and all." Annant challenged her duel with a duel of his own.

" Guide...uhh...like old Dev Anand. Try to be the Narayan types, then I would believe you, now come back least you drown into the river making it impure; remember it is the Kumbh bath tomorrow." Minnie held his hand and pushed him out.

"Leave me, you already have anyway." Annant wriggles under her control.

Minnie pulls him through the crowd and makes him sit on the steps of the Ghats. He offered her the packet and stared vacuously at the lights and the devotees lining for a glimpses of the priests conducting the mass prayers. Disciple soldiers falling in line for the blessings of the gods.

Minnie unwrap the packet and pulls out the tome of Russell. She leaves through the pages and seemed satisfied. "Where did you get it? Did the Bhatt guy at the Ganga Book Emporium at Rishikesh give you this?" She asked. "I had ordered the copy last week. Did he tell you about my order? There was a dictionary of philosophy, too. Did he get that? He doesn't try hard enough, like you." She drowned him in her verbosity.

"No. No no.. one of my students got it? I wouldn't go so far.. for you." Annant lied.

"Liar..Liar.." she caught him. "You poor soul, you went all the way…" She looked at him with her lovely eyes.

"No." He was adamant. "I did not have the requisite strength to hunt for your whim."

"Never mind it will do. Next time you go take me along." She continued her impassiveness. Russell or no Russell she would be so, Annant thought.

"You have your way; now can I go?" Annant asked.

"Where to? Do you have a place of your own? Living off the poor father of yours. And you are stoned at that. Sir what should I do of you? Have spoilt my life and all; dear Annant: Mister, today we have to decide about us." She had tears in her eyes but they refused to drop.

"Nobody decides for 'us'. It is always the 'I' on the bases of which the decisions are taken". Annant poked her.

"My father is hell bent on nipping in the bud my flight of Philosophy. Then a girl has to worry about aging too, you know youth is transient for a lovely lass like me. To top it all I hate the Poorie trade. Am I doomed to be forever serving two masters: my father and you?" Minnie made a point to beg with her vanity intact: an art the sole preserve of women.

"How is it that I am responsible for this all? There was time when you were a nowhere girl without a destination and with the sickness that afflicts the middleclass girls with Pseudo fathers; ambition. Then I came along and you have definitiveness, even if somewhat. Now what is it that you look for?" Annant shouted in the din of the prayers.

"There is this boy". She spoke softly.

"Oh! I knew." He shouted, the stoning makes one immune to shocks or else.

"He is a high ranking Provisional Civil Services Guy, keen to marry me." Minnie was always forthwith whenever she was unsure of herself. Her left hand fiddled with her right pocket of her blue Denims.

"Those Half-sweater guys! The Middle of the March to nowhere? Hierarchy Hooligans; not up but neither down; serves the ego alright." Annant spoke in his sarcasm.

"We are sought of attracted to each other. He is a Brahmin to boot; St. Stephen output."

"Why Phut? They usually end up ruining the country or writing about girls on a roll and their moll." Annant was bitter.

"He plans to serve his state; the motherland calling." She defended her father for all his wrongs.

"Good way to hide the tracing steps. When the world wakes to the reality of the globe, your paramour searches for mother's recipe; Good good doog god dog.." Annant shouted.

"Do I have a choice? He has agreed to sort out our traditional Poorie trade, maybe get a grant from the government or what to modernize the eatery. As for you? Well you are good for parts but as a whole you are a useless. Just the talk of being a Brahmins and the half-a- yoga of yours, that's all." She was calm and in control of herself as she warned Annant.

"But I am true to you or myself. And I rebel for my creativity. As for my guidance, the results speak for themselves." Annant defended himself in his entire sobriety. Kudos Karma.

"It doesn't show. My father is a practical policy man, seeking to insure my life; in his scale you score dismal points. Then there is the matter of your face." She hesitated for a brief moment before letting the cat out of the bag.

"What?" He cried over the jingle of the bells and the commotion at the Ghats.

"What scale and what face? He should have thought about that when he handed you to me. Bloody selfish man; a black spot on the name of a Brahmin. Drop the hat once the sun hides behind the cloud. But, of you, dear Minnie, you are..We are.." Annant searched for words but failed.

"I am a weakling, dear Annant, I can't go against the wishes of him, my greatest hero, my father. He has done a lot for me. He has no one to look after him." Minnie was in tears.

"There was a time when I was a father and mother rolled into one for you. Do you think it is my doing this with every other girl?" Annnant said. "I the King Lear stand betrayed by my daughter, but before you go can I live my oedipal fantasy, dear Minnie the queen who spades my heart." He lamented in a dramatic passion.

"Dare you say anything sacrilegious or else..." She was angry.

"What would you do? Get me arrested for harassing you?" He shouted back.

"There were times when we enjoyed each other, now...

'Now what? It is you who seek new grounds, morphing a relation according to your liking."

"Times change; and you have nothing in you on which I can hold on to. Driftwood seldom makes a castle. Even economically I am not illiterate like you; about to inherit an empire of Poories, as you say." She spoke calmly.

"Castle? Who needs one? I am a hut man and I see that you need a hunter who can pierce you through and through. The arrow of a man."

"And why not?

'Ownership of a soul; there were times when you rebelled against the very idea of spending life with someone other than you. And now you are ready to let the reins of your life in some unknown one's hands." Annant said.

"I am tired, Annant, I really am". She sighed in her despondency.

Now is the time, thought Annant. The forests are not far and the darkness can hide the sin. As it is with a sheath covering an embryo. Germination of an idea that was what is required. She is weak and so, I should strike a soft velvety strike. Girls are to be taken into confidence and then you can do the damn. Annant had tried it once and succeeded. Well almost. He hated the almost in his life. Things are to be perfect or they shouldn't be. To be means to be A-OK. But he is not he thought. Now is the time.

"Would you take a walk with me?" He threw a dice. "I am leaving the river town in a few days; next Thursday." He dangled a bait of going away. Absence is the best appetizer. Devour as there is no tomorrow.

"The Ganga-Prayer is about to begin. Let us wait for it to get over and then perhaps...but would it be proper." She sensed the danger. Girls have a knack for this and all else. It is in their mind all the time.

"Now. Prayers can wait, they usually do; more so when things don't go your way. In the heart resides the invocation. It is urgent." He showed his eagerness.

"Alright then if you insist. For you; I owe you a lot in life. It would take me a few re-births to return what you have done for me." Minnie told her disapproval in her own way.

Annant ignored her and held out his hand. She took it and stood up in slow movements. Both struggled to break the wall of humanity that surrounded them. They hustled through side stepping and over stepping the crowd. Annant pulled her in his passions which seethed in him like an inherited counter play. Minnie felt the pinch, somewhat; in a corner of her heart. Was she right in leaving the person who had stood by her when none believed in her? It is important to have one; at least one person who could stand by your faith. And Annant did precisely that. Five years ago. When she gathered courage to discuss her periods with him. Mothers are important during menstrual: but if they don't educate pubescence then one has to look for some outside support. That day she bared all to him. She had no choice but he had one, which he let go, for her. From then on she had had her way in most of the things. Love and Learning. Life and times. Now? She has to make a choice. She knew it that she had hurt him. Her father was like all fathers searching a safe alternative for her. See to it that she doesn't grow. Annant has it in him to rise to the limits: it was indubitable. He was the Brahmin of the old school. Knowledge chaser. But life has to be lived practically. Money is the oil which moves the wheels of society. Profession is the compulsion. He had tried to convince her that one day, one day he would make a global system. When would that day come? She was ripening at a feverish pace. Youth would wane soon. She knew the limitation of fecundity. In a few years time she would be a bag of flesh. A woman needs a family more than a man. Annant never did understand all this. Even if he did, he never ever hurries up with a settlement of some sort. To be human is to confirm to one's nature. Minnie had retraced her rebel steps. Conformity as a boon, she saw it and all.

Annant freed her from his clutching hand. Should I let her go or not or seek a rent or have my pound of flesh? His mind was claustrophobic in his cluster of thoughts. She has relented; he saw her tagging him as sublimation of her freedom and his hold over her. But? There is always the other hand at work. A nevertheless, like a second voice. Two sounds spoiling the tune of life. I would have my way. She had kept me waiting for no reason, pestering me with her refusal. Gentlemen always end up being too gentle on the curves, Annant smiled at the roadside directions to the drivers on the winding hill roads. He was an astute conductor; but a driver he was not. Now was the time. Hurry up he shouted on her, it will be dark. It was indeed getting dark. They climbed the hill on whose top stood the temple of Mansa Devi: the Goddesses who makes the wishes come true. If only she would shower her blessings on me, Annant thought. Afar, the prayers with a thousand brass bells tolling and a million earthen lamps floating on the holy river Ganga had just begun. A mesmeric moment hung between them. Both stood still as the words floated along. Hypnotized souls. Frozen thoughts. Consciousness culminating.

Hume hummed in his head. Reason versus Passion. David versus Goliath. Let the Goliath win for one last time. But the world is full of Davids; the begging Bastards; passing of their defeat as a win over the favorites. Why the world sides with the underdoggies, he never did understood. A favorite is nobody's favorite, but one's own. As if he has to pay a toll tax for his tolls. Success is very personal and very secretive. Annant was not an underdog and certainly not everybody's favorite. He was a chaser of dreams and destinies. A Goliath on the run. He hastened behind her butt, the swinging bell balls. A thin stitch line of her panty was visible as an outline to the shapely back. He cherished the sight despite the dark. Eyes find their own vision. He surveyed her. Almost voluptuous; like Indian woman. Not the stick of the west. But fat round and like ripe Mangoes, ready to be sucked and relished for long. He tasted her in his idea.

"Should we return?" She asked hesitantly as they entered a desolated forest path.

"It is dark." She said.

"Are you afraid of me?" He asked her suddenly.

"No and yes. Yes yes.. We should have a few quite moments for us, before you go." She held on to his hands and walked in small steps.

He was relieved that his intentions were not revealed. The baser instincts should be hidden till they find their final culmination. He had tried it a couple of times but she had caught him and refused to bite the bait. Boys are after all boys; she saved him the blushes. But Men-boys are worst, she added. True. At thirty if you have not lain then you better be stoned. The black diamond is the best friend of a middle of a nowhere man. Annant flung his arms around her and brought her in his embrace. He could smell her sweat smell: oils and lemons. Her hairs, black all, caressed his cheeks. He tightened his grasp. She wriggled and struggled to free herself but succumbed after a while.

Both continued to walk on a thin forested path which rose in a slow gradient. Good choice Annant rejoiced his half a victory. The bait often works, he thought. Nine out of ten times. The one worried him. What if? The bell toll before the cat is tamed of her curiosity. Mice fear for their life, that is why they are fast runners and live in Burrows. He was a Goliath, he assured himself and David has to lose. The David in him. Again two. Good old David Hume hummed again. He was father of real Psychology. The boss of Freud. It is this itch he wanted to itch till it bleeds. The greatest motivation of a man is Sex and all. Passions rules the minds and hearts of human beings. He was a mere human too. He let his left hand brush her breasts. It aroused him. He stopped her and looked into her eyes. She was impassive and yet, he could sense a red streak of lust in her black eyes. Need is a need; no gender wars here. The acme is the dilemma, he thought. Now is the time to …. Annant let himself free in the youth of the lass in his arms. Minnie snuggled and put her head in his chest. His heart beat a beastly beat. He let her stand still for a moment. Afar the prayers reverberated through the river town. Jingling brass bells and chanting rent the air. They listened to each other's prayers. Both blessed the other as an answer to the prayers. Annant touched Minnie's forehead with her hand. She looked up. He smiled. She was calm, like the river. Pure and ethereal: a washer of sins. His hands moved around her body, feeling her youth. She was the sacrificial offering in the *Yagya* of life. He could offer her to the fire. Let her burn. Pour her at the altar of his passions. She was ready. He savored his revenge. Once upon a time there was a boy called Annant who won a queen. He took her to a jungle and …the feeling of revenge is the sweetest of all. And when it is against the society, damn well: you are god. But when it is against one's own self then? Dilemma. Die. Even if the dye is cast; colors of life.

She waited for him to make a move. The prayers reached an orgasmic crescendo. Their souls attuned to its cacophony. He waited for the fire to subside. He held on to her for solace. It surprised him to fathom the depth of the calm: Sweeter than the one of the red revenge. The *Sattva* of the white- Peace. Passionless. This passion business, he thought, is good in parts; but as a whole, it is vain. A pain in the soul. As for reason, well Meta reason subsumes all- The destiny or the universal system.

She waited for his next move. Her head held low, resting on his bosom, her eyes closed in her own silent prayers. Faith needs a support system; a respiration of the will. She tested him in her teases. Her hard nipples lay on his broad chest. Her lips caught his ears. She bit him in her naughtiness. He sighed. She let her hands play with him. He let her have her way; like always. The puppet and the puppeteer- Two together- An embrace of the coital propositions. He smelled her hairs, running his fingers on the silky forest. His hands pressed her breasts. Squeeze of a sequester saint. His hands explored her forest. She unbuttoned herself of her burden. The moon played with her nakedness. She stood with her eyes dancing to the tune of his arousal.

Annant watched her with intent of a father. But her beauty charmed him in a strange manner. Hunger can be demeaning and more so. It seduces one with all its might. What is life without being hungry? It decides one's destiny. One is how one earns his bread or sex; the persona of gratification. Thou shall have bread through this or that; the god ordains. Annant let passions over take him. He moved closer to her, hiding her in his arms. Why should moon have a glance of her? He contemplated his actions. Always better to think first then act. It ends the ruing, later: if things do not turn up your way. Should he? He unbuckled his trousers, then his shirt; in slow spurts of action. In the left pocket lay the three jasmine beads, emanating a smell of their own. He stopped, as if caught in the act. The white witnesses smiled on him. He buckled up under the fear of being found. Not by none but by his self. One's voice is the strongest, provided one is ready to hear. One needs a will to absorb the soul words, in letter and in spirit.

Minnie waited for acceptance of her services. That was all she had to offer, she owed herself and she could make offering of the same. But he stood like a stone? The god of passions, suddenly numbed under the influence of a quandary. She played the cupid coy dancing under moon lit night enticing him in his thoughtful slumber. Would he play the cupid or not, would I measure up to his expectations, could she stop him, would he spare her; what next? She always had doubts abound. Never free from the fear. Maybe woman are like that, being afraid of the future. Nature; I suppose, she thought.

Annant stood stoned, this time under her influence. Women are the real beauty of the nature, if one has not seen them, this way, all naked; then one has not seen the creation. This is the real Maya. Magic of the unseen wand; god's very own lasso around the souls of men. What of if? One has to win over one's doubts, and then the road to victory is cleared. He was a winner. But? The white jasmine beads pricked his soul- All three of them. He had to decide and damn quickly at that? Hurried dreams: Without conclusions.

Yes conclusions; it were that he feared the most; if he makes a move then everything comes to an end. What of his being Annant? The endless. Love, like doubts, should be left hanging, without fulfillment. He needs to begin again; fresh sowing of the seeds of living; irrigating with soul water, the purity of the holy river Ganga. How to? Once one has traversed a path one has to retrace the steps if one is keen on changing the course. It is hard to change course. Midway. He would. That much he had in him to will. Anything is a possibility. He took a step back and eyed her. She blushed under his gaze. He displayed his maleness. And then withdrew. He took a white jasmine bead from his shirts' pocket and tied her wavy hairs with it.

She dressed up as he watched her from a distance. The river town grew quiet almost suddenly. No chanting, no tolling of the bells and no murmur of the crowd. The forest was alive to their acquiescence. They sat on a boulder for a long time, at peace with themselves.

"Shall we go?" Minnie asked.

"Remember; do you; the first time we had met and I had asked for a kiss, just a peck, I wished for?" He reminiscence the episodes of his life; now only memories would remain, he thought of his ensuing journey leaving everything hanging.

"Would you like to; now?" She asked her approval.

He took her in his arms and kissed her. His hungry mouth searching her being. Both drank each other under the moon gaze. A few stars eavesdropped on them. They were unmindful of all and sundry. Time stood like a hand maiden; cloaking them for eternity. A Frozen fable for the generations to come and live up to.

CONFLUENCE

Malashri always, without fail; weighed the pros with the cons, in whatever she did. Prevents the regret later on, she had her justification. It was a dilemma, though, which made her restive; wanting to move on; to find, to explore and to search: to be faithful to one's faith or to one's self? She doubted herself. It is always the doubt which has the last laugh until you put it to rest; or, still better; annihilate it. In her explorations she delved deep into the Upanishad texts of the Hindu Philosophy. The *Braham* and the concept of *Atman* had attracted her; but in her was alive the need to question. And she didn't agree with the universal concept. It is alright to believe in the duality of reality; the usual body and the spirit. But the one; THE ONE- spirit? Wasn't it one more effort towards subjugation of individuality? Why is there a need to claim this oneness of the spirit? Then the rest should be discarded forthwith? Was not Kierkegaard right in questioning the very basis of absolutism of the Hegelian variety? He damn well was. 'Truth is subjectivity: the way I see it'; he had said. She believed him despite his falling back on faith. Religion is just a hand maiden of this business of universalism bringing together people as a herd with no individuality of their own. Right O! The opium of the masses and the resultant of the mob-crazy. I got to experience the truth; she concluded. For me, the particularity matters, she asserted- Her Atman as her own; not a part of the universal spirit. How can there be oneness of the spirit when all of us are unique in some way or the other? She questioned the great *Acharya* Adi Shankara, himself. A modern Hindu saint who reinterpreted Hinduism in the eight century A.D. - Was he trying to defy Christianity or Islam? Maybe. He was the commander-in-chief of the Hindu army, wasn't he? - Resurrecting it from the onslaught of Islam and Christianity; and the home grown varieties of philosophies: Buddhism and Jainism. You had it coming old Sage, she smiled- Should have put your house in order first. Even now things haven't looked up for Hinduism; the soothsayers are up in arms for its militancy and its lack of secular values, she chuckled. Let us see what the modern Sankhara has to say, she smiled at the thought of meeting Agastaya. The concept of Particular is the contribution of the Western Philosophy; of the Aristotelian school of the Greek: her Professor Doctor Shaymal Chatterjee, at the J. L. Nehru University at New Delhi suggested. May be; she wasn't convinced, there must be some of particularism in Hindu line of thought, too. How would one be creative if one has no personality? What of evolution? She questioned. Souls are all; to each for own she proclaimed, no *Brahm;* of which each soul is a part of. No, the professor had contradicted her without convincing her. Academics sure make one as rigid as a dried log. Logged out of the reality, she concluded. A university is just a system of maintaining certain notions and no more. One cannot accept it to encourage lateral thinking; innovations or neo-liberalism. She moved on. Knowledge is the quest. What is there to living if one fails to find answers to one's queries? Half a life- A fly in a bottle. Philosophy should have a therapeutic value, indeed it should. Wittgenstein was right: The German legacy to science, language and philosophy. Logical Positivists- a modern temper of the science. What now? Spirituality and philosophy, superimposed over each other or both having an independent existence? Where does one put Science?

She hadn't planned her search. But one can. If one is devoted to find what one is looking for, one would. What of destiny? Destiny is for religiously minded; god and all. For her the zeal mattered. Find she would; the answers to her questions.

Her father saw in her his own reflection- His youth coming alive through his daughter. Meet Agastya, he advised her. Oh! Father one of those phony yogis; ochre robbed and vermillion painted, she said. I have had enough of them, she sounded her exasperations. He is none of what you think, Mr. Namgyal explained her. Meet him once and then decide, after all, being prejudicial won't serve your cause, he reasoned. Malashri had agreed; to stand on the judgment without the trail was not her way of going about it.

She read Agastya's SMS on her mobile; -"the Ghats for Confluence@ Aarti". Strange way for an invitation, she thought. A whim of a yogi, just a whim, she concluded as she sauntered towards the main bathing Ghats of the Ganga; the Har-Ki-Paudi; lord's own feet. The teeming millions put her off initially but she did become a part of them. The fervor caught her unawares and she mingled with the devotees enjoying the kaleidoscopic mass of humanity. How do I find you? She messaged him and waited for his reply- Her patience running loose. She clicked a few photographs, smiled at the Sadhus who took a liking to her and broke peanuts for solace. Nuts! What am I doing here? Shouldn't I be somewhere in the west, some university; or any of them; and know about the reality? Why Hinduism, for god's sake, with its ant-intellectual stance, should be a way to my search? What of science and all? A bitter pea nut soured her taste. Where to spit in this damn holy place? Bharat is the land of the Gods and Goddesses, her father had said and Haridwar is the focal point. A confluence of …so there it is; her father seems to be under the influence of this Agastaya. Puerile soul: my poor old man. But she would blow the smoke first; clear the haze and then decide. Hers is a free association of the will; none can force a point of view on her. I would deal with him. She thought. But where is he? The Aarti preparation had begun and she watched the priests light the huge brass containers; with hundreds of bowls engraved on them carrying clarified butter and cotton wick. A group of white *lungi* and saffron *kurta* attired boys clanked huge brass bells and bronze plates. On the banks sat the devotees waiting for the proceedings to begin.

What is it that keeps them glued to this mumbo jumbo? She thought. Ah! The detailed preparations: the play of the fire, incense haze and off course the music; all hypnotics of the highest category. Kant was right; reason and the categories decide knowledge. Religion or the god is the limit of reason; the ideas of reason, he calls them. His moral god: Categorical Imperative; is certainly reasonable and scientific. 'If you want A do B'. In his hands ethics became an objective requirement independent of what anybody may want. To this she could submit her free will: the objectivity of existence along with the quest for the spirit. The coming together of the Metaphysical with the physical.

Did it satisfy her curiosity? No. Just for a short while. She was up and again moving for finding newer pastures of Knowledge. One thing she enjoyed was meeting people; she smiled, that way one could get a peep into the evolution of a thought and not just the words narrating a given theory which would definitely be anachronistic in its attributes.

Agastaya would; talk to him, at least once. Her father had said. Would Agastaya? She questioned.

"Looking for me?"

It surprised her that in the clamor of the prayers she heard him. "Yes?" She asked turning her head to meet his gaze.

"I said were you looking for me?" Agastya repeated his query as he eased himself into the mass of humanity gathered for the evening prayer.

"Was I? It is a matter under duress." Malashri answered, eyeing him from close quarters.

"Indecision, I am forced to conclude. I am Agastaya." He introduced himself and extended his hands.

"Oh!" she took his hands. "My father insisted that I see you. How far is the railway station form here?" She asked nonchalantly. His forehead says all, she told herself.

"Two thousand five hundred yards to the docks." He replied in a matter of fact manner.

"You are precise." She said.

"It saves time and energy." He added.

"Precession perambulations." She added her might as she took a few tentative steps into the sea of people.

"Let us." He agreed and followed her.

Both sauntered on the stepped Ghats along the river Ganga. *Aarti*; the evening prayers had begun: A chorus eulogizing the Holy River; the mother to the entire humanity.

"Let us sit here." Agastaya suggested a diagonal point for better viewing.

Both sat in reverence, harmonizing their thoughts with the concert of piety. That goes for all religions, attuning one's self to the voice of faith. Agastaya closed his eyes in the acknowledgement of the power of devotion. *Bhakti* is soul song, he thought. Malashri watched the play of lights and sound enfolding before her and found it quite mesmeric. Her mind rested on the chanting and the clanking of the bells. Her eyes trans-fixed on the thousands of floating earthen pottery *diyas*; decked with rose petals, jasmine and marigold flowers and a cotton wick burning amongst them; placed in a Sal leaved saucer. They floated with the currents of the holy river like the stars paying a visit to the earth. She watched Agastaya with intent of a student. His aura and easy demeanor attracted her. There was something unique in his walk and the word he spoke; in measured tones that somewhat made her to sit with him. What surprised her, though, was the way a few moments under the influence of the prayers had arrested her mental confabulations. A sublime silence prevailed in her being. Agastaya sat still, without the pretentions of existence. He existed only as an experience experiencing the present and all else remained suspended, like it is when a tortoise retreats into his shell, closing the world around him.

"Hinduism is this and all." He began the conversation after the chanting had come to an end.

"This? It is nothing but a hocus pocus to betray the senses." She poked her.

"Is this an isolated incident?" He asked.

"I have heard that these prayers are offered every day." She replied carelessly.

"I mean our meeting."

"My father is the cause and our sitting here is the effect". She smiled.

"Ah! Every cause having an effect. But where does it all start?" He asked.

"Darwin has answered you a long time ago." She said.

"Good. You are awake to the reality." He said.

"I want to know more of it." She demanded.

"Would you like a cup of tea? It is cold." He offered.

"Certainty; if we conclude that every cause has an effect. Are cold; need warmth." She jested.

Agastaya called a tea serving boy who poured two steaming cups of milky tea into pottery tumblers and handed them to him. He offered one to Malashri and took a hurried sip from his.

"Sugary." He pronounced his verdict.

"Certainly." She seconded taking a gulp herself. "But beats the cold, with certainty."

"Opens up the thinking, too." He added.

"Helps in killing time."

"Brings people together." He said.

"Now that is something new, but I enjoyed your observation, I certainly did." She smiled. "And yes, it could be a matter of chance that I visited the Kumbh fair."

"Brings people together." He said.

"Opens up the thinking, too." She poked him.

"Helps in killing time." He laughed.

"Is this blasphemy?" She asked.

"Certainly: with doubt." He answered.

"What is this yoga? Dear Fakir of the Hindustan." She asked eyeing him slyly.

'All this and no more: with certainty." He answered her earnestly.

"What of sitting for ages meditating on the unrealizable? She asked.

"Stages." He answered.

"Are there two lives?" She opened up to him.

"Are there?" He asked instead.

"What is asceticism?"

"All this and no more; all what we live in a moment." He answered.

"My father has a high opinion of you." She said.

"He is a great man: Tarkeshwar Maharaj himself, the Shiva incarnate." He laughed.

"Is it jest?" She seemed miffed.

"Just jest." He smiled.

"But you haven't answered my question, yoga?" She said.

'You didn't ask." He replied.

"I did." She defended.

'Did you?" He asked.

"Yes."

"What does it matter? It is nothing to talk of."

"Still, a few of your precise word; with certainty." She cajoled him.

"An experience, perhaps: A practice to increase the consciousness of the being." He answered her.

"*Braham* or what, the spirit?" She sought a clarification of a seeker.

"I don't know." He was honest. "To intellectualize my experiences for they are not in the realm of the mind."

"How can one know without thinking?" She asked.

"How does one know with thinking?" He asked.

"Reason." She answered.

"Science." He added.

"Spirit?"

"Well! In all."

"God?"

"Spirit: The universal blessing."

"Why universalism?" She asked.

"I agree." He said.

"Good. Now we can talk. When can I see you again?" She asked.

"Do you wish to know more about the practice of yoga?" He asked.

"Certainly and more; more so the essential contradiction involved between the body and the spirit."

"What of it?" He asked.

"The truth of duality and the problem of suffering that ensue with it?"

"Physical is a reality; quite like the spirit." He spoke solemnly.

"And the suffering?" she was curious.

"What of them? I don't see them." He replied.

"Death, pain and all..

"Part of living; the world and its ways."

"Of the spirit?"

"Experience it; all should; at least once in their life time."

"How?"

"Practice."

"Just."

"Just without jest." He smiled.

"You make it so simple."

"It IS simple; just take god's blessing along."

"Doesn't it make the simple complicated?"

"God is the simplest of the simple."

"How?"

"How?"

"Why is that all invoke god every time?" She asked.

"I don't know: Haven't given god much of a thought, but yes, he adds to my *Annand*, the bliss, the final resting point of the soul." He answered honestly.

"Limit of one's knowledge, is it?" She asked in her keenness.

"I am not all that educated, you see; to try to know god and failing to do so; finding a cause for the same, without accepting my defeat in this regard. But as I said, I haven't given god a thought; or I have given god everything except thought." He elaborated.

"Are you escaping rationality; hiding behind the curtains of faith and all? Draw them open Mr. Agastaya, there is a whole new world outside this river town of yours." She poked him.

"You are right. Dare I defy youth and their times. No I can't; I shouldn't, I wouldn't. Yea... Yes you are right to the last drop of this holy river. Certainly you are. I fail to understand the world of jargons; you know, last night my daughter....

"You have a daughter! She exclaimed.

""Yes, like you talkative, and last night..

"You are married...!!

"So.. yes...off course, and last might my...

"Does it not go against the tenets of the practice of yoga...

"Can there be yoga without a union?" He asked.

"You surprise me."

"So, Kerrie; my daughter, asks me Baba what is McCarthyism; now you see a jargon laden childhood, so I ask her from where did she heard this burger word and she tells that it was in a quiz show. Now why would you quiz a child at all, to lay him low or to show off the power of inanities?"

"And did you explain it to her?" She tried to fathom what his diatribe meant.

"No. I don' know what it means. Seriously; or the other day Mr. Bardhan wanted to know about this business of Socialism in the writings of Kautilya and I said I will have to read his book, and then I pick up this book and having leaved for a few pages, fell asleep. Last Tuesday Himnash came to me and narrated story about a theory of closed spaces by Ouess..or Ouchpensky or what, see I cannot even pronounce it, like that burger Macdonald or what; I told him so and then replied that if there is a space why close it." He laughed.

"Is it not the frog and his well, syndrome?" she asked.

"Perhaps, you are right. I need to be aware of all this: Neo-liberalism, Philosophy of Kant.... Would you teach me all this?" He asked.

"What do you mean?" She asked instead.

"Modern science and the language of the internet have revolutionized the way we express ourselves- One cannot now not take these developments into account. Needn't I be update on all this?" He posed a question for her.

"What is the core, the one you claim to know off?" She asked after pausing for a while.

"Consciousness." He replied.

"Why?"

"Because it is the only common element in all that is- the living, the celestial and the universe." He answered.

'Tell me more, in elaboration, if possible." She pleaded.

"Why don't you elaborate it as a part of your Home work? Would you teach me? He smiled "the new ways of the world?" He repeated his request.

"You are a hard task master but a good student, I suppose." She observed.

"Not a master, no never, but ever a student, I suppose. Be on your own. I can guide you and help you solve your problems. Do not expect much from me. You get as much as you work for." He said solemnly.

"Rest as god wills." She taunted.

"You are a naughty spirit." He laughed. "Take a dip tomorrow and then let us see what emerges."

"Would something? I care a dime, as long as I get my answers." She relaxed on the steps of the Ghats, closing her eyes in her somberness. A pious calm seeped in her and she cherished it; till it lasts, she mused. This must be the famed un- framing of the mind: Meditation.

He kept quiet. She understood the silence. It surprised her to know that an understanding existed beyond the mind and its nature of thinking. I got to find the way to such knowledge, she resolved. Agastaya seemed a right kind of a guy: Had depth and all. The old man's judgment cannot be doubted. Fathers reserve the best for daughters.

The river had become quieter now; as if sleeping in its bosom. People moved in groups, visiting temples or their favored God-men; seeking blessings and a way about out of their miseries. Every now and then bathers would splash the Ganga waters on them. Both sat absorbing the happenings around.

"Knowledge is the real culture and no more." He mumbled.

"What is culture?" she caught his mumble.

"Yoga, I suppose."

"And yoga?"

"Culture."

"Are you working on your book?"

Minnie asked.

It irritated Annnat, to be pestered on matters of creativity. What does she know?- The daughter of a Pooriee trader. It runs into the streams of blood; this business of creation. Not oiled by vision and all. It is not commerce, for God's sake, he wanted to shout. But the night was beautiful and he didn't want to spoil her mood.

"I am on it." He answered laconically.

"That you have been for the past two years." She was back to her wifely bitterness.

That is what I hate; Annant lamented and cursed his destiny: A woman: one's woman; should be a partner in one's pursuit. An oasis or a shade. All that the great queen Minnie does is to pronounce her judgments, every now and then. Invariably all were detrimental to his progress of creating. If only she could be quiet for a few months, I would.

"Wait a little while. It would be a classic." He replied in his submission.

"Who knows? Time would tell. Up till now you have been a failure." She spoke quietly.

"I did help you out. What does one expects from a teacher but to teach, from a philosopher but to think or a yogi to provide direction and set standards." Annant rebelled.

Minnie was a facsimile of his father: boot the back till it hurts. Bleeding bumps. He kicked her and she him in return. Painful payback.

"Do you not want to stay with me?" She asked her threat.

"Has it not been decided?" He asked but wanted to run away from it all.

"But what are you doing for it? I had asked you to write a book and you…" She looked away.

The two were returning from the forest and had entered the Kumbh Fair area when Minnie asked clarifications of her doubts. It didn't find favor with Annant who was lost in the aftertaste of passions which lingered in him.

Damn well should have laid her. He thought. That is one language girls understand the language of physical pleasure. Rough them up and you are the king- *Prakriti* Passionate; matter over the spirit.

"You are a bottleneck to my flowering." He said with a degree of dignity.

"Flowering? She mocked. "Bud up first, dear, then we will see how much your petals spread."

"Bloody well, tie yourself with that Governmental guy; breed a breed, ill bred and all." He shouted.

"You are an irascible insect; yes you are: a bastard beetle." She shouted back as a few heads turned in the bazaar which was being wound up for the day.

"You are an insecticide." He was calm. "Spray of death."

"I have prayed for you. What else a girl could do?" She played the gender card.

"And what of your rebel against the hypocrisy of the society? What happened to your vows of fighting for the rights of daughters to choose their mates? Afraid of Honor Killing I suppose? Why don't you come and stay with me? There were times when you spent hours in that old structure; my mother's mother's Haveli." He was bitter.

"You!! Have you the guts to face up to the reality of the world? It is a high talk: no work for an artist; no money not at all: *Nishkama* karma and what not." She cried out her frustration.

"What is wrong with being satisfied with what one gets?" Is there a more subtle way of living than to be satisfied?" He asked. "I am not begging for my living and neither have I deprived myself of the material pleasures of living." He defended his lifestyle.

"I am a simple girl, Annant. It is hard for me to understand your ways or the ways of the world. Spare me my life. It is two lives I have lived; one for you and one for my father. Of my own I have known to fulfill my duty; to him and to you. I can't leave any of you." She was sad.

It is this vulnerability of women that digs the grave of many a man. I am no exception. It smothers my anger and the passions with it. Those dew tears hanging by the thread of my breath just whet my soul. Minnie crying and emotional is better; any day better, than Minnie passionate. Butter melts under soaring temperatures. Degree matters. And the depth of a relation is in the way it is expressed. Not in the way every emotion is saved or used in a miserly proportion. Blow up over the top.

"You bug me." He shouted over the mummer of the crowd.

"You are a screwed up and a bugger to boot. What you take yourself a Napoleon of all the Bohemianaparte of the world?" She shouted back.

"That was good. It surely was. Why don't you write?" These

publishers have a date with women and their washing of the dirty linens in the market of porn and puerility. But that is indeed a fine piece of verbal siring; Bohemian-a-parte: A –la-carte of free living. Dear Minnie do just one more thing to add a punch; practice before you preach." He laughed. "I should have sucked those taut nipples of yours." He delighted in pricking her.

"Look a beast talks like yeast and what have we here? A sermon of a parasite; Annant the man of my sins what would you take to leave me alone?" She said.

"A kiss like always; on your lips and no more. You see I come cheap…all in a heap. Committed totally…wounded fatally… by those black eyes of yours .. and the wavy serpents on your crown .. dear Minnie be mine…" Annant fell on his knees.

"Get up you father of the theatre of the street. Don't create a scene of a Shakespearean variety. What would the people say?" Minnie pleaded. Men are like kids; Unpredictable tadpole. She thought.

"To him, whom the world considers a god in matters of the theatrics, but my dear Veronica, say; did he visit the river town of Haridwar or took a dip in the fair of Kumbh, like Marky Twain? Then and then only, my angel would I believe your hearsay." Annant played on.

"Jester; mister Annant that is what you are." She replied venomously.

"You ignore Old Russell and bring in Shakespeare between us: between them: I am a fan of the former." Annant said.

"Russell? Wake up to Metaphysics or is it the physical you are charged with? Buttressed and Pine nipples."

"Please don't misunderstand me, the miss of my heart beat; but Russell was a true Christian of yore; held on to his wife for eternity: he owed up his longevity to his fifty years of married life; died at ninety-eight. Of Shakespeare I have heard a gossip." Annant said.

"What?" Minnie asked.

"Ah! The women and their Galloping gossiping." He teased her.

"As if men are all saints: keeping mum and digesting cud."

"That Anna hath a way away from his way ...you know… with someone who hath her way." Annant whispered.

"With whom?" She asked almost instinctively.

"So I finally have your total attention. But tell me how you concluded that she was… after a queen's consort?"

'Did I?" She asked. "All males are like this only. This Nina of yours: what of her?" She fumed.

"Minnie be mum. You hit me where it hurts the most." He was quiet.

"Oh! Poor innocent darling of his mother; it bleeds within. It sucks after you have sucked and mucked." She was vehement.

"Spare me." He pleaded. Women are full of this violence; it is the red-*Rajas* cycle they live through every twenty-four days, he concluded.

"Spare me too. Who wants to be saddled with such despair for a pair?" She stood piercing him with her eyes.

Both stood in a dark alley facing each other like spent enemies: Annant with slumped shoulders and a barely audible sob and Minnie with her haughty vanity, ignoring his pleas. She has to be a winner despite her being an unfair fighter. But would she relent? No, Annant knew his predicament; no confirmed loyalty before the seven solemn vows in this country. A husband is a women's best bet and her best friend. He waited for her balm knowing it was a vainless wait.

"Your perception may not be my reality." He whispered and walked slowly, clutching his back. The pain had reappeared in mild spasms, like waves in a despondent ocean.

"Hey you two, what's up.?"

Both heard a call coming from the crowd. An unseen voice; People know each other in small towns; must be some acquaintance. They thought but stopped in the middle of their angry foreplay.

"Come over here." A voice guided them towards the steps on the river around the crowded Ghats.

"Should we?" Minnie asked.

"It is Agastaya." Annant said. "Let us. Do you want to see him?" He asked.

"My father..err..It is late, and we haven't reached a conclusion about us." She hesitated and yet let out her complain.

"You represent a dream which was always on the verge of fulfilling but never really got fulfilled." He was indeed sad.

"I got to hurry, you were always a defeated poet, a morose soul; I err..my father." Minnie dusted her crumbled white top.

"Alarm Bells! Santa callow: The old man's head buzzes with ideas of the diabolical proportions. Jingle bell mingle bell; dingle all the way...Santa Sharma comes along riding on his sleigh." He let out his sarcasm.

"If things are so sour between us why don't you leave me?" She cried.

"He doesn't know how blessed he is having somebody to irritate him into happiness. *Parth*, complaining in our times is a sign of ageing. Hey Minnie come along meet Malashri from the university in Delhi; the Nehru Planetarium....I mean Nehru University. She has come for a gaze and a dip of the Kumbh. " Agastya joined them in their throes of familial discord.

"Hello." Minnie wished him in her awkwardness and extended a friendly hand towards Malashri.

"How goes life old chap?" Annnat shook hands with Agastaya. "Same; getting old by the day bag and the same old tricks." He eyed Malashri. "No grapes are sour for me". He replied to Minnie eyeing her in his hatred.

"You are the champ in matters such-. The town says so." Agastaya replied. "Meet Malashri, a seeker of *Gyan*: not Knowledge. Am I right Malashri? She is Minnie; and this is Annant Baba. Both the pride of this town; separately: though together; they would give rise to a whirlpool in the holy river." Agastaya laughed.

"The Yeti and the Rati..." Sameer spoke in his stoned voice. "What was this case of sourapes." He slurred.

"The gang gangs up here in the Kumbh. Good one and where is dear Jorden?" Annant said. "But Aagi, dear, you have a point, I am indeed a fawner of thing feminine. I find woman like art- needing patience of the highest order to come good."

"He awaits the *Darsan* of his Mother of the previous birth- The mother searcher Jew." Sameer said.

"Keep quiet. The father sits as a headman." Annant stared at Sameer.

"So Minnie, where have you been?" I had a pleasure of talking to your father in the afternoon. He searches hard for a legatee." Agastaya addressed Minnie.

"Does he regret not having a male of a Sharma tribe? Ancient instinct as wisdom; I was out for a walk with Mr. Annant . I got to go, have had enough of enlightenment already." She replied.

"What of the orgy of the tribal group?" Sameer murmured. "The world is an anthropological mess- rape of the genes. Wear your pants and down your hats- the *kshatriyas* are dead who would save us...O!! Rama rise from Ayodhya ."

"Who is he?" Malashri asked of him eying him with a disdain reserved for a scavenging sloth.

"Ask me Ask me Cask me Cask me. Johnny Walker or old monk: Red Angel or tangy orange: He roared. "I am the doctor of the universe". Sameer shouted. "Puff for swings Charak Maharaj longest live."

"I am back." Jorden announced his entry.

"I love all backs and blacks- White out of my sight." Sameer shouted again.

"Malashri do not pay him heed. You can if you want to; pay him in coins". Annant comforted the flustered girl.

"I saw her." Jorden continued his announcement.

"What does that prove? That she is hooked by you?" Sameer murmured. "Coin shoin loin moin doin; Pay me my color."

"You would know them all. Just attend a few of their sermons." Agastya replied. "Annant here is sane still, but he wishes to write." He said. "Then the Kumbh would be held every year."

"Is he? What is it that you are working on?" She asked. She turned to Agastaya, "Sermons? The doctor prescribes hearsay for medicines." Malashri was surprised. "Blasphemy as a soul cure?" She wondered.

"Well they are all harmless and full of witticism: the sole soul laughter." Agastaya said. "I enjoy their togetherness."

"All stoned." Malashri showed her disapproval.

"They are almost beastly, the two; have got an itch for knowledge but know nothing worth for a while." Minnie said.

"Sameer is a photographer first and Annant is creating something, I suppose." Agastya defended the two again.

"Jorden is from Londonium a part of the roam for the relics- Has flown for a dip in the Ganga." Annnat introduced the Jew. "He searches for the Raj relics."

"Are you a Jew?" Malashri suddenly became keen.

"I am the son of my mother." Jorden replied, his blood shot eyes piercing her.

"Is your mother Jew?" She ventured further.

"Off whites do not ask who the father is." Sameer the savant said.

"My mother is Meera." Jorden replied with all humility.

"The Saint-woman; a Krishna devotee of the highest order." Annant stepped in to hold the situation.

"The mother of all gods is his mother, too." Agastya said.

"Why all of you talk in riddles?" Malashri was exasperated.

"Precision." Agastya corrected her.

"Never mind them- A male bonding of some kind or some sought. Let me escort you to a safer place." Minnie offered to help her out.

"Ammmaa". Sameer shouted. "Rid my aches."

"Amm..Am..Emu." Jorden murmured.

"It is our Headman of this tribe's birthday." Annnat whispered secretively.

"Whattt..?" All shouted in unison.

"Yea-Bloomsday of the east....Goodbye of Joyce." Annant remarked.

"Happy birthday to you...may all gods bless you...." They sang in a chorus.

Two saffron clad, clean shaven head youth, crossed them looking cross.

"The government should ban these creatures." One of them commented.

"Nay ...They should be kept behind bars, call the police." The other spoke angrily.

"Let it be." The first one placated him.

The group continued to dance around Agastya singing songs.

It surprised Malashri to realize that how much she enjoyed this impromptu dance. Minnie was skeptical but bore it with a quiet dignity. After all one has to be a perfect figure in public. And what if my father comes to know of all this? Her smile faded and she stopped in tracks.

"What is it?" Annant asked.

"Let the Pea of the Cocks dance, do you want to come Malashri? We can talk while we walk back." Minnie ignored Annant's query and addressed Malashri instead.

"Her father awaits her arrival." Annant said. "For her the alarm bells toll in this maddening crowd, so her demand to go away to the far pavilions of Uncle Tom Tom."

"Wait for a few moments I am escorting you, all horned up…pee..peel..see." Sameer struggled to sit up but feigned a fall then sat with his eyes closed as in meditation.

"Beware the *Trenetra-* the third eye of the lord Shiva. She is the daughter of Tarkeshwar Maharaj, the ruler of Haridwar." Agastya warned them.

"Go you both can but not before a cup of tea and smoked peanuts. The treat is on my pocket." Annat announced.

"The rich of a man: Capitalist *Masti*-Viagra my Agra. Minni…ee Mum… Tazzz Wahh!. Remember your father has disowned you." Sameer said. "Patricide for a chicken soup- sole heir you are. But what be your inheritance, say?" He asked. " Taj Mahal of Horses or poultry poultice?" He cried.

"A few green backs to me. I offered all mine to the holy mother." Jorden begged. "Jai ho..Jai ho..Ekaba Muni..Jai ho..Jai…

"Al right; But better hurry up with your order." Minnie agreed with a caveat, as was her wont.

"Order..order…hurry get the best curry….tea-man serve us all your best tea…here Sameer get some best baked peanuts." Annnat stood up and shouted. "Drink and munch…breakfast or lunch."

They sipped starry sips as the night shone in its entire splendor. The Ghats were quieter now. People started retreating to the comforts of their tents after the hectic day. The police was cordoning off the main bathing Ghat for the early morning bath. The *Akharas* would be the first to take a dip. *Juna*, *Nirankari*, *Sideshwari*... Then only the Har-Ki-Paudi: the holiest of the bathing spot, would be open to the public. Order of a sect: glimpse of a religion- Teaser as a poser.

Agastaya thought of the wish list of Aditi that lay in his pocket like a forgotten letter. Now the shops are all closed for the day; will remain so tomorrow. His heart missed a beat. Another of her wish remained suspended. Kerrie too, had a wish that she should be allowed to accompany them to Mumbai. It is tough to be a parent; all wishes cannot be fulfilled. He feared the drift between the three of them. The signs were all too evident now. Got to keep the flock together, he resolved. What of Aditi's domineering conduct? Not the one to be tamed even by destiny. She could trip many a times and yet she would commit the same mistake. That was Aditi, the Socrates of his family minus the philosopher's adaptability, and without his emphasis on the maxim: Do thyself. She was a woman, after all, needing support and all. But why should the entire family drink Hemlock on her behalf? It is after all the women who run the society, not the men folk; who seldom flock together. Ego Egrets. Woman should be good listeners, that goes equally well for the males. Listening is half the interaction. But one needs the heart as ears to listen to the whisper of love. The coming of Annant had lightened his burden. At least he could talk. He remembered his day of birth. He should after all that they both had been through, together. A bond existed between them.

"I am done." Minnie got up and wished Agastya once more. "Got to go". She announced. "Are you coming Malashri?" She asked.

"I take your leave then; I would see you in near future: Would message you." Malashri addressed Agastaya. "And a very happy birthday to you." "Bye All". She held out her hand for Minnie.

"Buy me." Sameer said.

"Blyme." Jorden said.

The two girls giggled and rushed towards the Krishna lane leading to the Burra Bazaar. Both re-introduced each other and found a common point of discussion; Philosophy. Who is this guy Annant? Malashri had asked her curiosity. "Teacher". Minnie revealed minimum. "Quite a guy; you have some company here in this quaint religious town." She said. "Looks a ghost with his face and hairs: An ugly duckling; is he available, though, I wanted to clarify some of the points in philosophy; the ones dealing with deontological theories in ethics and the symbolism logic?" She asked.

"He must be, nowadays he doesn't have much to mull." Minnie replied in a jealous tone.

"What are his charges on a monthly basis?" Malashri asked.

"Charges? For what? For philosophy? Can one buy knowledge? Even if one can; he won't sell"

"It must be his living, to teach. He is a teacher, you said." Malashri said.

Both became silent giving time to understand each other.

Strange girl, thought Minnie. Metro megalomania: smaller the town lesser the knowhow. How come? What of villages? Dying India: Matricide. Cities are for marketing the wares; it is in the smaller towns that the creation takes place.

Strange town and stranger people, thought Malashri. This is one reason that India hasn't progressed the way it should have been. Why can't these towners' be professional? The old school still rules in *mofussil* places, she concluded. Or is it the way knowledge should be imparted? Got to find out, she resolved.

"You have lovely hairs." Malashri commented

"Do I?"

"Yes, tied by the Jasmine bead, they look divine."

"Do they?"

"Nice bums." Sameer was stoned in night.

"Four moons and sex pence, Doctor." Jorden said in his innocence. "Doctor Maugham; Summersault -Saint Annnat in a marooned island scribbling his heart out."

"Tarry stoned souls; father Agastya sits like the Buddha himself; with his smile and all." Annant said.

"Go on. On you go. I haven't the mind to mind." Agastaya said.

"Mind minding mind?" Annant asked.

"Can? Can of worm and vermin." Sameer slurred.

"Practice annihilating it." Agastaya replied.

"If wishes were a heart; the mind wouldn't flutter." Annant said as he sat cross legged on the Sand stone steps of the Ganga Ghats.

"Will it is. Let the Head pump rule and see life slither away from your grasp. Don't weigh the options, for you have none. Spray the vapors of herbicide to kill the germ before it lays eggs in a billion proportions." Agastaya spoke in his trance.

"Pray! What spray? I have enough poison in my ill gotten living that I need no more. It is venom that I have sucked from the breasts of my mother. Forgive me, the father of all: Nation-Parent; but I would exercise my options to opt out of the race of the hearts. Even Chitragupta; the keeper of universal records of all men and women, would vouch that whenever I have utilized the services of my heart I have landed in the deepest troubles. Now dearest Aagastaya, I have my head at the right place. It beats to the tune of pragmatism." Annant rebelled in his posture.

Sameer and Jorden listened to his and clapped. 'Good good we second the call given by Saint Annant , a Jesuit at heart." They chorused.

"No heart farts for me. James the Dean of the University of Opportunism was right: Pragmatism is the key to goof living: Willy the cow boy running a prairie philosophy." Annant borrowed a Chillum from Sameer and puffed hard. "Rotten men- only coal colas without fire, where is the real stuff?" He shouted. "Have heart and see it trampled under every goddamned foot." He spewed his venom on Agastaya.

"Don't exclude me. In the name of the lord Shiva, it is my birthday. Pass me the puff if you have an iota of respect for an aging sage." Agastaya joined them in jest.

"No we won't leave you at the altar of denial. It is my old Grand Man's day of birth, too- The Romeo who searched Kausambhi. Let us have a double dose." Annant laughed in a sinister tone.

"Jorden has it. Who was Buxom Kausambhi? Sameer asked innocently. "Daughter of Vatsanaya?"

"Jew, fill up the pottery of circa Indus civilization with some of your Ganja. Full Doctor fool- Kausambhi is an ancient city excavated and restored by my doctor senior; The Ancient, ancient relic of the family curse." Annant was bitter.

"A search is a search after all. Speak well of your legacy Annant." Agastaya admonished him.

"The father and grandfather have a same day birth. Try as one may but one can't be one's own judge." Annant said.

"What judge? All are fudge. Pine apple pie scoop it with all might as a matter of right. Lend us a few dollars and we get you the best of Ganja or the hemp to rule the universe, O! I swear on my Ba and Ma." Sameer stood up with extended hands.

"All whites are the Babas of the world and all blacks are sheep who weep, poor Jew only mew." Jorden stared into the dark waters of the holy river.

"And the browns?" Sameer challenged him. "Should they be thrown off this planet? A bag full of wool..yess suurr... yess suurr... push off the stool...into the fire of pool. "

"Remember the Jogi of Jeruselum, the color of mother earth is what; but brown." He eyed the Jew.

"The two are mayhem. Where did you find them in this state?' — The Rajaji National Park or some zoo else?" Agastaya asked.

"Pay them and get rid of them. I think something has gotten into their minds. A virus or what: comes out of its dormancy, every now and then. Here Sameer how much to get rid of the headache?" Annant offered a five hundred rupee note.

"That Five Hundred Bill would do; opens up the holy gates of Providence; a true Christian. But what have Father Agastyine against us? Would Gandhi challenge his own sins and doubters in his land? Sameer spoke with emotions. "We the creator are being disowned by all and sundry, including our fathers. Lest we can do is to drown in the holy Mothers Ganga . Oh! Ours is a lamentable tribe, tis would have been better had we be born in the state of Oxford or Cambridge; we could have been the authors of the million reports that come from the press printing of the world: Poverty, children, environment, female feticide, democracy, terrorism, tribes, gender..."

"Enough or I shoot you out. Dear doctor if you cannot digest the Ayurveda stuff why snuff the puff? Get some for us and be gone." Annant said.

"I need more of the same more of the name more of the shame more of the game more of the lame more of the tame more of the maim.... Jorden murmured.

"I take your leave the two tales and their cities; respected gentry of the heaven. Your humble servant does as ordained. Hey brother Jorden, these Hitlers are out to throw us in the fire of hell run away to save your life or else meet your fate". Sameer pulled Jorden with much effort and sat when he failed to shake up the giant.

"Jorden ..Jorden... wake up to the night of the Kumbh." Annant called.

"He won't; Have had his fill of things all. Let him sleep, you go and fetch the black diamond, go now before the senses hold us back." Annant let him be.

"Dear brother of mine I would ..I would." Sameer gave a forlorn look to Jorden and stepped on to the by lanes of the Bazaars. The stoning part is important he thought. In a few days it would be back to cutting flesh and the gore that comes with it: Just one color in life-Red. If only I could add more to it. Who can live a life of utter forbearance? He walked in haste; one has to make an offering to the gods, the two together. He was proud of his cousin defying the odds of middle class world, trying as he was, to create for posterity, untouched by the trend of the markets. He would to be a part of them, always, he thought. Togetherness is the greatest stoning. Yes it is. Relation is the strongest snuff.

"Aditi had packed her Chapattis a few too many; were you occupied in the afternoon? I waited upon you in the Sharmaji's Poorie shop." Agastaya asked.

"I was in the college. Then these honest souls joined me for a joint. It is one hell of a fair this Kumbh; millions on the journey onwards. How are Aditi and Kerrie? I met the little one last week." Annant sat near Agastaya and watched the dark river floating with a sound of a gargle.

"Both in their own world. They have gone to listen to Ekaba's *satsang*." Agastaya replied.

"I heard Kashi. She seems a misfit in all this- As if wanting to run away and all." Annant said.

"Aditi wants to run in to it; but before that to Mumbai for her art mart shard..*iti*..*iti* of creation." Agastaya opened up a little.

"What? What a way and what a what? I say Aagi, I have known and known for sure, that one who doesn't listen is the one who does not hear or see either." Annant said.

"She always had a different way of looking at things. But this time it is her dissatisfaction with her present state of being that worries me. Kerrie, too, needs her, but does it matter to her?"

"She may have a point it is just that you are averse to what she wants. Her history is a set of complex tales, unlike Minnie with her silver spoon." Annant suggested.

"Yes I agree. It adds to the challenge of living as I have to work overtime to iron out the creases, if I may say so."Agastaya replied.

"How about the Practice: *Sadhana*?" Annant asked.

"What of it? Goes on without a break. It has become a part of me; so much so that I have stopped thinking about this all. I enjoy it and, more importantly live it to the fullest possible joy." Agastaya said.

"I wouldn't agree with you; no less. It sure takes a lot to achieve the stage. You have made sacrifices, I know." Annant said.

"I was lucky. Then god willed my progress. What of you? How goes the system of evolving?" Agastaya asked.

"I trudge along with failures and successes; a toss for a life. I do bear up with all rather stoically. You know Nina died: Karma or the Karmic cycle questions me; I try to find answers but fail. Sometimes I wonder if this world is of my liking or not." Annant reclined on his back, rubbing it softly.

"One has to meet life as has been given. Can't change much of what one has got. Are you continuing with your practice? Learning is all about keeping up with new situations." Agastaya said.

The night deepened with alacrity. Not the darkness, though, lit up, as it was, by an aura of religious activities. Both sat in the silence of knowing. All questions lay suspended. The banks wore a deserted look. Few mendicants wandered about; ochre robed and vermillion smeared. A battalion of the elite commando force had taken the charge of the sacred banks and the chief of the unit marshaled his troops with dexterity of a teacher. Two of the commandos stood behind them.

"Is he asleep? You cannot lie down here." One of the two informed them.

"He is ill." Annant said. "We are waiting for the doctor."

"Looks like a *Firangee*. This Kumbh wouldn't suit them. What happened?" The other asked.

"Got stoned of Hinduism." Agastaysa answered.

"Who is he?" They asked.

"Sage Vashisht." Annant replied. "Has twelve *Siddhis*; Take his blessings and the Kumbh fair would be your final Pilgrimage." He added.

"*Baba ki Jai ho.*" Both chorused.

"*Khush* Raho.. *Kumbh raho*..Be happy…but do not call me *baba,* I am a *Rishi*." Agastaya lifted his right hand and blessed them.

"We are indeed blessed that we were put on duty at the Kumbh Fair. Mother Ganga has called her to serve her." They said with their eyes closed in reverence.

"Yes you are. Take a dip early morning and let the waters cleanse you of your sins and all." Annant said.

"We would sit here for a while and then we will go." Agastaya lay to rest their fear of duty.

"Not a problem at all. Sit for as long as you want. Both of you sit in meditation and who has the temerity to disturb a meditating soul." They bowed and moved on.

It was quiet now. The stars stared at the unfolding religious drama. Dew hung like hopes. The troops lighted small fire on the right corner of the bank and kept themselves warm.

When was the last time he had sat with Annant at the Ghats like this? Agastatya thought; last year but not on his birthday; it was summer time and he had come to ask him a question regarding yoga.

The first time I had loitered around the town with Annant when he was no more a three year old and I, a teenager. Little Annant wouldn't let go of his finger and walked with small, but careful steps. Doctor vet. -Was a known of Mr. Vashisth and had come to the vet's place bringing me along. Annant a tiny creature then had crawled onto to my shoulder and played with my freckled face. We had gone out for a saunter. Baby Annant was treated to cotton fluffy pink sugar candy by me, paid, as I did, out of my meager savings.

Then on a wintery and cloudy December day, the town was under a curfew and he had accompanied the sub Divisional Magistrate to the Ghats. Someone somewhere had been over zealous with his religious leanings and had given it a politico-nationalist hue. The river town, with its religious trappings was the nucleus of such activities. A saffron army was organized and dispatched and sent to the land of Lord Rama's supposed birth place. Annant was one of them. His youth burned under the fire of religious nationalism. He wore a saffron headband and carried a trident. I am young and full of my love for my religion. It is blood we have to shed to free ourselves of this Mughal yolk, he shouted. A pimpled, rabble aroused teenager with a mission of an inverted identity. I had had accosted him in his rebel. Right on this very Ghat- in the winter of discontent as the nation shook under a cultural churning. Let me go Agastya brother elder, he had shouted. But is this all Hinduism? I had asked him. For which he had had no answer. Yes I am, if I am, blind with my love for my religion, he had argued; where is your this very logic when they do the same? He asked in his blinded zeal. Let peace prevail, the only true religion, I had replied. The police had come and put Annant behind the bars. He was a hero alright, back in his school in the hills, Agastaya smiled.

He use to have long vacations for the winter season which he spend at his mother's mother's haveli-the Nanku Havelli with Jung Bahadur; until his father was transferred to the plains. This broke his routine. It made it tough for the two of us to spend time together. I got busy with my college and then the pursuit of Yoga; the usual degree courses and then the PhD.

They met again, when was that, Agastaya tried to remember. When was it? eight years…no six it must be, or more? Perhaps eight; when he had decided to take a dip in the river Ganga for the Kumbh fair. Annant, pimpled faced and passionate about philosophy and wisdom had met him by chance. I want to learn, too, he had announced his grand plans. Would you take me along as your disciple? He had asked. No was the answer he got, I learn yoga for my own evolution not to teach, I justified. It made him angry, not just on me but on the entire gamut of people who weeded his life. He was being ignored for no reason of his. By all- Family, friends and I - Damn well, I would go on my own.

He had said; and gone away-to wander in the hills. It became an annual routine for him. The summers were spent on trekking across the Himalayas and crossing innumerable valleys and rivers. In one of his trek, when was it? five or –six or even four years, he had saved me. I had fallen in a deep pit while climbing a steep hill, one night. When I woke up he was there preparing some herbal concoction of his. I smiled as he practiced yoga in the sublime peace of the hills. They were friends now. It was he again who had brought Aditi to him, his love and Annant acting as the messenger of love. Now he is like Kerrie to me.

Both sat on the banks of the river waiting for the Kumbh twilight.

Annant sensed Agastaya's thoughts.

"It has been a while since we sat under the stars like this." He struck a conversation.

"That day on the mountain, when you saved me; six, was it six years? Whatever it is. " Agastaya said.

"You remember it.?" Annnat asked.

"My mind overworks today." He replied.

"How come?" Aditi is it?" Annant asked with an alien compassion.

"Lot many things I suppose." Agastaya replied.

"The family Ashram taking its toll." Annant smiled.

"I love Aditi." Agastaya was candid in his reply.

"The sage falls for the forbidden. Well then tide is well neigh against you and the dice would invariably roll in your disfavor." Annant laughed.

"You have become a cynic of late. That happens if you seek rewards of your labors. Aditi has sacrificed a lot for me I feel under her obligation all the time. It is not that I sought what happened to us both. A quirk of destiny I suppose, but then I haven't really stood up to shoulder my responsibility. Kerrie too grows with rapidity of adolescent girls." Agastya said in his lament.

"Aditi has his penchant for things big. That much I know of her. Religion, philosophy or yoga: she would dare not have faith in the good old way of research and learning by doing." Annant said.

"At least she has a leaning towards matter spiritual." Agasataya said.

"Yes. And she has an understanding of the basics." Annant agreed.

"It is Ekaba; to whom she owe her life- who pulls her from her ordained path; add to it her fascination for this guy Tulli, who lay dreams for her in the Metro."

"How?"

"By weaning her away from the familial responsibilities and showing her a chimerical world of religious grandeur and fake faith; in Ekaba's case and the Mumbai guy giving her a lesson or two in the marketing of art." Agastaya said.

"Do you think that this organized system of Hinduism is the most important challenge the oldest religion of the world faces?" Annant asked.

"In a way; yes and add to this the ignorance of the scientific yoga and what we have? - Truncated, half knowledge about Hinduism and all." Agastaya replied.

"Agreed. There is an increased tendency to leave the normal challenges of life and lead a closed so called *Ashramic* life. We sit here in an open ashram. No wall to hide ourselves and a starry sky to cover us up." Annant said.

"True; the rest are half a system, though, they do some philanthropy; but it is nor spiritual education. No. Not at all." Agastaya spoke passionately.

"Of all people Aditi would fall for the charms of such systems, I am unable to digest. Or is it some other issue?" Annant asked.

"Ambition, blind one at that" Agastaya replied.

"What of that?"

"Of the class difference and the emerging capitalism; of which we all are a product now- cannot escape the potency of it. It feeds the appetite to consume without an emphasis on creating .All production is mass based, hence the tastes and needs fit in to the product available in the market." Agastaya said.

"It does give an individual a freedom to learn and grow."Annant said.

"Fine for me; this system of markets; as long as it does not erode the basic values of a society and preserves the culture and identity of people."Agastaya said.

"But it does, is that what you mean?" Annant asked.

"In a subtle manner. Unless one is aware of it one cannot find how it alters the basics of living." Agastaya replied.

"One has to live with what is on offer." Annant said.

"It has stirred a storm in my household, though. Aditi wants to leave the destiny of a family and move on to seek the proverbial greener pastures. She paints well, but to paint for the bazaars is a different ball game altogether, the rules are different and so are the shades and strokes. Would not religion and all this that we savor sitting here on the sacred Ghats become a part of the burgeoning market? What of Kerrie? Is bringing up a child not creative enough? Agastaya asked.

"Let her go then- Kerrie has her destiny to live up with, she would manage. You are there to look after her." Annnat consoled him.

"What of me?" Agastaya questioned for himself.

Things were silent again, like the crest of the waves or the swings of the mood. It bridged the divide of age. A few swans waddled on the banks feeding on the offerings and flowers which floated on the quiet banks. Street smart kids dived deep into the river to pluck coins and small idols which the devotees had thrown in the river. They gave a cry once in a while when they struck upon a bounty- A five rupee coin or a brass statute of Shiva. A tea- man carried his basket of cups and glasses and the tea container and hurried to a corner and sat with a sulk on being refused to serve the guarding commandos by the deputy commandant of the unit. The temple doors were shut and the priests wound up the day's proceedings but not before overseeing tomorrow's preparation of the bath.

"How's your writing going on?" Agastaya asked.

"I haven't begun." Annant replied rather tersely.

"Are you serious about this writing business?" Agastaya poked further.

"No." Annant said.

"What would you do then?" Agastaya asked.

"What do you mean I would do?" Annnat asked.

"For a living and for growth. Karma is a part of us all: *Nishkaam* and all." Agastaya replied.

"Can one live a single moment without doing Karma? If yes then I am whiling away my time. If not then I do what I am supposed to do." Annant was irritated and prepared to leave.

"Is it hunger that has worked you up? Or is it the hangover of the joint? Or Minnie, who is a combination of the two and a potent one at that."Agastya relaxed with a joke.

"None of what you think. No. Not at all of all that I care." Annant replied in his anger.

"Let us go to my house, I owe you a treat, let me cook up something for you. What do you say?" Agastya said.

"I wouldn't mind your stewing. It depends on what you put into the broth. And if it opens up the buds of my taste." Annant spoke with faith.

"Ah! Taste my friend; the fair weather friend. How can one faith upon senses?" Agastaya stood up from his squatting posture and dusted his clothes.

"What would be life; nay, living, without them. As for the taste: primary one doesn't alter its ego much." Annant said. "You are a devourer too, of the essence. I have seen your nectar sucking: like bees from flowers."

"You have a fetish for a taste; quite a taste, lasses not from the masses: Greek goddesses for amour. Annant you are the Romeo of all the Juliets of the world." Agastya smiled and walked on. "I prefer the refined taste of all things those surround me. Yes I am a consumerist myself and I consume nature; the plentiful production of god, priceless and the most valued."

Annant followed him. They crossed the somnolent bazaars and the silent streets and reached the compound of the collector's office. Kripa wished them in his yawns. Agastaya dusted his motorbike and kick started it.

Both rode through the Chandi chowk through the Chandhi Bridge. The town looked a one huge canvass of dotted lights and colorful camps. The black moon reflecting river intertwined through the town with peace- devoid of the pomp of the morn.

A few loudspeakers espoused the causes as night sermons, disturbing the silence. They left the town behind and entered the forest road.

"Damn well I forgot to full fill the wish list of Aditi. Should we go back? It would be tough to get the provisions tomorrow; it being a Kumbh day." Agastaya noted his loss of memory. "Your idea of stoning got me." He laughed.

"You were in the market in the afternoon. You should have thought of it then. Now the shops are closed. Then those Rapid Action Force commandos wouldn't let us through. Got to wake up some local provisional store guy- He would help you out. But manage it somehow; you have the market all by yourself after the day after tomorrow. It was in the papers. Did you hear a gem of Old JDB- Annant thou shall be the sub-editor with 'Beware-Haridwar; the evening daily. The man, a fan of my old man; has quite a gut. As big as a gutter." Annant laughed.

"Good idea; media is the pulse of the public. Why don't you pick up the cudgels on behalf of the society and that of the brothers' Chaudhary. We are leaving tomorrow afternoon?"

"I wish to be creative and more. Newspapers! Uhg… suppliers of the filth of the disdain. But come again, what is this leaving business?" Annant asked in his surprise.

"What isn't creativity? You are going the Aditi way. If all is all then nothing is held in exclusion." Agastya fumbled in his pocket for the keys to the apartment. "I lose my keys somehow; managing to do it with amazing regularity. There I have it. It was hiding in my pocket like a lost idea." Agastaya fumbled for the keys.

"You didn't answer me? Are you two leaving the town?" He was sad.

"Not for good. I will be here to prick you every now and then." Agastaya climbed the creaky stairs. "Be careful." He called out.

"Do you need to go?" He asked.

"Aditi orders; wife is supreme once you are married. Think of yourself, get organized. Do you have a plan?"

"I have my teaching to go back to. But times have moved on to internet and all; closed learning- half a dose or a wrong pill. I agree with your observation that all is creativity- Entire system of living and non- living. It is simple as that. My breath is creative enough to give me life and so is yours." Annant followed him into the dimly lit staircase.

"Once a teacher always one- let us lecture for food. What is it you order? You look a person devoid of protein and vitamins; good though, you are fatless. Take some *Triphala* for your hairs- Your head wearing a white cap." Agastaya said as he climbed the creaky stairs. "Careful of the hanging bride, catch the railings as you climb" He called.

A few pigeons fluttered their wings on being disturbed from their sleep .Early risers. 'Shh..sh…" Agastaya called out in low tones. They ducked the birds' flight and tip toed to the main door. Agastaya searched for the latch in the dark and after a while caught hold of the lock. He unlocked it with some effort and opened the door with a push. "Jammed doors..Oh! I forgot to tell you about my meeting with Mr. Srivatsana for the new housing scheme that the government is coming up for its employees. The man has a finger in a deep pie, he gave me a hint; something about the government taking over the Siddeshwari Ashram once Ekaba goes."He said as he entered the room and fumbled for the switch. "It is switched on when I reach home. I seldom put the lights on." He defended his fumble. "Ah! Got it." He switched on the light and adjusted his eyes. "Little messy and in a big mess; my house holding, you know, Anne, peace is a matter of legacy, some families are inheritors of battles." Agastaya laughed. "But you are a free birdie; can perch on any nest- enjoy it son as long as it last. Hunt for a seat and sit and mull. I heard from a chirpy bird that you seek a nest of your own? Leaving the barn of the Vet?" He asked.

"No; nothing of that sorts. I love my roam: Rome prescribed it long ago- the state wives. Sire a son and the state owes up the responsibility of the upbringing. Free association- Plato the Plutarch of Utopia; but I put up fine at the Nanku Havelli."

"Utopia! Get a wife and know how the family works. Look at me how I struggle to find a way out of my present impasse. May be I fail but I wouldn't be accused of not trying." Agastya opened the small kitchen and entered it, searching for the vegetables and fumbling with the array of cans and jars. "It seems we have run out of provisions. Ah! The list of all wishes." He called out. "I will have to make do with what I have."

"You are a great cook. Like good old Brahmins of yore- an inheritance of what else but taste- refined and defined. A natural born chef of the highest order. Culinary conjurer." Annant sat on a wooded stool and picked up a jug of water gulping mouthfuls. "Water is food, too; sweet, liquid and digestible." He remarked as he stretched his legs. "Are those Aditi's paintings?" He asked pointing to a collage of abstract paintings on the wall of the only room along with an array of Ganga River in its many moods.

"Relax and don't' pay compliments for obeisance. But they are worth a first look." Agastaya was miffed. "They come at a price which is born by me solely- an ill-kept house: order less."

"You sound a jealous husband. She does a fine job despite the limitation of an Indian bride. I say, you ought to be proud of her strokes of colors." Annant said.

"It is Kerrie that is my worry at the moment; poor girl has had a nightmare for a childhood, but could I do or would have done; fate is an untrusting accomplice." Agastaya sat with slumped shoulders.

A thin line of aging crossed his broad forehead. He stared vacuously at the walls of the kitchenette; His aura sublimating under the fire of his duty. He looked tired and frail. Fallen fruit.

Annant held out his hand and silently consoled him. It is men who face the challenges of the world and they are discredited for that, he thought. Women are born mothers and hence divine. Fathers have to work every moment for an iota of respect. He longed to meet his father. The poor vet. Had managed the household with all he had; sacrificed all he could. But still he was faulted. Work has to be *Nishkaam*- fruitless aspirations. He held Agastaya's hand for a long while. The night suddenly grew cold and the two shuddered under its influence. Agastaya lighted a fire and the two sat around it rubbing their palms for warmth and helping the fire to gain in strength. Presently Agastaya lighted two Tobacco- *Tendu* leaf rolls and passed on one to Annant. Both puffed in silence. A somnolent clock ticked in the room and they attuned their thoughts to its Tic- Tock. Tick

The two sat like an aging couple, each praying to leave before the other; lest the memories haunt the one who is left behind; like a howling owl. They turned into the ashes of a pyre burning in their fire.

"You were quite a young fellow, weren't you? Agastaya asked. "Ran away for all that the world cares- a rebel in the middleclass milieu: Good I liked that washing utensils at where was it?"

"Luxar, now nearby, at that time it looked like I had escaped to the third of the seven heavens. Annant replied puffing and feigning coughing on the cheroot.

"Your Uncle brought you back. Good to rebel. Did something fruitful come out of it?" Agastaya asked.

"I enjoyed it. Living in a shanty and working in the roadside eatery. We waited upon the trucks and the public transport buses and served the travelers. All had stories to tell and I delighted in their little sonnets of life." Annant smiled a smile of a lost in the woods soul.

"Tell me one." Agastaya took a swig of the water and wetted his lips.

"Oh! My memory fails me. Yes there was this one of a dwarf ghost, who still visits the small eatery I worked in; Charan Dass the owner told me when I met him a couple of years ago. At that moment, though, I enjoyed them like a childhood soiree. I was pulled back after that; Back to the mediocrity of living. Why complain? But it is you who face the challenge of the family and love- The dark horse winning the race." Annant said.

"It was never the race and I didn't aspire for a win as the way you perceive it. Let us hope for the best. What would you have for dinner? I suggest we cook *Kichdi-* rice and lentils: gods' food" He offered.

Annant kept quiet, fiddling with strayed utensils. Agastaya opened a plastic jar and took out a handful of rice. He measured four handfuls pouring them on a steel bowl. He soaked them in water and searched for lentils. A green lentil attracted his attention and he took a handful of it and mixed it with the soaking rice. Next he put a pan on the gas stove and lighted the burner. He poured a table spoon of mustard oil in the pan and waited for it to be smoked and burnt. Then he sprinkled it with cumin seeds and let them crackle on the boiling oil. He quickly drained the water from the soaking rice and lentils and poured them on the pan. It hissed and the vapors filled the kitchen. He sprinkled it with spices: turmeric, coriander, salt and chili powder. Lastly he poured a tumbler full of water in it and covered the dish with a steel plate.

"There we are done up with cooking- As simple as living. No hassles and no trappings and yet fulfilling. Would you like to climb up to the roof?" He asked.

"Yes." Annant said as he coughed out the vapors of the dish. "Roofs are the heavens in the homes." He said.

The night lay bare under the stars. A gentle cool breeze blew across the town. It was quieter now as things settled for another day.

Occasionally; with the gust of the wind, words, voices and the hymns flew across and tapped them in their thoughts like eager visitors on the door. The duumvirate sat without purpose and with a poise of a thinker. Like long lost neighbors settling an old score; making up of a bond.

"They wouldn't be back until the midnight?" Annant asked.

"Hopefully, my Uncle and Aunt may come a little early" Agastaya replied.

"Is your dish done?"

"It will take a while. I have simmered the flame down. Slow motioning the moments."

"I feel famished; but the world must be a nice place with a family. I never really had one. I wait for a twist in my script of life; hope... Aagi, is life a trail by fate?" Annant asked in pauses.

Agastaya kept quiet. Time elapsed without being noticed-like a milestone which needn't be taken note of-the journey having just begun. It was the journey that Agastaya longed for. Aditi was wilder then, he smiled a sly smile. Little wildness is like a chili powder in the *Kichdi* of life. Why not? Got to tingle the taste buds. What has goddamn years got to do with it? Fun is fun. Funny if one is not: a serious business. One cannot pull the shutters down before the shoppers come, poor Aditi and poorer Kerrie- it is his fault. There has to be a mix and a match of the merry in the carnival of life. Am I not humorous? Poor me. How would people around me live? I would crack them into nuts. Time was when I was the nucleus of a gathering; harnessing laughs and pokes; but; a big but- now I have been rendered a Baba of the morose. Is it bringing up the family which has truncated my jest of living? Agastaya thought. Got to learn it and learn it damn quickly. Before Aditi goes. I can beg her to give one more chance; a chance what can be this journey to Mumbai before she takes a plunge into the nether world of religion. A monk in a Hindu system? Life is a system of four Ashrams. Everything is Ashram: the idea behind living. Why then create an outside system? Pseudo reflections.

"What is it?" Annant asked.

"Nothing. Sometimes mind attacks with a vengeance; today is such a day." Agastaya replied.

"Let us pray." Annant said and closed his eyes.

Agastaya laughed. "That was a good one you pulled on me." He said.

"No ..No I am serious. I need the blessings of the almighty."

"Who doesn't? But you pulled it fine." Agastaya continued to laugh.

"I am going down. It is cold out here." Annant got up in a hurry.

How would one judge a man who lives in moments? He has no history, no past, present, future, ambition, longings, cries, regrets and memories. But Aagi babu is a bit disturbed today. Well one cannot remove all the shortcomings in one birth, some imperfections remains, clinging like mortal disease. He climbed down carefully in the dark and entered the dimly lit room. Clothes lay sprayed like used bullet covers. The sheets on the bed were crumbled and soiled. A few books on religion and spirituality lay in half open poses; posing questions. On the right corner lay a heap of clothes; half wet and waiting for a dose of the sun. The wall on which the lone window was attached like a photo frame was adorned with posters of Shiva with Parvati- his consort: Hanuman; the constant companion of lord Ram; Saraswati- the goddesses of learning and lord Ganesha- the harbinger of prosperity.

On the wall opposite this wall a few framed canvass on oils were neatly nailed; over them hung a blue bulb with a pointed face. He gazed at them and then came closer and adjusted his pupils. Aditi is a genius; she certainly is- the Amrita Sher Gill of the town. Dam well she is right. She should run away and hire an art gallery to exhibit her efforts. Here in this town only the flow of the years exists: the priestly river and its myths. Life is what one experiences. Today's menu for the thoughts; no left over or carry forward-debit or credit. Cash as long as you have something to sell. She has the world of talent. Then why waste? Go and set up a wall mart of art. "Agai..Agai." He shouted.

Agastaya rushed downstairs and headed towards the kitchen. "I am here, don't worry." He shouted and ladled the mixture of rice and lentils. "Another ten minutes or so. Wait." He called out.

"I want you here, in the room you have for a living."Annant called out again.

"What is it?" Agastaya entered the room and stood beside him dusting his hands.

"You have a treasure for all that you care for." Annant rebuked him. "No wonder Aditi wants to dump you. You are a closed store; Aagi dear. That is what you are."

"They are nice. Aren't they?" Aagastaya murmured his doubt.

"Nice. But you were never known to express anything. They are world class. If a Majumdar can do, so can our very own Aditi." He said. "Look at the abstraction of the blue canvass.- A motif of life." He spoke excitedly.

"That one is by Nina." Agastaya whispered.

Nina. Nil. A nil life: Extinguished fire without the smoldering remains. What of this?- A blue coffin hanging on the wall? Remains of the footsteps. Nina hung on the noose of nihilation. Nothingness beckoned her like chasing crows. If only? Only if?

"Is it?" He sounded tired to himself.

"She came here often; brushing herself on the white canvass the life as she saw it. She had a mind of her own." Agastaya said.

"And she was much more; her going away leaves a vacuum in me. But life doesn't stop for bygones. She was fun though." He smiled a weary smile.

Agastaya held him in his hands. "You should worry about yourself; emaciated as you are. Come....Wash your hands as I lay the food." He directed Annant like a child and proceeded to the kitchen leaving Annant in his sorrow.

"I knew... she was... going but I couldn't do ....anything." Annant mumbled incoherent words. He pulled out a Jasmine bead from his pocket and laid it over the blue canvass, closing his eyes in reverence.

The water was cold as he splashed a palm full on his teary face.

Agastaya pulled out two steel plates and poured ladle full of *Kichdi* on them and called him twice.

Annant sat on the stool and stared him like a child; His eyes moist with emotions. He looked at Agastaya with forlornness; "Would you give this to Aditi?" He handed him the white Jasmine bead.

"I would, now eat." Agastaya took the bead and kept it on one of the jars of condiment.

"Eat." He repeated a little sternly.

And Annant followed orders. It burnt the inner linings of his mouth but he didn't mind the pleasure that comes with pain. He savored the taste of red puffs and small boils that appeared in his palate. Nina was gone now Aditi was queued up to go. Next Minnie would follow. Good. All should leave all. None should stay with none. Himalayas were better than all this leaving and longing.

"What is it?" Agastaya blew air over his helping.

"One has to hold on to a vacuum to reach somewhere...to begin a journey...to reach...so as to... dig the end .....

ADITI

I have never taken it the other way the way he had cut the cabbage into thin shreds and the potatoes in slices like apples, he was almost keen to cook too, but how would I be the boss then; that is what a woman is and I realized it now when he tried to enter my domain that is what is with me that much I know of myself. It was his birthday and I should have at least wished him, well why I have to do the need full, always; have done it enough, carried his burden in my womb for nine months and even now for last so many years. I wasn't on the way; a smooth way, as I see it right from the day I was born as an unwanted mole; as the story goes in the family, I was found on the railway dockyard but my other siblings brother Siddhartha and sister Roli were the womb born duly spending the requisite months in the amniotic sac. They were young, still are and hence I was the older one, still am; right from age three when one of the two was two years and the other my sister three months old; yes I was the older parent of my brother and sister my parents were younger parent to me learning the ropes. It was I who inherited the orphanage and gave parentage in return off course if you are the elder you have no gender, you swing from being the son to the motherly elder daughter. When I was four or five for age, I didn't read much into the drift between me and my parents. But it came suddenly, like a deluge of the most unexpected force; I realized that I was the one who caused misery to my mother; for my father was busy with the way the world works and so one day he was laid off due to the economic backlash of the nineties after the Kuwait war and the invasion of Iraq. So it were dark days for a lower middleclass family like ours, we were lucky to the extent that we stayed on in a village and had a roof to cover our heads not droop our shoulders but it was I who shared the blame with the ruler of Baghdad; my mother simply and it came damn simply, stopped talking to me as for my father, he roamed the streets of the town in search of a job and advised for free to anybody who didn't seek his advice on matters all sundry. One advice he gave me, on the sly and with necessary bitterness of an out of work householder, was to get head on towards finding a job and get in to the mould of competition, early work results in rich harvest, he spoke with a certain sinister undertones, giving me back which he suffered. So it was a life of a slog for me waking up at four in the morning, when I was five, cycling uphill for a good ten kilometers and attending to the tuitions and all then rushing to the school English medium and Christian one at that and then rushing back to the house. I would be tired when I reached the house and saw the sullen faces of my parents but the smiling countenance of my brother and sister unwound me and I lived on to fight another day. I remember in this childhood of mine there wasn't a child present I was over aged for my age and that was the only thing I had to show off in my wonder years, for, I was a shabby ill-dressed and ill-tempered girl all thin as a stick of golf and dark as a brown bread. I grew quick, without a pause and hence hadn't the time to think on as to how I should conduct myself for I was knack less and foul mouth which made me unpopular in the school. It is easy to adjust in a joint family though and my cousins listened to me I being the elder one but the cousins were all boys and it gave me boyish insight to living. Of the cousin's Aseem was the nearest I had to be called a friend; it was he who was besides me listening to me and providing the solace of a companion; that is what a girl wants, somebody who listens to her and understands her, it also helped me fit into the huge joint family that I stayed with. So it was like this for me; an assembly of sisters and brothers to lord over and a friend in Aseem to share the little foibles of living till I grew up enough to be on the radar of my fathers' ambition. This was how I was sucked into the whirlpool of mindless pursuit of a career I detested and abhorred both at the same time, for, I was keen to make a mark in matters creative, the academics were a spanner in my effort and pulled me into the mire of failures. During the same time Assem died the most untimely deaths, in hindsight though all deaths are untimely coming a shade early or a little late, but it was the going away of Aseem that pushed me into the laps of Philosophy and the enquiry of matters spiritual; first the *Anekantvad* of Jaina attracted me, knowledge is relative none can have a complete view of things like the seven blind men and an elephant each one of them interpreting the animal in his own way; then the Greek idealism of Plato. It was escapism for all that I care of but I needed to mend myself; from the pushing and prodding and the jostle of the worldly pursuits. I became a girl soon once I attained an age of pubescence, liquidating my manliness with white fluids and red botches botching my privacy, the blood didn't make me run for cover but my mother's ignorance of her daughter, who was after all a daughter and in need of an education in matters of growing up, the oozing wet me so did the tears. But I was in a schooled school so we had video sessions of how to manage during puberty; it was the loss of the boys in my class when they saw their leader, that was me, attend such sessions, but it was I who could supply furtive leaks to them regarding the pads and all and the cramps that accompanied the menstruation cycle; the teenage rebel of a woman. The pains still linger in me and so does the mood swings; it proves that woman has to suffer due to the nature without the compensation or an indemnity. This whole business of womanhood made me sulk so did the small round mounds on my chest which was up till now flat as a paper; it made me uneasy and shy of myself. I retreated into a shell not alone but with the Enid Blytons and her famous fives; an age when books seem more adventurous than the real living. I devoured them like a hungry bird and that was not the end of it. I lived the ventures at my maternal grandmother's house in a small village of Bhagpoor; there I was the queen with the hunter and the army of cousins that I had were my courtesans and together we raised a ruckus in the quiet village in our summer vacations. We had lush mangoes and juicy litchis to gorge upon and steal them for fun and then be chased by the Nepali watchman Bahadur with his huge bamboo pole; he is no more now, dead long ago, served us for a good thirty years and died on *Sankranti* day. Of him I remember being carried on his back riding my childhood with a gay abandon; but growing up takes away the foibles of childhood and for a girl there is a shorter version of youth, that was the case for me too. I returned to the books for solace this time mathematics and reason; the numbers giving me a cold rationality which still lingers in my paintings; one cannot let go of the images of childhood so easily and live them through your siblings; they grew slowly slower than I, never catching me. Even now, when I am old and they are youth personified, it though helped me live life in a periphery away from the gaze, though my father would pester me with his ambition the one which he always wanted to fulfill but never could, so his failure became my destiny. He did what he knew best not what was good for me; the prodding went on till I succumbed to the pressure of the middle class aspiration and one day it all came crashing down .My father, his wife, my youth and the relations; I failed. For good though; on hindsight every failure is the best medicine, bitter but effective. At that moment, however, when the wound is fresh it hurts; more so when you are reminded of the hurt time and again. That was the case with me and there was no Aseem to listen to me as my best of the friends he had died as I have told you earlier of a bike crash on a not so busy crossing, death by chance. I cried alone that was the last time I cried, it happened to be the first time too, not on failures but on failing the faith that my father had on me; it is sin I thought at that time, to cheat your nearest ones.

I did and was dumped in one of the thousands of colleges that have cropped up like ferns of monsoons as the country opened up and globalised for good or worse that was a matter of conjecture. I was made to feel like garbage in a plastic bag, black and tied up to be thrown in the master dustbin that was life for me at that time. Like a cloud in a silver lining I met Timothy, a convert Christian who was as snobbish as I, but on matters physical, so one day in a party we danced a tribal dance and he pulled me under a staircase and roughed me up breasts and all and he kissed me on the lips, that was alright the kissing business for explorations, not for passions, but I didn't like the roughing up bit and slapped him hard so that he bled from the lips and looked like a red Macau monkey. My breasts hurt after the incident and it made me rebel a bit more this time; though in a constructive manner for I picked up paints and let the brush stroke freely on the white sheets. It colored my life along with philosophy but the later lost a shine and I fell back to the colorful pursuit of religion as an art form of rebel; I thought at that time. Was I right or not I still don't know but it was that way for me for a long time in the history of me; a recent history of me, though at my age at that time history means knowing your elders. I said I was a grown up long before the grownups were the grownups but who listens to you when you are at your lowest lows? No one; but it is the best time when you should listen to your calling. I did as the century came to an end and a new one began I moved on flowing with the tide of the river waters the holy river flowing from the Himalayas through the entire country all rivers are the proverbial life line of the populace this one was the mother of all, the holy Ganga, supposedly, feeding millions the manna of spirituality. Was this my calling or not I didn't give it a thought and let my instinct take me over it is good to live a life of an instinct, you have nothing to fear, no failure, no successes, just a gut and the beating of the tiny heart. Let it see the world, it said in its beat, like the haloed *Damru* of Shiva; come out and enjoy the *Maya* of the so called God; now this was one mystery I couldn't fathom; wait there was one more; destiny. To these I added a third; faith, not in these two but in my Self..the *Atman*. There was the usual mess of the family, for the family and by the family. What was I, a twenty something girl do? Fight off course, one last time, for my existence. What is this decade or nay the whole century stands for I asked? Freedom, I replied and did not listen to my father for the first time. He had killed me already so I was let go off all. My mother was repentant though, as my family raised, in the scale of a middle class living, good job for my brother and my little sister, my cycle mate, the pillion rider, riding the romance waves with someone out for her caste, for her rebel. So I was the spare part, hence the parting wasn't' painful. When I look back I know that the first episode of my life was as it should have been a truncated affair in which hope was the only thread in which I swung for survival and survived. I did but then everybody does until the call comes to leave the physical form and free the spirit, little did I know that a whole new life lay in front of me, full of surprises, turns and the cliché of twists.

How a sip of water from a brass cup or a few drops from the brass spoon of the size of a finger or how one can keep rose petals and marigold spreads between the pages of one's book for years or how the fresh shoots of barley could be put behind the ears or how a dot of vermilion on the forehead or how fasting for a day could or how praying could or how chanting can or how lighting an incense stick does or what lighting a cotton wick soaked in mustard oil brings or how being blessed by the priests and yogis or how sitting on the crossed legged posture, the lotus posture or how reading Gita could kindle in one that thing called faith. I wondered one day, the day I stepped out from the rickety state transport bus blue and white painted on to the river town of Haridwar, the door of the abode of gods. Temples and more temples welcomed me as I mingled with the crowds and did what they did, a dip in the holy river, mandatory visits to the shrines and meetings with the holy men, the Sadhus, Babas and the yogis. It was a world very different from the one I inhabited up till now. It freed me from the Sui generics of my life and sought of, only sought of made me anew. Did I say new? Well, yes I changed course and my attire, a saffron Sari and my appearance, vermilion dots and Turmeric paste on my forehead and Rudraksha beads garland across my neck, name was new, too, Meera; after the ardent devotee of the lord Krishna. I sang the songs of love and compassion and moved about with a group of ochre robbed clean shaven headed whites singing Hare Rama Hare Krishna. It was fun and the nights were a little stoned, I must confess, that I looked forward to this part, for it helped me dilute the longings that remained of my family, not that they were a worried lot, my parents or brothers and sisters; the group of my childhood. They slowly dissolved from my memories like butter on a hot day, liquid legends, story less. I added more to my repertoire of religion, travelling and reading a lot, even Gandhi, could you imagine! But I did it was the good old Gita I stuck to. Krishna the sage and his Karma concept, *nishkam* and all was good and so was its dualism of the *Sankhaya* Philosophy of the Sage *Kapila* the incarnate of lord Vishnu himself.

Prakriti and the *Purusha* was a good enough explanation but why was *Prakriti* passive, though, the sage makes it clear that the creation takes place only when the both combine and alone they are like the blind or the lame, it didn't satisfy me neither was Jorden satisfied, a Jew wanderer whom I met at the Ghats of Rishikesh. I detailed him of what I knew and I knew that he didn't knew nothing at all so I sermon him and listened to his questions was he impressed, yes he was, to a damn extend so I became a teacher at the age of twenty- three in my first year at the holy twin river town, the mother Meera Amma the divine sage and an expert on matters spiritual. I travelled a lot and attended conferences organized by the BHP and other Hindu organizations. Now as I look back I find it hard to understand my affinity to them, leads me to question as to what is Hindu in them. That apart, I did meet a few genuine souls who added to my search of them one was a yogi who was pursuing a doctorate in Meditation and was keen to explain to the west the scientific aspect of yoga. He was good damn good but I differed due to the high I got from the commune living of the sect and all the adulation I got after every *Satsang*. It was heady, the mixture of religion, a mass following and music and it led me to pay a visit to Beatles' temples where they made their best music for the soul and all at Rishikesh. It went about like this for years three to be precise, though in the corner of my heart the rationalism of the yogi who pursued Meditation doctorate and accosted me from time to time lampooning me at my and that is what he said puerile attempts at understanding the spirituality concept. I fought with him from time to time and then didn't see him for quite a while, though; Jorden came back every year like a keen student and lay on my feet for hours as I sat on the banks of the holy river Ganga. He brought a fresh set of visitors every year with him who listened to me with a deep devotion trying hard to get into the business of Hinduism. They did or not I never could know but of Jorden I knew a thing that he somehow developed strange leanings for me or a set of familial feeling, not that I cared of but it made the woman in me come alive to the need of the realm of physical. So our *satsang* turned into some sought of romance by the riverside holy and all a saffron color and sprinkling of red rose petals, life was full of little joys of differing shades, I thriving on them till it lasted, for I came to know of the dangers of such communes only when Jorden, in his stoning one day proclaimed in front of all that I was his mother of the previous birth and that through regression analysis he had found this out and also one of the Swami at Badrinath had said so. I was shocked to hear his outbursts and retreated to reasoning, finding causes for the cycle of birth and death and the theory of reincarnation. Son Jorden, I finally said to him, I don't have a belief in your analysis but yes I do believe that we met through some connection of the universal system. He was downcast by my observations and cried the whole day that day sitting on my feet. I let him and then explained to him the concept of selfless service and the value of fulfilling one's duties; it was my way of saying him my final good bye. He made the parting less painful by disappearing one fine moonless night leaving a strange void in me and when he didn't turned up the subsequent year, I was sure that he had left me for good. But after him a lot of men turned up claiming to be my sons from the previous birth and as the word spread I was a universal mother without actually siring child of my own. Leave alone siring I hadn't had a touch of a male for a long, long time and it made me long for the rough touch of a man. I waited upon that boy a Christian convert but he didn't turn up. How would he it was my wish full thinking but I wasn't hungry the way I was supposed to be, just wanted to explore and the scientific yogi was a good prospect for his aura and all but he disappeared too, leaving me in the throes of my conflicts. It was the time when the attraction of religion waned in me and I delved deep into the development of science and the way renaissance had changed the way the humans lived and more importantly behaved and interacted with one another. It opened up the flood gates of new learning for me and I thought of moving on but it was not so simple for the system and the town had crystallized in me and I stuck to it for the security it provided to me, after all a woman needs the security of a home so I lingered on, on the periphery of half a existence, moving in and out of a wish for the sameness and something novel. It was a sort of stratagem, a locked thought and whom do I turn to during the interim of my life? No one. That I found despite looking for someone. What does one do but to listen to one's voice? It is like going back to the class room. How many voices are there to listen to; head, heart, gut and the fourth one that I found on the day when I lay hot and sweating on my bed, a strange warmth like currents of electricity ran through my veins and my throat was parched and the lips dry and eyes burning. It worried the heck out of me for I know when you are self-dependent then you owe yourself up, good or bad doesn't matter. So, if I was ill then I have to look for myself. I went to the doctor of physical and he pronounced that it is the hormones' disharmony, Meera Amma. I found, despite my dismay, that apart from the God and the Spirit the body hangs with all its paraphernalia and needs. It sought of forced me to listen to the call of the hormones as well, not that I could do much about it except ignore the boil of the estrogens and other esoteric names, but now the voices overlapped, all in a mix and all crying for attention. So what I do but to acknowledge the process and the inevitability of aging and the addition of years like unwanted hairs which crop up in your underarms, upper lips or between your legs. I lived through the cacophony of the voices creating mayhem; a confluence of head, heart, soul, hormones, the great *Sangam*. I bided for time letting the storm pass by. I found out during this interregnum of my living that when you need someone to glide by you, you will never ever find one so you have to trudge alone through the maze all by yourself, falling and rising and then perhaps falling again. Each falling making one stronger or weaker, I cannot be the judge of my struggles or even escapisms for it was the later one that I fell for. Religious songs day and night and night and day, *Satsangs* and lectures on Krishna and the legend of Rama, the lord of Ayodhya; a folk lore living that was what I lived. It did make me forget or ignore the voices that slowly but steadily and surely controlled me and my basis but this was also the time I longed for the doctor of yoga now *Acharya Neeleshwar*, who dropped by but walked with a gait of someone who had stumbled upon a treasure, not his own, but now his due to some divine providence Ah! The yoga ego I poked him but he ignored me even when I was open to him and all to the extent of sharing with him my voices. Hear them he advised without owning up the responsibility for the same and disappeared for what else but detachment that was what I concluded but what didn't end was my misery which led to my getting cynical about life in generality and in particularity, leading me to conclude that it was an early onset of Menopause. That was then the end of a women's fecundity and hence destiny, I thought my own set of conclusions, though, on my face and on my conduct seldom a shadow passed and I kept a smiling countenance attracting devotees to the sect and travelling far and wide to spread the message of Krishna but the lord was not competent enough to satisfy my search and the questions raised by my voices from time to time. A haze of doubts hung around me mingling with the aura that abstinence had brought on to me giving me a strange demeanor which was lapped up by the people but it was I who seethed at my own incompleteness which pricked me like unseen and unnoticeable thorns and blood oozed from my invisible wounds. I sucked the red water and salted my taste, my tongue became numb and I was sucked into the quagmire of illusions. At precise this moment of my annihilation I heard a voice among the multitude of voices that cackled in delight on seeing me fall from the proverbial grace. It was the voice of my conscious, a soft whisper it was, almost a sign for a language which I caught in one of my long walks on the beaches of the river Ganga. It was a voice which comes once in a while and almost invariably is a result of a prayer or one can say an answer to one's prayers. I heard it and ignored it but it came back the next day and the next and the next and the next till I thought I was going insane. So, one day on the banks of the Ganga, I sat crossed legged in a lotus posture and fixed my gaze on the vacuum that lay ahead of me. After the elapsing of unaccounted time I knew that I had reached a conclusion. When I came back the voice was no longer there and a deep peace had spread inside me which was sweet and strange for it had come a little late but the fault was entirely mine I should have listened to it when it was young, nubile and decipherable.

The month of February in these parts of the globe is like October, part cold and part warm, almost incomprehensible, as the seasons overlap and become amorphous, hence open to question; but the birds are back to their chirpy self and chase the dull insects which emerge from their hibernation, the leaves fall like stray boons and find their nemesis in their purposelessness, the rains are intermittent and fall in little droplets and never in a shower, though there are occasional bursts of wild intensity and indecisions hang like the loose ends of a story to be tied up when things become clearer. On such a month I took my decision despite suspended moments, waiting people and winding seasons. I walked on leaving whatever identity I had in the river town and where was it I was headed to, towards the Himalayas which is the birth place for all knowledge or so the legend said. At that moment I had to, as in, had to, find things for myself to satisfy my own quest and what better way but to be on one's own. It was lingering in me now from quite a while, this idea of trekking up the hills from which emerged the holy river Ganga but I never really had a will to walk on just like that. So what made me walk the call was the call which I heard after much ado. Out went the conformity of years and I tip toed one fine morning into the dense forests along with the entwining river. I was welcomed by the trees and the forest dwellers and I breathe my freedom with an ease of a yoga exponent and that day I found out that the real ashram or whatever it is, lies under the blue skies or the verdant shades or starry nights. Though the nights were a little scary for me, so I made it a point to camp near a village or if possible stay with the friendly hill folks. They found me a holy person which I was and was treated well but as I dwelled deep into the mountains then I found that the terrain was unfriendly and even dangerous. What made the effort worthwhile was the wondrous play of nature, of little streams and trees and birds, insects, shrubs, ferns, all existed in a perfect blend of the master blender, God; being lorded over by the majestic snow bound Himalayas. There were huge waterfalls and quaint villages, temples of Shiva and many a Goddesses. Hidden amongst the mountain trails were animals but I was never attacked or what, though I was careful and once I accompanied a group of *Gaujjar* tribes who are the cattle bearers practicing transhumance. They were all six feet tall and red bearded mostly faithful Muslims and all were sweet tongued and friendly. I had asked them about their journey and they said that in the lands which are accessible the government rule rules and off course they would be pushed out and all and hence they hunt down the areas where the government cannot set its foot, hence their trek uphill. No government and all so come summers and they trek to the green pastures like the Alpine meadows which are called *Bugyals*. It was the individual versus the state debate that caught my fancy and I laughed loud on their predicament and at the folly of the modern governments, democratic or not but certainly Bureaucratic and I was happy for their rustic charms as they searched for their place under the sun away from the gaze of the Orwellian eye. One thing I liked about them was the way they loved their cattle more than their family and also the way they treated me with freshly udder frothy milk and huge round mound of what they called Chapatti. I was well looked after and I travelled with them for quite a few days and followed them as they climbed up the Himalayas in search of fresh and greener pastures for their cattle folk deep into the mountain ranges and into the alpine meadows. On the way up I met their fellow tribes of *Bhutias* who were a some sought of a specialist in matters of the sheep and with them were thousands of sheep, furry and fleecy and their little ones with whom I played like a child of yore. These shepherds were not more than five feet tall and the Gujjars who were over six and a half feet towered over them but there was all camaraderie and a just distribution of pasturing rights without the arbitration of the government. I noticed one thing that highly evolved systems do not require an external force to live peacefully. Peace yes, there was all round me and the wondrous nature which beckoned me with its splendor; the wild geraniums, balsams and bunches of the red and pink Rhododendrons in full bloom, led me into a mesmeric world of wilderness. However, the long treks and a strong March sun, sought of tired me. I camped in a village on a ridge and stayed with an old woman who and that was what she told me about herself, was at the fore front of the *Chipko* movement which she had launched along with her mentor Gaura Devi in the early seventies. Now this woman was in her late eighties and a part of the folklore herself but her lore about the *Chipko* really brought into light a forgotten tale of the first organized fight to preserve the environment before the blood and the Gore of ecology set in. She often narrated her tale, a tale of valor and grit. She told me from her memories and with wistful eyes that how the contractor of the forests have come to their village and marked the trees to be cut. Then Gaura Devi, along with her bands of village women, hugged the trees, when the wood cutters came the next morning. They hugged the trees as if they were their children and despite the threat from the contractor and the police they refused to let go of the young trees. Soon it became a mass movement and perhaps the first one, long before the globe rose to the need for awareness of preservation. Now, she lamented, that the government has become a thief itself and all good reforms movement are run like a theatre of the absurd. I was wonderstruck by her erudition and stayed on for her snippets from the life she had lived. This led me to stay in a village for a couple of weeks more and I grew accustomed to the ways of the hill people, eating Ragi and stinking nettle vegetable broth and making drawing on the floor from turmeric powder, vermillion and rice paste. Ah! It transported me back to the time when I painted and colors returned in my life through the spring season too and the valley where the village was situated was resplendent with flowers and their fragrance. This was the real trance I thought and nature is the ultimate god, move over Krishna, I called. The old woman, she was called Jamuna Devi, asked a religious song of me one day. I sang a Krishna *bhajan* and the village was spellbound, hailing me the incarnate of Meera. I knew then and there that the time had come for me to resume my wander. Which I did, crossing many a streams and valleys and climbing mountains, meeting people and paying obeisance to the local deities, devouring fresh fruits and plucking the wild berries. The nature way opened my mind and heart to the magic of living and it made my plump figure into a taut and sun baked cake. My walk grew wild and I had dream in my eyes that is how it is with a woman I suppose, dreaming of a guy like a knight in a shine or what and sweeping me from my feet. I must confess I was more than ready for the romance of my life but I was not prepared for an accident. Yes I would call it that, now when I have decided to move on after seven years of subjugation. At that time, though, it was a sweet occurrence, almost natural and I loved the beauty of its spontaneity and purity, like the river on which I stood that day early in the morning, as the sun had just tickled in, in the narrow valley, across the village. I was washing myself with certain gayness when, afar, I saw a man in his not so young youth, standing on one leg and gazing at the sun. He was erect as a stick and stood in the middle of the stream unmindful of the currents. I watched him off and on as I played with water. He stood midstream for long and finally hit the ground and started his practice of the twelve posture *Suryanamaskar* Yogic exercise. It was a beautiful dance that he enacted and I being the only audience hidden from the practitioner; enjoyed his movements and his toned body glistened like a pearl under the sun and his forehead was soon sweat bead smeared. I watched him with intent as he lay on the grass in the posture of the dead, finally sitting on the lotus posture with a fixed gaze, as I enjoyed his surreal company. When he opened his eyes he found my gaze meeting his and he sort of made faces in all jest, I thought, not scorn and I smiled the most beatific smile of me. This he ignored and started to move on. I followed him and asked him his permission to accompany him and he said why I ask and I replied that because he walked on earth as if the mother was his alone and none's. This seems to thaw his resolve of keeping me at bay and he smiled and said yes to my question. We walked together without the exchange of social pleasantries for we were in the wilderness and we delved deep in to the forests leaving the gurgling call of the river-stream. He was a quiet soul and I chirped like a free bird, pausing for his nodding and then blabbering all over again. He didn't seem to mind it, I concluded and walked along till the night fell with an alarmingly freedom, deepening a strange fear in me, though his gait was assuring enough. Still a lingering doubt arose in me as I found myself alone with him and worse was the case when his furtive glance caught me in my blush as red as the setting sun and the lazy summer evening. He smiled a terse smile and asked me where I wished to be dropped, at my house or a police station nearby. It fumed me and I let him know of my flames and told him, Mr. whatever I can look after myself, don't need your help or bloody advice and asked him in a huff do you know who I am. Whosoever but a woman certainly you are, he said and this was certainly the pulling of the fuse of the grenade that he had hurled at me and a beautiful one at that, he added. I went all liquid in my knees; it was the first time someone had called me beautiful. I called him a liar in my mellowed tone which surprised me but I think that is what all women want, the appreciation of their beauty. I told him he needn't worry and that I would go back to the nearest village if he wants me to. He said that a Himalayan bear was on a prowl and that I had to stay back for the night with him in this jungle if it will be alright with me, he asked for my permission, otherwise we can have a night trek he suggested. No, no, I am comfortable let us camp here at a safe place and I can go back early in the morning I said. He laid open his olive green rucksack and picked out a hunting knife, the one which is used for clearing forest paths and as a Talisman against no particular evil and sliced a few branches from the nearby trees, most of them dry, but also some young branches, for which I admonished him, remembering the *Chipko* movement. What was he up to, ignoring me? It ignited me long before he lighted the fire; before which he laid a neat stack of the tree-sticks and arranged them in a cone shape dome and covered it with limply dew leaves and he then put a few stripes of rosined bark of the pine trees and then pulled a matchstick from his pocket. It was with the third matchstick that the bark caught fire, followed by the moist leaves, hissing like the engine of steam, slowly the branches hissed too, catching fire. His careful guidance guided the nascent flames and within no time a huge fire rose like a phoenix through the contours of the wooded dome making the dark forest come to life. The fire spread with an alarming speed and it worried the hell out of me as I had heard the dangers of the forest fires in the summers. The spreading fire burnt all with which it came in contact with, leaves, mosses, peat, trees; he was quick as a rabbit as he drew a fire line around the fire and the two of us stood in the circle with fire in the middle but in control. The thought comforted me and I relaxed in his company. On his part he put a forked bamboo across the fire and let an aluminum kettle dangle over it with a tea mixture in it. The strong flames made it come to a boil almost immediately. He let it boil for brief moments and then poured the broth in two terracotta cups, he handed me one and himself sat under a tree with large leaves which formed an inverted umbrella over his head collecting dew drops. I remained near the fire and we both sipped quiet sips and kept to ourselves, neither sharing nor caring. I wasn't aware who slept first me or him or the humming bird that hummed for company, but when I woke up the embers were dying and the darkness caught me unawares. So did the eerie of the night, all humid and windless, like a suffocating embrace of someone not up and close. I saw him sleeping in his abandoned glory, like a soldier who had fought and won a war. I confabulated as to whether I should wake him up or not and let him peep into my fears; I decided otherwise and prayed for the night to pass quickly. My eyes dropped under the influence of the day's trek and I was somnolent when the thunder and the roar of the clouds woke me up. Again this time I was determined to do something, so I crept near where he lay, he wasn't aware or even if he was, he kept to himself and let me lay besides him. Presently it started raining and he finally woke up and found me near him but I knew that he knew I was snuggling around him. He didn't speak a word and pulled on my arms. It angered me, this owning business of his, just like my father owned my mother, so I told him to keep off. He smiled, which I caught under the play of lightening. It angered me all the more. I think he sensed my coming to a boil and so he relented and begged me to rush under the tree shades or search a place of hiding. I said all right, and he picked his bag. We ran for cover, however, the forest was dark and even dangerous, so our progress was slow, but we nevertheless entered the forest and after much beating about the bushes literary, we found an abandoned cave. He was delighted and entered it without fear and got down to light a fire but I was circumspect, which is natural for a woman, alone with a man to be. He comforted me, as if reading my mind and maintained safe distance in the cave which had strange roots inside, its walls giving it a look of a shady joint with figurines on the walls and it looked all so out of this world, the nature dancing an unruly dance outside and I with a stranger. We had no choice, yes, even he looked a bit bemused, so I struck a conversation and asked him where was he heading to and he said that he had a search of his own and that he was keen to reach the source of the holy river Ganga and before he reaches there, he wished to visit the temples on the way. I was surprised by his religiosity and told him so. He seemed offended and said that he had travelled so that his mind opens up to the things he wished to know and his quest was more spiritual and yogic in nature. I asked him that if both religion and spirituality were different and he said a firm yes. It tired me, his rigid resolve to be all spirit and I asked him that whether he totally had disbelief on matters material and again I got a firm yes in reply. It irritated me all the more and I shouted at him saying he was half a guy and that everything was spiritual, including matter. He challenged me to seeing my own ghost and I was afraid of him now, as the fury of the storm gained momentum and a hailstorm ensued, he laughed a hoarse laughter saying that I was stuck up with him and that the god has conspired against him and send me to test his patience for inanities. I shouted in my dread and threw a stone at him. It caught him on the temple and little drops of blood oozed out smearing him like a vermillion. He became quiet again and lay with his back to me I tried to take a wink but failed and kept all ears for any sound, but the deafening sound emanating from outside the cave had rendered my olfactory useless. I didn't let my guard down. I don't know when I lost my consciousness and sleep crept like a creeper entwining by very being. It was still dark when I woke up, infact, very dark, like in a pitch black hole and the rain fell with an ease of a swimmer, almost like a float. I looked around and saw the fire that he had lit when we had entered the cave now lying in its last rites as a thick ash cover covered the smoldering coals. The cave was dark and he was nowhere to be seen. A panic entered me and I shouted out for him. There was no reply and I shouted again almost in my tears. It was the first time I had experienced such danger to me. I sobbed for long till a heavy hand rested on my shoulders. I shuddered with fear and looked up and found his eyes piercing me with contempt. What is there to fear he said, I had gone out to get some dry wood if I could, the fire is out can't you see. He seemed angry which made me all the angrier and I threw a handful of leaves on his face and he pulled at my hairs with a vehemence of rebel. I gnawed on his bare skin with my nails wetting them with his blood. He pulled me closer to him and bit my ear. I pulled at his clothing. He, in turn, as if taking a cue from my violence, shouted abuses and pulled at my cotton dress, pulling my warp first and then the shirt it revealed my mounds on the chest and it somewhat mellowed him. He withdrew but all this anger had made me intimate with him and so I pounced a feline pounce and brought him to the ground. He lay still for a brief moment, as if contemplating his next move and so did I and I found it strange as I waited up on him to take a lead. Our hearts fluttered in the darkness as the rain fell with a sublime regularity, like a meditative music. I heard his hoarse panting and I heard mine too so we are both in it together, I thought, which he seemed to acknowledge as he moved closer to me and looked a shy look into my eyes as if asking for my go ahead. I let my lashes do the talking. I felt his breath closing it on me like a hunter going for the kill and I lay with sweet expectations as his hands moved with a cottony touch all over me. His nails pricked me to submission and I snuggled into his strong arms in surrender. It was then he made his wild moves like the swirling pith and tones of a musical note as he explored me like an errant musician, making me one, too. I followed him in his actions and tore into him with a wild abandon, my legs lay lose and wide all full of juices and shook under his passions. He tore my clothes off, every last bit of the livery, exposing and getting enthralled in my nakedness. I was bewildered by his manliness almost ugly and yet satisfying. We danced in the early morning hours and like children made love till both of us were tired of the foreplay and then he pushed himself hard and like the thundering clouds came in a deluge on to me, a deluge like a flood, which I couldn't handle. I lay in a state of semi-consciousness. He lay in his fatigue as we disowned each other and slept. I regained consciousness after a while and saw the twilight broke through the maze of morning clouds. It was a fresh sun waking up after a cataclysmic night. He lay like a child coiled in his nakedness, sleeping in intermittent snores, a content soul. I thought of waking him up but decided against it, as the morning opened up the world for me. I let the experience linger in me and came out of the cave walking on the wet leaves and splashing water from the puddles that had appeared like a bequeath of nature. I drank the nature's manna to my heart's content and walked on ignoring him, though I had feared abrupt conclusions all my life, but I had to move on and own up the fact that life cannot be burdened by carrying histories and it is the future that one has to look up to and that morning I woke up to one more fact that abrupt conclusions are inevitable to one's existence however much one tries to avoid them.

I struggled to open my eyes as the white flakes of mucus glued on the margins of the eye lids, matting the lashes together, with white crust and they felt like jammed and rusted bottles refusing to uncork. I went back to the slumber land in which I had been, for god knows how many days, so it surprised me when a deep voice called on me in my state of dormancy asking me to wake up or what. It irritated me somewhat and me thought that if I could wouldn't have I, but kept quiet knowing that I was dependent on the soul who called on me. This soul became my keeper and he fed me all those herbal concoctions and applied oils on my body as it ached. He sat on my bed side like a nurse, nay mother, least I undermine his effort. Now these were long and lonesome days as I lay without moving or seeing anything, I think he realized what I was going through and one day he took me out for a walk and I walked with his support. I could even mumble a few words, he laughed at my effort and said that the day I talked he would rush back mount *Meru* or *Neelkanth*; it is sheer luck that I found a woman who keeps quiet, doesn't roam about and prefers to be quite like the three monkeys of Gandhi. I admonished him but a piercing pain shot through my throat and I vomited. Blood it must be, for the deep voice was worried and he called on the other voice, I heard a woman's, Kashi.. Kashi he called, come quick and bring my bag. I heard footsteps rushing towards me and he administered some injections and washed my face and gave me a liquid to drink. I was back to bed but this time the woman, Kashi was there to keep me company. As the days passed I became restless and demanded to be handed over to my family. I missed my parents and wished for someone with whom I could share my pains and the hibernation, the voice admonished me and told me to rest and leave everything to the gods. A feeling of helpless and dependency engulfed me for the first time in my life as I lay in a sulk. The woman, Kashi though, did her best to enliven the proceedings and one day she introduced me to a dog Chiru saying he was the one who had saved me. Now this was news to me and I concluded that I was in danger or something, from whom, I didn't know. I mumbled my query which Kashi seemed to understand and said that all I could do was to pray. I followed her advice and mumbled my celestial songs of Krishna and no sooner had I whispered the words I knew I had an audience as the voice appreciated it and Kashi clapped and I think the dog Chiru wagged his tail in acknowledgment. It sort of encouraged me and I resolved to be fit again and so I asked for Kashi's help which she readily agreed to do. The two of us embarked on a mission fitness for me which bore fruits in the first week itself and I was able to see the world one day, after how many days, I didn't knew. When my eyes opened I found myself in a hay hut surrounded by a beautiful woman in her twenties and a thick haired lazy looking dog wagging his tail in joy. Indeed joy it was for me too and I laughed as my voice, too cleared. Then an old man, tall and white bearded and in a white robe entered the hut and offered me flowers and white sugar balls. I looked at him with a humble gratitude, thanking him with my silence. I had never experienced such surrender before, not even when I was deep into the Krishna Bhakti. My eyes were tearful and my heart gay; he smiled a calm smile and said that he was Ekaba. Strange name was my immediate reply, which was rude of me but now on hindsight I realize that my reaction made our bonding a possibility, for a relation needs certain disdain to be able to grow above the mundane. He seemed to like my openness, despite my predicament and he laughed and directed Kashi to cook a delicacy for me. That night we had a feast of sorts and Kalpi the master of Chiru joined us. He was a fisher man and had brought a catch from the river Alaknanda; he was rustic and *Pahari* to the core, the real hill man so he was on a high of country made liquor and sang songs in the local dialect and in his inebriation he narrated how he had saved me, one day when he found me floating in the river. He boasted of his expertise on netting but I wondered how I fell into the roaring river, to which Kashi suggested that I might have had an accident. I feared she knew of my night spend with the stranger so to way lay her I told her that I was on a trek and a wild bear chased me; I had heard it from the villagers that to save one's self from the bear one should run downhill and I ran so. Then I must have slipped, I spoke a lie with the conviction of a story teller; and that was how I must have fell into the river, I concluded. I proceeded to thank Kalpi to which he smiled and went away. The old man listened to us and ate in silence, which somehow worried me and so before signing off for the night I asked him what was wrong with me. He said everything. I flared, listening to his pronouncement and let go of my steam, demanding to contact the nearest police station. In his calmness he asked me to bloody well shut up, which I did under his aura, for he was a yogi of some repute. Kashi had told me that, I wept and then slept and when I woke up in the morning I found the villagers on my door applying *Alapna* on the hay hut verandah, they drew lovely floral patterns and colorful squares and triangles and Lord Ganesha's portrait. I stood up and joined them and drew patterns to my heart's content. Then I slowly went to the local temple and sat through the prayers. This made me a part of the village which was named as *Gau-Char*, the place for the cows to feed. It was a village life for me as I recouped from my fall but in a few weeks I was aware that I missed my periods and I thought I was old and that menopause had set in. Then I felt sick in the morning and my nipples pained and I felt bustier on the hips. I was real worried now and confided in Kashi who was not keen to divulge the details and so I called Ekaba and asked him whether I was dying or what; to which he laughed and said that in the contrary I was about to beget a life. I felt the shattering of a million mirrors and shouted aloud, now what, He was calm as ever and said that between us I was the woman and that I should best know the womb. What womb I shouted I was dropped from the sky. He laughed a soft laughter and bid me a good night, saying none can fall from a vacuum. What a night it was in my life as I regretted meeting the stranger, however, as night deepened I longed for his arms and a tear drop hung in my left eye, a love tear perhaps, or so I thought. It was Kashi who caught me in the morning and insisted on knowing the details. I was secretive but soon gave in to girlish gossips and the two of us sat on the river banks talking about him. She teased me further and I did not mind, in fact I quite enjoyed her company which made me forget my fear. I relaxed in the tutelage of the saint Ekaba who looked after me like my mother never did and directed me like my father never did. He even appointed a maid for me called Suddbhuddi and said that she was the wise one in matters of midwifery and was responsible for the birth of entire generation of this village. All set to go for the final lap, was how she announced her intentions and then rather surreptiously asked who the hell was I.

Meera, said I, so she demanded who Krishna was and I realized that I didn't knew the name of the stranger I had for a paramour. This made me keep mum for a few days which led Suddbhuddi to smell a rat I suppose. But she was a true follower of Ekaba and so kept her suspicion to herself and so did the villagers who seldom questioned the lack of the father the *causa sui* around me during my pregnant days. Not that I cared much for proving them or to any one for that matter, for the inception had made me a rebel all over again, taking me to a new high of motherly expectations. I think that women are born to be mothers and the more they go away from their basics they become the hand maiden of men. This mother business is their spirituality and I was no different, as a glow descended on me which attracted the attention of the old Ekaba, who was happy for me and asked me of my family and all and became my friend. Though he never called me by my name but just Baba which I quite liked as it gave me a sense of pride to be in his good books he re-taught me Geeta and read ancient books of wisdom which I listened. He said that he wants her to listen and I asked who, to which he replied the one in my womb to which I asked that how come he knew that it was a she and not a he. This made him laugh and he said that what do I think who he was. Now this was funny, for, I really could never fathom his depth or whatever. He was mysterious and secretive. I tried Kashi's good offices to know of him but she was a true Ekaba bred girl and kept quiet. The other woman Suddbhuddi didn't know a thing but divulged a detail that a long time ago then when Ekaba was young he had dropped anchor in this river side village and since then he had stayed here, though he travelled to the river town of Haridwar downstream to attend some meetings. Ah! I thought there must be some skeletons in the cupboard of this white bearded guy so one day I chided him that if he was such a highly qualified person in matters spiritual why doesn't he set up a system for the world to learn and know. I would he replied, though in the bottom of my heart I need not do the needful but still I would even at my age. Oh! Age Baba Ekess you are young I exclaimed, what if you were born with white hairs and they slowly turned black and people would say you are getting old and all, it is all a perception, dear Baba black without sheep. Now.. now; he seemed miffed, your sense of rumor or humor is palpable and black, you laugh for fun and not on being funny, but dearie of mine stop pulling the leg of a seventy seasoned man years. One yoga year is equal to thrice what the rest live Blah..Blah. I laughed, hugging him for reconciliation and kissing his forehead. I said that he was all for me, my mom, dad. I lingered for long as he waited for me to complete my confession; lover I said and this time he laughed and said that now he believed that I was a true Krishna prodigy talking as I was of lovers and..Son I cried, I wished for one but now I have to be satisfied by a daughter. This made him serious and he rebuked me for being a gender bender. To hell with all this, yes I am; for a woman would always aspire for a son, that much was true of all and I am no hypocrite. I left him in a huff and pendulated towards Kashi who, it seemed was more of a poetess and sat on the river boulder writing some poems or what. Tell me some, I requested her once and she turned hot and red and stammered her no. I insisted and she finally relented by taking out an old diary on which she said she had written her scribble, go on I egged her, so she ruffled the yellowing leaves of her tome and selected one to read it to me. It is a stray writing and I am not a writer she begged. I told her to go ahead and let me be the best judge, her eyes dropped seeing no escape route so she began her rendition as we sat on the river side one evening when the sun was playing hide and seek with the clouds and a few cranes hunted for fishes.

I have often walked…
And walked alone…
Through the years…
Journeying across the temporal…
Into the labyrinth of moments…
I have walked
And walked alone.

On days when I sit
And reflect in my solitude
Reclining against nature's rest
I find I have reached
The end of the road
With no more journeys
And no more walks
But a voice calls me
And I walk
And walk alone.

With every single breath
And every flutter of the eyes
With every beat of the heart
And every hope for a wish
I walk
And walk alone

On days when I trudge
On dry dewy leaves
And the sound of my feet
Tail me in my walks
I realize I am not alone
My walk walks behind me.

It matters little
Where I reach
Or where I am
Laid finally
For I will walk alone...
Into the realmless…

I found her in her wistfulness as soon as she completed her recital. She stared vacuously on the angry white waters of the river; she was deep in her contemplations and I thought it best to leave her. I searched for Ekaba to know more of her mystery; that I did with both, Kashi told me about the old saint. He was not forthcoming when I pricked him to tell me about her. He dithered and changed the course of the conversation. This made me all the more curious like the cat and I decided to Sherlock them both. Now as I think of my whim I blame it to my pregnancy which somewhat had chained me and Kashi's poem haunted me because I couldn't walk alone now, never could, now as I was a mother and like all mothers, not mine though, she being an exception. I have to dove tail my child and so the bulge grew in size as the day neared. It was Suddbhuddi who kept me in good health and spirit for Ekaba had gone to the river town for some workshop on yoga. During his absence Kashi retreated more into her cocoon making me realize that she was an ardent follower but she had something in her which she kept all bottled up, away from the worldly gaze. He returned before the rains began and was agitated on being ignored by the organizers. These Babas have blasted the country; he was furious, what do they know of yoga? Bloody selling it like a commodity of the west. This is a *Sadhana* and not some social work or an exercise in politics, he said. I told him to calm down and challenged him to set up a system of his own; to which he replied that he would, one day and whether I would be with him. I replied my yes; saying where would I go, otherwise. He was happy but said that one has to marry for the society and that knowledge was an individual pursuit. I was firm though and said that I would help him along with my daughter; for whom I waited all monsoons, sitting by the hay-hut window with Chiru as company and watching the rains pour from the prison of huge nimbus clouds, like children emerging from the hibernation of their classrooms once the final bell has been rung. It made me a child too, my heart running after the drops, chasing them. Then they were gone, the monsoons and my bulge widened so much that I had a difficulty in walking. I lay all day and walked with the support of Kashi, who took me out for autumn strolls and when the festive season began I sat through the entire drama enactment of the story of Rama and Sita. It was fun to be up and awake all night and see the villagers perform the roles of Ram his brother Laxman and Sita the poor soul and the evil ones Ravana his sister Supernakha whose nose Laxman had cut and the brothers' Kumbhakarna the sleep- devil. What was fun was that the clapping and whistles were seemed to be reserved for the evil ones, the villains of the show, along with the cash rewards, which the public gave for performance and which were announced on the public address system. It was like this; that Rama and Sita would get ten rupees from someone whereas Ravana would get rupees fifty. I found it damn funny people eulogizing the demons as demi-gods. How thin the line is between the good and the evil we can seldom know. It was entertainment of the highest level, though, lot of value education and character building, making me an aware would be mother. Now, these would be mother days, are critical for the child as the womb gains in awareness, the child learns inside it like Abhimanyu learnt how to break the *Chakravhuy* in his mother Subhadra's womb; but, as the legend says, when technique to break the last of the seven circles was being narrated she fell asleep and the womb-child couldn't listen. Poor he, for, it was in the last schemata that he was killed by Kuravas; the poor son of Arjuna died due to the ignorance of his mother. This made me all the more self-conscious of my impending motherhood. One day I asked Ekaba the destiny of my child whom he claimed to know about. All I said was to tell me my worry. He was quiet for a while and then said that the girl would be some unique creature pestering me day and night and that soon she will have a father of her own. What of her life I asked. To which he replied that I needn't worry as my daughter would be some kind of a savant and I should be now called Aditi, the mother of gods. Hence the name Aditi stuck to me even before Kerrie (Ekaba called my daughter thus) came along on a cold wintery morning. Her birth is a story in itself, one which worried me dead, though this business of being a mother and all seems all exciting and fulfilling but I knew the dangers and the pain I have had to go through. I was nervous throughout so when the day came to deliver I held Ekaba's hand and meditated upon my labor. Suddbhuddi used her domestic science and got warm water and cloths' rags ready. Finally the time to push came early in the morning. It was blood and sweat till she arrived in silence, pretty quiet, without the mandatory cry. It worried the heck out of me. It was Ekaba again, the savior, who pulled a trick out of his bag, making her cry out. She seemed to be a harmless girl at the beginning, playing on her own and sucking my nipples without the gum bite. However the pranks came early, even when the village was cold and wintery dark, she would slip out of my bosom and hold Chiru's attention, which wagged his hairy tail without giving a warning signal. So both souls talked without words and with much understanding, mumbling acknowledgements. It made me a worried mom but Ekaba laid to rest my doubts about the mountain dogs. This made one thing clear that the little girl would have her way in her life. Kashi, too joined in the fun to bring her up and composed a poem which Ekaba liked; what I liked was that little Kerrie, very little, with tiny arms, eyes, fingers and mouth had a huge spirit. She laughed with her eyes closed but when these very eyes opened it gave me a cause to live, for I saw life in them, like lights from a holy candle or from an earthen bowl with a burning cotton wick dipped in mustard oil. Under her I grew, which surprised me. Why would I mind as I was enjoying myself; true that a girl has to have mother business of her so that she lives according to her nature. I realized it a little late into my life. There is one more thing I noticed, that I never really missed a father for her or another wheel to run my system. I never missed him, neither any information cropped up regarding him. Ekaba did bring up the issue but I ignored his enquiries as I was enjoying the foibles of the devil for a daughter. This often made me wonder why my mother couldn't really enjoy me, I being her first daughter. Suddenly I missed my parents and one day I demanded Ekaba to arrange for my journey. He advised me to wait till the naming ceremony is complete. I agreed and then stayed back for the whole year; now this year was the shortest I had lived up till then.

Oh! To bring up a child is a back breaking and a futile exercise; why? - For all of it falls in the realm of a duty without a quid pro quo. It dawned on me then, the sacrifice mothers make to rear their children, all mothers, including mine, though all mothers are reluctant mothers at the beginning, you know the grime of child rearing getting into their nerves. Why I call it futile is purely hindsight; Kerrie grew on her own terms and reared herself better than I did. It was fun alright as I found in the first years; usually it is the first year and the year after that that a child is a child, after which it grows into an adult damn quickly at that. What of it; I ignored the soothsayer in me and went ahead plunging into this bringing up a girl kind of challenge. My days were filled with Kerrie and her fumbling nuisances; feed on time, continuous peeing sessions accompanied by burps, vomit and excretion, without the discipline, almost anytime, day and night and her sleeping sessions were the most awkward; daytime snooze and play at three in the morning. Good way Aditi I laughed on my destiny from being a mother universal to mothering a particular, a task impossible. It was left to Kashi to be her second mother; that goes for all of us, having an alternative mother, more competent and reliable that the first, though, I showered my love to the little one, she was always on a look out for Kashi and Ekaba whose beard was her favorite swing. This made me relax a bit and as the spring came I picked up a paint brush and painted her childhood in myriad hues like the wild flowers of the Himalayas. It was in spring that Misti; we named her thus; a black, yellow eyed, fat and furry, lazy and languorous cat; not curious at all, joined us at the village, dropping on us like a long lost relative and eased herself into the household. Finding the little girl easy to placate she hovered around Kerrie much to the dislike of Chiru who chased the cat away, but at the end it is the cat who wins and at the family meeting it was decided that Misti could stay, which made Kerrie cackle in delight as if she understood the whole business of expanding families. I think she did; children understand everything through their consciousness; like the need for a father. This Ekaba pointed out to me, adding his might to my motherly nervousness, like it is when you own up things. To this Ekaba the savant that he was said that children owe themselves, their good or bad. It is their cycle of Karma and they bring their destiny with them. What of me then I cried, keeping someone's egg for nine months and then feeding her, only to know that she doesn't belong to me. This made him angry and in a huff he shouted that why women cannot be reasonable and follow the diktats of the duty. Now I have never been shouted upon like this; it made tears flow from my eyes in a stream and I picked Kerrie and said that it is parting time Mr. Ekaba. It was Kashi who played the meditating soul and brought me back but I didn't talk to Ekaba for quite a while. My attention was towards Kerrie and Kerrie alone. It was summer season so fruits ripened quickly and succinctly in the valley village. I took Kerrie to the small stream which flew through the community orchard and in which ripe mangoes floated like wishes. I gorged on them and let Kerrie suck on the yellow milk. I tell you, the little devil that she was, was quite delighted by the taste and when we returned we were splashed all in yellow colors. It was Ekaba who felt ignored by both of us but damn to him I had my best friend with me, yes it is true, a woman's best friend is a woman and it is divine if she is her daughter. Into the fold we got Kashi and the threesome set siege on the fort of Ekaba who sulked; poor man or poorer men when it comes to matters of woman bonding it was three versus the lone old man and we teased him to which he replied that still at seventy-three years of age he had in him to bring as many girls as he wanted as he had a line till *Kadhukhal*, which was a village nearby. We challenged him to show us at least one, this really angered him and he spent more of his time in the temple or reading the sacred books. His absence wasn't missed by me as I became Kerrie myself despite the misgivings I had about motherhood and it being a noose around which a women's fate is tied to and suffocated till death. To hell with all that I told myself, let us have fun and children are the funniest element on earth, a spiritual laugh, that is what they are. On her part, Kerrie was a keen child even in her pranks she lay a detailed plan involving us all. It was fun till it lasted for sometimes it got into my nerves and I rebuked her, once slapping her when she refused to tow my line, she was obviously angry and refused to talk to me, just snuggling on me during feed hours. It was Kashi who was her companion then, giving me time to think on our future, this our business pricked me like pine needles, where was the I in my life, strange ways of living and he what of him? Ignore or search, a daughter needs a father, if he is like mine, god save Kerrie, poor girl. She was lucky no pressure to handle, no other's ambition to live for, though, my being was annihilated forever, Ekaba had a different view on this saying that my existence had in fact expanded to include all. A mother is a mother of all. I laughed on him telling him to keep mum on this mum business. He wasn't a father I said. He kept quiet, realizing that my anger had grown in these past few months. I noticed it too, hormones I concluded so it was back to Ekaba's classes learning the ropes of Pranayam; the breath control exercise. My condition improved and so did my relation with Kerrie as I played with her when the rains arrived in the village she would, in her little strides slip on the soft wet earth, her tiny claws gnawing on earthworms and snails, squashing the poor creatures. Children are like that, little knowing that they are snuffing a life; they play with animals, Kerrie doing the same. Misti never retaliated nor did Chiru when Kerrie pinched them or clawed them. A turtle was swept away by the river current and Ekaba brought it to the hut. We all were surprised with this gift of the monsoons. He was named Chintan, the thinker, because he kept to himself and seldom moved; when he did it was the slowest canter one could see. Kerrie took a liking for the new inhabitant, her wild cackling growing with time. The rains receded quickly and the fall set in, with leaves flying all over without someone to guide them. Kerrie picked up the after rains butterflies for her play playing with their colors and flights. Her perception grew wildly and she demanded to go on long walks. In stepped Kalpi, who, in his slur volunteered to take her to the higher hills in the clear weather. The hills are the most verdant after the rains and the snow bound peaks are visible after the haze and dust had been washed by them, the skies are azure and the native birds are joined by their migratory friends from central Asia. Autumn season also brings the white apple, pink orange flowers which add to the mystic of the Himalayas. It lend its aura to Kerrie who grew under the watchful gaze of the mighty mountains, the abode of learning. It was learning I missed and it was the time when Kerrie seemed a burden to me. I distanced her from myself and delved deep into the library of Ekaba, reading with a voracious appetite like an act of vengeance. This made Ekaba happy and he encouraged me to complete my education of life. Kerrie was happy with Kashi, who it turned out, was quite a singer as well and sang lullabies for her. The rest of the time nature's splendor kept Kerrie occupied. She wouldn't remember any of these moments, Ekaba said, adding that the saddest part of a one year old was that they don't have a memory to hold on to moments like these. I was surprised to know this fact, that Kerrie would forget all this; yes Ekaba said but they will grow as a part of her consciousness. It was this very consciousness I sought to develop on the day I had met him. He had said something to this effect; so he was on to such things I thought. What of leaving me I questioned him? Making love and disowning the child of love, I admonished myself. No business of love or emotions; just a hunger or hormone hooliganism. I was a well entrenched single mother holding on to our daughter as my daughter-ego danced, I stepped up the isolation which Ekaba noticed and invited the villagers to share the little girl, saying a child needs to grow in a crowd, being alone is death. So are you I challenged him, no family or a wife for the oldie. Would no longer be alone, he challenged me back, my system is being set up and soon I would have followers from all over the world. Good I cried, do it if it pleases you. He said it doesn't, but it has to be done, as all incompetent people are working overtime to bring disrepute to Hinduism. You are the new Sankara I said and he became serious. Time that you stop making fun of me, he snubbed me. You are getting old I snubbed him back; snobbish at seventy, I laughed. We were back to we -are –not-in- talking-terms relation and remained like that for a long time during which Kerrie was often rebuked by the old man. Kashi kept the frayed tempers in check, this time by her culinary talent, cooking a varied spread for us all. Winters had set in, working up an appetite for us all; it was a strange period for me, as I drifted away from my daughter slowly moving back to where I had begun- philosophy and painting my first love, long before Kerrie had come, making a mother out of me. She felt like an outcast though and often cried in the long wintry nights without any reason. I knew it though, but couldn't do anything. I was driftwood who knew the banks but could not dock. Why? I never could answer myself. Why did I not hold on to my daughter? Perhaps I gave back what I got from my mother. Kerrie suffered and grew fast; an adult in the first year of her life on this earth, her sucking my breasts was the last of our relation. She sucked my nipples as if under an obligation. I knew it dam well, I am the mother. I tried to bridge the gap but ended in widening it; slowly she refused my milk or I retreated in my shell. What difference it makes now? But at that time it pained me to see my little girl search solace outside my bosom. Kashi it was who provided her calm; the two it seemed shared a childhood. Ekaba tried to intervene but I refused to listen. I needed space to grow, always, even now, when I had certain responsibilities to keep up with. The choice was there, it was my picking that mattered, I did give it time to think and find the proverbial middle path. O! Buddha, the first of the Pragmatist I fell back on Buddhism and its invocation of Nothingness as given by Nagarjuna. So it was Monk living for me which angered Ekaba all the more. He said that when I was a born Hindu why have I to fall back on other religion. Look at all these people who visit our country they search for Buddhist temples ignoring Hindus in their own country. I listened to him with patience and replied that Buddhism is the religion of the world whereas Hinduism was full of trite education and snobs like him. He stopped talking to me that day and for days to come. I lived in a hostile environment; all the forces being aligned against me. It did not stop me from carrying on with my research but one day, I would never believe that I lived a day like this. Kerrie came on her fours and sat beside me giggling like a baby monkey. I ignored her and kept to my books. She wouldn't' stop, in fact she climbed on to my lap, her fingers playing with my hairs. I let her. She saw it as a sign of encouragement and proceeded to explore my shoulder and head climbing them as a staircase. No sooner had she pulled a leg up her left, on to my shoulder she fell with a thud on the rough ground I sat on. Her head came crashing down. She was as still as a wicked night without cries or the tears. Her mouth open wide as if her jaws had been locked she had stopped breathing. At first I thought it was some trick of hers but she lay like that for a few moments longer worrying the heck out of me. I ran out to look for Ekaba. He was nowhere to be found. I shouted his name with tears welling inside me but he was not there; next Kashi I searched her hut but it was empty too. Seeing me in a state of panicky Chiru started barking which attracted the attention of a few villagers who were passing by they stopped and I told them the problem. They panicked too and ran to the village square to get help. Kerrie's eyes were turned inside out. So was this the end I begged god, praying in my cries as tears rolled from my eyes. I lay on the hut door for a long time how long I don't remember but soon Ekaba appeared with a motley group of villagers and his magic worked, as always, for Kerrie was up and crying soon. That was the best music I have heard for my entire life none can surpass the peace it gave, no amount of prayer or god's songs would, just a loud cry of my daughter was enough to make me live again and I hugged the little girl saying I was sorry and cried myself like a flood. Kashi had come and she cried too and I could see moisture in the eyes of Ekaba who laid a hand on my shoulders as I looked up meeting him in the eyes and said sorry to him. Promise me you would look after that girl, never leaving her the way you did, he demanded. Never, I said as a promise or an injunction but I said never. Soon it was her birthday then that we all, meaning the entire village looked forward to. There was huge preparation and Kashi cooked up delicacies, the villagers decorated the hut, in the temple a prayer meeting was held and abulations offered to the fire. It was the feast time at night, a large fire was lit and the entire village danced till late into the night singing songs and Kerrie was loaded with presents: homemade sugar candies, embroidered frocks, crochet hankies, dolls with colorful dresses, a wooden cartwheel, red ribbons and pink pajamas, baby soap from the city. Ekaba presented her a copy of the Bhagvad –Geetha. Kashi had knitted beautiful tiny woolen socks for her, which little Kerrie grew found of. So that was my daughter's first birthday. I missed my parents that day but thought it wise to keep the secret for a little longer. I sat outside the hut beside a fire thinking of him when I heard a voice. I was too tired to answer it so kept quiet. It came again, a little frantic this time but I kept to myself refusing to leave the comforts of the fire, thinking of my parents and of him and questioning myself that wouldn't it had been beautiful had he been with his daughter. The voice came from my back again, right into my left ear startling me. I called Chiru..shooo…shoo. I said. The lazy Bhutia dog wagged his tail, gave a look of scorn and went back to his slumber. I picked up a burning wood and turned to face the intruder.

Cover your head least the dew gives you a headache, a voice commanded. An uncouth, ill dressed, youngish man in early twenties stood behind me with a shiver for a language. Cold it is and the fire looks all so you know what he said; can I he looked into my eyes. I was taken aback by his over the top ways so did not answer him. He sat nearby and extended his hands over the fire warming them like one cooks chapattis over the coals, each side one at a time. I am a traveler, he announced with magnanimity of a king. I am Meera I replied almost instinctively, which surprised me, looking at him through the corners of my eyes. The tiredness of the day getting into me, making me sleepy, I, nevertheless felt a tingle pass through my spine. I am Krishna then, he laughed, you certainly look like one, except a marked one; have you seen her, I asked. No, he replied but all girls are Meera; your mole on the right cheek just below the nose makes you a slightly different Meera. But are all men Krishna I asked? He laughed and said that I knew how to handle men, this made me laugh too; you are interesting I said. You are beautiful he replied, looking at my turned back, piercing me with his gaze. I knew I glowed under my motherhood and the fire threw its redness on my cheeks, like the sprinkle of embers, my hairs waved in the winds, like untamed passions. The village stay had made me fairer and despite my pregnancy my figure was taut and slender. So you find me attractive I asked of him? Like an oasis in the Himalayas, he spoke in a husky hungry voice. What sought of simile is that I asked? I have been walking for months across the mountains but found none as mesmerizing as you, though people talk that the *Apsaras*- the celestial nymphets live in the higher Himalayas you are the first one I found, he was huskier now. This is called flirting if I am not wrong in expressing myself. Cavorting, he corrected me. Oh no! but you are simply out of this world he whispered. I know I whispered back. We both laughed in whispers. In my heart a flutter had taken root growing ever so slowly like the wintery night or a monsoon climber or like an intense dream which seeks immediate fulfillment. I reclined with a sigh on the surface near the fire, my wrap falling from my bosom revealing my round mounds. He seemed embarrassed and looked the other way. I closed my eyes feeling secure under his gaze. The wind had gained in velocity and blew from the snow bound mountain ranges beating on the faces of us both like foreplay; needling us with the sharpness of passions. It put me into a state of blissful somnolence, my eyes failing to keep the lids open, so despite the freezing night I slept under his watchfulness and the orange warmth of the fire which was kept burning by him. The dew fell like rain but I lay in half a slumber, like a sleep refusing to sleep. The sweet intoxication of a man's company making me wet from inside. It was a pleasant night; the one in which I slept with a strange wish in my heart. His youth was wild and pungent like a mountain herb whose qualities are a matter of conjecture unless a closer scrutiny is undertaken. Off course it could be poisonous but then what is life without a little danger or an awakening of a primeval instinct. When I woke he was not around and I looked for him expectantly. He, it seemed had vanished in thin air. It was Kerrie then I didn't tell him about. Nor did I share my night's excess with anyone, keeping it as a secret of a phantom heart. I lay under the sun catching up with the lost last night's sleep when suddenly he appeared all drenched in water. Are you mad I shouted at him it is cold and you dipping in the Alakahnanda aqua, I admonished him, which he seemed to enjoy like an errant child. He smiled and said that the water was warm like last night. I blushed at his insistence. He saw Kerrie and asked who she was. What do you mean who she is; my daughter off course, I challenged him in my own way. Or, the princess number two he asked in all his innocence; his eyes piercing me with their urgency. I told him to shut up as the old man Ekaba is around. At that precise moment Kashi came out of her hut and I was a sought of fumbling like a teenager and introducing him to her; he is Krishna I stammered. Am I? Just because you are Meera doesn't give you a right to call every other man Krishna he said in a ruthless tone. Then he turned towards Kashi and wished her a Namaste by folding his hands in humility. I am Annant he announced, the corners of the eyes looking at my reaction. Are you? I shouted before Kashi could reply; he is lying I said. I am Annant he repeated. Kashi turned blue under his antics and mumbled her reply then got busy in her daily chores. I accosted him saying why he had lied to me. So had you he said. To which I asked him that whether he was a clairvoyant he laughed for a long time; your eyes are a giveaway he said laughing. Worst liar, but the best lair; he said. All are, including you, who is this girl? He eyed Kashi. Dare you, I warned him. I have met your Ekaba he seemed impressed with me. Oh! He is a gullible old yogi I said but I am not. What, may I ask is the purpose of your visit I asked him. Do you know the purpose, he countered me. Offcourse I replied with a dignity; I have read a lot, has been a *Sadhavi* and now a mother. I showed off my achievements like trophies. Good for you but where the father is he poked me where it hurt. I winced back at my defeat, he is out there busy with his quest, I answered him quietly. Has he left you he asked? He picked Kerrie; that is easy you weigh things way to much but this little girl is a blast I wish I were a little younger he smiled. Mr. Annant, I shouted now. Only if you could mind your business, I warned him. How about you mend your ways? He was calm as he played with Kerrie, who took an instant liking for the youth. How dare you I said, I am fine, I cried. Then where is Mr. Meera he asked? I am Aditi I called out loud and now get out of this place, I shouted in my exasperation. I will but let me rest here for a few days; he suddenly became sober and begged me. I relented, all right I said you can, but keep up to yourself, I will feed you, then can sleep in Kalpi's hut. Feed! he eyed my mounds; who is this Kalpi, he gave a sly smile. A fisherman I laughed and left him in his wonderment. This, then, was Annant, I must confess, I liked his wild ways; my kind of guy, impulsive and sensuous. In his company I felt all womanly all over again; going out on long walks with him and in one instance holding his hands. It was like seducing the youth; even Kerrie took a liking to him finding in him certain fatherly touches, though I thought he was quite unlike a father would be, you know the vagrant, or the proverbial vagabond, not the settling types. He was a philosopher, pursuing yoga, his common refrain being; creativity is the real thing, he lived his hypothesis with a disdain for testing the same. Is it I asked him one day and he said yes advising me to take up some. I said I was a painter; he was pleasantly surprised and we got down in to talking about the neo- art movement and even Hussein; for whom he advocated a Bharat Ratna; what of the respect for sensibilities of the religiously minded, I challenged him. What of them; damn, creativity is the supreme religion, the oneness of all being, he shouted. But painting the gods in nude is taking this art bit a bit too far, I ventured. Let an artist be his own judge, surely the old painter would find a way, he conciliated. It was Ekaba who kept a distance from him, finding youth as a competition tough to overcome. Kashi took a liking for him and sang songs for him; her moroseness lifting its misty presence for a brief while. It was a smooth winters, passed as they did without the rancor or repellency of nowhere moments; till he decided to move on, as the spring knocked. He had become a part of the amorphous family that I had now; so his going would leave a vacuum. I told him so; come along with me, he said with a straight face. I was surprised by his nonchalance. Come on he coaxed me, maybe we find him he smiled. Would we I asked? He whispered something which I didn't hear but his offer made me think. I knew Kerrie could be looked after by Kashi. It had been a long time since I set foot out of this village. I sought Ekaba's view; he was too busy in his world of an organized system he was planning to put up at the holy river town so he treated my enquiry as a matter of minor nature which strengthened my resolve to go with Krishna or Annant, or whosoever he was. On a springy morning with the sun rising in its summery slumber, we hit the trek, so to say. The first thing he told me was that he was Krishna and not Annant so I am Meera or Radha and Aditi all rolled in one and I am proud of my motherhood, I sought of warned him off. In the wilderness we walked, climbing on the mountains with ease, at nights we camped near the villages, separate tents though, because I wouldn't trust his instincts. He pinned for me I could see it and once in those tough climbs I offered him my hand and he refuse to let go once he held on to it. At night we sat around the fire under the starry sky I could see the smolder in his eyes but that is what is youth all about I said to myself and told him so. He laughed aloud, you are young too, he said and then he told me that he had met him, my paramour or a night's stand in. This surprised and irritated me all at the same time, why the hell did you not tell me this before, I cried at him. Why I should have, he said, what I get; I have given things for free all my life now no more. I am least concerned what and how you have lived, I was livid. Then to hell with you all he said and slept in a huff. I didn't sleep the whole night, sitting by the fire and thinking how destiny makes one to face situations like a fiction. In the morning he was somber and said sorry. I met him in my treks last year, he said, I know him from my childhood Agastaya that is what he has for a name, works in a government department at Haridwar, he told me all he could. I was on a trek one day, when I heard a sound of a fall. It was he, lying in the bushes all bruised up. I brought him out, and we walked across the mountains for a few days, together. We went to a village got drunk on the local liquor and he said something about meeting a girl and things happening all on their own in the morning she was gone, he was crying. Poor Agastaya searched everywhere and then went back taking it as a one off case of a deathly destiny. I was wandering along the mountains when a strange force pulled me into your village, then you know the rest, he closed his eyes under the sun. I went to him and ruffled his hairs. He melted in my arms and sobbed like a child. I know how men are and what they seek, so I let him snuggle in my bosom till he was back to his cheerful self. Let us go, he got up in a hurry, we have to go to the river town and meet him, that much I owe it to him and to you. Would you do it for free or is there a price I have to pay I asked eying him and teasing him with my slipping wrap, revealing my clef of the breasts. He grew red and flushed in his nervousness scratching on his pimples. Don't, I ordered like a mother and he pulled me closer, looking into my eyes, his lips twitched in a queer way, his heart beating with an intense regularity, then he embraced me for a while and let go. Let us go, he said. We trekked for days again, this time with a definitive destination. He seemed irritated with this business of definiteness and told me that he has wanderlust and doesn't like fixed targets, but then things are to be done, focus on the journey. We would I suggested which made him happy and he gaily ran across the verdant valleys chasing butterflies and plucking flowers. I followed him and both of us became children creating mayhem of sought in the wilderness. O! He made me live the fun and freedom, coming as it did after my first child, opened me to the life I had envisioned for myself until Kerrie had come and now I was going back to the system which would ultimately chain me for good. I told him of my fears. It was then I came to know of him as a born rebel; dam to Agastaya or Kerrie he slogan-shouted; you lead life the way you want he said. Isn't what this century stands for he asked? Like me he was; this glued us both for the rest of the journey, keeping us close and in a healthy camaraderie, though I knew in his heart, deep, deeper than he knew, I could perceive there was a tinge of longings for me. A few years separated us, he being younger and full of brim and trim I was a woman on a wane after motherhood. I told him so, he said that the glow on my cheeks was lovely like a morning blush or like the buds of red roses or, I smiled and told him to shut up. He didn't and held my hands as we climbed down the valleys, closing it on the river town and my daughter's father who, according to Krishna or Annant was a long way away from matters of the world. Would he be able to live up to your or Kerrie's expectations; he created a doubt in my mind. Stop pestering my soul I told him and he sulked like a child. Look it has been like this with me for ages I do good to others and in return I get kicks on my ass, he complained. I listened to him patiently and said that it has been like this for ever for everyone, none would be good to you, so better stop all this and lead your life and I went on to narrate my story of life. He heard me with an attention of a student and then bowed to me and said that he has decided to work for himself, from now onwards perhaps create something, write a book, and even teach for a living. I was happy for him, following him, as he led me to the one with whom destiny had tied me to. It was at the end of the seventh day of our trek that I realized that his feelings for me were much more than I had fathomed. He searched a parent in me and I being a fresh recruit on matters parenting readily obliged him with my love and care. It was a dangerous path I had tread, for with passionate youth one can never be sure of trust. It so happened that we ran into a cloud burst which was rather unusual for spring but it rained in torrents and we sought refuge in a dilapidated building on the outskirts of a hill township. It was dark and the thunder played a truant. We hid ourselves under the falling walls, without food or light, in the pitch darkness; we were a kind of close and his hands brushed by breasts. I ignored it owing it to the dark night and the fearful rains. Slowly his hands moved closer inside my clothing, his touch tingling me to the core, caressing my womanhood. I laid back and enjoyed his touch, then he bent down on me and kissed me on my lips and I entwined around him like a climber. He was excited and almost uncontrollable like a horse and pumped up all over me. I let him and then he lay all spent and wet. The rains fell with a sweet intensity. I was feeling fresh in the morning which was sunny and glowing, when he came up to me and apologized. What for, I cried; for everything he had said. I sat down in a thump and looked at him. Your guilt childhood has been ingrained in you; stainless it, then can only you move forward, I said. I was cold and he was quiet for a long while and then he spoke in a soft tone as if accepting defeat from what, I didn't ask, nor did he tell. We resumed our journey, this time a distance having cropped in between us, each kept to oneself. I was, though, a little excited, going back to the river town of Haridwar, for a different reason this time. He was morose and even irritable; now, that is a problem with youth, downcast once they see that things aren't moving their way they fall back to imploring themselves and blaming the rest. Like in Annnant's case, so he pestered me with his complains about his friends, his family and all the girls in his life. It sought of got in to my nerves, so I let him have a piece of my mind saying that he can very well cry if he has to, in hell. It bugged him and he said that I was all talk and no concrete, a balloon full of pseudo air and that even my paramour was not looking for me, it was up to him to find him and all that. Heck! I cried you are a male for a bastard; until married, all women are bitches, he let go. We fought all along the way, seldom putting of the ignited passions of that night, though, he had a way with woman I knew and kept a safe distance, never nearing me. This country and its culture is safe for a woman, no machismo to deal with, I concluded and told him so. This made him laugh finally, why girl you are right, I hadn't given it a thought, he said and held my arms, drooling his voice and sang an inane song about my eyes being beautiful and my hairs like clouds and so on, then he told me that sensuous world is a real is not a no no . *Maya* all

Kaya- the physical and the soul, is a part of it; it could be the other way too, I countered. Yes you are right, he agreed, matters spiritual usually come first he said. Ah! The man has something in him I thought and said that one day he would be a great man; funny man you are, he said, where are the men in this century he asked all are appliers of the cream white, they play cricket and watch television he said. I laughed right O! I said males are consigned to the flames of womanhood; damn dim wit, seed sowers, who needs them anyway. You do, you are looking for that guy without a gut, he teased me. O! him, that is for Kerrie, I fumbled for a reply. Is it, he asked or you want an encore of the date blind. Shut up, you are a devil I said and held on to his arms; his proximity giving me a sense of safety. I think all woman need that, despite all this talk of feminism, they are born to live an organized life and not on the wilder side of things, hell they need a dose of conformity in their lives, so what; they are the champions of humanity, though it all depends on what sought of companion they get. It made me circumspect regarding, what was his name, Agastaya, a one off night could be a sweet accident, but to be together for the remaining of the living days with the same guy and god knows what sought of guy, he was a zombie, thought I. I asked of my apprehensions to Annant, he said I was right, that guy is a yogi, only he knows what he wants and usually gets it. See he did not look up for you, having had the pluck of the bud, let it suck, he said, in an alarming tone, adding to my fear. That is a fact my darling of detours, he said, but now we take a rickety hilly bus from here, he announced as we reached a small town on the national highway-72. Do you have any money he asked? I said no; neither do I, he laughed. Aren't we living a life of wrong, even in an era of capitalism, no money, then how do we travel he asked. We borrow, isn't capitalism all about borrowing, right from the government to the business, men all borrow and then lend in return, I replied. Point noted he smiled so we searched for some nice soul to lend us the dough, no one did. Are you an anti-social element I admonished him, nobody coming forward to help you. What of you; you are a woman, act as if all is lost and the world would be at your feet, he suggested. You mean beg, I was incredulous. Yes it is monk style you see. We sat with our haggard looks on the pavements begging for a few hundred rupees but by the evening we collected eighty-six rupees; good going let us eat something he said and we spent all in having a sumptuous dinner at a *Dhaba* and slept in a temple. Next morning I told him that I wouldn't beg for the life of me and that he had to find a way out, so he said that his father is the boss of animal kingdom being a vet. He was so why not ask the help of the resident vet he might, my old man is a Good Will hunter you see, let us cash some, he said. Dam you, why didn't you think of it yesterday, going through the embarrassment of begging. Two reasons, he reasoned: one, that now you are going to live a life of your husband asking him for money to spend and two, begging breaks the check dams of ego. Ah! The savant Mr. Annant I shouted at him as we entered an old building which housed the hospital for cows, a few of them stood on line waiting to be inseminated artificially from the best bulls of the West of Germany province of Helid..urbg, the poor doctor missed his pronunciation, though he was proud of the yeoman services he was doing for the people of this hill state. I stay in the remote, sitting alone and looking after the cattle he said but are you paid I asked him. Yes he said; good Annant said lend us a few, we got to reach Haridwar. Why spend money, he suggested, he was the saver, another misnomer in a capitalists system, spending is the game; but I would arrange for a lift in a truck which brings our medicine, you both will be comfortable in it. I eyed Annant and nodded my head in a no but Annant seemed to like the idea, a wild ride would be perfect end to this journey he said. I wouldn't have agreed no less, it started early in the morning with the mini-truck, phenol reek suffocating me and the driver all alcohol laden like a sponge, driving on the long, winding road with hair-pin bends and the road without the parapets or filled with boulders from landslides. He is an expert Annant consoled me as I hung for the life of me on the nylon thread that was tied across the hollow of the truck. Is he I queried? Yes, in matters of the drink, look how he drives drunkenly, he laughed with gayness. You are a carp I scolded him, we could have hired a cab and told him to pay, your friend I said. He laughed, forget him and save yourself; he was enjoying the journey, more so my uneasiness. Let the truck fall into the valley, I shouted over the gurgling of the diesel engine. He continued to laugh and said that poor guy, his friend, wasn't lucky, will not die before being pestered by me. You suck! I cried as if I am so, we bantered along; he was not a not very nice guy but good in parts. I didn't wish to know his whole, for he was under the process of evolution. I was happy I did business with him, what with his humor and an easy demeanor; like sadism, he whispered, as if reading my mind, in my ear when the truck turned on one of the bends bringing him closer to me. Yes, I agreed, so much for your machismo.

"*Rama* was the next to come out of the churning of the ocean", Ekaba continued his ponderous rendition of the Kumbh story. What off me? I thought, never really got a chance to, but the goddesses *Rama*, whom we know as *Luxmi.* She chooses lord Vishnu as her paramour amongst the gods that stood waiting for her benedictions; Ekaba said. Who choose him for me? Destiny perhaps, I must be aging; laying the blame on this maiden of fate. He received me rather coldly or so I felt. Maybe I had wished for a different degree of warmth; anyways the way was clear for our knowing each other on a mundane plain, I thought I knew him what he was. I am Agastaya he said in a matter-of-factly tone. I am Aditi I said in a reply. We sat for long hours on the banks of the river Ganga and I told him about my life as Meera or about certain mundane details. He heard me with a patience of a lover; then he asked me about Kerrie which made me long for my daughter. Yes you are a mother now, he said. So we went to his parents' and finalized a date to get married. My parents had come to complete their duty. We got married in a temple according to the Vedic rituals; all mandatory seven vows with seven times encircling the fire and the offerings and promises and all. It was all very nice to hear the priest render the chants and the mantras. Then he applied a vermilion strip on my forehead and I touched his feet. Why? I did give it a thought but at that moment it seemed all to justified, so I went by the flow. On our first night, the first after nuptials, we talked the whole night holding hands and watching the stars. Early in the morning he sat for his yoga and I joined him. Good for me I thought, getting something to learn. He took me as his student, which I did not mind, he being the loadstar. For his first sermon he decided to bring Kerrie back from the mountain village. This time we took a cab and reached the village where Ekaba had planned a little party for us. We visited the temple, with Kerrie holding on to Agastaya who seemed a trifle ill at ease but managed to put up a brave face. Kashi was impressed on my choice when we gossiped like girls. You should tie the proverbial knot too, I told her, she smiled wanly, then who would look after Ekaba she asked. Yes she was right, only that Ekaba was getting younger, as he discussed his plans with Agastaya who wasn't' convinced but kept up a straight face. It was soon time to go back and we departed with a promise to meet whenever any of us was willing and not pressed by matters of the world. I had a few tears in my eyes as if I was leaving my home, my family. It matters a lot for a girl, her house, before she acquires one of her own and raises a family. It was tough, he made it easy though, not fun, for he was rational being lacking the in depth emotionality of relations. All relations are spiritual, he claimed. I didn't argue, getting sucked into the whirlpool of a home. Soon his parents came to live with us and Kerrie had a second mother in her grandmother. This is how this country functions two mothers and many fathers to look after a child. I was free to join painting classes and soon the brush strokes gained momentum. He was alright with my passion but I was not agreeing with his *Sadhuness* and his emphasis on fate or his concept of satisfaction. It was on a Diwali day that we had our first tiff, not argument I had told you, he never talked. I blabbered along then he asked what it was I wanted. I said a decent living. He said we already had one. I said more money, some fashion wear and a travel. He said that I was talking like those socialites who wasted themselves. I argued that women are like that, never satisfied with what they get; it is the way god has made us. He was silent and left in a huff. I was surprised by my diatribe; so this is what to be a woman is I thought and then busied myself in the pursuits of Kerrie, who I must confess grew fast and quite like me ignoring me and keeping to her group of toddlers. I was back to painting and to supplement the family income started tutoring the neighborhood kids. It was fun, the business of teaching, it raised my level of consciousness; with time though I felt a need for a bigger stage and I told Agastaya so. He said that I should be patience. I blew my top on his remark; to hell with you and I went off sat on the banks and wept. It is hard to face up the reality of being stifled. It was the time when I drifted from Kerrie, who found solace with her grandparents. I objected, saying that they were spoiling my daughter. This flared up a family war of sorts. I lamented on my dependency. Agastaya took me to a movie that day and we had some *Chaat* at the Burra Bazaar he bought a jasmine flower bead for me. I was happy now; that is what with woman is, easily placated or even gullible, but he was my husband so he must be right, I convinced myself. Kerrie, it was, who pulled at me when I had decided to move on from this joint family routine and pestered Agastaya to look for a separate roof. He was angry and said that how two homes are justified in the same town. I said to hell with your rational views or sense of duty, I need space, you have only check dams; they are in the mind he said; your yoga sucks I said, my future has been blackened by you, so it went on for long creating an air of tension which effected Kerrie, who became a recluse, shunning her friends. It made me feel guilty and Nina was the first to point this to me. I included my daughter in my creations, not leaving her on the mercy of the destiny; all creative mothers tend to ignore their children I told the class one day. I don't agree Nina stood up saying that parents have a way with sucking all from their children and that every child is sick, at the most, if it has unsupportive parents. She was right but her death is an example for us all, though at that time I fought for parents' rights and said that it is they who make all the sacrifice, to which Nina replied that children don't need nothing but a little compassion and understanding not pushing and prodding towards the wrong mountain. I shut her up saying that she was creating a hill out of a mole. She missed the classes for a few days and then came, one day, painted a rebel on a canvass and said that Annant sir is right. So now I knew who her influence was, the wild eastern boy, now a Sir! Well, strange, but I longed for the youth as Agastaya polished his practice. I did meet him once when he was smoking a joint, his beard was little grey and he had dark marks on his face giving him a look of a cowboy; rugged and tough. He was happy and offered me a cigarette; come of it I said, dare I dare myself, then I took a swig; you sure have a way of spoiling women I said. He laughed hoarsely, I make them rebel he said, at least they would rise from the mediocrity of the society; a horde herded mentality, but you are mother, good, no need to be a wife, that is the work of the man, to make a wife of a woman. And a mother I added. No not at all, mother they would be, look at the Hindu mythology, all characters were created by divine intercourse; like Arjuna or Karna or even the lord Ramchandra, all were test tube babies, none having a steady father, but a divine and a truer mother. Your theory is blasphemous at best, I said. Get stoned and you would be singing my paeans he challenged me. I was, indeed, after a few pulls on the white stick, filled with a Marijuana punch, you are a fuckin ladies man, this Nina I asked. It made him twitch his lips, you too, he was suddenly sad, she has a streak, like you, I just want her to succeed, he said. Or else, I asked. He was quiet. This emotion, shun them for good I said. Yes *Mata Hari* he smiled and went away. In my home things were not normal, I tried but found that this family system was not for me and I told Agastaya. What can be done now he asked; live with what you are ordained with. I was pissed off and cried that he could be my husband at least once and not a teacher. What difference that makes, he asked. I kept quiet and vowed to not to talk much; when the man is not ready to listen then why waste words. It went about like this for a few weeks then one day I was down with what I thought at first was flue, but the fever refused to subside and my strength waned. He was worried as hell and took me to a doctor, then used all his knowledge of Ayurveda and yoga to cure me. I liked the way he was punctual in giving me my daily medicine or maintaining a strict regimen of diet and all, the best part was how he held my hands when I was in a delirious state, often waking up at night, but he never left my bedside all these days sitting on a jute couch, backless and all but he was erect in his glow, going about through the duty of looking after me. It was a month for which I lay in bed and he did all he could to bring me back to life. He succeeded but the moment I was normal he was back to his reticent best. I understood him better this time around that is what it is with staying together and interacting one tends to know more of the same person. I soon forgot all about my illness and was back to my rebel ways painting and all. Annant helped me arrange an exhibition at a local community hall and I was able to sell a few of them for a few thousand rupees. I was happy but not content; I knew I had in me to do more. One day I mailed a guy from Mumbai who ran an art centre, he asked me to send some photographs of my paintings, which I did and the very next day, when was it? Yes, last week, he invited me for a show at Mumbai. This was my big break, I said so to Agastaya. He was quiet; why not evolve a bit more, there is a room for much improvement. I was aghast this man is insensitive I thought; you are not a judge of art Mr. Agastaya, I said people from Mumbai have given me a call and here you are jealous of my achievement, go to hell. I stomped out from the house. I thought it over and found that it was the whim of my husband to criticize me, not in a constructive manner, though and I should do something. So I called the Mumbai guy Nicholus Tulli to pay a visit to Haridwar. He was more than willing sightseeing, on the sly, he said and he was on the next flight. I received him and put him in a hotel at my expense. So this is it then, he said when I said that my husband doesn't have a high opinion of me. He said that in India it is this way only, male ego, you should go ahead and be a winner, your paintings are so religious he said. I was flabbergasted, religious I said, man are you from arts or do you represent a church, I asked. I paint feelings and perceptions. All the same he said, they should sell, make money like the Hussian guy, why not paint something controversial, he said. Man this is Haridwar, we could create a storm you and I; he laughed. Would it be good I asked him in doubt. Leave it to me, he held my hand, I would manage, you just paint better still, go where the market is, this town is good for the business of spirituality but the metros are the best to sell your talent. What of creativity I asked him? What of it; paint as is your wont, it is your duty to present it to the world, for people to see. Now this man was a good salesman, selling his idea to me, I fell for him sooner than I had thought, the glitter catching me when the hormones were subsiding. The first thing I did was to inform Agastaya, who was reticent with his views, try it he said, laconically. I would, I definitely would, I raised a ruckus, which made my mother-in law intervene; this was something new, for his parents kept to their religious pursuits and seldom commented on our tiffs, but this time my mother-in-law sat with me during the kitchen chores and said that it is the duty of a wife to care for her husband like Sati or later Parvati did of lord Shiva. Old times mother, I said and I have my aspirations too. I left her in a huff she followed me and said that her son is a patience man but one day he might blow over. Are you threatening me, I shouted and left the house, roaming on the Ghats, listening to the temple bells and the chanting. When I came back I saw Kerrie sitting on her own; Agastaya's parents were nowhere to be seen. My daughter informed me that they had gone to the village, up in the hills. I was quite on the back foot now and when Agastaya came I told him what had happened. He laughed it off saying that this is an age old problem in India; war of the women, then he was serious suddenly, it is Kerrie who is being slighted, he remarked, yes I agreed. I can take her to Mumbai, I offered, she has a world to see, here she is just a frog in a well. Take her he said, as if laying down arms. That night he was on the roof for a long time, till the wee hours of the morning. I was worried when I saw him the next morning, drooping shoulders, inflamed eyes, wild hairs and parched, swollen lips. What happened I asked? Nothing, he smiled weakly; maybe you are right I, have not in me to be a father or a husband, I am like that he said and went to his office without having a bite. Now I may have been against him or what or demanded things like a child but dam he was my husband and seeing him like this awakened in me the need to stand by him and that is how we wives in India are touchy about their husbands. Enough is enough I thought and took Kerrie with me to the village and begged his parents to come back saying that I was sorry and all. When we reached our home late in the evening Agastaya welcomed us with a straight face and handed me a packet from Mumbai he announced. I tore open it with expectations and found two tickets and some amount of draft money. The journey begins yet again; I was happy, so was he and said that he was ready to accompany me to my goal. It was three days ago and I thought life has finally come to a logic conclusion; yes just three days ago and in these three days everything would again be turned upside down, bringing me to the point where I had started.

" Next emerged Dhanvantari with a pitcher containing the nectar of immortality which was snatched by the Devils so the *Devas* requested the lord Vishnu to do something; the lord did, Ekaba spoke with labored albeit measured tone like a general who may have been defeated in a battle but who knew that the battle could have been won only by losing, "the lord took the Avatar of a beautiful damsel who oozed sensuality thus blinding the *Asuras* with passions; stop fighting the damsel said and let me help you in distributing the nectar, so the damsel told them to line up and let the *Devas* join you, she ordered, so the gods and the devils lined up and the damsel started distributing the nectar beginning with the gods"

It was not the first time I was hearing the story but for Ekaba it would be the last time. He told me this. That was three days ago. You are the only one I could fall upon he said as I sat in his huge and ostentatious ashram; a modern oxford he claimed. What of this Hindu business, I asked? Yes, it worries me, though when I started it I was keen to make it in to a *Gurukul* based learning system, slowly though and I don't know when it became overtly religious, he said with pain. You could stop and restart I said. Too late, he replied, my time has come, won't live in a physical form through the Kumbh fair. I was quiet, not that it made me sad or what, after all life and death are hardly different. This is it then, I said, the endgame. No, he said, it starts now, look after this ashram when I go; you have it in you to do so. Kashi could I suggested without refusing his last wish. No she can't nor could Swami Chintan nand, for he has a political axe to grind, you are pure and then Agastaya can help you. I thought for a while then said that I have to discuss the issue with my husband, what I didn't tell him was that in a few days I would be chasing my dream of childhood and in the process open a window for my daughter to see the world, away from the claustrophobic existence of the small town. How could I? The old man was running his final lap and I owed my life and my daughter's too, to him. We would go after the dip in the Ganga, the one o'clock flight from the Jolly-Grant airport, near Dehra Dun, tomorrow Agastaya had told an excited Kerrie.

" the damsel distributed the nectar in such a way that when the turn of the *Asuras* came the pitcher was empty but the devil *Rahu* sat between the sun god and the moon god and drank a few drops of the nectar and became immortal," Ekaba was keyed up, "the gods pointed this to the lord Vishnu who beheaded him; even now, because *Rahu* was immortal, he eclipses the sun and the moon who had pointed his presence amongst the gods. "So how does it all make Kumbh an important festival." he asked the stunned audience. "Well," he answered himself his question "during the skirmish between the devils and the gods the nectar from the pitcher called the Kumbh fell at four places; the holy river Ganga at Haridwar being one of them and from then on anybody who takes the dip in the waters of the Ganga during the Kumbh fair gains immortality" Ekaba fell silent, his eyes were closed and he breathed with difficulty. I watched him as the devotees shouted *Jai Maa Ganga…Har..Har.. Mahadeva…Jai Vishu Baghwan…* It was Kashi who rushed to his aid as I sat among the crowd with red rose petals being showered on them. I closed my eyes in a prayer.

Kerrie pulled at my hand Maa..Maa… Ekaba..Baba Ekababa…. She cried.

GATHA

It has been a tiring day, Kashi thought. But then the next four months would be so. Four; she shuddered. Karma comes at a price. Ekaba insisted on her joining him for the Kumbh Fair. What for? She had asked with due regards reserved for the teacher- And then followed him. One has to listen to the guru and not question his ways. It had been like this since she was a child-when Ekaba had taken upon himself to Parent her. He found her in one of the river fairs; pink frocked, red ribbon tying her hairs and a doll lying on her shoulder; its hairs disheveled.

She cherished the quiet life of the village: Gauchar. The river Alaknanda flowed through it. Legend has it that once up on a time the queen of Indore, on her annual pilgrimage to the lord Badrinath, camped near the banks of the river amidst the vast green fields and Mango orchard. On one of her evening stroll, she sees a villager beating a cow with all his might. She calls the man and asks him the reason for his violence against the holy mother of the milk. She enters my fields and eats up my standing crop, the villager answers in his anger. From today all these fields will belong to the cows; who would be free to graze on them, saying this she hands him a bag of gold coins. Since then the village is called Gau-Char: the land of cows' grazing. Kashi liked the idea of a place belonging to the cows; no ownership of human ego. A snow fed blue stream divided the village into two, before it drained into the main river of Alaknanda. On one side of it was the human habitation of twenty-five families and on the other was a mango orchard; a nature's present, and hence owned by none; with a spattering of a few Lokut and Lithchi trees. Kashi swung between the religious cacophony of the river town and the quietude of the village on the Alaknanda stream village. It was the freedom to move about in close proximity of nature and be able to contemplate on life and the ensuing vagaries that attracted her. For long hours she sat under the mango grove and, in the summer season gnawed on the yellow fleshy fruit. She took long walks across the valley, collecting the wood figurines; which had floated downstream with the flash floods of the monsoon and lay like fallen treasures on the slopes of the hills or on the banks of the stream, hidden under the loess and sand: A bird, a spear, a snake, Hollow bamboo for a flute, a natural candle stand, an eye, roots like an old man's head, wood bangles and ear rings, Characters from Grandma's tale. She collected them all along with polished lime stones and granite pebbles that lay like bounty on the banks. Isolated Families.

In her spare time she scribbled her thoughts; wishes and dreams; life and times. It kept her sane despite her loneliness. And she had time for her Practice; the yoga *Sadhana*. Life, despite the accompanying loneliness, that afflicts human without any umbilical attachments; was one to be cherished for the sheer joy of nature. With Ekaba to guide her, she evolved. Then Aditi came along followed by Kerrie, and Ekaba changed.

In the autumn; he was all of seventy-five years; of his life, had a wish to establish a sect of his own version of Hinduism. Time to have a following of my own, he announced it to Kashi. Is it necessary to have a formal system of imparting spiritual education? She had questioned him thus? Dear girl, the market calls, if we won't somebody else would. Capitalism requires some sort of organizational set up. How are we to work without an organization? Yoga is after all, all about Karma and the excellence therein. He was adamant. You would be the secretary and head the Discourses Division; he directed her as a CEO of a newly formed firm. She followed.

Today she was the story-teller; in the mould of the popular and traditional mode of rendering the stories from the great scriptures: Puranas, Bhagvad, Rama Charitra Manas, Mahabharat, Shiva Purana.

The stage was set. Ekaba worked swiftly. And within no time he ran a huge system patronized by the rich and the famous. Media was used effectively and the Public Relations Unit worked overtime. Old Ekaba of the Mango stream village was the new God-Man.

Today Kashi had to render the story of the birth of the River Ganga. She rehearsed the folklore she believed in as true. It had to be done, she thought, in the best possible manner. She would sit on the wooden, muslin covered stage, sprinkled with red Rose petals and Marigold flowers. A public address system would be at place and thousands would sit attentively to listen to her.

She wondered at the use of technology to further the cause of religion. Television, mobile phones and the loudspeaker had made religion a household passion. Once upon a time they were at loggerheads. Foes turned friends. She smiled as she applied vermillion dot on her forehead, followed by three layers of turmeric finger-prints. Her hairs were tied on by the beads of the white Jasmine flowers. She wore a yellow saffron bordered sari. Over which a cream colored woolen shawl lay, in pleats. The sudden rains had made her nostalgic about the mango stream village. It had made her live, like longings do; make one feel lively; the human touch of emotions. Only women understand the sensitivity of the soul, she concluded. Men are ambitious and ruthless. Ekaba was a man first then a Yogi.

"So you are ready for the occasion?" Ekaba asked as he entered her changing room.

"As commanded by you; my master." She answered with a subtle sarcasm; arranging the pleats of her Sari.

"It has to be done, Kashi. Life is not all black or white. Grey is the shade; like shadows." Ekaba straightened his white flowing beard. He wore an Ochre rob and turmeric and vermillion lines adorned his wide forehead. He shone under the glory of the Practice.

"Sham-doors, the shadows and all." She replied tersely.

"What? What do you mean?" He was sad when he asked.

"A farce for a fair." She said. "But that is not my calling. I have to seek your blessing." She bowed down and touched his veined feet.

"*Ayushman*." He mumbled.

A pause hung for a brief moment. Ekaba sat on a gold rimmed chair. His own; or of his anointed heir. Kashi stood quietly; like a fawning servant. She thought of Ekaba of yore without the paraphernalia of this all- Religion taking over the wheels at the end of his life cycle. What for? She searched for a reason. Yoga subsumes all; God, Religion and Philosophy. Then why was there a need to build up a system of followers or add the paraphernalia of detailed rituals? Purity of the being was being challenged. What of the Karma? Why? Her mind twirled under her doubts.

"Does all this seem inconsequential to you?" Ekaba sensed her dilemma.

"No. I have faith in you and in my practice." She answered.

"Maybe it all is so jumbled and fluid at the same time that you cannot fathom the depth of it all. Dear, be prepared for your sermon; your first, and remember it has to be done." Ekaba said.

"I would not fail you." She answered.

"The whole town would be here. So would Aditi be; with Kerrie." He informed her hesitatingly.

"Oh!" She mumbled in her surprise and then regaining control over herself she said, "You have indeed travelled, Ekaba, indeed you have: in the last four years."

She had reached a point from where she couldn't have possibly returned. All doors shut. There was something sinister in Ekaba when he said told her that Aditi and Kerrie would be present at the discourse. She had to move fast, least he succeeds- To fight against her guru. It was the Mahabharata that she was a part of- A battle for the ethics. But Ekaba ought to be given one last chance. Maybe he had a reason for it all. What of his bait to Aditi? Poor Kerrie. Kashi was preoccupied in her confabulation. A buzz of the crowd wakes her up from her thoughtful slumber. Time.

She sat on the Padmasana; the Lotus posture, on the adorned stage. A mass of humanity sat with expectations of a Katha: A story with a Moral. Kashi was the avatar of the Mother Ganga, herself. She began:

"Blesseth am I who tell this story of Mother Ganga...
Blesseth are you all who listen to it...
The gods have ordained us for this day...
Have faith on thee and on you, come what may.
Once upon a time, a very long time ago it was in the Tretya Yuga...
There ruled a king by the name of Satyavarta
Who became known by the name of Trishanku....
He was guilty of offences three:
Displeasing his father; the famed Tribandhana;
For forcibly carrying away a..
Brahmana girl who was recently married..
For the first sin.
Of the second, it is said...
He killed a cow belonging to his preceptor; Sage Vasistha,
The third: he ate meat without having consecrated it by sprinkling holy water...
His father cursed him turning him into a Pariah...
A Chandla fit for hell only...
Sage Viswamitra, the teacher of Satyavarta..
Through his sheer meditative power...
Sent him to heaven instead..
Gods, though, became an angry lot....
And sent him back without a thought...
Sage Viswamitra was the one not to take a defeat...
And through his extraordinary powers...
Stopped him in mid air, thus, challenging the gods.
Even to this day; the king, now known Trisanku
The one who dangles in between...
Hangs between the heaven and earth...
In the form of a star...
Trisanku's son was Harischandra...
famed for having stuck to his vow...
To pay up the Dakshina; of Sage Viswamitra

As payment for conducting a Rajasuya sacrifice...
The sage stripped Harischandra of his belongings..
Kingdom, wife and his only son.....
Sage Vasistha, King's preceptor, flew into a rage
Knowing this; challenging Sage Viswamitra for a duel....
A battle raged between the two..
Ending in a mutual curse of transforming the two into birds...
Thus Sage Viswamitra turned into Adi, a species of cranes..
And Sage Vashtitia turned into a Heron...
Emperor Harischandra, the symbol of uprightness...
In his sadness, for he had become issueless...
Sought the advice of Sage Narada, the travelling one....
The sage advised the Emperor to seek God Varuna the god of water....
The Emperor did as advised and prayed...
O! lord let a son be born to me....
And I shall propitiate you by sacrificing him to you....
And through the agency of Varuna...
A son, who was named as Rohit, was born to the Emperor..
Varuna said, O king, now that a son has been born to you sacrifice him to me ...
As promised by thee..
The king said, O lord, my son would be fit for sacrifice only when...
He becomes of the age of ten days..
Lord Varun appeared after ten days....
O! lord, the king said, my son would be fit for sacrifice...
Only when he had teethed...
And so on... and on...the king..blinded of his love ..
For his only son..
Refused to sacrifice him to Varuna as promised...
Rohit grew in years and understanding took to the woods..
To save his life...
Varuna, was angry and cursed Emperor Harischandra....
Who developed the disease of Dropsy...
On hearing of his father's predicament....
Rohit prepared to go to his home...
But was accosted by Lord Indra, the god of gods...
You will be surely sacrificed if you return....
The lord of the lords said..
Undertake a pilgrimage of all sacred lakes and rivers...
To free your father of this curse..
Rohit did as counseled....

And returned after six years with Ajigarta, whom he bought…
The lord Varuna was propitiated through him..
Relieving Emperor Harischandra of his disease..
Rohit bore a son Harit…
Champa was born of the loins of Harit…
The builder of the city of Champa….
Sudeva was born of Champa..
And Vijeya was the son of Sudeva….
Bharuka was Vijeya's son….
Whose son was Vrka…
The son of Vrka was Bhauka…
Whose land was usurped by enemies..
And forced him to retire to forests…
He died and on his pyre his wife…
Who was enceinte, prepared to ascend the burning pyre…
Sage Aurva prevented her from immolation…
The co-wives of Bhauka, out of jealously..
Administered poison to the pregnant woman..
No harm came to her due to the blessings of the Sage Aurva..
Instead a learned son, by the name of Sagara,
The one born of poison, was born..
He was a universal Monarch…
Conquered; Talajanhas, Yavanas, Sakas, Haihayas, Barbars…
His sons dug up the oceans…
On the advice of the sage Aurva…
He conducted the Ashwamedha sacrifice…
Fearing his increasing power…
Indra, the god of gods stole the consecrated horse..
Looking for the horse; the sixty thousand sons of Sagara..
From his wife Sumati…
Excavated the earth down…
While excavating, they perceived the horse…
Besides Sage Kapila: the Avatar of Sri Hari Narayan, himself…
Let this wicked fellow be killed, they shouted….
And rushed towards him with weapons…
At that moment the Sage…
Opened his eyes..
Reducing the sixty thousand sons, in all..
Into Ashes: not by Sage Kapila's anger…
But by the fire of their own body..

As the Sage was pure Sattva..
And couldn't possibly burn anyone.
There was another son of Emperor Sagar..
Born out of his second wife, Kesini..
Asamanjasa; whose son was Amsuman..
He, Sagara's grandson, was devoted to his grandfathers' interest..
Asmanjasa, though, was an evil ruler…
And threw children into the Saryu River…
He was made to depart from Ayodhya, the capital.
Emperor Sagara then commanded his grandson, Amsuman…
To look for the sacrificial horse…
And to find out the fate of his uncles.
Amsuman fixed his mind on the Lord Sri Hari…
Seeing his complete devotion…
Sage Kapilla blessed him mentally…
This horse, meant for sacrifice by your grandfather…
May be taken away by you…
But the uncles of yours lie burnt…
In need of the water of holy river Ganga…
To be redeemed; and nothing else.
Sagara completed the sacrifice and retired to forest..
Amsuman, too abdicated the throne, in favor of his son Dilipa..
Who was unsuccessful, like his father…
To bring the Ganga down to earth..
From heaven..
Bhagiratha; the son of Dilipa;
Undertook severe penance…
Goddesses Ganga; pleased from his efforts said…
I am ready to confer a boon on you…
Emperor Bhagirathi, bowed with humility and said…
Respected Ganga Mata, I need your blessings …
To propitiate my granduncles, whose ashes lie…
Without being immersed in the holy waters…
Goddesses Ganga replied, I would descend on earth…
But someone should sustain my force…
As I descend on earth piercing the crust….
I shall penetrate the sixth subterranean sphere from above…
Moreover, I am not inclined to come down…
As people will wash away their sins in to me.
Mother, Bhagiritha replied, pious souls who have..

Given up attachments to actions...
As well to their fruits...
Are pure of mind, nay...
The knower of Brahma..
Hence capable of purifying the whole world...
Shall wash off their sins ...
In your waters..
Again, Rudra, the very self of the embodied soul...
Into whom this universe is woven...
Warp and woof, as a piece of cloth into threads...
Will bear your force.
Having said this, Bhagirathi proceeded to propitiate Lord Shiva..
And in a very short span to time...
Shiva became pleased, and said, "so be it".
So said Sage Suka, while narrating this Bhagvad Story to King Parikshit.
Mother Ganga descended down to the earth...
And sat on the long hairs of the Lord Shiva.
King Bhagiratha, led the Ganga..
To the spot where his granduncles' ashes lay...
The Ganga bathed the burnt sons of Emperor Sagara...
Though burnt by their own offensive behavior towards a holy Brahmana; Sage Kapila...
The sons; all sixty thousand of them..
Ascended to heaven...
By the mere touch of the holy water.
What can then be said of those who regularly take a dip...
In the holy river...
When even the ashes of the sons of Sagara..
Rose to heaven when it came ...
In contact with the Goddesses Ganga.
What can then be said of the river...
Which has emanated from the feet...
Of the Lord Sri Hari...
And whose water has...
The power to shake off the identification with the body...
And hence...
With the three Gunas of the Prakriti.

Kashi closed her eyes. Her lips quivered under the emotions of her Bhakti. The crowd of devotees was quiet as well. Silent Seekers. Tear drops hung from the corners of their eyes.

"*Jai Maa Gange..Jai Ma Gange..*' they shouted in unison.

Aditi joined the chorus. So did Kerrie, in all her innocence.

Mr. and Mrs. Vashistha closed their eyes and clapped.

Mr. T. Namgyal sat on the front row. I could join Ekaba's ashram, after retirement, he thought.

On the last row, sat, Sameer and Jorden, stoned.

Pankaj Bhuria contemplated on religion and its mass hysteria.

Mr. Y. D. Bardhan waited for Ekaba to emerge, even when his mobile rang in a silent mode.

Swami Chintan Nandji dialed Mr. Bardhan's mobile, pick it up Babu, he swore under his breath.

Ajay Pardhan yawned, twice in quick session and wished to go back to the Naga Baba camp.

Dr. Bhardwaj saw Sameer and searched for Annant in the crowd of thousands. Mrs. Bhardwaj sat with closed eyes sipping on herbal tea which was being distributed by the Akahara. Annant walked out with wobbly steps.

Ekaba prepared for his act after waiting impatiently like a nervous actor who is relieved that finally the stage was his. He hurried to fine tune his script in the mind and cast a furtive glance at the mirror arranging his ochre robe and white flowing beard, appearances are important he thought. Last time he had conducted a Satsang and a sermon, the public had appreciated them both and donated liberally for his cause. Today it should be better, it is after all Kumbh time and like all fairs, a time to approach the market and extract the best price. He smiled not an evil smile but a scheming one. Just that now the time has come to disown the physical form-*Deh-Mukti-* the Moksh without the physical. Karma has to be done, to the last moment, he thought, there is no way of escaping the world once one is in it.

The silver white hairs floated with him as he entered the raised wooden platform that was the stage. He lit a lamp and paid floral tributes to Goddesses Saraswati and sat on the cross legged posture. One of his devotee showered rose petals on him and sang a song eulogizing him. The crowed which had swelled since evening sat in silence with closed eyes and folded hands.

"*Ayushman...*" Ekaba raised his voice and both his hands in the posture of blessings and froze for a few moments. ..Then he began.....

-My respected devotees of the lord I feel a sense of fulfillment at being given a privilege to render from my humble mouth the tale of the Kumbh which is the most important tale for us Hindus I need your blessings to carry this onerous task at the best of my ability...*Jai*

Hari..Jai..Shiva...Jao Ganga Mayyia..

The Bhagvad-katha was rendered by Sri Suka to King Parikshit and in that story an episode of the churning of the ocean occurs, today I would tell you all the tale of the churning and the flow of nectar and how the gods were able to win back the pitcher which contained the immortal manna and how a few drops sprinkled upon four different places in the country and how every six years an Ardh Kumbh and every twelve years a Maha-Kumbh is held to commemorate the event and also to give us mortals the chance to gain purity and immortality by taking a dip in the holy river of Ganga.

OooMmmm....Ekaba closed his eyes and began:

—The great king Parikshit with folded hands requested Sri Suta...O Great sage narrate to me the cause for the churning of the great ocean of milk and how nectar was obtained and what happened thereafter... ..

The pious sage welcomed the query of the King and proceeded to tell in detail the tale.

In the battle between the gods and the Asuras the demons had gained an upper hand and a large number of gods lay dead in the battlefield and upon the curse of Sage Durvasa they were hapless infront of the might of the demons(once Sage durvasa was returning from Vaikunth the residence of Lord Hari who presented him a garland. On his way he met Lord Indra and gifted the garland to him, Indra; in his arrogance; threw it on the head of his elephant, Airavat ,who latter tore it playfully and trampled it under its foot. On seeing this, the Sage grew angry and pronounced a curse on him that he would soon be divested of all his riches and glory).

On seeing their army of Gods being killed in a heap by the Demon army, lord Indra and lord Varuna and other Gods deliberated amongst themselves and decided to seek the advice of Lord Brahma. So they all went to the court of the lord of the lords. Seeing the great Gods devoid of the powers and splendors Brahma grew worried and started contemplation with a concentrated mind.

He came back with a smiling countenance and told the Gods present that lord Hari, the creator and sustainer of the entire universe should be extolled to seek his blessings at this critical hour- saying this lord Brahma closed his eyes and prayed, extolling the virtues of the supreme lord.

On being extolled by the gods the lord Sri Hari revealed himself with the lights of a thousand suns tailing him. Lord Brahma prayed to him and made him aware of the dangers that the Gods faced from the demons. The lord Vishnu listened to the woes of the Gods and said, O lord Brahma and lord Shiva and all the other Gods- go forth and let peace be concluded with your cousins, the demons who are favored by the time. Then, once you have won over your enemies- efforts should be made to get nectar from the oceans, by drinking which even one who is in the jaws of death would be immortal. With my help the demons would reap toil and you all shall enjoy the fruits. Say kind words to the demons and befriend them, you would need them for the churning; leave your anger aside and do not be afraid of the poison; *Kalakuta* that would come out of the ocean.

On hearing the lord, the Gods returned to their abode and called on the great fighter King, Bali- the emperor of the Demons for talks. King Bali sat on a throne after having won over the three worlds. Lord Indra, with a very polished tongue spoke about the proposal of the lord Vishnu. It found favor with the King Bali and after a few conciliatory gestures from both the sides, a mutual friendship developed between the warring groups.

Together the gods and the demons uprooted the mountain Mandara and carried it to the ocean. But on the way they dropped it, unable to carry it any further. Lord Vishnu then appeared in the form of Garuda- the king of the birds and carried the mount Mandara, which resembled mount Sumeru-the mountain of gold.

Lord Vishnu then summoned Vasuki- the lord of serpents and after assuring him of his share in the nectar, twined him round the mountain. The demons were given the head of Vasuki to hold and the gods held the tail and together they started churning the ocean. However the mountain started sinking as it had no base to hold on to. Seeing this lord Hari himself took the form of a giant tortoise and plunged into the water and bore the mountain- which was 800000 miles long. Then the lord, oversee the churning helping the demons, by lending them the quality of Rajas and the gods that of Sattva and to Vasuki suspended consciousness, so that the god of snakes does not feel the pain when his body was being rubbed against the great mountain Mandara.

Ekaba stopped and opened his eyes. The audience listened to him in rapt attention. He sipped water from a brass tumbler and resumed his discourse.

-The churning continued for long and yet there was no sign of the nectar; then the lord himself rose up and began churning along with the Gods and the Demons. The first that came out was the most deadly poison- *Halahala*. The Gods and Demons were equally frightened and ran to the SadaShiva who sat on the mount Kailasa. They prayed to the Kailasa-Pati who was under deep meditation. Seeing his devotees in distress, the lord Shiva said to his consort- O Bhavani, look how distressful these are, I must provide them security by drinking the poison. He then proceeded to drink *KalaKuta* (*Halahala*) poison, but did not swallow the whole and stopped the flow in his throat. The effect of the poison was so great that the lord Shiva's body turned blue and even today he is worshipped in this Avatar. The snakes, scorpions and poisonous herbs took whatever drops of poison fell from the palms of the lord when he drank it.

On being safe from the deadly poison the gods and the demons gave a war cry and redoubled their efforts at churning the ocean. Then emerged the cow of the plenty-*Kamdhenu-* the principle source of milk and ghee used for oblation into the sacred fire. Seers who were exponents of Vedas took it.

Next sprang the celebrated horse-*Uccaihsrava*, which was white as a moon. Bali longed for it and took it.

Next emerged the king of elephants *Airavata* –Indra took it for himself.

Next emerged a jewel of a type of ruby-*Kaustubha-* lord Hari himself longed for it and took it to adorn his breast.

Then appeared the tree –*Parijata* –the ornament of the celestial world which immediately gratifies and wish- Indra took it for his court.

Then sprang the *Apsaras-* the celestial Nymphs who were propitiated by the Gods for heaven.

Rama, the goddess *luxmi* herself emerged next and stood like a streak of white lightening; she was beauty personified and all the gods longed for her but she, holding lotus wreath in her hands with a swarm, of black bees humming over it and smiling bashfully, her breasts were in perfect symmetry and she moved with a slender gait; she searched for a husband free from blemish; she deliberated upon and then chose the lord Vishnu himself and placed the lotus wreath on his shoulder. Lord Vishnu gave her a permanent abode in his bosom.

Then emerged the goddesses of wine; *Varuni*, in the form of a maiden with lotus eyes, the Asuras caught hold of her with the approval of the lord himself.

Then emerged a most wonderful personage; youthful and a conch shaped arms, broad chest, long and plump arms. He carried in his hands a jar full of nectar. He was *Dhanvantri*: the one who had revealed the science of medicine to the world. Seeing him all the Asuras were eager to grab hold the pitcher which carried the nectar, they succeeded in snatching the jar and carried it away. The Gods were dejected and resorted to the lord for help. Be calm the lord replied. Soon there arose a quarrel amongst the devils on the issue of who shall have the first sip of the nectar. This was the chance the lord sought and appeared in the Avatar of a damsel, so beautiful that all the Asuras ran behind her. Would you trust a wanton woman like me she smiled in her innocence as she enticed them with her beauty and sensuality? Are wolves to be trusted? She asked. They laughed what harm you can bestow on us they said and chased her. Then let me treat you to the nectar she said. Alright they entrusted the task of distribution of the nectar to her. But you have to promise me that whatever I do you will have complete faith in my act whether right or wrong, she said. Agreed the *Daitiyas* said. Then the demons, after having bathed and worn the best of clothes and having prayed, squatted on the *Kusa* grass waiting for her to distribute the nectar. On the other row sat the Gods waiting for their turn to drink the nectar of immortality. The lord in the form of damsel poured the nectar for the Gods first; *Rahu*, the devil, entered the God's row and drank the nectar, which was pointed out by the sun and the moon god, then the lord Sri Hari chopped off his head with his *Sudarshana* Chakra; at that precise moment, so that the head got the nectar and became immortal but the body fell dead(Trunk), lord Brahma then made a deity of the head who presides over the planets and who is the cause of the sun and moon eclipse, even today as he wears animosity towards them.

The pitcher of the nectar was empty when the turn of the *Asuras* came and they did not get the necessary result for their work though they had worked in the same way as the Gods. What they lacked was devotion to the lord.

Ekaba became silent for the moment- Very silent. His breath was labored and his eyes closed. He opened them which much effort and he mumbled- "how did the Kumbh Fair came into existence?" he asked the devotees. No one answered him; instead waited upon him, for an answer.

"A few drops fell during the skirmishes between the Gods and the Demons, in four places- Haridwar being one of them and therein lays the importance of taking a dip in the holy river Ganga where the drops fell. One who baths gains immortality." He said and stood still in his Padmaasana, without the *Prana*; the breath.

People clapped and shouted *Jai Maa Ganga...Jai Shiv Shankar... Jai Vishnu...Jai Ekaba...*

Red rose petals fell like pious rains.

It was Kerrie, who shouted in the din.... Ekaba..baba.. as she rushed to the stage.